"I don't like leaving you here alone."

She cleared her voice and seemed to push the worry from her expression. "I will be fine. Call me as soon as you can, though."

"I put a gun in your purse that I had in my glove box in the pickup." He saw her glance toward her purse, which she'd dropped on the table in the corner of the bedroom. "It's a point-and-shoot handgun. All you have to do is pull the trigger." He could tell by her expression that she didn't believe she could do that. He hoped she was wrong—should she need to fire it.

"Eleanor, I..." He realized he was going to tell her that he loved her. It was on the tip of his tongue. This woman had stolen his heart. But for so many reasons, he couldn't say the words. Not now. Maybe not ever. "Be safe."

B.J. Daniels is a *New York Times* and *USA TODAY* bestselling author. She wrote her first book after a career as an award-winning newspaper journalist and author of thirty-seven published short stories. She lives in Montana with her husband, Parker, and three springer spaniels. When not writing, she quilts, boats and plays tennis. Contact her at bjdaniels.com, on Facebook or on Twitter, @bjdanielsauthor.

Books by B.J. Daniels

Harlequin Intrigue

A Colt Brothers Investigation

Murder Gone Cold
Sticking to Her Guns
Set Up in the City

Cardwell Ranch: Montana Legacy

Steel Resolve
Iron Will
Ambush before Sunrise
Double Action Deputy
Trouble in Big Timber
Cold Case at Cardwell Ranch

For a complete list of books by B.J. Daniels, please visit www.bjdaniels.com.

Visit the Author Profile page at Harlequin.com.

B.J.

NEW YORK TIMES BESTSELLING AUTHOR

DANIELS

SET UP IN THE CITY & RESCUE AT CARDWELL RANCH

HARLEQUIN
INTRIGUE

ISBN-13: 978-1-335-44978-8

Recycling programs
for this product may
not exist in your area.

Set Up in the City & Rescue at Cardwell Ranch

Copyright © 2023 by Harlequin Enterprises ULC

Set Up in the City
Copyright © 2023 by Barbara Heinlein

Rescue at Cardwell Ranch
Copyright © 2014 by Barbara Heinlein

For questions and comments about the quality of this book,
please contact us at CustomerService@Harlequin.com.

Harlequin Enterprises ULC
22 Adelaide St. West, 41st Floor
Toronto, Ontario M5H 4E3, Canada
www.Harlequin.com

Printed in U.S.A.

CONTENTS

SET UP IN THE CITY

Prologue

Vernon "Spark" Murphy couldn't wait to get out of Lonesome, Montana. If the money hadn't been so good… Maybe too good. He tamped down his misgivings about coming back here. Too late now anyway. The job was almost over.

Never do two jobs in the same town. He called it his code. And now he'd broken it. No wonder it made him uneasy. That and the amount he'd been paid. But he also never asked questions, priding himself on always getting the job done.

Now he hurried across the street in the cover of darkness to wait out of harm's way against an abandoned building much like the one he'd just left. It was an odd neighborhood. An old industrial area near what had once been a railyard. The tracks had been removed and the weeds had taken over, giving the whole place an eerie feel that he didn't particularly like on this very dark night.

Counting under his breath, Spark didn't turn around until he reached a safe enough distance out of the way to watch the conclusion of the job. He focused on the three-story brick shell of a building he'd exited only minutes ago. This job was unusual in his line of work because the building was in such bad shape. It made him wonder. He was still counting, reminding himself he wasn't getting paid to wonder or question why.

The first explosion lit the ground floor in a flash of bright orange, streaking across the entire lower level. He looked up to the next floor, still counting. Another flash, this one filling the second floor with a burst of light as it blew out what few windows were still intact on that level.

Even with his reservations, he couldn't help but smile. He did love his line of work. He had always loved explosions and flames. He'd been hypnotized by campfires as a child, so much so that he'd tried to hold the flames. He still had the scars.

Spark felt the growing heat as he looked to the third floor and waited. The entire deserted area was aglow now. He could feel the heat on his face, hear the crackle, smell the fire eating away at anything combustible inside of the structure as it raced across the dry wood floors to rush up the stairs. A faint glow shone even now through the windows of the top floor.

A movement caught his eye. The image of a woman with long dark hair suddenly filled one of the windows. Her features were twisted in raw terror, her scream silent from this distance, her mouth only a gaping, dark hole. Yet he recognized her. *He knew this woman.* She fell against the glass, her wrists bound, her hands frantically beating against the window as if she saw him standing across the street and thought he could—

The flash of bright light rippled across the third floor, engulfing everything in heat and blinding light. The other two floors were already burning. He stared at the window where only moments ago the woman had been standing. She was gone.

Spark heard the too-soon sound of sirens, but he couldn't move. He could hardly draw his next breath. The building had been empty when he'd set his charges, hadn't it? Otherwise, he would have seen her. Unless someone had hidden her, but then she'd somehow gotten free enough to make it to the window? He leaned back against the warm, worn brick of the building, fighting to keep down the meal he'd consumed earlier.

The sound of sirens was growing closer, clearly headed this way. He knew there were no alarms in the building because he always checked. With this abandoned industrial area a good distance from the town of Lonesome, he should have had plenty of time to get away.

His already frantic heart dropped like an anvil. Someone had to have called in the fire even before the first explosion. The same person who'd hidden that woman somewhere in the building so he wouldn't see her, wouldn't even know he'd killed her until the cops pounded on his door?

This was supposed to be a quickie job. In and out. Piece of cake. And the money… He'd been right. The money had been too good on such an old building on the outskirts of this tiny Western town.

Move! He quickly turned away from the flashing

lights coming up the street and ducked behind the building. His rig was parked close by. He wasn't worried about getting away since he always planned for just such an unforeseen complication. It was why he was so good at his job.

Until now.

He felt the weight of the woman's death on him, making it hard to think since he had no idea what was going on. But as he drove, one thing became abundantly clear. He'd been set up and he had no idea why. Had it simply been about getting rid of the woman? Or was Spark himself also the target?

Not that it mattered. He'd been in this business long enough to know that even if he avoided capture by the cops, someone more dangerous would be coming for him.

Either way, his life wasn't worth a plugged nickel right now.

Chapter 1

Willie Colt was having the best ride of his life on the back of a rank bull with a reputation for maiming cowboys. All Willie had to do was hang on and wait for that eight-second horn to sound.

But just as the horn blew, everything went wrong. He realized his hand was caught in his rigging. Hanging by his arm off the side of the bull, he was being tossed around like a rag doll. Two rodeo clowns were trying to free him and keep the bull's attention as he was dragged across the arena. Then suddenly, the bull stopped, twisted around, horns gleaming in the arena lights as it lowered its head, and—

Willie jerked awake at the sound of an alarm going off. Two nurses came running into the room. One rushed to his bedside, the other shut off the machine next to him as he attempted to sit up. He blinked, part of him still caught in what he realized had been a nightmare from his former career as a bull rider on the rodeo circuit.

"Deputy Colt, you need to calm down," the nurse was saying. "Dr. Bishop is on his way. You're fine."

He doubted that. He was lying in a hospital bed with a bunch of devices attached to him. What the hell was he doing here? "Where am I? How did I—"

"Seattle General Hospital."

He tried to still his raging heart. Moments ago he'd been on a bull about to be gored. He touched the bandage on the back of his head and grimaced. Whatever had happened to him, it wasn't a bull that had done the damage.

"How long have I been here?"

"You were brought in yesterday afternoon."

He'd been here since yesterday? "How did I get here?"

"Ambulance," said the larger and sterner of the two nurses checking his vitals.

His brain felt fuzzy, but two things became clear. He hadn't been riding a bull because he'd retired to become a deputy sheriff—in Lonesome, Montana. He could see his Stetson and his sheriff's department jacket on a nearby chair. And he was in a hospital in Seattle. What the devil was he doing in Seattle and how did he end up in this bed?

"What happened?" He saw the nurses exchange a look.

"I believe you were attacked. Mugged," the smaller, nicer of the two said.

"Mugged?" His head felt filled with cotton. "But what was I doing in Seattle, Washington, in the first place?"

"Picking up an extradited prisoner. At least that's what we were told."

Her grim-faced coworker shot her a look and said, "You received a blow to your head. That's probably why you're a little confused right now. You have a concussion. The doctor will be in shortly if you have any more questions. Just try to remain still."

As they left the room, he lay back against the pillow, wincing, and closed his eyes to ease the killer headache. Slowly, he recalled the drive out to Seattle from the sheriff's office in Lonesome, Montana. The nurse was right. It had been to pick up an extradited arsonist named Vernon, nickname "Spark," Murphy and bring him back to Montana to stand trial for arson—and the death of a young woman who'd died in the explosion and fire he'd started.

Willie, the newest deputy on the force, had gotten the job because no one else wanted it. No one wanted to spend that many hours in a patrol SUV driving all the way to Washington and back—with Spark.

"Trust me," one of the other deputies had told him. "I can promise you that he won't shut up the entire way. You may have to gag him. Seattle can't wait to get rid of him."

They'd all laughed, wishing Willie good luck.

He hadn't known what to believe, but he'd told himself it was no big deal. He liked road trips. Living in Montana, where travel was measured in hours rather than miles, a man had to like driving distances. He remembered thinking he wouldn't mind the company, either.

Willie had known that he wouldn't like the city, though. Born and raised in Lonesome, he liked wide-open places, disliked crowds and hated traffic. Nor was he a fan of water and, after a childhood boating accident, you couldn't get him on a boat.

All that aside, what had happened after he'd arrived in Seattle to land him in the hospital with his head nearly split open? And where could he have gotten mugged? His plan had been to go straight to the cop shop, pick up his felon and head back to Montana as fast as possible.

So, what had gone wrong?

Chapter 2

By the time the doctor stopped by, Willie had remembered a little more of the fifteen-hour drive from Lonesome to Seattle. He'd stayed at a motel in one of the smaller towns outside of the city and gone to the police headquarters in downtown Seattle the next morning.

The traffic had been bumper-to-bumper. He couldn't imagine driving in this every day. In Lonesome, if you had to wait for three cars to go past before you could pull out, then something big was going on in town. There were no stoplights in Lonesome, hardly any stop signs. For miles outside of town it was just an open, two-lane highway as far as the eye could see. Traffic was unheard of until you got to one of the larger cities in the state, and there weren't many of those, either.

He'd found the cop shop with the nav system in his patrol SUV. After signing a few papers, his prisoner had been brought out. He'd only seen Vernon "Spark" Murphy's mug shot, so he'd been surprised when he laid eyes on the slight, five-foot-eight man he was transporting back to Montana. In the photograph, Spark had the look of someone who lived in his mother's basement and played video games all day, only going out at night to light fires and set explosives.

That someone had dressed him up was obvious in the way Vernon was tugging at the collar of his white button-down shirt. His hair had been cut more recently than Willie's own and he wore clothes that looked expensive—and also clearly not his, by the way he moved in them.

If it wasn't for the slight trembling of the man's hands, Vernon almost looked like a man on his way to the office—instead of a man headed for another cell and a murder conviction. Spark climbed into the back of Willie's patrol SUV as if he'd ordered an Uber.

As Willie slid behind the wheel, he glanced in the rearview mirror. His eyes locked through the metal grid with those of the fugitive from justice. "You all right, Vernon?"

"Spark. No one calls me Vernon except lawyers and bill collectors."

"All right, Spark. You might as well settle in for a long ride." He started the engine and didn't hear what the man said. "What was that?"

"It won't be a long ride. We'll never reach the Montana border. They'll kill me before that."

Willie stared at him. "That shows an almost insulting lack of faith in me, Spark."

The arsonist laughed, though the sound held no humor. "You have no idea the people you're dealing with. I didn't, either. Until it was too late." He shook his head. "I told my fancy lawyer that by extraditing me I was being sent to my death. No one listened. But this ride? It's a death sentence—for us both. They'll be worried I'm telling you everything right now. You're just as good as dead and you don't even know it."

"On that positive note," Willie said, and motioned for the cop standing next to the big garage door that they were ready to leave. The deputies back home had been right. Spark was a talker. A depressing one at that. "I can't imagine *that* many people want you dead."

"They're all in on it—the cops, the lawyers, every last one of them. I shouldn't have trusted any of them." He shook his head and nervously pulled at his collar until he finally shrugged out of the suit jacket, ripped off the tie and undid the top buttons on the shirt. "I'm not sure why they sent you to pick me up." His eyes flew to the rearview mirror. "Unless they've already paid you off to help them."

"I'm not on anyone's payroll except the sheriff's department in Lonesome."

"Then your boss must not think much of you."

"Look, believe it or not, I'm going to do my best to make sure nothing happens to you." But Willie couldn't help being a little unnerved.

"Good luck. These people… You won't even see them coming."

"Are we talking about the people who hired you for your last job?"

Spark looked out the side window, clearly not going to answer. He was probably saving that information to make a deal once they reached Lonesome.

As the Seattle officer finally opened the overhead

door to let them out of the building, Willie had given him a nod and pulled into the street, anxious to get back to Montana and the open road. He remembered being a little concerned, but not all that worried. His big fear was that Spark was going to keep talking.

After that, things got more than fuzzy. He was guessing that he hadn't gone but a few blocks when they'd been attacked. So where was his patrol SUV? And more to the point, where was Spark, the man he'd not only been paid to protect, but had promised to keep safe?

His head still ached, but Willie was anxious to get out of the hospital. He had to find Spark—if the man was still alive. He kept thinking about how convinced the arsonist had been that he would never reach Montana. Clearly, he'd known what to expect more than Willie had.

But that brought up the question of why someone wanted Spark to never reach Montana.

The attack raised even more questions. Whoever had ambushed them knew the time and place. Where had they gotten that information?

His cell phone rang. He checked it and groaned before he took the call. "Sheriff Henson." He'd never liked Frank Henson, a buddy of the past two sheriffs, who'd made a hobby out of harassing all four of the Colt brothers.

"What the hell is going on out there, Deputy? I just heard that you're in the hospital and that you've lost your prisoner. How in blazes did you do that?"

"I'm fine, but thanks for asking. Just a concussion," Willie said. He took a breath, reminding himself why he took this job, why he still needed it. "We were ambushed. Had to have been an inside job. Don't worry, I'm going to find out what happened and take care of it. If Spark is alive, I'll find him and bring him in."

The sheriff scoffed. "What you need to do is get back here and quit wasting taxpayer money. Let the local law handle it."

"The local law could be who gave the attackers the information about where we would be and when. I was set up and I intend to find out who did it."

"Doesn't sound like you're in any shape to do that."

"Don't worry about me. I've been kicked in the head by bulls that hit harder."

Sheriff Henson swore. "As soon as you're released, I want you back here or you won't have a job. The Seattle police are looking into what happened."

Somehow Willie doubted that.

"I should have known you couldn't handle something as simple as picking up a two-bit arsonist."

He would have argued with the sheriff, but the man had already disconnected. He had a lot of questions about this whole mess. For starters, why would someone want a two-bit arsonist dead, even one who'd killed someone in the last building he'd blown up, before he could stand trial? Because the person who'd hired him worried he would talk? Or was there more to it? Spark had mentioned he'd had a "fancy" lawyer. To Willie that meant high-priced. How had Spark managed that?

There was no doubt that the arsonist had been terrified of being extradited back to Montana for the trial—and with good reason. The ambush to abduct Spark had definitely been planned and executed with help. Willie had to find out who was behind it—and quickly. Spark might still be alive.

He made a call to the police station. He was told that while his patrol SUV had damage—the driver's-side window and the right rear window had been knocked out—it still ran and would be taken to a storage yard. The windows were being replaced as per Sheriff Henson's instructions.

Hanging up, he wondered how he was going to get around until he had wheels. He called the police department and asked to talk to the police officer who'd taken the call on the attack. Fortunately, he was available and filled Willie in what he'd found at the scene—Willie on the ground bleeding and unconscious and the prisoner gone.

"I'd wondered when I saw that the driver's-side window had been knocked out and so had the back seat right-hand passenger-side window," the officer said. "I'd assumed there'd been someone in the back."

"An arsonist I was extraditing."

The officer had called for an ambulance and written up a report.

Willie thanked him and made another call, this one to Colt Brothers Investigation back in Lonesome, Montana. James answered on the third ring. "I need your help," Willie said without preamble.

"Let me put you on speakerphone," his brother said. "Both Tommy and Davy are here."

He quickly filled them in on as much as he could remember that had happened.

"Sounds like you were set up," Davy said right away.

"I need to know why. Could you find out everything you can about Vernon 'Spark' Murphy and what it was about this case that it appears someone doesn't want him to stand trial?"

"Well, you know a woman died in that fire," Tommy said.

"I suspect she's the key," Willie said. "What do we know about her?"

"Very little until they get a DNA match," Davy said. "Otherwise, we might never know who she is or why she was there."

"What if Vernon didn't know she was there? My gut says he didn't and that's why he ran scared. He realized he was set up," Willie said.

"What are you going to do?" James asked.

"Find the people who ambushed us, and hope Vernon is still alive. Either way, I want answers. Sheriff Henson is threatening to fire me if I don't return to Lonesome as soon as I'm released from the hospital."

"How are you feeling?" Tommy asked.

"Angry." His brothers laughed. "I'm getting released right away—no matter what the doctor says. Call me when you have something."

He disconnected and made yet another call as he found his clothing in the closet and began to dress. Within minutes he had the name of Spark's attorney, E.L. Shafer. He looked up the office address, wondering why the attackers hadn't bothered to take his wallet and his phone. Because all they really wanted was Vernon. They'd probably thought that they'd left Willie for dead. Based on the way his skull felt right now, he knew he was lucky to be alive. If he'd been hit just a little harder...

"What do you think you're doing?" demanded a male voice behind him.

"Leaving," he said as he reached for his Stetson and the sheriff's department canvas jacket. "Thanks for patching me up, Doc, but I have to go."

"I'm not releasing you," the doctor said. "If you walk out of here—"

Willie didn't catch the rest as he left. The clock was ticking—especially for Spark, if still alive. He'd found out that E.L. Shafer had an office downtown with a list of other highfalutin lawyers. He thought about calling but preferred a face-to-face with the man. Fortunately, the office was only a few blocks away.

He arrived at the high-rise, asked what floor E.L. Shafer was on and then headed for the elevator, with the man at the desk calling after him. As he entered the elevator, hit fourteen, he saw the man making a hurried call, either upstairs or for security, or both.

The all-glass interior was impressively furnished with thick carpet, a swift elevator and a great view of Puget Sound, he noticed as he got off on the fourteenth floor.

"Can I help you?" the receptionist asked behind a half-moon desk that gleamed.

"I need to see E.L. Shafer."

The receptionist looked at the time. "I'm sorry, the office is closed. Do you have an appointment?"

"I know Shafer's still here because the security guard downstairs called up. Tell E.L. that I'm the cop who was taking Vernon Murphy back to Montana when I was almost killed and his client taken. The name's Deputy Willie Colt."

The woman made the call. A few moments later a woman in a suit and high heels came down the hallway. He groaned. How many people was he going to have to go through to see Spark's lawyer? He was losing his patience. If Spark was still alive, he needed to find him, and quickly. Even if he wasn't, Willie had to know who'd set him up and why. Once he knew that, then he'd deal with it.

The clack of her high heels on the polished floor drew closer. He'd been pacing in the reception area, but now stopped to watch the woman approach. She was the kind who could turn a man's head. Classic features, great body, long, amazing legs. All of it tucked compactly into a business suit with a blouse buttoned all the way up, to go with the buttoned-up look on the woman's face.

"Deputy Colt?" she asked as the brunette stopped only a few feet from him. Not a hair in her topknot was out of place. He wondered if she was born this uptight. "I'm afraid—"

"No offense, but I'm not interested in speaking with another of E.L. Shafer's gatekeepers. Tell Mr. Shafer I want to speak with him. *Now*. It's urgent."

Her wolf-gray eyes narrowed. "I'm E.L. Shafer."

He was seldom at a loss for words. *"You're Vernon Murphy's lawyer?"* He couldn't keep the surprise out of his voice even if he'd tried.

"You're surprised because I'm a woman?"

Willie shook his head. "It's not your sex that has me surprised. It's that Spark was able to hire any high-powered lawyer from your firm. But I do question why you in particular?"

Either Spark was a bigger player than he'd been led to believe or something was dead wrong here.

"I'm afraid our offices are closing. If you'd like to make an appointment to return during regular business hours—"

He cut her off. "Unless you want Spark's death on your hands, you will talk to me. *Now*."

She bristled at his tone, her cheeks reddening slightly beneath her perfectly executed makeup as she slowly turned to the receptionist. "Hold my calls." She barely looked at him as she said, "My office," before she did a one-eighty on her heels and headed back down the hall-way, back ramrod straight.

He followed, trying to focus on her perfect twist of mahogany hair and the way it wound at the back of her slim neck instead of her compact, perfectly round behind that was impossible not to notice in that skirt. He'd love to get her in a pair of snug-fitting jeans, he thought—a stray thought that told him he was still suffering from the blow to his head.

E.L. Shafer's office was as luxurious as the rest of the floor. "Please close the door," she said as she took the large leather chair behind the huge teak desk.

He closed the door and glanced around. The woman had a corner office with one hell of a view of the city. On the wall behind her were numerous plaques for one award or degree after another. The carpet under his feet felt four inches deep and the entire place smelled of money.

He shook his head, more convinced than ever that something was suspiciously wrong here. "How was it that Vernon 'Spark' Murphy could afford you?"

"Deputy, do I really have to explain client-attorney privilege to you?"

She was angry. She contained it well, no doubt priding herself on never losing her temper. But there was the slight tightening of her full mouth, the tiniest flare of her nostrils and an almost indiscernible twitch next to her left eye.

Willie believed that anger wasn't a bad thing. Maybe he felt that way because right now he was angry as hell. "Look, Ellie—"

"It's Eleanor, but you can call me Ms. Shafer."

He cocked his head. "Let's try this again. How did you come to represent a man like Spark, a small-time arsonist from a town no one has ever heard of in Montana?"

"Like I said, that is privileged information."

He stepped to her desk, flattened his palms on the smooth-as-a-baby's-behind teak and leaned toward her menacingly. He gave her credit. She didn't flinch; she didn't move an inch. Those gray eyes merely bored into him as if she'd faced down much worse than him.

"Let's cut to the chase. If Spark had walked in off the street, he wouldn't have gotten past your security guard downstairs—let alone to your fourteenth-floor executive suite office. And if he had, you wouldn't be representing him—even if he had enough money to hire you." He took a breath. "So, who paid you to represent him?"

That beautifully classic face turned as cold and hard as marble.

Willie rocked back, shaking his head. She hadn't had him thrown out or arrested, yet. But he wasn't getting anywhere with this ice queen. "Look, this is some messed-up sh—stuff. Vernon said that he would never reach Montana. He was right. I'm assuming he meant whoever hired him for the last job. I'm guessing he begged you not to let him get extradited." Something changed in the granite-hard flint of her gaze.

"The men who attacked me and took him had done

this type of thing before," he continued. "They weren't a bunch of his rowdy friends breaking him out of the hoosegow. You understand what I'm staying? Vernon was terrified of being sent back to Montana because he knew the people who hired him would kill him before they'd let him drop a dime on them—let alone ever testify against them. Whoever he feared didn't want him returned. This was a *setup*. They knew the time and the place to attack us. That means that someone in the know told them. Someone in the police department or in *your* office." His gaze met hers and held it in a viselike stare. "So, I'll ask you again. Who hired you? Because I'm betting that's who you told."

Chapter 3

Eleanor knew the moment she spotted the cowboy cop with his ten-gallon hat, butt-hugging jeans and dress boots that Deputy Willie Colt was going to be trouble. She should have gone with her first instinct and let security handle him. Outside her window, the sky began to darken as the long day promised to finally end. If managing partner Phillip McNamara hadn't asked her not to leave until he talked to her, she would have already been gone.

"Excuse me, but you didn't just accuse me of setting up my own client, did you, Deputy?"

He gave her a grin that she suspected made some women melt like expensive chocolate. "If the Jimmy Choo fits," he said, locking eyes with her.

"My shoes are Louboutin."

His laugh eased the tension between them. She'd been

ready to have him shown out of the building. But her instincts told her it wouldn't be the last she saw of him. There was another reason she didn't have him thrown out. Something about Vernon Murphy's case had felt off from the start. This cowboy had just pretty much told her the same thing.

She leaned back in her chair, crossed her legs and asked, "Does your brand of charm work back in Montana?"

"About half the time. Look," he said, pulling up a chair, sitting down and leaning toward her. "You seem smart." She raised an eyebrow but said nothing as he continued. "There are apparently those who want to shut Vernon up before he rats them out. They couldn't get to him while he was in jail, so they waited until he was being extradited. They had this planned all along and now they have him. He told me when I picked him up to take him back to Montana that this was going to happen."

"You're saying you lost Mr. Murphy."

He removed his hat and turned his head so she could see the large bandage on the back of his head. "They tried to cave in my skull. I need to find them. Maybe they haven't killed Spark yet. Maybe they have. Either way, I owe them and I need your help."

She opened her mouth to remind him again of attorney-client confidentiality, but he cut her off before she could speak.

"You'll help me *because* you're smart. By now, you realize that whoever wanted Spark won't stop until he ties up all the loose ends. That's right, you are now a loose end. These people figure Spark took one look at those amazing legs of yours and spilled his guts. You think it's an accident you were given him as a client? They figured that if there was anyone Spark would bare his soul to, it would be a good-looking woman with mesmerizing gray eyes tucked nicely into an expensive suit."

"I resent what you're implying, Deputy."

He scoffed at that. "Like I said, you're smart. If you didn't know the score, you do now. The people who took him will think the same thing I did—that Vernon talked to you. That's put a target on your back. Basically, you're screwed."

"You have such a wonderfully blunt way of putting things."

"Lady, you haven't even seen blunt yet. What I'm trying hard to tell you is that your life is in danger. I need you to help me before they come for you. Because quite frankly, you'll be worthless to me once you're dead."

Eleanor rose with a sigh. "I'm sorry, Deputy, your time is up. Since we're being blunt, would you like to leave on your own or be dragged out by security?"

He smiled as he shook his head and gingerly replaced his Stetson on his head of thick dark hair. "Damned shame," he said as he rose from the chair. While not an overly large man, he still seemed to dominate the huge office.

"With or without your help, I'm going to find your client—or the men who took him and are probably torturing him—if not killing him—as we speak. I wonder how much time you have left before they come for you? I really doubt you've dealt with men like these before. But if you should somehow get away from them…"

He reached into his jacket and took out his card. Leaning over her desk again, he picked up her pen. The movement made her want to draw back, but she held her ground, determined not to let this man intimidate her even as he did. He wrote what she assumed was his cell phone number on the back of the card and tossed it toward her. "Call me. I might be able to get to you before they do. Otherwise, they'll torture what they want out of you before they finish the job. I'd hate to see blood on that fancy suit, let alone that white blouse on such an uptight, buttoned-up woman."

With that he turned and walked out, leaving her door open.

Eleanor stared after him, surprised that she was shaking inside. She didn't like being bullied. It made her angry. Uptight, buttoned-up? She took a deep breath and tried to still her raging pulse. Deputy Willie Colt actually thought he could walk into her office, offend her and use scare tactics on her?

A tone sounded as a message popped up on her monitor screen. Her assistant reminding her about the meeting upstairs.

She glanced at the time and rose, shaking her head as she snatched up his card from her desk. He was a deputy from a place called Lonesome, Montana? She'd never heard of it or him. Another message. This time it was Phillip McNamara. He must be anxious, since he, too, was reminding her of their meeting. Still gripping the card the cowboy had given her, she quickly pocketed it in her suit jacket. Her boss would want to know about Deputy Willie Colt, she thought as she headed for the elevator that would take her to the top floor.

On the way to the main downtown police station, Willie found a quick mart, bought a bottle of over-the-counter painkillers and took three for his headache. He was beginning to question leaving the hospital. The tablets only slightly took the edge off the pain.

He found himself going over the case more critically than he had when he was assigned the job of picking up the fugitive. Seattle police officer Brian Kemp had arrested Spark after pulling him over for a taillight violation, and had been surprised to find out that there was a BOLO out on the man for arson and murder.

But when Willie asked to see Kemp, he was instead sent to the police chief's office, where a large man with a face and voice like a bulldog sat behind a massive metal desk that took up most of the room.

Police Chief Ted Landry motioned the deputy into a chair, but Willie passed. He walked up to the desk, his headache still pulsing, and demanded, "Who the hell set me up?"

Landry was taken aback for a moment before he growled in a gravelly voice, "What the hell are you insinuating about my department?"

"I'm not insinuating anything. I was set up. Those men who attacked me and took my prisoner knew exactly where I would be and what time."

"Well, they didn't get the information from this office."

"I'll ask them when I find them," Willie said.

"I don't know who you think you are, cowboy, but you have no authority out here. You are way out of your jurisdiction. I asked for a rush job done on replacing the broken windows in your cruiser so you can return to Montana as soon as possible."

"That was quick," he said. "Why the bum's rush out of town?"

The chief scowled. "As I told your boss back in Montana, we'll be handling this case from here on out."

"I've seen the way you handled things so far," Willie said, knowing he'd probably said more than he should have. But he was angry, and his head hurt like hell, and he had a bad feeling that no one was looking for Spark—let alone tracking down the men who'd taken him.

"Pick up your rig when it's ready and go home," Landry said, shoving to his feet threateningly. "Otherwise, I'll have you arrested for interfering in police business. Am I making myself clear, Deputy?"

"Perfectly." Willie turned and walked out. It seemed everyone wanted him to go back to Montana, including his own boss. Like hell he would.

There were four partners in the office when Eleanor reached the top floor suite. They rose and left, nodding to her as they did so. Whatever had been going on, they didn't look happy. Neither did McNamara, the managing partner. She'd already been intimidated today by a Montana cowboy. Now what?

She was a senior partner in the all-male partners' group. Her suggestion to bring in more female attorneys had been shot down even though her parents had started the firm and always thought she'd be the managing partner one day. McNamara had hinted at a co-managing partnership, but things had been strained between the two of them lately. Which made her anxious. Why did he want to see her?

Phillip McNamara waved her into his office. He was a striking man seven years older than her, with gray at his temples that only added to his good looks. He offered her a chair. Usually, he kept things quick since he preferred her to be adding up billable hours instead of warming one of his office chairs.

He'd been especially abrupt at their meetings since he'd made his feelings for her known and she'd had to tell him that she didn't feel the same way about him.

Now she sat, noticing that he wasn't meeting her gaze.

"Just wanted to keep you up to speed on one of your clients," he said, glancing at his notepad as if to recall the client. She could read the name written on the notepad from where she sat. "Vernon Murphy."

"Is there a problem with his extradition?" she asked, even though Deputy Willie Colt had pretty much already told her the problem.

"No, no, you did a great job. Everything was in order. Unfortunately, he has escaped," the managing partner said. Not quite the story the cowboy had told her. "I really doubt he will contact you, but if he does, let us know at once. We'll take it from there. He hasn't contacted you, has he?"

Eleanor shook her head. She thought of the deputy's card in her jacket pocket.

"Just let me know if he does. Everything else all right with you?"

For just a moment, she thought about mentioning her visitor, but something changed her mind. "Fine."

"You look tired. You should go home."

She said nothing as she rose from the chair, wondering why they hadn't done this over the phone. As she left the room, one of the other partners who'd been in the room earlier returned to McNamara's office, closing the door behind him. When she glanced back, she saw the two having an intense conversation.

About Vernon Murphy? Or about the cowboy cop who'd lost her client? Or something entirely different?

As she returned to her office, she saw that the receptionist had left for the day and her assistant, Christie, had her coat on. Eleanor was surprised she hadn't left already.

"Vernon Murphy is on the line," Christie told her. "He says he has to talk to you. It's urgent."

Her first thought was that the cowboy deputy had been overly dramatic about Vernon's life being in jeopardy if the man was able to make a phone call to his attorney. "I'll take it, Christie. You don't need to stay."

As she heard her leave, Eleanor entered her office, sat down and took the call. "Mr. Murphy," she said without preamble. She thought about McNamara's admonition that she call him at once if she heard from her client. Now she would have to call upstairs before she left tonight—if any of them were still around. She couldn't keep this phone call to herself. But it did make her question what was so important about this alleged arsonist-murderer. *"Mr. Murphy?"*

She heard a groan of pain. Her heart lodged in her throat even before he spoke in an agonized whisper. "They're coming for you. They think I told you. Get out before they—" There was a horrible shriek before the call ended and then nothing.

From down the hall, she heard the elevator door open with a ding, followed by the sound of heavy footfalls.

Chapter 4

Eleanor replaced the phone with trembling fingers and stood. Her first instinct was to hide. Or run. But there was little place to conceal herself in this fishbowl of an office building, with all the glass. And running? The stairs were at the other end of the hallway. The quickest way off the floor was the elevator.

She stared at her open doorway and tried to breathe as the sound of someone stomping down the hallway grew louder. The emptiness of the entire floor seemed to echo as if she needed reminding how alone she was right now. Maybe McNamara or one of the partners was still upstairs. She felt the deputy's card with his cell phone number in her pocket. Too late for that. Too late as well to find a weapon on her immaculate desk.

Suddenly the bulk of a man filled her doorway. With a swallowed gasp, she felt relief wash over her like a tsunami as Deputy Willie Colt stormed into her office. She'd never thought she'd be so glad to see the rough-neck deputy.

He stopped abruptly, his blue eyes taking her in. "What's wrong?" He was moving toward her before she could speak. But it wasn't until he laid one big hand on her shoulder that she let go of the edge of the desk she'd been gripping. He eased her into her chair and hunched down, turning her chair so she was facing him. "What's happened?"

Eleanor swallowed, her years of study and work as a lawyer warning her not to confide in this man. If she was going to tell anyone about the call, it should be Mc-Namara—not this cowboy cop.

"Ellie?"

She didn't correct him. She knew he'd seen her fear. Only moments ago she'd been terrified that whoever had Vernon Murphy had sent someone for her. The cowboy was no fool. He'd known she was in trouble long before she did. Was that why he'd come back? "What are you doing here?" Her voice only slightly betrayed her true emotions.

"I realized that if Spark was still alive and had a chance, he'd contact you," Willie said, those blue eyes narrowing as if he could read her like a book. "You've heard from him, haven't you?"

Something she'd learned even as a child was to follow her instincts. It made her a good lawyer. It made her able to think fast on her feet. She told herself to trust those instincts now. This deputy's story rang true compared to what McNamara had told her upstairs only minutes ago. Not to mention the bandage on the back of his head as even more proof that he'd been telling her the truth.

"Mr. Murphy just called." She cleared her throat, recalling the terror as well as pain she'd heard in his voice and wondering what McNamara would say if she told him about the call.

The deputy met her gaze. "Tell me exactly what he said."

She swallowed as she made a decision that could destroy her career, ruin her life—or save it. "He said, 'They're coming for you. They think I told you. Get out before they—' Then I heard him shriek in what sounded like pain and the call ended."

Willie nodded. This explained the terrified look he'd seen on her face when he'd entered her office. She'd been scared and with good reason. He rose from beside her chair, removed his Stetson and raked a hand through his hair as he turned to look out at the city, twinkling as far as the eye could see. Wasn't this exactly what he'd feared? Whoever took Spark wanted to know not only what he knew—but also whom he'd told. He turned back to study the attorney.

She wasn't as pale as she'd been a few moments ago. But one thing he sensed about her was that she was strong, and that was good, because she was going to need that strength—especially if she didn't do exactly what he told her.

"We need to get out of here." He didn't like all the glass in these offices. Nor did he like feeling trapped up here on the fourteenth floor. "You need to come with me." She didn't know him from Adam, so why would she believe anything he told her? He expected her to put up an argument, but he was ready to throw her over his shoulder and carry her out of there if it came to that.

She hesitated, but only for a moment, then opened her desk drawer. He wasn't surprised when she pulled out her purse. He'd already figured that if she had a weapon in there, she would have had it out before he reached her office.

He saw her look toward her phone on the desk as if thinking she should make a call. The police? Her boss upstairs? But apparently she changed her mind as she stood and walked toward a closet set back in the wall. She withdrew a long coat and hesitated again as if re-alizing she might not be back here for a while—maybe not ever.

"If it helps," he said, "I'll do everything in my power to keep you safe. You have my word on that."

She met his gaze as she pulled on her coat and then walked past him, her back stiff as a board. "I bet that's what you told Vernon Murphy."

He groaned inwardly, knowing it was true, as he fol-lowed her down the hallway toward the elevator. "We need to take the stairs. Do you have some other shoes?" he asked, and looked pointedly at her designer high heels. She gave him a stop-underestimating-me look and turned toward the stairs.

That she was trusting him at all surprised him. But she'd told him about the call, he thought as he followed her. That was progress, right? But then again, she'd been afraid. Once that fear wore off, she'd probably change her mind about him.

As he watched her quickly descend the stairs with little effort in those impractical shoes, he wondered if he'd met his match. He'd have to watch her closely. She was far from believing him. Somehow, he had to con-vince her that her best bet was with him.

Good luck with that, he thought. His track record right now wasn't good. He might have been able to keep her safe if he was on his home turf back in Lonesome. But in this city, a crowded, unfamiliar and so far unfriendly environment that was already trying his patience, he wasn't so sure. Spark was the perfect example of how well he could be trusted to keep her safe.

They reached the ground floor. He glanced at the security officer's station that had been manned earlier. It was now empty. Willie's gaze shot to the elevator. Someone had just gotten off on the fourteenth floor—Ellie's floor.

"Had you been expecting anyone to stop by your office?" he asked as he saw her follow his gaze.

"No," she said, a tightness in her voice as he took her arm to hurry them toward the exit. "Stay close to me." He could feel the muscles clench in her arm as he steered her out of the building and onto the dark street.

The moment they hit the street, the night air, redolent with the smell of the Sound, enveloped her. *What was she doing?* Now that they were out of the office, she began to question what she'd just done. Why hadn't she called upstairs? Maybe McNamara was still around. He would have known how to handle this. Hadn't he said as much when he'd told her to call him if she heard from Vernon Murphy?

The deputy still had a tight grasp on her arm and was leading her down the street in the wrong direction. She needed to get her car from the parking garage. Earlier, she'd panicked because the frantic call from Murphy had frightened her. It hadn't helped to see that someone had taken the elevator up to the fourteenth floor... She realized it could have been anyone. It didn't mean— She recalled that she hadn't noticed any security personnel at the desk on their way out. Too many coincidences?

A horn honked somewhere in the steady stream of traffic, making her jump.

Eleanor stopped walking abruptly. Several people had to dodge them on the busy sidewalk. But the deputy didn't let go of her arm. Instead, he turned in front of her so they were facing, inches apart. She saw him look over her shoulder.

"I know what you're thinking," he said.

"You have no idea."

"You can't go back to wherever you live," he said so close to her that she could see the lighter blue flecks in his eyes beneath the thick dark lashes. "You can't go get your car, either. They're probably watching us right now."

He was scaring her, but maybe that was exactly what he wanted. She had no reason to put her faith in him. She couldn't even be sure his version of what had happened to Vernon Murphy was true. She should have called McNamara right after Vernon's call. Or if not him, the police. Just the reminder of her client's shriek of agony and what the men who'd taken him were capable of…

"I need to go to the police," she said, determined to take control of this situation.

He shook his head as he pulled her out of the flow of pedestrians and lowered his voice as he moved even closer. "I already went to the police. If you didn't set up Vernon, then one of them did. They aren't going to help you any more than they helped me. Nor do I believe that they are actively looking for Spark and the men who took him, no matter what they say. I'm your best bet to stay alive. I know you don't believe that right now, but it just happens to be the truth."

In the time she'd been an attorney, she knew that the Seattle police force was overworked, undermanned and underpaid. But was she seriously going to throw in with this cowboy?

"Come on," he said, gripping her arm a little tighter. "Trust me, you don't want to do this on your own. Whoever hired you to represent Vernon threw you to the wolves."

She looked into those blue eyes. Trust him? Did she dare? She thought of McNamara and realized that she trusted anyone more than her boss right now. What choice did she have if the deputy was telling the truth?

"Let's get a drink." He drew her toward the door of a nearby busy pub.

The last thing she wanted was a drink, but she was smart enough to know he wanted to get them off the street. She glanced around as they headed for the bar, but she had no idea who might be after her or what they might look like—or if she was even really in danger.

As the deputy closed the pub door behind them, Eleanor felt a jolt. If someone really wanted her dead, they might even come in the guise of a cowboy cop.

Chapter 5

Willie found a corner at the back of the noisy, crowded pub where he could watch the front door as well as the back entrance near the restrooms. When the waitress came to take their drink orders, he asked for a beer. Ellie ordered something he'd never heard of. She looked nervous, as if ready to sprint to the back door and out of here.

He leaned closer, his lips next to her ear. He caught a whiff of her perfume as he said over the roar of voices, "Whoever hired you to represent Spark is the one who's put your life in danger. Not me." He pulled back to meet her gaze. She did not look convinced. "I'm in the same boat you are, except they already tried to kill me."

A large man came through the back door. He was dressed nicely enough, looking almost too clean-cut, but there was an agitated air about him that struck Willie as wrong. The man was looking toward the front of the pub as if searching for someone. As his head started to turn in their direction, Willie pulled off his Stetson and quickly leaned over in front of Ellie, cupped the back of her head with his free hand and kissed her.

Just when her mouth began to respond and the kiss was starting to get interesting, she jerked back, her right hand coming up fast. Just not fast enough. He caught her arm before she could slap him and then checked the spot where the man had been standing. He was gone.

"What do you think you're—"

He let go of her. "A man came in the back door looking for us."

Her eyes widened in alarm as her gaze shot to the back hallway. As she realized there was no one standing there, her eyes began to narrow.

"He was there. Big guy, hair cropped short, close-set eyes, dressed nice but not quite right." He shrugged. "I acted on instinct. But for a first kiss, it wasn't that bad, was it?" he asked. "Sorry, I was just trying to lighten the mood."

She scowled at him as she moved farther away from him. "I don't believe a word from that mouth of yours." She reached for her purse just as the waitress came with their drinks.

He laid a gentle hand on her arm. "Ellie, have your drink, then we'll decide what to do."

"It's Eleanor," she snapped, but he saw her hesitate as he slid the colorful drink she'd ordered toward her.

"I know you're scared. I am, too," he said quietly. "Just tell me this. Someone at your firm assigned you to Spark's case. Someone you trust?" He saw the answer as her lashes dropped over those Seattle-gray-sky eyes. She took a sip of her drink.

"Are there other female lawyers in the firm?" he asked. "I'm betting if there are, none of them look like you. Isn't it possible that's why you got the case?"

When she looked up, her eyes darkened with storm clouds. Anger pinched her lips.

He hurriedly raised a hand in surrender. "It's just a theory." He picked up his beer, took a drink, watching the entrances, his mind working. "There had to have been a red flag. You didn't think there was anything strange about the case?" He saw her hesitate and got his answer. "I'm guessing that whoever hired your firm offered too much money for a simple extradition of an arsonist, even one facing homicide charges. Or, someone at your firm has a connection to Spark or the person who did the hiring."

"You can't really believe that everyone in Seattle is part of this," she snapped. "Do you realize how paranoid you sound?" He could see that she was having doubts, and not just about him.

He watched her take another sip of her drink. She didn't look as confident as she had earlier. Was she wondering why she was given the case? Had she been suspicious from the onset?

From the sick look on her face, Willie suspected she was realizing that her boss had done exactly that—thrown her to the wolves.

Willie took a long draw on his beer and realized he hadn't eaten anything other than some green gelatin at the hospital. "You hungry?"

The look she shot him was incredulous, as if he'd asked her on a date. Or worse.

He signaled the waitress and ordered an appetizer plate and another beer. Ellie shook her head, still holding her not even half-finished cocktail. She looked more than ready to leave, but he had a feeling that the man who'd stuck his head in the back door might still be waiting outside. Let him wait a little longer. Willie ordered her another drink. For the moment, they were safe. Once they left this pub, all bets were off.

"Is there somewhere you could stay that no one at work knows about?" he asked.

"I work with attorneys. They can find anyone."

"I hope that's not true." But he suspected it was. "What do you suggest we do then?"

She side-eyed him. *"We?"*

"I'm not going to hold you against your will." He saw her disbelieving look. "I won't kiss you again unless I'm forced to."

"Thank you, I think." Was that just the tiniest of smiles?

"But I'm still your best bet for staying alive." She mugged a face and tipped more of her drink into her mouth. It was a very nice mouth, he noted, and checked his phone so he didn't think about it or the kiss. "I have my three brothers looking into the case back in Lonesome."

She put down her glass. "Your brothers are deputies, too?"

"Colt Brothers Investigation. They're private eyes. My father started the business after quitting the rodeo. We all have pretty much followed in his boot prints."

She considered him for a moment before she picked

up her drink and finished it. As she put the glass down, she seemed surprised to see another one waiting for her. The alcohol had taken the edge off her just a smidgen. She picked up the second drink, cupping it in her hands as she said, "So, you're a rodeo cowboy."

"I was a bull rider. I quit to join the sheriff's department. I'm actually looking for my father's killer." He saw her surprise. "It's a long story."

"Now you and your brothers are looking for the men who took Vernon."

He figured all lawyers had to be skeptics. "You can check it out on your phone if you don't believe me. Colt Brothers Investigation. Or just Colt Investigation for when it was only my father."

She put down her drink and dug out her phone. He watched her out of the corner of his eye as he scanned the crowded pub. No sign of the man from earlier, but that didn't mean that another one wouldn't come walking in the front door and neither he nor Ellie would realize it.

By the time the appetizers arrived, she'd put her phone away and picked up her new drink again. "Your father's death was ruled an accident."

He nodded as he helped himself to some food and pushed the platter closer to her. "The sheriff back then was a mite crooked and didn't like my family. My father was working on a case the sheriff didn't want him working on." He shrugged. "My gut tells me it wasn't an accident."

Eleanor found herself studying the cowboy next to her. There was more to him than she'd first thought. Three brothers in the investigation business. As an only child, she'd always wished for siblings. Now his brothers were working to help him. She envied that kind of loyalty, that kind of family.

She realized that she was starting to relax. Probably just the alcohol. It certainly couldn't have been the cowboy, as charming as he was. Or that kiss, as interesting as it had been. But she was glad to be in a public place surrounded by people. The cowboy was convincing. Still, she would be a fool not to have doubts about him.

Since she'd had a yogurt at her desk and that was about it all day, she nibbled on one of the appetizers. The alcohol had mellowed her. What she kept asking herself was how much of this she believed. She knew the only reason she was still sitting here with this cowboy was because of the call she'd earlier received from Vernon Murphy.

She thought of her conversations with her client before today. The deputy had been right. Vernon had begged her not to let Washington extradite him back to Montana. But he wasn't the first client who didn't want to go back to the state where he'd committed the crime. She could guess what information the cowboy wanted from her. That she was here with him already made her feel disloyal to the firm, not to mention what her betrayal meant as a lawyer sworn to uphold client-attorney confidentiality.

"I have to use the restroom." She rose, half expecting him to either try to stop her or go with her. "I won't be long." She started to step away when he reached for her wrist. She turned to look back at him with one of her perfected stares that had worked many times with so-called witnesses on the stand at a trial. "You don't trust me?"

"Probably more than you trust me." He brushed his calloused thumb over the tender skin on the back of her wrist. The look in his eyes suddenly felt dangerous. Her heart responded with a flurry of thumps that hurt her chest. At the same time, heat ran along her veins, warming her blood. He let go. "Be careful."

Willie sat debating as he watched her walk away from him. Maybe she was just going to the ladies' room. Maybe she'd come back. He doubted it. She was hard to read. He reminded himself that there was nothing he could do if she took off on her own. The thought made him swear, since he was convinced that she really didn't know what she'd stepped into when she'd taken Spark's case.

His cell phone vibrated in his pocket. He pulled it out and saw that it was the call he'd been waiting for. "I tried to call you earlier, but your phone was off," his brother James told him. "I have information. Spark worked as a blaster for a mining corporation out here in Montana. He was still working as an explosive expert in North Dakota when he took the job in Lonesome. The interesting part is that the mining corporation is based out in Washington, near where you are."

Willie found himself watching the opening to the hallway that led to the restrooms—and the back door—growing more anxious. "That is interesting."

"It gets better. The woman who died in the explosion he set? Her name is Zoey Bertrand, twenty-eight, a former receptionist at Cascade Extraction Corp in Gig Harbor, Washington—the same company Spark works for. There's a chance he knew her."

"Thanks," Willie said, getting to his feet. "Gotta go, will get back to you." He disconnected and headed for the back door. He told himself that there was nothing he could do if the attorney took off on him. But at the same time…

Eleanor relieved herself. As she stood at the sink minutes later, washing her hands, the doubts surfaced with a vengeance. As an attorney, she wasn't required to consider whether her client was guilty or innocent. All she had to work with was the evidence and the restrictions of the law.

What evidence did she have that Deputy Willie Colt was telling the truth? Had she let his badge persuade her? Or was it his cowboy swagger? Maybe she should call McNamara. She had his cell number. She dried her hands and pulled out her phone, but then changed her mind. She felt confused, and the two cocktails she'd had weren't any help on an almost empty stomach.

Her instincts told her that the cowboy was dangerous. Clearly he was a loose cannon who played by his own rules. Shouldn't she get out of here and go somewhere until she had a better grasp of what was going on? She could go to a friend's if she really believed her life was in danger. Didn't that make more sense?

Worried she'd waited too long to make up her mind, she started to open the restroom door when it flew open. She jumped back, expecting it would be the deputy. A couple of intoxicated young women came in laughing as they rushed past her. A line was forming in the hall with more intoxicated young women all wearing Bachelorette Party T-shirts.

Eleanor had to smile, remembering nights out with her friends, some preceding one of them tying the knot. Her big-city independence made her even more determined to go her own way and figure things out on her own—no matter what the cowboy said.

Once out of the bathroom, she headed down the hall, past the men's lavatory and out the back door to the narrow alley. As the door closed behind her and she stepped out in the darkness, she had a moment of uncertainty. She stood on the wooden steps just outside the door, the sudden quiet almost deafening after the noisy pub.

Before she could step down to alley level, the pub door swung open, knocking her forward. She fought to stay on her heels as she dropped down the few steps to the alley. She spun around, cursing Deputy Willie Colt, whom she expected to see in the doorway.

Her breath caught at the sight of the large man standing in the lighted doorway before the door swung shut behind him. He matched the description the cowboy had given earlier, of the man he said was looking for them. She froze at the sight of him, unable to move even as he pulled on a pair of black gloves.

For those brief seconds, she told herself that the man wasn't after her. The cowboy had just been trying to scare her, maybe hoping to get a kiss.

She started to turn, knowing that once she took a step, she would run. But the man had read her movement. He lunged down the steps, grabbing her arm before she could move. She watched him pull a syringe from his jacket pocket, her pulse rocketing. There was nowhere to run, nothing in the alley she could use to defend herself. Even if she screamed, she doubted she would be heard in the noisy pub.

Her pulse took off like a supersonic jet at Sea Tac. She tried to pull away, but he only held her tighter as he dragged her to him, clearly determined to inject her with whatever was in the syringe.

Willie pushed his way past the line to the women's restroom, stuck his head in the door and called her name. No answer but giggles and smart remarks from all the women inside. He peered under the four stalls to even more squawks from the women. No Louboutin high heels. He swore as he pushed his way back out and started down the hallway to the back door.

Hadn't he known she would run? Why would she trust him? More important, why had he believed her and her steely gray eyes peering at him from behind the dark lashes? No, it had been the feel of her mouth under his that had made him think he could trust her as far as the ladies' room.

Swearing, he shoved open the back door, expecting her to be long gone and only himself to blame if something happened to her.

What he saw chilled his blood to Montana winter ice. A large man was struggling with the attorney. She'd taken off one of her shoes, using the spiked heel like a weapon as the man appeared to be trying to inject her with the syringe in his hand, all the while swearing profusely.

Willie pulled his weapon. "Police, stop!"

The words had barely left his mouth when the man let out a cry of pain. He swung around, bringing Ellie with him. He shoved her. She crashed into Willie on her way to the ground, blocking him from taking a shot as the man took off down the alley, turned the corner and vanished. But not before Willie saw the damage that had been done to the man's left eye—apparently by the lethal heel of Ellie's shoe.

He wanted desperately to go after the man, but Ellie was on the ground—the syringe next to her. If the man had injected her with something that would kill her— He holstered his gun and quickly crouched down next to her. "Did he inject you?"

She shook her head.

"Are you sure?"

"I'm sure," she said as she pulled herself into a sitting position, then to standing by pulling on his arm. She stood on one shoe and one bare foot as she reached into her purse to pull out a tissue. He watched her wipe blood off the heel of the shoe she'd been using to hold the man off. He could see that her lips were trembling even as she tried hard not to show how frightened she was. Or how nauseated by what she'd had to wipe off her shoe.

He wanted to shake her. Or at least yell at her, telling her what a fool she'd been to try to leave without him. But as he watched her struggle to put her shoe back on her foot, he couldn't do either. There was no need. Instead, he offered her an arm as she slipped on the expensive heel.

"Can I have one of those tissues?" She didn't question why he wanted it, merely reached into her purse and handed him one. He saw that he didn't have to chastise her for her foolish behavior as she leaned against him for a moment before she straightened and began to dust off her clearly expensive suit. Except for one lone tear on her cheek and a little smeared mascara, she looked like the professional she was. There was no doubt that she was a woman to be reckoned with, he thought as he leaned down and used the tissue to carefully pick up the syringe. He felt a surge of respect for her even as he wanted to throttle her.

"You're sure he didn't prick you with it?" he asked again. She gave him an impatient look before she shook her head. He examined the syringe. "Probably little chance of fingerprints since he was wearing gloves." He considered it a moment longer, then pocketed it. "Got to try to get a print off it anyway."

"I thought you didn't trust the police?"

"I don't. You know any cops you trust?"

Chapter 6

Eleanor considered that for a moment. "I might know one." She'd expected the deputy to lecture her, warn her again about how dangerous this all was. As if she didn't know since she'd been fighting for her life only minutes ago. Maybe he was smart enough to see that his point had been made, she thought.

"We have to get out of here," he said, looking down the alley where the man had disappeared. "The next time he comes after you, he'll bring help." He met her gaze. "He didn't expect you to fight like that." She swallowed, surprised herself.

"We can't take your car and I'm unable to pick up my patrol SUV yet."

She pulled out her phone.

"What are you doing?" he demanded.

"Calling an Uber. One will be here in three minutes.

He's picking us up on the other side of the block where there is less traffic this time of the evening."

"An Uber," he repeated. She suspected from his expression that he didn't have the app on his phone. He'd probably never had the need, or Lonesome didn't have Uber service. Did the town even have a stoplight?

They quickly walked down the alley to the other side of the block as a car pulled up. "E.L. Shafer?" the driver asked. She nodded and they climbed into the back of the sedan and the driver took off.

"Where are we going?" the cowboy whispered.

"I had to give him an address. Right now we're headed for Sea Tac. We can pick up a taxi from there or another Uber. The whole idea is not to be followed, right?" she whispered back.

He glanced behind them. "Right." She could feel his gaze return to her.

Eleanor tried to relax. She was safe. At least for the moment. She leaned back into the seat and fought to calm her still thundering pulse. She'd never experienced anything like what had happened in the alley. Although she'd wondered what she would do if she was ever attacked. It was something a woman living in the city thought about occasionally.

"What do you think is in the syringe?" She knew it was still in his jacket pocket. Did he really hope to get prints off it? Or had he been worried that she was mistaken and had been stuck and might need an antidote?

"More than likely a drug to make you more manageable. Whatever it is, it probably wouldn't have been strong enough." Was that something like admiration she saw in his gaze? Or a rebuff because she'd tried to get away from him?

She looked away, shuddering inside at the memory of her heel puncturing the attacker's left eye. They drove in silence. The lawyer in her tried to put together everything that had happened since she was asked to take Vernon Murphy on as a client. Given what had happened in the alley, there seemed no denying the fact that her client and the deputy weren't the only ones who'd been set up.

As she considered that, she also wondered how much—if anything—to tell the deputy. He was right about one thing. Her life seemed to be in danger. "Vernon didn't tell me who hired him."

He seemed surprised by the admission. "He was probably trying to protect you. Unfortunately, the person who hired him to do the arson job might not believe that."

Eleanor thought of her client, remembering how nervous and afraid he'd been—and with good reason, as it turned out. She could still feel the effects of the two cocktails she'd consumed. She wished now that she'd eaten more of the appetizers he'd ordered.

"Who do you think has Vernon?" she asked.

"Whoever gains the most by him not standing trial."

She thought about that. "If they wanted to get rid of him, why not kill him while he was in the process of destroying the building?"

The cowboy smiled at her. He did have a killer smile. "Too dangerous. Spark knew what he was doing. Whoever hired him didn't, or that person would have done the job himself." He shrugged.

"If he was taken by the person who hired him, then why torture him?"

She saw him consider that and suspected he'd already been asking himself the same question.

"Could be they don't know if he had any contact with

the woman in the building before it blew. Maybe she passed him a message somehow—that's if he even saw her. I don't know. More than likely they didn't expect him to run. I wonder why he did. Makes me think he did see the woman and possibly recognize her. The sheriff's department got the tip even before the building went up in smoke. Instead, he managed to get away and now the person who hired him has no idea who he's talked to and what he's told them." He sighed and looked behind them again.

"Are we being followed?"

"More than likely, but who can tell in this traffic?" He turned back around. "I don't understand why Spark didn't tell the cops out here the name of the man who hired him."

"You asked earlier if there was a Seattle police officer I trusted. Vernon told me that he trusted one of the cops, but that he wouldn't make that mistake again."

She saw from the deputy's surprise that this was news.

"Did he tell you the cop's name?"

She could feel the alcohol humming in her bloodstream. What if the deputy really was the only one looking for the men who'd taken her client? If she ever wanted this to end… "Alex Mattson."

"Then I'm going to have to find Mattson. If he isn't working for the bad guys, then he's probably already dead, since I imagine Vernon has been persuaded to talk by now."

She pulled out her phone, tapped on the keys and said, "Mattson lives in West Seattle." She looked over at him and lifted a brow in question.

"Maybe you didn't hear me correctly. Mattson might

be working with the bad guys. Or he might be dead and the bad guys waiting for us."

"And if he's not working for them and not dead yet? I've met him. I got the impression he was an honest cop."

"What's the address?" He repeated it to the driver, who changed course.

Eleanor felt a rush of adrenaline even as she questioned how getting in deeper was going to get her out of this mess.

"Anything else you want to share?" the cowboy asked close to her ear.

She didn't look at him as she said, "Vernon *did* see the woman. He said she rushed the window." Feeling his surprised stare, she finally looked over at him. "He swore that the building was empty because he was checking it as he set the charges. But just before the top floor exploded, he saw her." She cleared her voice. "He said her wrists were bound together. She was beating on the window, her mouth open as if she was screaming. He figured she'd been secured in the building but had managed to get free and couldn't escape for some reason."

The deputy swore. "There was a piece of burnt bicycle cable still attached to her ankle when her body was found."

Eleanor felt sick at the thought as she watched him studying the traffic behind them again.

She suspected he couldn't tell if they were being tailed or not. If they were, they could be leading the bad guys right to Alex Mattson's door. She hoped that wasn't the case, but she'd feel responsible if it was.

"Maybe you should call Officer Mattson. He might not even be home."

"You're probably right." She gave him the number

and he placed the call. She was half hoping Alex Matt-son wouldn't answer the phone, so she was disappointed when the cowboy spoke. "Alex Mattson? This is Deputy Willie Colt from Lonesome, Montana. I was the deputy sent out to take Vernon Murphy back for trial. I'd like to ask you a few questions." He held the phone where she could hear the conversation.

"I don't know anything about Vernon...what did you say his name was? Murphy?" Then, a pause. "This isn't a good time," Alex Mattson barked, and the line went dead.

The deputy looked over at her as the driver said they had reached their destination.

Eleanor felt weak with guilt over everything she'd done since the cowboy had walked into her office. Until she reminded herself that there were still people out there who would torture her apparently and it was the deputy who'd saved her in the alley—certainly not her boss.

Still, she felt as if she was only getting in deeper and with a man she wasn't sure she should be trusting. Yet, as the cowboy had pointed out, he seemed to be her best bet to stay alive right now.

The cop lived in a small bungalow with a freshly mown tiny front yard. Willie had the Uber driver go past the house and drop him a block away. He didn't think they'd been followed.

"Your first Uber ride?" Ellie asked him as he tried to give the driver money. "I have an account. It's all taken care of, including a tip. Don't worry, he'll wait for us."

"There's no Uber in Lonesome," Willie said in his defense. "And I own a truck, so I have my own ride. The rest of the time I drive a patrol SUV."

"Welcome to the twenty-first century," she said, and started to get out, but he stopped her.

Just as he'd suspected, she'd bounced back from the incident in the alley. At least temporarily. He figured it wasn't something anyone could throw off that easily. The trauma of it would probably hit her sometime in the middle of the night when she least expected it. He wondered where they would be then.

Or if they would even still be together. Once he got out of this car, she might tell the driver to take her home.

"You've proven that you have no trouble moving in those high heels and that tight skirt," he said. "So I'm guessing that if things go south with Mattson, you'd probably outrun me back to the Uber. But let's not try out that theory, okay? You need to stay here with the Uber guy and let me handle this. If things do go south, you tell him to take off like a bat out of hell. But not back to your place."

"You call that a plan? If Alex Mattson is dirty and a deputy shows up at his door this time of night... What could possibly go wrong? But if an attorney—"

"If you're suggesting what I think you are, forget it." He caught the flash of taillights behind them up the block as someone backed out of the garage at the Mattson house and turned in their direction. A moment later the car roared past as if the devil himself was riding shotgun.

"Change of plan," Willie said, and flashed his badge as he asked the driver to follow the car that had just sped past them with a man he suspected was Alex Mattson behind the wheel.

Chapter 7

Eleanor hated being caught up in something completely out of her control. She'd once tried surfing in Hawaii, on a trip with friends. She'd fallen, tumbling into a wave that wouldn't let her go. She kept tumbling and tumbling, convinced she was going to drown, before the wave spat her out on the beach.

She'd never wanted to feel that helpless ever again. Yet here she was, in a car speeding through the streets, feeling as if she was caught in that same wave. The deputy was leaning forward and giving the driver instructions, complimenting the man on his ability to keep the other vehicle in sight despite traffic. From lane to lane, they rocketed through the night, lights blurring past.

Eleanor told herself that this wasn't happening. This wasn't her life. For so long her every thought as well as most of the hours of the day had been spent at work. Her parents had both been lawyers. She'd wanted to make them proud, and that meant nothing less than taking back the firm they had started, which Phillip McNamara had somehow wrangled from them. She wanted to see her family name up there again, so she'd worked night and day, head down, only that one goal in mind. She would change that all-boys club if it was the last thing she did.

As she hung on in the back seat of the speeding Uber, she could almost hear what her parents would have said if they could see her now. *"What would ever possess you to do something so irrational and dangerous? Why did you even consider leaving your office with such a man? Didn't we teach you to always follow the chain of command? You should have called Phillip. He promised to look after you."*

"Are you all right?" the cowboy asked.

She had no idea how long he'd been studying her. She nodded, shoving away the voices of her parents as the Uber took a hard left, throwing her against the door.

"Stop here," the deputy ordered. In the rearview mirror, she saw that the driver looked exhilarated. She feared he, too, was risking his life and job for this cowboy cop.

"Give me your phone number," the deputy said to her. "I'll text you the address once I know it. We need to know who lives here." He handed her his phone and she keyed in her number before handing it back.

"Terry, our driver, is going to need a big tip," Willie said.

Eleanor could only nod, thinking she would probably never be able to take another Uber again if the driver gave her a bad review. But if she didn't have a job, she wouldn't be going anywhere, would she?

The deputy gave her a warning look. "Stay here," he said, and was out of the car.

"Is he really a cop?" the driver asked as his adrenaline waned. He sounded nervous.

"Believe it or not, he is. Apparently, this is the way they do things back in Montana."

"That explains the hat," the driver said as they both watched the deputy disappear into the darkness toward the house where Alex Mattson was now parked.

Her cell phone rang, startling her. She checked the screen. McNamara? It rang again. Her heart pounded. Should she take it? The driver glanced back at her as it rang yet again.

"It's my boss," she said, staring at the phone again. "I can't imagine why he would be calling at this hour." Actually, she could. She declined the call to let it go to voice mail, hoping that hadn't been a mistake, and waited for a message or voice mail, but one never came.

What had he wanted? Was there news on Vernon? She highly doubted he would call her if there was. She tried to breathe. Where was the cowboy and what did she do if he didn't come back?

That thought only increased her anxiety. There would be only one reason Deputy Willie Colt didn't come back.

Chapter 8

Alex Mattson's car was parked in front of the garage at 30478 Seabrook Lane. The house was huge in a line of huge houses that overlooked Lake Union. Lights were on behind the drapes of what Willie assumed was the living room. Another light shone from an upstairs room.

He texted the address to Ellie and checked the time. Late enough that Mattson might have had to wake up whoever lived here. It didn't take her long to cross reference the address with the name of the owner of the house in a database her firm subscribed to. She texted back the name. Jonathan Asher.

The name meant nothing to him. Who's that? he texted back, but didn't wait for an answer as he cautiously approached the house.

Standing in the flower bed, doing his best not to trample the flowers, he peered through a narrow gap in the front drapes. The open-concept house allowed him to see all the way from the living room through the kitchen to the back door. He could see two men standing in the kitchen at the island.

Willie guessed the slightly balding, younger man with the paunch was Mattson. He was talking fast, waving his hands, clearly agitated. He appeared upset about something. After Willie's call just minutes before the cop had taken off like a shot from his house to come here?

The older, more distinguished man with his head of white hair filled a glass with something dark and shoved it toward Mattson, who quickly picked it up and drained it.

From this distance, Willie couldn't hear what was being said. He'd have to go around back to get closer to the kitchen. But that meant going through the gate. There was always the chance Jonathan Asher had a dog. Or security.

Before he could decide, Mattson slammed down his empty glass. It appeared that Asher was attempting to calm the man down—and failing. Asher reached into his pocket, pulled out his wallet and handed the cop some bills. Mattson threw them back in his face and turned to leave.

Willie had to scramble to get out of sight as the cop stormed through the house and out the front door to his vehicle. Hiding in the bushes, he watched the man drive off before returning to the flower bed so he could see what was happening in the house.

Just as he'd suspected, Asher was on the phone. He, too, was now talking fast. Willie moved through the shadows to the sidewalk, then leisurely walked back to the waiting Uber and Ellie. All the way, he couldn't imagine what this might have to do with Spark—yet it felt like the arsonist turned killer was the catalyst that had set something much bigger than his own crime into motion.

Willie just had no idea what it was. But until he found out, he and Ellie might not be the only ones in danger.

Eleanor felt a wave of relief as she spotted the cowboy coming out of the darkness. She hadn't realized that she'd been holding her breath until the sight of him finally let her breathe again.

The back door swung open and he slid in, bringing the crisp night air with him. "We're going to need a motel," he said to the driver. "Something out of the way and cheap." The driver got the car moving.

As if sensing what she was about to say, the deputy—like a magician—produced with a flourish a long-stemmed red rose, making her wonder where he'd gotten it. "The motel's just for tonight until I can figure out what we do next," he said as he handed her the rose.

We? She stared at the rose, feeling suddenly close to tears. She should have been curled up in her king bed in her apartment working at this hour. The last thing she wanted to do was to spend the night in some cheap motel—let alone with this charming, handsome, loose cannon of a cowboy.

But the memory of Vernon's call and the vile man in the alley with the syringe had her scared as the Uber driver began to work his way back to a commercial part of the city.

The deputy pulled out his phone. "I'm calling Mattson. I suspect he's in over his head and knows it by now. I want to make sure he does. Maybe if we rattle his cage…" He leaned toward her so she could hear, bringing with him his male scent and the warmth of his strong shoulder against hers.

She heard the ringing stop. Alex Mattson had declined the call. It went to voice mail. "It's Deputy Willie Colt. I missed you at your house tonight. Whatever Spark told you, it's going to get you killed if you aren't careful. Seems Jonathan Asher isn't going to be of any help. You have to know that you could be next. Call me when you're ready to talk. Hope you don't wait too long."

Before he could pocket his phone, it rang. "It's Mattson," he said, and took the call.

"How did you get my number?" the cop demanded.

"I need to know what Spark told you and who you told. I suspect you're the one who gave the information to the people who attacked me and abducted him."

"I don't know what you're talking about."

"I know Spark confided in you. But how does Jonathan Asher fit in?"

A few beats, before Mattson said, "Who?"

"The man you visited tonight. Looked like a pretty intense conversation."

Silence. Then a shocked *"You followed me?"*

"I'm a cop, too, remember? I'm going to find out what's going on—hopefully before bodies start stacking up. I'd hate one of them to be yours."

"Are you threatening me?"

"Of course not. I suspect you have enough people threatening you, am I right? I'm offering to help, starting with you telling me what Spark told you in confidence before it's too late to help him—or you."

Mattson let out a nervous laugh. "Don't call me again or I'll have you arrested." He disconnected.

"What if he goes to the chief of police and tells him that you're threatening him?" Eleanor asked.

The deputy shrugged as he straightened and pocketed his phone. His shoulder moved away from hers, taking the heat and what little comfort it had offered. "I need to find out which side of the law he's on. I don't think he'll have me arrested, which means he's one of the bad guys."

Eleanor stared at him for a moment, then closed her eyes. Her life was out of control. The only way to stop this was with facts, she reminded herself. She opened her eyes and pulled out her phone. "Jonathan Asher is retired," she said as Willie balanced his Stetson on his knee and, leaning closer, watched her fingers moving in a blur on her phone. She tried to ignore his close proximity and the sweet scent of the rose resting next to her thigh on the seat. "Asher apparently made his money in real estate and investments."

"Can you find out if one of those investments was in a mining corporation called Cascade Extraction Corp out of Gig Harbor?"

"That will take longer than this Uber ride, but I'm sure I can," she said as she pocketed her phone, her gaze going to the rose again. He had to have picked it for her out of someone's yard. Asher's? "Are you going to tell me what happened back there?"

He turned to look at her, drawing her attention to him. Even in the dim light coming from the dashboard, she couldn't help but notice how blue his eyes were or how dark his lashes. He had a couple days' growth of stubble. He looked dangerous, like a man on a deadly mission. A man who could not be stopped when he wanted something badly enough. She thought how different he was from any man she'd ever known as her body warmed to the sexy, diamond-in-the-rough cowboy. She blamed those two cocktails she'd had. No more drinking around this man.

She thought he wasn't going to answer, but after a moment it was as if he realized he owed her more than a flower. "I couldn't hear the conversation, but Mattson was worked up about something. Asher was trying to calm him down. I'm not sure he succeeded. He tried to give the cop money, but Mattson threw it back in his face. How all this ties in with Spark—or if it even does—I have no idea."

"But you suspect it does."

He nodded. "Spark confides in Mattson. Spark is taken. After my call, Mattson races over to see Asher late at night, clearly upset."

"How does this mining corporation fit in?"

"I heard from my brother James. Spark works as a blaster, an explosive expert, for Cascade Extraction Corp. The woman who was killed also worked for the same company."

"I don't see arson as the next step in an illustrious career."

"I suspect someone offered him a job on the side that paid more than blowing up rocks," he said. "If we look into arson cases that involve property owned by the corporation or its subsidiaries, I suspect we'll see a pattern."

"This is the first time Vernon's been arrested for arson," she said.

"He's either been lucky or he's good at the job. Which is probably why he knew he'd been set up and ran the moment he saw the woman at the window."

She frowned. "If Vernon did reveal the name of the

person who hired him, and Mattson didn't go to his boss…'"

"He might have seen blackmail as more lucrative. But a very dangerous business. I hope he knows what he's doing if that's the case." He shrugged. "Or he could have gone to Asher because he heard that I was coming looking for the men who took Spark—and those behind it." His grin, even in the dark, destabilized her already weakened emotional balance. The man was alluring, especially after everything she'd been through today. He'd saved her life. How did she deal with that, let alone the fact that there was something so appealing about his rough-edged cowboy charm?

She couldn't. Not tonight. "My boss called while you were…picking flowers."

"Is that something he does, call you this late?"

"No." She could see he was waiting to hear what McNamara wanted. "I didn't take the call and he didn't leave a message. Maybe I should have."

"No. If you had, your cell would have pinged and he would have known what neighborhood you were in. You were smart not to take the call." But she could tell that like her, he wondered what her boss had wanted—and probably suspected it had something to do with Vernon.

"Sounds like they are expecting you to get a call from Spark."

"Can you please call him by his real name?" she snapped.

He looked over at her, his expression softening. "You think Vernon is better?"

"It is his name."

"Fair enough," he said with a nod, his gaze staying on her a little too long for comfort.

She gave the driver an address of a hotel in Seattle. Out of the corner of her eye, she saw the deputy raise a brow. Fortunately for him, he didn't comment. She was tired, dirty and not staying in some out-of-the way cheap motel with this cowboy lounging in a sagging bed next to her. She was taking charge and they would definitely *not* be roughing it.

Chapter 9

PI James Colt felt as if he'd fallen down a rabbit hole. He stared at the computer screen. Since Willie's call, he'd been following Cascade Extraction Corporation's maze of subsidiaries, divisions and multitudes of holdings.

The mining part of the corporation had been involved in numerous lawsuits and paid millions in penalties for environmental mishaps at their mines. The state of Montana was still involved in several lawsuits over the mining company pulling out and leaving a mess behind.

It was nothing new for Montana, which used to be called the Treasure State. Since the beginning, corrupt companies had come in, ravished the land and left. This corporation seemed to be no different.

"Are you coming to bed?"

He turned to see his beautiful, pregnant wife standing in the doorway. Realizing how late it was, he shut down his computer and rose to go to her. James couldn't believe that Lorelei Wilkins had agreed to marry an ex-rodeo bronc rider turned private investigator. He'd never thought he could get that lucky.

"How's our daughter?"

"Jamie's sound asleep." Lori had insisted on naming her after her father.

"And our son?" he asked as he laid a hand on Lori's swelling belly.

"Growing every day."

He bent to kiss her, drawing her to him. "We should go to bed."

She chuckled. "My thought exactly. What are you working on that has you so engrossed anyway?"

"I'm doing some investigating for Willie."

Lori frowned. "I thought he was out in Washington picking up an arsonist."

"He was. Unfortunately, he was attacked by a couple of men who took his prisoner. Now he's determined to find them and get the man back." He didn't mention that the fugitive might already be dead.

"Is Willie all right?" she asked, studying him, no doubt knowing there was more to the story. There usually was in this business.

"Concussion, but you know how hardheaded he is. The doctor wants to keep him overnight for observation."

"He's in the hospital?" she asked in alarm as they reached their bedroom suite in the house he'd built for her on Colt Ranch.

"Maybe," James said noncommittally, making her groan. "Probably not. By now, he's probably checked himself out."

"Oh, you Colt brothers," she said with a shake of her head. It was a familiar refrain.

Willie didn't know what to do with the attorney. He'd all but kidnapped her. But he couldn't keep her. The smart thing to do would be to talk her into visiting some friends in another state until he got to the bottom of what was going on. The problem would be convincing her—even after what had happened in the alley outside the pub.

Also, even if she was agreeable to leaving the city, he had to admit she'd been helpful. He didn't know anything about the city and, worse, he didn't have the resources she did, because the Seattle police weren't offering any help nor was the sheriff back home.

Terry dropped them off in downtown Seattle at an expensive-looking hotel, from what Willie could tell. He shot a look at Ellie. "You can't use a credit card."

"I used to live in the penthouse as a child," she said with a sigh as Terry jumped out to open her door. "I won't use a credit card and I gave our driver a large tip."

"The county will reimburse you," Willie lied as he climbed out and they walked toward the waiting hotel doorman. He'd have to dig into his savings, but he would pay her back.

His cell rang as they entered the lobby. Ellie went straight to the reception desk. He saw that everyone seemed to know her, from the doorman to the clerk behind the desk. As he took the call, Willie tried not to worry that her boss would also know she might come here.

To his surprise, it was the local cop shop letting him know that his patrol SUV could be picked up at the yard in the morning after paying the towing fee. He disconnected with a curse.

"Something wrong?" Ellie asked.

He shook his head. "Everything is great. You did get just one room, right?"

"You still don't trust me?"

"I could ask you the same thing," he said, their gazes locking. She looked as tired and worn out as he felt. But it hadn't dimmed that spark of rebellious determination in those gray eyes of hers. It reminded him of a wolf he'd stumbled across in the middle of a trail some years ago. The wolf wasn't getting off the path. Willie had quickly considered his options before he stepped off and gave the wolf a wide berth. He'd made some mistakes in his life, but he was no fool.

Letting that wolf get the better of him was one of the smart things he'd done. But he wasn't so easy when it came to the buttoned-up attorney. She didn't know the kind of men they were dealing with. He did. There would be no stepping off the trail to appease these men. Things had gone too far. While Willie was looking for them, they would be looking for not only him, but also Ellie. Spark's call to warn her assured him of that.

"I got a suite with two adjoining bedrooms. I think you'll be pleased," she said as she turned on her heels and headed for the elevators.

He saw she still had the rose he'd picked for her from Jonathan Asher's yard. He couldn't help smiling as he followed her.

Eleanor watched the cowboy take in the suite she'd gotten for them on the sixteenth floor of the four-star hotel. He'd let out a low whistle even before he'd walked to the balcony to take in the view of Puget Sound. It looked like a photograph from a brochure, complete with one of the late ferries' running lights glittering on the dark water.

"You're just showing off," he said as he turned to look at her.

She chuckled. "Maybe a little. Maybe I just like to pick my own…motels."

He smiled at that. With the night sky behind him, his blue eyes seemed to sparkle. She felt him sizing her up as he slowly removed his Stetson and raked a hand through his hair. It was thick, collar-length and as shiny black against the skyline as the piece of obsidian a friend had sent her from Yellowstone Park. There was no way the man could have been more handsome.

But it was that hint of wild about him that was most appealing. She could tell he probably would have been more comfortable in a tent in the middle of a pine forest. She'd seen that primal look in those blue eyes of his the moment he'd walked into her office. All her instincts had told her to beware and yet here she was alone in a hotel room with him.

She'd faced down criminals before without batting an eyelash, but the intensity of the cowboy's gaze forced her to lower her eyes. "Your room is that way." She pointed to the right as she dropped the two key cards on the counter next to the door. "My door locks. Nothing personal but I want a hot, uninterrupted bath." She pretended she didn't see the slight lift of his eyebrow or the widening of those blue eyes as she turned toward her room. "You can order something to eat for us from room service."

"What would you like?" he asked.

"Surprise me." She didn't need to see his face to know that he was grinning.

"Enjoy your bath." When she turned before closing her door, she saw that he had moved back to the wall of glass and was looking out at the city lights and the dark water. In the reflection, she saw his forehead furrow before he turned away to find the phone and call for room service. She couldn't imagine what he would order for them as she closed and locked the door. She smiled at the thought since she didn't care. She was starved and her life was out of control and had been ever since he'd walked into her life.

Tossing her purse down, she took off her coat. As she did, she saw that she'd missed a text. It was from Phillip McNamara.

You have me worried. Call me.

Willie had kicked off his boots, removed his holster and sprawled on the couch after ordering room service and then calling his brother James and filling him in on what little he'd discovered. He found a news station on the television, but there was nothing that he could find about Spark... Vernon. He'd turned it off, worried that he was trying to save a dead man.

He couldn't help but question why he was still in Seattle. It wasn't his job to find Vernon—or the men who'd attacked him and taken his prisoner. If he was smart, he'd return to Lonesome—just as his boss had ordered him.

But how could he? He glanced toward the closed, locked bedroom door and thought about the buttoned-up attorney in the next room, neck-deep in bubbles. He quickly pushed that particular image away. Even as he felt guilty, he told himself that she wasn't his responsibility. He hadn't gotten her involved in this. Her boss had.

But he couldn't convince himself to leave her to her own devices. The man in the alley had been planning to drug her and take her—of that he was certain. What other answer was there? They wanted to know what Vernon had told her.

Nor could he back away from finding Vernon and the men who'd taken him, any more than he could desert Ellie.

There was a knock at the door. He picked up his weapon, tucked it into the back of his jeans and went to the door. Room service. "I can take it from here," he said to the young man, pulling out a few bills to send him on his way.

When he dragged the cart full of food into the room, he saw Ellie come out of her adjoining bedroom wearing nothing it appeared but a large, fluffy robe. What flesh he could see had a rosy-pink glow. Even in the robe she looked untouchable, although there was a lightness to her gray eyes.

"Enjoy your bath?" he asked. She looked away in answer and tugged the sash on her robe tighter around her. "I hope you're hungry," he said, and smiled because she looked like the bath had done wonders for her. He noted that her long hair was still wet. She'd pulled it up in a ponytail. Did this woman ever let her hair down? Not around him, he thought ruefully.

Eleanor's stomach growled loudly, making Willie laugh as she joined him at the table by the balcony windows. With a flourish, he removed the covers from the food. She couldn't help but laugh when she saw what he'd ordered. Two beautiful fat, juicy-looking beef burgers, two beers and a basket full of thick-cut French fries.

"If you tell me you only eat lettuce, it is over between us," he joked.

She shook her head. "I've been known to eat beef."

He grinned and handed her a plate. "Smart. You never want to tell a Montanan you don't eat beef." They each dove into their meals. She got the feeling he hadn't had much to eat all day, either. The burger was delicious. She indulged on the fries as well, not feeling even a little guilty, although she'd only been able to eat half of the huge burger. She could feel him watching her as she dragged a fat fry through a puddle of ketchup.

"I thought maybe everyone out here ate salmon," he said.

She looked at him. "What's wrong with salmon?"

"Nothing. I just happen to like the rainbow trout I pull out of a stream back home, fried up with potatoes and onions and served with baked beans and homemade bread." He smacked his lips comically and she laughed.

"I'm noticing a fried theme."

"I might have some coleslaw with my trout sometimes."

Eleanor shook her head. "Who does all this cooking? Don't tell me you do this frying yourself."

He raised a brow. "If you're asking who I share my kitchen with, I don't. I never stayed anywhere long enough to get serious about a woman."

"I believe I asked about food, not your love life."

He grinned and shrugged. "Sorry. When I'm home I cook, usually over a Coleman stove outside a tent in the woods. I got sick of fast food on the rodeo circuit."

He dropped his gaze to what was left of his fries. She watched him dredge one through his ketchup.

"But now that you're a deputy, sounds like you'll be staying in one place."

"What about you?" he asked before he took a bite of the fry. "Who cooks for you?"

She smiled, knowing what he was really asking. "No one in my kitchen, either." She laughed. "Not even me. I live in a place where I can order anything I want almost any hour of the day."

He shook his head as if in wonder. "I live in a town that rolls up the sidewalks at eight every weekday night, ten on Saturday. Sunday, after church, most people get a meal at the family restaurant. Chicken-fried steak is its specialty."

"Fried, of course," she said with a laugh.

They ate in companionable silence for a few minutes, Willie finishing off his fries and Eleanor moving hers around the plate.

"You might like Montana," he said, shoving his plate away. "You might even like trout. I suppose you've never had elk or antelope or venison?"

She shook her head. "I tried buffalo. It was okay. I think I prefer beef."

That made him smile. But then his eyes darkened as his gaze locked with hers. She felt her breath catch in her throat at his look.

"You need to leave town until this is over. I'll let you know when it's safe enough for you to come back."

"I thought that was what the chief of police told you to do."

"I'm serious, Eleanor."

It was the first time he'd called her by her name and

not the nickname he'd come up with for her. It gave her a strange feeling in the pit of her stomach. She could hear how serious he was. He was trying to tell her that as dangerous as this had been, it was about to get worse.

"You could go out to Lonesome. My brothers and their wives and girlfriend would make sure that you were—"

"I'm not leaving." She rose. "Thank you for dinner, but you don't need to babysit me. Nor do I want to cramp your style, so you're free to leave and do your own thing." She pulled her robe tighter around her, already missing the teasing comradery between them from only minutes ago as she walked to her open bedroom door. Stopping, she turned to look back at him. "Good night, Willie." Then she stepped in, closing and locking the door behind her.

Her heart pounded and she wasn't even sure why she suddenly felt like crying. She blamed the long, exhausting day, the fear, the lack of control over her life. For a while, they'd merely been a man and woman sharing a meal and conversation. It was so companionable that it had let her forget that her life was in danger—or that Deputy Willie Colt was only here to find the criminal he'd come to Seattle to collect—and then he'd be gone, back to his life out in the wilds of Montana.

Willie swore under his breath as he picked up the dishes, put them on the trolley and left it out in the hall. As he walked back into the suite, the city twinkled beyond the balcony doors. He'd never felt so much like a fish out of water. To make it worse, he'd dragged Ellie into this.

It didn't matter that she was already neck-deep in this

mess before he'd even met her. Still, maybe she was safer anywhere but with him. Going to his room, he left his door partially ajar so he could hear if she decided to take off in the night. As he showered, he had to rein in any thoughts of attorney E.L. Shafer in the next room—let alone that image he couldn't banish of her earlier neck-deep in a bubble bath.

He removed the bandage from the back of his head to wash his hair. After a long shower, the last part purposely ice-cold, he got into bed. He doubted he would be able to sleep a wink—even in a bed that was so soft and high up off the floor that it was like climbing up on a cloud.

He'd left the drapes open, and lying in bed on the sixteenth floor, all he could see was the glow of the city and the glittering water. No stars like back home. He missed the wide-open spaces, the smell of pine and clear streams, and the magnificent show the galaxy put on almost every night above the treetops.

He thought back to everything that had happened since he'd landed in Seattle. He thought of Spark…Vernon and Ellie and what little he'd learned about her. He tried to make sense out of it all but none of it did. Yet.

He must have drifted off, because when he opened his eyes it was morning. He didn't know what to expect as he dressed in his jeans, boots, Western shirt, and picked up his sheriff's department jacket. He had a change of clothing, but it was in his patrol SUV.

Last night he'd taken the syringe out of his pocket. He planned to take it by the cop shop, not that he had much hope of getting prints from it—or the cops helping.

His first thought was that Ellie would be long gone. Even after the scare last night outside the pub, he figured

her stubborn, independent streak would have her prefer-
ring to be on her own than to stay with him.

So he couldn't help being surprised when she came
out of her side of the suite. She was fully dressed in
a different suit, white blouse and high heels. She saw
his surprise. "I have my ways," she said of the clothing
she'd somehow obtained. "Don't worry, I didn't use a
charge card. Here." She reached back in her room and
came out with a bag brandishing a gaudy logo on it he
didn't recognize.

He took the heavy bag as if he expected to find rattle-
snakes coiled up inside ready to strike. He peered in.
"You bought me clothes?"

"I figured you probably hadn't brought much with you
considering that you hadn't planned to stay."

"Ellie—"

"Don't make a big deal out of it."

He held her gaze for a moment. "Thank you, but how
did you know my size?"

"I guessed. Try them on and we'll see how accurate
I was."

He couldn't help but feel touched. "I've let women
undress me before," he joked. "But you're the first I've
let dress me." Chuckling, he turned back to his bedroom, but not before he'd seen the flush that had risen
to her cheeks.

Eleanor had to admit that she was definitely out of
her realm—not to mention her comfort zone—with this
cowboy and the turn of events. She had considered being
gone this morning when he woke up. But right or wrong,
she felt she was safer with him. She'd never met a man
like Willie Colt. There was a coarseness about him, from

his stubbled jaw to his rough hands to his language and lifestyle back in Montana. He was nothing like the men she'd grown up with, the men she'd dated. Nothing like her father.

That he'd called her Ellie this morning shouldn't have pleased her as much as it did. If it had been anyone but Willie— She realized that she was no longer thinking of him as the deputy or the cowboy. He was now Willie, another sign that she was in dangerous waters—on more than one front.

"You have a good eye."

She turned to see him standing in his doorway fully dressed again, only this time in the clothing she'd ordered for him. One look at him and she could tell that everything fit, no small task given his broad shoulders and slim hips and that behind that made his jeans sexier than any trousers she'd ever seen on a man.

"Thank you," he said, actually looking a little embarrassed. "But I can't have you dressing me or—"

Or undressing him?

"—paying for expensive hotel rooms, although I have to admit that bed last night was a little piece of heaven."

She nodded, a smile easing from her. "Just as I can't have you taking care of me as if I'm helpless."

"You're far from helpless," he said, holding her gaze. "But as long as you're in danger I can't let you prove just how independent you are." As if he could see that she was about to argue the point, he continued quickly. "We need to go pick up my patrol SUV, drop off the syringe with the cops and then put you on a flight to somewhere safe. Your choice. I just thought with my family… It has to be a place that no one knows about, especially your boss and his associates."

Eleanor merely looked at him, waiting to see if there was more he wanted to say. "I thought I made myself clear last night. I'm not going anywhere." As he opened his mouth, she held up a hand. "You need my help. Even you should be able to see that."

"*Even* me?"

"As you've made abundantly clear," she continued, "you don't know Seattle. I do. Since going back to my office or my apartment isn't viable, I'd rather take my chances helping you stop these men than having them track me down elsewhere." Her gaze locked with his. "You're apparently my only option."

"I'm…touched," he joked.

She picked up her purse and raincoat. "My boss texted me last night. He's insistent that I call him." She turned then to look at him. "What do you suggest I do? Since I think you might be right about him throwing me to the wolves."

Willie had been ready to argue that she couldn't stay in Seattle and she especially couldn't stay with him, but her words and the no-nonsense look on her face stopped him. He saw that he could argue with this woman until he was blue in the face, but she wasn't going to change her mind.

She was right. He'd abducted her from her office yesterday after she'd told him about her phone call from Vernon. He'd saved her life from the man in the alley. Now she was his responsibility, but he knew better than to say that.

Anyway, she was right. He had no idea where he was going or how to get there. He needed her as much as she needed him. It was an odd pairing, no doubt about that.

Had he not come to Seattle, their paths would have never crossed. Even if they had, they would have given each other a wide berth—clearly seeing at a glance that they were nothing alike and had nothing in common. But being thrown together, they were now forced to work together to get out of this situation.

"Let's pick up a burner phone," he said, making the decision. "And see what your boss has to say."

She raised an eyebrow as if he was overdoing the precautions. "And if he asks where I am?"

"Tell him you were unexpectedly called away. A sick parent or—"

"He knows that both of my parents are deceased. They started the law firm that he now controls."

Willie picked up the bitterness in her tone. "I'm sorry."

"Phillip McNamara was my father's protégé."

Still, he thought, there was something not quite right there. Not that it mattered in the grand scheme of things right now unless the man was neck-deep in this. "We'll pick up a phone after we get my ride from the pound."

"You aren't worried that we'll be followed?"

"We'll just have to make sure they don't corner us in a dark alley."

She nodded. "No dark alleys. Got it."

He wasn't sure she did. "If you're determined to see this through, then we just need to stay together so—"

"We can protect each other," she said. "That is what you were going to say, wasn't it?"

That wasn't what he was going to say. He thought of the lethal end of her heel. She was a fighter, no doubt about that. But the next time, the men wouldn't be armed with nothing more than a syringe. "Sure," he said, and had to fight the urge to put her shapely butt on the next plane out of town—one way or another.

They caught another Uber to the towing lot. Once in the patrol SUV, Ellie riding shotgun, he made a quick stop at the police station to drop off the syringe. As he drove away, they both kept watching the cars behind them. Would she even know a tail if she saw one? Willie wasn't all that sure he would in this busy city.

He found a drugstore outside of the main downtown. He worried about leaving the patrol SUV for very long, convinced they had been followed from the tow yard. But if a bad cop had wanted to screw around with the rig, he could have already done it.

It didn't take long to get a phone and return to the SUV. As he walked toward the patrol car, he looked around, telling himself he'd recognize the kind of men after them. He didn't see anyone who seemed in the least bit interested in them. Nor anyone like the man who'd jumped Ellie in the alley last night.

But that didn't mean that the two of them hadn't been followed. Or that they weren't being watched. He bent down and inspected the undercarriage of the patrol vehicle. He didn't see a tracking device. Nor did he see explosives. Maybe they hadn't been followed.

As he climbed inside, he thought about Vernon and the men who had taken him. By now they would have gotten whatever information they wanted out of him. Would he have cleared his attorney? Would they have believed him? Was he even still alive?

He handed the phone to Ellie. "Call your boss. Let's see what he wants."

* * *

Eleanor couldn't help being nervous about the call to Phillip McNamara. She thought about a time when he was sitting at her family's dinner table. Young, intelligent and very hungry for what her father had to offer, Phillip had been the nervous one back then.

Once he'd taken over the firm, he'd changed. Or was she the one who'd changed once she found out that he'd been after more than the firm? He'd promised her she was on track for managing partner when he retired—or co-managing partner before that, but as she prepared the burner phone the cowboy handed her, she knew the offer had come with strings. McNamara had wanted her as part of the deal. Once he'd realized that wasn't going to happen, he quit pretending he'd ever made other promises he wasn't going to keep.

Now she wondered why she'd stayed at the firm as long as she had. Because the firm meant something to her. But maybe giving her the Vernon Murphy extradition case had been McNamara's way of getting rid of her. Had he known there were going to be problems with it? Or had he known the people who hired Vernon to begin with—people who could ruin her reputation and destroy her career, if not kill her? The thought made her angry and less nervous.

She swallowed, her throat dry, as she called the main number at the firm and asked for Phillip McNamara. "It's E.L. Shafer calling." She waited, not wanting to believe that he'd thrown her to the wolves, as the deputy had so succinctly put it. But all indications were that he had.

This phone call would be the deciding factor, she realized. Was she ready to face the truth? She looked over at

Willie, knowing that she had already stepped over a line she couldn't recross. Like the minor quakes that often shook the city, Willie rattled her and the solid ground on which she'd believed she'd built a life.

Now, as she waited for McNamara, she feared that in the next few minutes, she was about to destroy that life.

Willie leaned closer so he could hear the conversation as McNamara came on the line.

"Eleanor, where have you been? Your assistant said she hadn't heard from you. Didn't you get my message?"

She took a steadying breath. This was unnerving enough without Willie so close. She tried to think like the composed, confident lawyer she'd been until she met Deputy Willie Colt.

Just from her boss's tone she knew he was alone in his office. He would never have spoken like this in front of the other partners or junior attorneys. Did that mean that his guard was down? Immediately, she decided to go off script, no matter what the deputy had told her to say.

"What's going on, Phil?"

Silence. She hadn't used his first name since she'd told him she didn't share his feelings. He'd become McNamara to her.

"Why don't *you* tell me, Eleanor."

A knot formed in her stomach at his tone at the same time it made her angrier. "Vernon Murphy called me last night right before I left my office."

He let out an exasperated sound. "I thought I told you to call me the moment you heard from him."

She felt Willie a breath away. This was not the way he'd told her to handle the call, but he wasn't trying to stop her. "I was upset. I walked down to that pub you like, you know the one, where you propositioned me, promising me a managing partnership that hinged, as it turned out, on whether or not we were together romantically?"

"Eleanor—"

"As I left the pub, I was attacked by a man who seemed determined to abduct me."

"Are you all right?" His tone didn't carry much sympathy or concern, though.

"Why did you give me the Vernon Murphy case?" The accusation was clear, but he seemed to want to ignore it.

"We don't discuss cases over the phone. Why don't you come up to my office?"

He had to know she wasn't in her office or even in the building. "That's not possible right now. Surely the reason for you giving me this case isn't a secret, is it, Phil?"

McNamara made a distressed sound. "I'm going to have to call you back."

"Before you hang up, I want you to know that I borrowed a phone since my cell phone was lost last night in my struggle with my attacker. I damaged his left eye in case you run across him."

"Eleanor." He dragged the word out with obvious impatience. "You can't think I had anything to do with—"

"What have you gotten me into, Phil?"

His voice sounded strained when he finally spoke. She could imagine him gritting his teeth, his free hand tapping on his large mahogany desk nervously. "I highly doubt the attack on you had anything to do with the case, Eleanor. I certainly wouldn't have put you in such a position. These things happen as a lawyer. I thought you were aware of that."

"Are you forgetting I was raised by two lawyers, the

same ones who put you in that chair you're sitting in right now with that great view of the city?"

"I can tell that you're upset. I am, too. But if you're still interested in ever running this firm, we need to meet and discuss this like two rational human beings."

"We could talk about whether or not you knew the time and the place that Vernon Murphy was being extradited." She thought of the man in the alley. "I'm going to get to the truth, Phil. Enjoy your view from that penthouse office because if I'm right about you, you won't be sitting in that chair when I'm done."

Eleanor disconnected and tried to breathe, the phone still gripped in her hand. She felt the deputy's fingers gently pry it free. She sensed his gaze on her, but he seemed to be giving her time to recover.

"You were right," she finally said, breaking the silence. "He fed me to the wolves." She was shaking inside—not with fear, but with fury. "I meant what I said about taking him down."

"Let's nail the SOB's hide to the wall."

She looked over at him. "I like the way you think, Willie."

His grin eased the knot in her stomach from earlier. From the widening of his blue eyes, she saw that he'd also noticed that she was now using his first name. "All we have to do is stay alive," he said, and put the patrol SUV into gear.

Chapter 10

Willie watched Ellie out of the corner of his eye as he drove. He was waiting for the fury to burn off, afraid that once she realized what she'd done, there would be tears. He wasn't good with tears. Hell, he wasn't good with most things to do with women when there was a problem.

And there was one hell of a problem right now. While he feared that she'd just burned bridges with her career, he was more worried about keeping her alive. He glanced in his rearview mirror. What were all these people doing driving around at this time of the morning? Certainly not going to work. He'd already decided he had to get off this main thoroughfare, even before his phone rang.

He took the first exit and was dumped into a neighborhood. Parking was impossible, he saw at once. He pulled down a side street and stopped in the middle of it to take the call.

"Are you okay?" his brother Tommy asked at Willie's impatient hello.

"Sorry. It's just…everything out here—the traffic, too many people, no parking, and thugs trying to kill us."

"Another day at the office, huh. I found out something that might help. I tracked down Zoey Bertrand's family. She had been having an affair with the head of Cascade Extraction Corp. Seems he has a cozy ten-thousand-square-foot cabin out here in Montana and an even larger home on Vashon Island out there. His name is Lowell Carter."

"Did the family have any idea if the romance had gone sour?"

"They said that the last time Zoey was home they could tell she was upset. She said there were things going on at work that she couldn't talk about. They knew she'd been seeing Lowell and had warned her that because of the age difference—Lowell's in his sixties and married, Zoey was twenty-eight—the affair might not last. They thought maybe she was starting to come to her senses."

"And that's why she's dead?"

"They think it had something to do with the business, something she might have learned, and that she was killed before she could tell someone. They have no idea what it might have been, though."

"Either way, it might explain why Lowell needed to get rid of her. Do we have any idea where Lowell is right now?"

"I drove down to Bitterroot Valley, where the cabin is. I talked to the on-site property caretaker. All I know is that Lowell isn't there."

"Then he could be out here," Willie said. "At least we have an even stronger connection between the mining company and its owner and Zoey Bertrand—and possible trouble in paradise. It's a start." He wondered where Jonathan Asher fit in—if he did at all.

"I have some good news," Tommy said. "Bella and I are pregnant!"

Willie knew they'd been trying. "Congratulations! That's great news. It makes my day."

"Just take care of yourself, Uncle Willie. We're going to need you. It's twin boys!"

Willie laughed, told him he couldn't be happier, and hung up. As he turned to Ellie, he said, "My brother Tommy and his wife, Bella, are having twin boys." He couldn't help smiling at the good news.

"Congratulations."

His smile waned. "Are you all right?"

She nodded, but he could see that although the fury had passed without tears, it had left her hollowed out.

"We're going to get to the bottom of this. And if you're right about your boss, he's going down."

She nodded again.

"The woman Vernon saw in the window before the explosion? She was having an affair with Lowell Carter, the owner of the mining company she was working for." He told her the rest. The news seemed to perk her up.

"When do we interview Lowell Carter?" she asked, sitting up straighter, that determined look back on her classically beautiful face. The buttoned-up attorney was back and ready to take on the world. She was right. He did need her.

"As soon as you tell me how to get to Gig Harbor—and out of this neighborhood, wherever we are."

"Doesn't this vehicle have a navigation system?"

"Not one that's worth a damn."

She shook her head. "Fine, I'll get you there."

The headquarters of the mining company was a nondescript building on the edge of Gig Harbor, surrounded by pines and old, used equipment. There were no cars in the small lot or in front of the building. While not surprised, since his attempts to call the business had all gone to voice mail, he was disappointed that there didn't seem to be anyone around.

He climbed out and walked to the door, expecting exactly what he found—the place locked up tight, the windows dusty. Peering in one of the dirty windows, he saw that the inside was deserted. No one had been doing business here for some time.

"Wasted trip," he said as Ellie joined him.

"Not necessarily," she said, opening the metal mailbox next to the door. She sorted through the flyers and junk mail for a few minutes before handing him a car warranty extension offer.

He took it, frowning until he saw the name, Lowell Carter, and what appeared to be a home address on Vashon Island.

He grinned at her. "Nice job. So, how do we get to this Vashon Island?" he asked as they walked back to the patrol SUV.

He saw that she was glancing around just as he was. He wanted to believe that the bad guys had quit looking for them, which would mean they no longer felt threatened. Which, he feared, could mean that Vernon was dead.

But from what little he knew about bad guys, they usually didn't stop—not until they were stopped. If they hadn't been followed, it was probably that they weren't seen as a threat because they were on the wrong trail. That thought bothered him more than he wanted to admit. What if he was wrong about the people involved with the mining corporation being the culprits?

"We'll take a ferry," she said.

He shot her a look. "What?"

He thought of the ferry he'd seen last night from the hotel room, crossing the huge, dark water of Puget Sound. "We have to go by boat? There must be some other way."

She laughed as if he'd said something funny. "You own a helicopter? Or would you rather swim?" She pulled out her phone and thumbed the keys for a few seconds. "The shortest ferry route is from Fauntleroy Cove. It will take us right to Vashon Heights. The boat ride is only twenty minutes, but it looks like the best time to go would be after the rush hour. There's one at seven twenty-eight p.m."

"In the dark?"

"Ferries have lights." She pocketed her phone. As she did, she turned to him, frowning. "Do you have something against ferries?"

Willie rubbed a hand over his face. He should have picked up a razor at the store earlier. "I've never been on a ferry and don't have much experience with boats in general since falling out of a canoe when I was five and almost drowning."

Out of the corner of his eye, he could see her looking at him as if he was a species she'd never seen before. "You do know how to swim now, though, don't you?" She didn't give him a chance to answer. "Oh, for crying out loud. You can wear a life jacket and if the ferry goes down, I'll save you."

He chuckled. "Thanks, but I'm not counting on that since I doubt you can swim in that skirt."

She made a disagreeable sound. "This from the man wearing a ten-gallon hat and cowboy boots? You'd be amazed how quickly I can get out of this skirt."

"Now, that's something I'd like to see," he said with a grin, and turned back to his driving.

At the ferry, Eleanor suggested they leave his patrol SUV and simply ride over to Vashon as passengers. "According to this address, Lowell Carter doesn't live far from where we depart the ferry. We'll be harder to follow on foot."

Willie nodded, his gaze bright with something close to respect. She turned away, telling herself that looking into those eyes was what had helped turn her life upside down and now had her on the run from possible killers.

"Let's go up on deck," she said once they were on board. "It's a beautiful night." She saw him hesitate. "Easier to save you up there."

He smiled at that and followed her topside. In truth, she needed the fresh air right now. McNamara had texted her as they were boarding: You have no idea what you're involved in. You need to come in.

He was definitely right about that. She didn't have a clue.

She shoved McNamara out of her thoughts and concentrated on what they knew. On the surface it appeared that Lowell Carter had been having an affair with a young woman who worked for him. There were problems, her parents had said. Did that mean he'd broken it off by having her blown up by a demolition expert who also worked for him? Vernon Murphy was that demolition expert, but he'd been abducted and was presumed dead.

If Willie was right, then whoever was behind all of this was afraid of what Vernon had told first police officer Alex Mattson and Eleanor herself as his attorney.

The ferry pulled away from shore, and she hugged herself from the chill as she stood at the railing, staring out at the dark water. There had been a few people up on deck, but now most of them had gone inside. Willie had moved next to her as if to block the wind. Or maybe he wanted to stand this close in case she had to save him should he go into the water.

She could feel his body's warmth, with him pressed against her. They were so close they could have kissed. Did he ever think about that kiss in the pub? Or had it only been a ruse, quickly forgotten? She met his eyes and swallowed. He hadn't forgotten. Her breath caught as he reached over and brushed back a lock of her hair from her eyes.

Her chignon had come loose in the breeze blowing off the water. As she started to reach up to repair it, he laid a hand on hers and shook his head. He slowly turned her, pulling her close again, as he backed her against him. She felt the heat and the hardness of his body. Closing her eyes, she concentrated on his fingers in her hair, on the bare skin at the base of her neck. His big, calloused hands surprised her with their gentleness as well as their dexterity. Willie Colt was a man of many talents.

She realized that she'd been afraid to move as he finished. It felt good having him behind her, knowing he had her back. It felt too good. She turned, instantly missing the comfort of his nearness as the cold, damp night air hit her. She could hear the chug of the ferry's engines, the slosh of the water as the boat cut through the waves, the steady thrum of her revved-up blood in her ears.

"The boat ride isn't bothering you?" she asked, surprised at the tightness in her throat as the lights of Vashon Island grew brighter.

He shook his head, locking eyes with her for a long moment before he dragged his gaze away and turned to look toward the island. "I worry more about keeping you safe."

His voice was low, his words trying to escape into the wind skimming across the dark water. She attempted to swallow around the lump in her throat, not knowing what to say because there was nothing to say as the ferry began to slow. Looking into the lounge, she tried to see if there were passengers who looked familiar. Was there a killer among them? She didn't recognize anyone. No sign of the man she'd injured last night.

No one looked dangerous, but she knew she could be proved wrong once the ferry docked and those inside prepared to disembark. She hoped this wasn't a mistake, coming out here to confront Lowell Carter in person. Willie had been almost pensive on the ferry ride. Was it his fear of water? Or was he concerned about their safety out here? She couldn't tell which.

He placed his hand, fingers splayed, on her lower back as they left the ferry. They'd let most everyone go on ahead of them. Now there were only a few stragglers at the edge of the shore, people apparently waiting for a ride. None of them seemed to pay her or Willie any mind.

As they walked into Vashon Heights, the streets were

still busy with people hurrying home for the night. Willie walked on the outside, keeping her closest to the building side of the sidewalk. She could tell that he was on alert, expecting an attack at any moment.

Eleanor took a shaky breath. She'd felt safe, as if breathing rarefied air before this. She'd worn her attire and her you-don't-want-to-mess-with-me persona like armor. Now that armor had been pierced—and not just by what was happening with the Vernon Murphy case. She glanced over at Deputy Willie Colt, hating that he made her feel vulnerable in so many ways and had her heart beating faster because of it. Now she felt powerless in ways that made her ache.

Willie seemed to have seen through her, like he'd stripped her naked the first time he'd walked into her office. This cowboy with all his jagged edges had been the first man to do that. None of the men she'd dated had been able to evoke the kind of feelings he had, she realized as they wound through the residential streets of Vashon Heights in the deepening darkness. It made her question why the universe had sent him crashing into her life, since he couldn't wait to flee Seattle. Once he finished his job here, he'd be gone.

Only if they both survived, she reminded herself as Willie grabbed her suddenly and pulled her back into the dark shadows of a tall hedge. The kiss fresh on her mind, she thought for sure—

"Stay here," he whispered, and then he was gone.

Chapter 11

Willie moved along the hedge, keeping to the deep shadows until he reached a spot where he could step off the sidewalk and not be seen. He waited, hearing nothing but the thump of his own blood circulating. After a few moments, he told himself his instincts had been wrong. No one had followed them.

Then he heard footfalls on concrete, someone moving fast. He pulled his weapon, determined to find out why they were being followed. From up the street came the shine of headlights. A vehicle moving fast.

He crouched down, no longer sure where the attack might be coming from. The driver of the vehicle hit his brakes, coming to a skidding stop only yards from Willie. A window whirred down and a female voice ordered, "Get into this car right now!"

For just an instant, Willie thought the female driver

had seen him and was talking to him. But then a sullen figure dragged his feet up the sidewalk, crossed in front of Willie's hiding place and slunk over to the car. "I told you that if I had to come looking for you again—" Willie exhaled. It was just a teenager being berated for not coming home when he'd said he would.

He heard no more as the teen disappeared inside the vehicle and the driver hit the gas, peeling out and leaving rubber tracks as she took off. He stayed hidden for a few more moments to let his heart rate return to near normal before he peered out.

Across the street, a man had come out of hiding. Willie realized that the man had been standing in the shadows between two houses. Willie watched him look around, almost as if he was lost, before he turned back down the street—in the same direction they had come from.

He waited until the man was out of sight before he went to get Ellie where he'd left her. She stepped out at the sight of him. "False alarm," he said as he pulled a dead leaf from her hair.

She gave him a look that told him she'd seen the man across the street and had inferred the same thing he had: they'd been followed. If it hadn't been for the wayward teenager and his angry mother, they might not have seen him tracking them in the dark from the other side of the street.

Eleanor still felt foolish for her earlier thoughts of their kiss, when their lives were in so much danger. Seeing the man come out of the darkness across the street had brought her back to earth with a thud. Fear had stolen her breath and kept her immobile as she'd waited and prayed for Willie's return.

When she'd seen the man turn back, she'd finally taken a breath. As Willie appeared she'd wanted to throw herself into his arms. She hadn't, but only by sheer strength of will. She suspected he'd seen how scared she'd been. The cowboy noticed everything. She felt her face heat in the darkness at her earlier stray thoughts. This was not like her. It was annoying and humiliating and distracting, when now more than ever she needed to keep her head.

They stood in the shadows for a few more moments. The man she'd seen didn't come back up the hill in their direction. The night pressed in on them as the ferry left, and the only sounds were doors closing, people talking on their cell phones, music playing as they walked through the wealthy neighborhood. She thought she smelled meat barbecuing as they made their way up the street to Lowell Carter's address.

Like Jonathan Asher's house, this one, too, was impressive, but at least triple the size of Asher's. It had a wrought iron fence with spikes along the top around the property and a wide, matching gate at the entrance. She saw a security camera over the gate.

Glancing at Willie, she knew that he, too, was assessing how they were going to get inside—especially without being seen. That answer came like an unexpected gift as a car pulled up and was buzzed in. The deputy moved quickly to keep the gate from closing and the two of them slipped inside before it clanged shut.

Rather than take the curvy drive up to the house, Willie took her hand and they cut across the wooded lawn.

Another set of headlights flashed behind them at the gate and moments later drove in.

"Seems they're having a party," Willie said as they neared the house and saw a valet approach the last car they'd seen arrive.

"Seems so," she said. A couple dressed in suit and gown exited the car and headed up the wide front steps. "Formal attire? I wonder what they're celebrating."

From the front, the massive house appeared to be made of all glass. They could see inside all the way through to the lights on the mainland on the other side of Puget Sound.

"I hate to think what they might be celebrating," Willie said. "Come on, let's go ask them." She hesitated and he added, "All they can do is throw us out."

"Or call the cops." They smiled at each other like conspirators as they walked up to the door and Willie rang the bell.

A staff member answered the door, and no surprise, the uniformed woman's eyes widened at the sight of the cowboy.

"We're here to see Mr. Carter," Willie said as they stepped in, forcing the woman back. "Tell him he'll want to talk to us."

"May I say who—"

"Deputy Willie Colt from Lonesome, Montana. He'll know," Willie said with a wink.

The woman gave a nod of her head, adding, "Wait here." It sounded more like an order than a suggestion.

Eleanor had come to know Willie well enough that she was anticipating a scene. She hated the thought that she might have to call an attorney friend to get them both out of jail as a well-dressed, distinguished-looking older man appeared, his brows furrowed in displeasure.

"You aren't an easy man to get to see," Willie said before Lowell Carter could open his mouth. "We need to talk." He flashed his credentials, strictly for show since he suspected this man knew exactly who he was and that he had no jurisdiction out here in Seattle, let alone on this island.

"I'm afraid you've caught me at an inopportune time, Deputy," Carter said without even glancing at his ID and badge. "We're having a few friends over tonight."

"We didn't come to visit," Willie said. "We're here to talk about Zoey Bertrand."

Carter frowned, as if trying to recall the name.

"Come on, Lowell," he said. "You didn't achieve all of this—" he waved his hand to encompass the house and grounds "—by playing dumb. I want to know why someone abducted my prisoner, Vernon Murphy. And when I find them, I'm going to bring down this whole house of cards. I have a feeling you're going to be under it when it falls. So, if you have nothing to hide, how about you tell me who hired Vernon to get rid of your indiscretion—if not you."

The older man smiled slowly. "Deputy, there must be some mistake, since as you know, you have no jurisdiction out here. All I'd have to do is tell the police chief that you're harassing me—"

"All I'd have to do is tell your wife about Zoey Bertrand," Willie said. "I'd hate to spoil your party, especially with all your close friends here, so maybe you could spare us a few minutes of your…valuable time to talk to us."

"You really aren't threatening me with blackmail, are you, Deputy?"

"Perhaps I can help," Ellie said. "I'm attorney E.L. Shafer. I think it would be to your benefit to speak with us."

Lowell's eyes shifted to her, as if he hadn't noticed her before that moment. His eyes widened in surprise. "I'm familiar with your firm."

Eleanor nodded, hiding her surprise better than Willie was doing. "The deputy here came all the way from Montana to extradite Mr. Murphy, only to be attacked and his prisoner abducted. He is determined not to leave until he finds out who hired Mr. Murphy to commit the act that ended in the death of a young woman who worked for you. I'm sure we can clear this up quickly, especially if you're the one who hired my firm to represent Vernon Murphy, also an employee of yours."

Lowell Carter hesitated but only for a moment as another car drove up. "If you'll follow me to my office," he said, turning on his heel to lead them in the direction away from the noise of the party—and the couple now exiting their vehicle outside.

Willie shot Ellie an appraising look. She merely shrugged and followed Carter down the hallway and into his office. Carter closed the door behind them.

"Let's get something straight," he said as he took a seat behind his large desk and waved them into the club chairs facing it. "I wasn't even aware that Vernon Murphy worked for my company. I found out when I got a call from the sheriff's department in Lonesome, Montana, telling me that one of my buildings had been destroyed and a woman killed inside." Lowell Carter cleared his voice and looked away for a moment. "When

I learned who the woman was…" He shook his head as if he was unable to finish.

"And you didn't question what she was doing inside the building?" Willie demanded. "Or why an employee of yours had blown up your building?"

"Of course I did. I'm not a fool," he said haughtily. "I certainly didn't hire him to destroy one of my buildings, let alone—" his voice broke and he bit his lower lip for a moment "—kill Zoey. I was in love with her. I was planning to get a divorce and marry her. Nor did I hire your firm to represent him," Lowell said to Eleanor. "As far as I'm concerned the man can burn in hell…and as for my wife…" Again his voice broke. "She knows everything now about Zoey and my plans to divorce her."

"And she's good with it?" Willie said, unable to hide his disbelief. "That what you're celebrating tonight with your party? That all's forgiven since Zoey Bertrand is dead?"

"Not that it's any of your business, Deputy," Lowell Carter said indignantly. "But Angeline is still determined to divorce me. I'm attempting to work things out, but I'm not sure we can overcome this… I'm hoping we can."

Eleanor had once thought that she could look into the faces of clients and tell whether they were guilty or innocent. She no longer believed that. Lowell Carter was very convincing, but there was a good chance that he'd gotten rid of his girlfriend. She could have learned something at work that she shouldn't have or he could have just gotten tired of her. Also divorces tended to be expensive and the man clearly had a lot to lose.

"When did your wife learn about your affair and your plans to leave her?" Eleanor asked.

"She learned when I got the call about the explosion and Zoey's death," he said. "I was in no condition to keep it from her after the call. I confessed everything."

"And if she doesn't forgive you?" Willie asked.

"Then she'll divorce me, take half of my holdings, all of our friends and my reputation and my dignity with it," he said. "I deserve to lose everything we built together. It's what I get for falling in love with someone younger than our daughter."

"You sound like a man who is sorry he got caught, not like one who is truly remorseful," Willie said.

Lowell Carter looked close to tears. "I loved Zoey. I would have done anything to be with her. I understand the police are looking into suspects, including a former boyfriend of Zoey's."

"How involved was your wife in the mining business?" Eleanor asked.

The man looked surprised. "Not at all. Angeline took care of our home, our children, not to mention she was the consummate host. She had no interest in business."

"You're that sure she didn't suspect you were having an affair?" she pressed.

"I'm sure. She was happy with the arrangement we had, her taking care of her part, me mine. She took the news badly. I never meant to hurt her. With Zoey gone, I've pretty much lost everything that mattered—except Angeline. I can't lose her, too." Lowell sounded defeated.

"So, you have no idea who hired Vernon Murphy to destroy your building—and kill your girlfriend?" Willie asked. Lowell shook his head. "Would Jonathan Asher have reason to want to destroy your life?"

"Jonathan?" Lowell's brows rose. "I can't imagine why. He invested in numerous businesses of mine."

"How will the divorce affect his investments if your wife goes through with it?" Eleanor asked.

The man frowned. "I hadn't really considered that. If we divorce, I would imagine Angeline will get rid of the mining corporation, selling it off piecemeal to be rid of it and me. So, if anything, Jonathan will be able to buy it all up if he's interested."

"Except for the half you will still own," Willie pointed out.

"I can't afford to buy her out, so whoever picks up her share can pressure me to sell for pennies on the dollar. I'm afraid I'm caught between a rock and a hard place, wouldn't you say, Deputy?"

"Maybe that was someone's plan," Eleanor said. "Who else would have been affected if you had left your wife for Zoey?"

Lowell seemed to consider that before shaking his head. "Why would anyone go to this much trouble to destroy me?"

It was a good question. Eleanor had one of her own. "You said your wife had considered filing for divorce. May I ask who her attorney is?"

The man was apparently surprised by the question. "I thought you already knew. Phillip McNamara, the managing partner at your firm. My wife contacted him after learning about my…indiscretion, as she is calling it."

The office door opened and a young woman with eyes shaped like Lowell's stuck her head in.

"Sorry to interrupt, but Mother is looking for you."

"Tell her I'll be right there." He rose as the door closed. "I'm afraid that's all I can tell you."

"One more thing," Willie said as he and Eleanor both got up to leave as well. "Do you have personal security, bodyguards? Did one of them have an accident involving his left eye?"

"Just because the man who attacked me works for him doesn't mean Lowell Carter is involved," Eleanor argued as they made their way off the property. "I tend to believe him."

Willie shot her a look. "The man is a confessed adulterer. You don't think he hasn't lied and cheated and maybe even killed to get where he is?"

"I'm just saying I believe him in this case," she said determinedly.

He scoffed. "I'm not buying it. I want to talk to his wife. I got the feeling that she's the one who threw that shindig back there tonight. Who throws a party after finding out your husband was in love with another woman, a much younger woman, and that he was about to leave you?"

"A woman who wants to show the world that she'll survive after the divorce. Otherwise, all her friends would be whispering behind her back about her."

"You don't think they are anyway?"

At the gate, she shrugged. Just as Carter had told them, it swung open before they reached it. "Depends on what all she tells them tonight. They probably already suspect that he's been running around on her—unless he kept all that out in Montana. Still, a woman knows."

Something about the way she said the last made him turn to look at her as they passed through the gate to the street. "Are you speaking from experience?"

She shot him a look, but clamped her lips shut and kept walking.

He surveyed the street. There was less traffic in this pricey neighborhood than there had been earlier. Maybe everyone was at the Carters' party. He didn't see anyone loitering around, but that didn't mean they weren't being watched.

"Are you doing this for Vernon?"

Her question came out of the blue and struck at gut level. "Do you mean do I hope to save him?" He shook his head. "I suspect he's already dead, so no."

"Then why?" she asked, stopping to stare at him. There was just enough light from the neighborhood lamps that he could see her features. She wasn't the buttoned-up bulldog attorney right now. There was a softness to her that he found equally attractive and unsettling.

"I'm angry and I want justice," he said truthfully, then softened his voice. "But I also want to make sure that you're okay before I can leave Seattle." He didn't admit that protecting her now outweighed his anger and his need for justice. E.L. Shafer had gotten to him in a way that kept him off balance, and he didn't like it. The sooner he finished his business out here and got back to Montana, the better. He preferred his boots on solid, stable ground.

She started walking again, seeming to avoid his gaze. "Does any of this make sense to you?"

He hated to admit that it didn't at this point, but he was more comfortable talking about the case. "What do you make of Angeline hiring your boss to represent her?"

"It makes me suspicious."

"Me, too, especially since he gave you the Vernon Murphy case. Even if he hadn't known that Vernon had worked for Carter's mining corporation, he would know that the destroyed building was his client's husband's—and that the woman killed was her husband's mistress. I suspect your boss is up to his neck in this," he said. "Have you heard from him again?" She didn't answer fast enough. He swore and stopped walking. "Why didn't you tell me?"

"He texted me to say that I don't know what I'm involved in and I need to come into the office." She turned to look at him. "It's true. I don't know what I'm involved in."

He heard something break in her voice. He'd seen her angry and scared. Right now, she was more vulnerable than he'd ever seen her. "I'm sorry." It was all he could think to say as out of corner of his eye, he saw the lights of a ferry docking at the shore and a handful of people waiting to get off. He didn't see a man with a bandage over one eye, but he still knew they weren't safe. So, how could he promise Ellie that he would solve this or even that he'd protect her? He couldn't, but he realized that he would die trying. He'd come to care about her, making them both vulnerable.

The night breeze teased stray locks from her chignon. She brushed angrily at them as if her hair was just one more thing she'd lost control of because of him. He suspected that her hairdo was a shield, like her buttoned-up-to-the-neck blouse, like the look she gave the world from those wolflike gray eyes. *Don't get too close.* He doubted he was the first man she'd held at arm's length.

But right now, he could see that if he reached for her, she would come to him. The question was what would happen once he held her in his arms, felt the supple parts of her against him, let the thought of kissing her again go beyond merely his imagination?

He swore silently. Seeing her vulnerability on this sultry night, the lights twinkling on the water, the faint scent of her perfume filling his nostrils, and feeling as lost as she looked.

Even as he stepped closer to her, he reminded himself that he'd sworn he wouldn't go down that path, that he couldn't, that there would be no turning back if he did. He reached for her, throwing caution to the wind.

Over her shoulder, he saw a man come off the ferry, hesitate, then head right for Ellie.

Chapter 12

"Eleanor?"

Willie had reached for her, his hand brushing her sleeve as he started to draw her to him. She saw her need mirrored in his eyes. Her body leaned toward his, yearning to be in his arms—a place she felt she'd been headed since she met him. She wanted desperately to surrender to it. The thought came with relief, as well as the knowledge that whatever she was feeling was temporary and so she had to be careful. She could get hurt.

Yet, she didn't care. She wanted to feel his arms around her, to relish in the warmth and strength and scent of him. To lay her head on his shoulder and not be afraid.

"Eleanor?"

She hadn't even heard her name being called. But Willie had. She saw his hand, which had reached for her, drop to his weapon. She turned, her disappointment an ache, and recognized the man coming toward her.

Surreptitiously, she touched the deputy's sleeve, signaling him that it was all right.

"Eleanor? *That really is you.* What are you doing on Vashon?" A tall, blond athletic man, Lionel was dressed in a suit as if he'd come from work. She realized he was probably waiting for his wife to pick him up. He glanced at Willie with interest.

She took a moment, her emotions in free fall. "Lionel, this is a…colleague of mine." Had Lionel walked up only a few minutes later, she would have been in Willie's arms. The ache became agony. "Deputy Willie Colt from Montana."

"Lionel Hayes," he said as he shifted the briefcase to shake hands.

"How do you know Ellie?" Willie asked.

Lionel raised a brow at the nickname as Eleanor groaned inwardly. He shot her an even more questioning look as he said, "How would you describe what we were to each other, *Ellie*?"

"Lionel and I lived together for a while," she said as smoothly as she could manage. "I think I heard you have a son now?"

He brushed a nonexistent blond lock from his forehead, the gold of his wedding ring catching the light. "Joshua. He's almost a year now."

"Congratulations." She looked at where the ferry had finished unloading passengers. "We really need to catch this ferry."

"It was good seeing you." Lionel looked as if he wanted to say more, but Eleanor had taken Willie's arm, drawing him toward the ferry.

As they hurried away, she could feel Lionel's gaze on her back, a burning sensation that made her nauseous.

"Let me guess," Willie said as they boarded. "Things didn't end well with the two of you."

She looked over at the deputy, her practiced stare relaying everything she had to say about Lionel and the past.

"You can tell a lot about a man by his handshake," Willie said. "You can do a hell of a lot better than him."

She couldn't help the laugh that escaped her as they hurried aboard the ferry. Moments later, deckhands began to pull up the walkway in preparation for departure. She moved to the railing, gripping it hard as she refused to look back toward shore.

Willie joined her. But he was smart enough not to say a word as they headed for the mainland.

They'd disembarked and were almost to his patrol SUV when Willie got a call from his brother Tommy.

"I'm putting this on speakerphone," Tommy said. "James and Davy are here."

He shot Ellie a look as they climbed into his rig. He could tell that his brothers had learned something important. He put his phone on speaker as well. "Let's hear it."

"I talked to Zoey's sister," Tommy said. "It seems that before she hooked up with Lowell Carter, she'd been with a thirty-four-year-old heavy-equipment operator named Kevin Yates. The relationship was off and on—mostly off, the sister said, because of Kevin's temper. Zoey called the cops on him twice after she started seeing Lowell Carter and ended up getting a temporary restraining order against KY, as his buddies call him."

Lowell Carter had mentioned an old boyfriend of Zoey's. "What are you telling me?" Willie asked, knowing there was more.

"I did some checking on KY, and guess what?" Davy said. "He used to work for the same mining company Zoey and Vernon did, near Lonesome and then later near Butte—and at the same time."

"We're assuming the three of them could have known one another." Willie frowned as he looked over at Ellie. "Which means that when Vernon saw the woman in the window, he probably recognized her. Even if he hadn't known why he'd been hired before that, he would have guessed then. It could be another reason he ran."

"I know you like the idea of bringing down the owner of a mining company that pulled out of Montana, leaving a mess behind, but you could be barking up the wrong tree," James said. "Take a look at Zoey Bertrand's former boyfriend. Kevin 'KY' Yates is an abuser with a history of assault. He had been threatening Zoey and he either knew Vernon or had heard of him and what he did. KY could have set up the whole thing."

"Where is he now?" Willie asked.

"That's the thing. He's out your way," Davy said. "He's working at a mine out of Ellensburg—just over the mountain from you. I checked. There's a bar in Ellensburg the miners often frequent. The Shaft."

"Sounds like our kind of place." He looked over at Ellie. She cocked her head at him as if to say, *Your call.* "We'll pay him a visit."

"We?" James asked.

He met Ellie's gaze. "My colleague and…me." He disconnected, smiling. "We're going to have to get you some real clothes before we go to a place like The Shaft."

"I beg your pardon?"

"Leave it to me." The truth was, he couldn't wait to see her in a pair of tight-fitting jeans. "I think it's time to go shopping."

Before she could put up an argument, he started the patrol SUV. As he did, her cell phone pinged. He watched her check the text she'd gotten, then look up at him.

"It's McNamara again. He insists we meet in person."

Eleanor saw McNamara waiting for her at one of the outside tables the next day. A stiff wind brought the scent of rain. Over the city, a bank of dark clouds announced a thunderstorm before the day was over. The approaching storm had chased off late diners apparently. The other outside tables sat empty.

As she approached Phillip, she could see the cup of coffee he hadn't touched. Instead, he kept looking at his phone, as if expecting a call. From her? Had he really thought she wouldn't come? With his other hand, he tapped the table nervously.

Looking up, he saw her and seemed to relax, pushing his phone away. He smiled as if posing for a photo. There was no warmth in it, though—or in his eyes. She realized he might have gotten her here to fire her. Could he do that? He could. Her father had given him control of the firm. Phillip could do whatever he liked within the all-male firm, which was one reason she was the only female lawyer.

Her parents had liked Phillip, trusted him. Clearly either they hadn't seen beyond the veneer or they were too busy and distracted to look deeper.

She slowed, afraid this had been a mistake even though it had been her idea and had taken some persuading to talk Willie into it. She felt her phone in her pocket. He would be listening and watching. If anything seemed at all hinky, he'd promised to pull her out, so she knew he would be close by.

Keeping her expression blank as if facing a jury, she walked to the table. His smile faded as she took a seat opposite him. The wind tugged at her hair. She brushed back a lock that had come loose and faced him, waiting.

"What are you doing?" he demanded, clearly exasperated with her, but then quickly softened his tone as he saw her stiffen. "I've been worried sick about you, Eleanor. You know I still care about you."

"Is that why you gave me the Vernon Murphy case?"

He groaned. "I had no idea any of this would happen." He looked toward the pub. "Do you want something to—"

"No. Who hired the firm?"

He met her gaze but said nothing.

"Who are you protecting?"

"Client-attorney confidentiality."

She shook her head and started to get to her feet.

"Where are you g— Sit back down. *Please*," he added quickly.

"Tell me what's going on or I'm done." She was still standing, still ready to leave. This had been a waste of time—just like staying with the firm after she'd turned down Phillip's advances. She'd thought she could change it within. She'd been wrong.

"You aren't going to throw your career and your future away over something this trivial." She said nothing. In ten seconds, she was walking. "Angeline Carter wanted my best lawyer. That is you."

She frowned. "I know she came to you about a divorce, but…" She saw his surprise that she knew. She slowly sat down in the chair across from him again. "Why would she hire the firm to represent the man who killed her husband's lover unless… Unless she had hired Vernon to kill Zoey Bertrand and wanted to make sure he never talked."

Phillip shook his head. "I don't know where you get your information, but it's just the opposite. She wanted to know who hired Vernon Murphy and set him up, fearing it was her husband and she might be next."

Eleanor scoffed. "That's ridiculous. Why would he kill his own girlfriend?"

"Because things had gone sour between them, and she'd become a liability."

"How could his wife know that?" she asked.

He looked away for a moment, no doubt uncomfortable with sharing what would have been client-attorney privilege. "She said she didn't know who the woman was that he'd been seeing but she'd been through this kind of thing with him before. Only this time, the affair was ending badly. She'd overheard him on the phone. Apparently, Zoey Bertrand knew things he'd done at one of the mines that could have gotten the mine closed down and him thrown in prison."

Eleanor shook her head. She wasn't buying this.

"She believes her husband got rid of his girlfriend for good and if she tries to divorce him, he'll kill her, too. She said she's had several close calls after contacting me."

This certainly wasn't the story her husband had told them. "Why would he want her dead?"

"Money. Lowell has a ten-million-dollar policy on Angeline and himself. Lowell made no secret of the fact that he was going to marry the woman. He'd purchased her a very expensive emerald-and-diamond ring—which I'm told wasn't found on the body. It's possible that Vernon Murphy took it, since no one believes he didn't know she was tied up in the building before he demolished it."

Eleanor thought of what Vernon had told her about seeing the woman with duct-taped wrists, hands banging on the window, mouth open in a scream. It was more believable than Phillip's story. "Let's pretend this is all true. Whose idea was it to put me on the case?"

He held her gaze for an uncomfortable length of time before he said, "Angeline wanted my best, so I guess it was my idea. I also wanted someone I could trust on it."

"Trust me to what?"

"To tell me everything Vernon told you. You've always been so…professional. I just assumed you would come to me if there was a problem with the case—before you took off with that cowboy cop. I had security check the cameras in the building. Why would you leave with the man?"

She ignored the question. "The men who attacked Deputy Colt weren't Vernon's friends. They wanted something from him. What do you imagine that was?"

"How would I know? Maybe the ring. It's worth a small fortune, according to Angeline. He didn't say anything to you about it?"

She shook her head and waited.

His eyes widened. *"You can't believe I had anything to do with Vernon getting away."*

"Someone tipped them off as to when Vernon was being extradited and where."

"What are you insinuating?"

"That you know more than you're telling me. Why did you really give me the case?"

"Damn it, Eleanor," he said, lowering his voice as he leaned toward her, even though they were alone out in the wind and growing cold. The air grew damper by the minute. "I thought he might confess everything to you. I told you when I gave you the case that I wanted updates. I was only concerned because Lowell Carter was involved and I was representing his wife."

"Wait, Angeline Carter hired you *before* Vernon blew up the building in Lonesome, Montana, and killed her husband's lover?"

"No, not hired me. She knew Lowell was having an affair and she said it felt different this time. She wanted to know what her options were. When the woman was killed in the demolished building and Vernon was caught out here, she wanted to know if her husband had hired him to do it. The case was a simple extradition."

"But it wasn't a simple extradition case and I suspect you knew it."

He groaned, shaking his head as he avoided her gaze. "Did Vernon Murphy tell you who hired him or not?"

"Not." She saw his disappointment, then his distrust.

"You're sure he didn't mention a ring?"

Eleanor thought about what Willie had said about Vernon taking one look at her long legs and unburdening himself. Phillip had obviously thought the same thing when he'd thrown her at Vernon. They were both wrong.

She got to her feet again but paused. "I want to believe that you didn't realize how dangerous this case was when you gave it to me. Or that you weren't the one to tip off the men who took Vernon. Tell me I can trust you."

"Do you really have to ask?" He met her gaze again and she saw such regret in his eyes that it made her heart ache. He *had* loved her. Maybe he thought he still did. But she hadn't loved him and was no longer sure she could trust him or anyone else. Anyone except Deputy Willie Colt.

"I hope now that we've talked, this means you're coming back to work." Phillip sounded impatient with her, as if she was being childish. Was her life still in danger? Willie had tried to send her away so she'd be safe. Why hadn't she gone, if she truly believed she was in danger?

A thought stopped her cold. Was she going along with Willie because she was still scared or because she was starting to enjoy the cowboy's company?

The roar of a car engine and the squeal of tires on pavement made her turn in time to see a dark SUV speeding toward them. As it roared past, she saw a masked man half hanging out the window, a gun in his hand pointed in her direction.

Eleanor froze, unable to move as glass shattered on the table next to her, the gun's loud report filling the air as the SUV sped past. In those seconds after the car took the corner and disappeared, tires squealing, she didn't know if she'd been hit by the gunfire.

In the equally deafening silence that followed, she heard Willie come running up to her, heard him swear and saw his expression. She looked down expecting to see holes in her body, blood leaking out.

There was blood, but it appeared to be splatters. With a horrible dawning, she knew it wasn't hers. She turned slowly to see Phillip McNamara slumped over. The wound to his head had formed a lake of blood in the center of the table.

Chapter 13

Eleanor felt numb as she sat in a corner of the restaurant with one of the officers. She'd already given her statement. Willie had cautioned her to keep it brief. She was having lunch with her boss and managing partner at the firm. She had no idea why someone would want to kill him. Or her.

She'd remained calm, spoken clearly and kept her inner turmoil from her expression. Years of practice had paid off. But every time she closed her eyes, she saw it happening again. The man wearing the black ski mask, the black SUV, the gun, a semiautomatic, also black. It all happened so fast.

That was what she'd told the officer.

Outside, through the shattered front window of the restaurant and the driving rain, she could see Willie with the police chief. She could tell just from their expressions and postures that the chief was chewing him out. It appeared that his time in Seattle had run out.

Yet, she couldn't imagine him walking away from this. Walking away from her, knowing she might still be in danger. Had those bullets been for her? Had the shooter missed and killed Phillip by accident? Or had her boss been the target all along?

Willie finished his conversation and headed for the front door of the restaurant. She tried to read his face as he approached, but he was as good at hiding his inner turmoil as she was, she realized. Their gazes met through the rain and held for a moment. He winked and pushed open the door.

A wave of relief washed over her. She had no idea what he'd told the chief, but Willie wasn't the kind of man who gave up. She felt warmth radiate through her— even as she warned herself not to get too attached to this man. Once he completed what he'd come to Seattle to do, he'd head back to Lonesome. Nothing could keep him in the big city. Certainly not a "buttoned-up" lawyer.

That thought brought the fresh reminder of Phillip slumped over the table, dead. She felt tears burn her eyes. What was going on?

Willie took off his wet jacket, slung it on the back of the booth and slid in next to her. Without a word, he put an arm around her, pulled her into his chest and began stroking her back. She'd been allowed to wash up in the restroom, but her clothing was still splattered with Phillip's blood. At first she was tense in Willie's arms, but after a moment, she felt herself let go. She breathed in his outdoor scent, her cheek warm against his shirt, his arms reassuring around her.

After a few moments, she pulled back. Being in his

arms felt too good, too comfortable, too safe when she knew different. "The chief—"

"Don't worry about him."

"I'm not. I'm worried about you."

He chuckled. "I'm fine. How are you holding up?"

She nodded, swallowing. "Do you think…"

"That you were the target? I don't know. Maybe both of you were. I wounded the shooter. Hopefully that will make him easier to find."

Eleanor stared at him. "You were firing, too?" She'd heard all those shots, but she'd just assumed the man in the speeding SUV had missed her, the shots going wild. Of course Willie would have fired back. "Is that why the chief is upset with you? You don't have any authority out here."

Willie nodded. "He's threatening to put me in jail if I'm not out of town by sundown."

"What are you going to do?" She waited, heart in her throat.

"Get out of this restaurant, for starters. Come on." He stepped from the booth, pulled on his jacket and then helped her with hers before leading her to his patrol SUV parked a block away. Once they were inside, buckled up and moving, he asked, "What do you want to do now, Eleanor?"

He only called her Eleanor when he was scared, she thought.

Willie wouldn't have blamed her if she was ready to catch the next plane out of Dodge until this was over. He knew the feeling.

Ellie looked over at him. He'd seen emotions wash over her face—shock, fear, sorrow and now anger. But no tears. He thought she might still be in shock. "I want to catch those sons of—" Her voice broke. "Don't try to send me away again. I'm going to see this through one way or the other."

The determination in her voice didn't surprise him. She was strong. Still, he didn't like the *one way or the other*. "Are you sure?"

She nodded, catching her lower lip in her teeth for a moment. "If you're right about someone at the police station tipping off the men who attacked you and took Vernon, then we can't trust them to stop these people."

"You're sure your boss didn't tip them off and that's why he's dead?"

Willie listened as she filled him in. He was surprised at the information she'd been able to get out of the man. The missing ring was a whole new twist. So was the wife's claim that her husband had been behind the killing of Zoey Bertrand—and instead of wanting a reconciliation, he was trying to kill Angeline, too, for the insurance money.

He'd wanted to dislike her boss, but now wondered if the man really hadn't known the case would be this dangerous for Ellie. He got the feeling that Phillip McNamara was still carrying a torch for her and had been hoping he might have a chance with her after all.

"What do we do now?" she asked.

He gave it only a moment's thought. "For starters, call Colt Brothers Investigation." He pulled out his phone. The rain had slowed to a patter that danced on the top of the patrol SUV, running like tears down the window. Outside, the day was a bruised variation of grays.

James answered. He filled him in on what had happened and the ultimatum the chief of police had given him.

"Sounds like you've worn out your welcome in Seattle."

"Does seem that way, but I can't leave yet."

"Willie, I don't like what's happening."

"Nor do I. That's why I need you to check into Lowell Carter's finances. His wife, Angeline, seems to think he knocked off his girlfriend to get back a very expensive ring he'd given her. She also believes he wants to get her, too. Something about a ten-million-dollar possibly double indemnity insurance policy on her life for accidental death?"

James let out a low whistle. "A nice cash payout, if he's short on funds."

"I need to know more about this engagement ring Carter allegedly bought Zoey that is allegedly worth a small fortune. Ellie's boss said it wasn't found on the body. I don't remember seeing anything about it in the police report. If it exists, someone has it. Could be why Vernon might have been tortured by the men who abducted him."

"Seems like a stretch," his brother said.

"That's my feeling, too, but it does add a new wrinkle."

"Am I going to have to get you out of jail?" He could hear the worry in his brother's voice. Jail was nothing compared to what James was really worried about. This could get him killed and they both knew it.

"Possibly," he said, looking over at Ellie. "If that happens, I need you to make sure attorney E.L. Shafer is safe." He smiled and winked at her. "Thanks, I knew I could count on you."

"Be careful."

"Always." He disconnected and considered her. He

hated to even ask, but time was running out. "You still up to going to Ellensburg to have a talk with Zoey Bertrand's old boyfriend KY? I'd like to know more about her. Was she the type of woman who'd turn him in to the authorities? Also, we still need to get you some real clothes for the occasion."

She cocked a brow at him. "I can't wait to see what you consider *real* clothes."

Eleanor stared at the woman in the mirror. She felt like the city mouse gone country in a story her nanny used to read to her. Willie had taken her shopping, sending her into a dressing room saying he'd bring her what she needed.

"Don't you want to know my sizes?" she'd asked him.

"Trust me," he said with a grin. "Let's see if I'm as good at dressing you as you were me."

She did trust him. Now, looking in the mirror at the clothes he'd brought her to try on, she had to admit he'd been almost too good at guessing her sizes. The bootcut jeans fit like a glove. She'd never owned a pair of cowboy boots in life. The leather was soft, the boots surprisingly comfortable. She couldn't imagine what they'd set him back. The Western snap shirt was gray-and-white check, the gray matching her eyes, something she knew hadn't been an accident.

When she came out of the dressing room, she saw his eyes widen. He seemed at a loss for words as he gave her a thumbs-up. "But the hair…" She stood perfectly still as he moved to her and removed the scrunchie she'd used to pull her hair up into a messy bun on top of her head.

A shiver moved through her as she felt his fingers running through her hair. She had to bite her lip to keep from sighing with pleasure. The man had nice hands. He drew her long hair into a low ponytail to one side and took a step back to assess her. His smile told her everything she needed to know.

Willie tossed her a jean jacket and paid the bill. "You ready?"

As they drove over the mountain to Ellensburg, they discussed everything they'd learned and agreed that there were too many holes in the information they'd gathered. They still didn't know who'd hired Vernon or who had him now and why.

"I'm hoping KY will fill in some of those holes," Willie said. "This place we're going, it could be rough."

She smiled. "Don't worry, power suit or not, I'll be fine."

The Shaft turned out to be a metal building in an industrial area. A half dozen pickups were parked around it. Ellie had managed to find a recent photo of Kevin Yates online. His Facebook page showed a blue-collar drinking man, most of the photos taken in bars with KY clearly overserved. From what they gleaned on his page, Zoey wasn't his first failed relationship.

Willie pushed open the door. A roar of loud voices, the smell of stale beer and the clatter of pool balls rushed out. They stepped into the dark bar, blinking until their eyes adjusted. Willie led Ellie over to a table in the corner, then went to place their orders at the bar. A skinny woman with a hoarse voice asked what he wanted. "Two beers. Whatever you have on tap." He tossed down a twenty, and she took it and headed down the bar.

He spotted a group of raucous men, KY at the center and clearly the loudest of the group. The bartender returned with his beers and his change. He passed her a ten-dollar bill and, leaning in, said, "Would you tell KY that we're over here and want to buy him a drink? Thanks." He turned, taking the two beers to the table and sitting down across from Ellie. She'd made herself comfortable, putting her boots up on an empty chair and leaning back against the wall.

He couldn't believe how different she looked in the clothing he'd gotten her. Even her attitude was different. If anything, she looked stronger, more confident, more determined than she'd been in her power suit and heels.

Willie had known she would look kick-ass in jeans and boots. She did. She'd left the two top buttons of the Western shirt undone, exposing her throat and a patch of lightly freckled skin. When he met her eyes, he had to laugh. Nothing buttoned-up about this woman tonight.

Like him, she'd spotted KY.

He watched the bartender give the man the message. KY looked in their direction. Willie raised his glass and smiled. KY glanced at him, frowning. Then the man's gaze landed on Ellie. KY took a long drink of his beer, said something to his buddies and extricated himself from his friends to saunter over.

Kicking out a chair for the man to sit down, Willie said, "This is Ellie. What are you drinking?"

KY took the chair and sat, grinning at the lawyer. "I'd take another beer." Willie signaled the bartender. The group of men KY had left were watching them closely. So was the bartender. Willie pointed to KY. She got the message.

Ellie dropped her boots to the floor and leaned toward the heavy-equipment operator. "We have some friends in common," she said to him as Willie returned from the bar with the man's beer.

"Is that right?" KY said.

Willie set the beer in front of him and took his chair again.

"You used to work at a mine in Montana, right?" she asked.

KY nodded, took a gulp of his beer and asked, "How did you know that?"

"Vernon Murphy. He told me if I was ever out this way, I should look you up."

"Spark?" KY sounded surprised by that, but not sorry. The man gave Ellie a lecherous look. "How is it you know Spark?"

Willie decided to move things along. He leaned forward, placed his badge on the table where the rest of the bar couldn't see it, and said, "Tell us about Zoey."

KY jerked back at the sight of the badge. "What the—" He started to rise.

"We just want to ask you a few questions," Ellie said quickly, touching his arm to keep him seated. "You know Spark's in trouble, right?"

"I don't know anything about it." Maybe he didn't.

"But you used to date Zoey," Willie said.

"I didn't have anything to do with her death. Spark's the one who blew her up. Not me." So he knew that much.

"We want to know who hired him, who set him up," Ellie said, drawing KY's attention back to her. It wasn't hard. KY was clearly smitten with her, and Willie knew the feeling. "I'd think you'd want whoever did this to pay."

"Zoey and I weren't together anymore," the man said sullenly. "Why would I give a fat—"

"I know you still cared," Ellie said. "All the times you tried to see her."

"Until the bitch got a restraining order on me." KY finished the beer he'd brought over to the table and put the bottle down a little too hard.

"Still," Ellie said. "I can't imagine that you wanted her dead. But I suspect she really hurt you when she hooked up with Lowell Carter. That had to be hard to take. If it was me, I'd be furious. Good riddance to bad rubbish."

Picking up the fresh beer, KY took a gulp before putting it down. "Yeah, maybe she got what she deserved."

"Any chance you had her killed?" Willie asked.

KY swore and reached for his beer again. He'd clearly already had enough to make his face flushed and slack, his eyes slightly unfocused. "Everyone knows Spark killed her." He mumbled something unintelligible, then said, "Blasters always think they're better than the rest of us. That little sawed-off, loudmouthed Spark was way too big for his britches." He drank some of his beer. "Guess he got what he deserved, too," he said, licking the foam off his lips.

"Are you saying he's dead?"

That stopped the cocky, heavy-equipment operator. "How would I know? I just meant he's got the law after him *finally*. Everyone knew what he did on the side."

"Did his boss Lowell Carter?" Ellie asked.

KY laughed. "He didn't have a clue."

Willie jumped in. "You hire him to kill your girl-friend?"

The man shook his head. "If I wanted her dead, I

would have killed her myself with my bare hands." Willie got the impression KY had given this some thought before tonight.

"Except she had that restraining order on you and this time you would have gone to jail if you got near her, let alone touched her," Willie said. The man brushed that off, as if going to jail was nothing. "You told her you'd see her dead before you'd see her with Lowell Carter." He didn't know this for a fact, but he knew KY's type.

The man shrugged. "I say a lot of things, especially when I'm mad." He snorted. "Or drunk." He took a long pull on his beer bottle. His gaze went back to Ellie. "You a cop, too?"

She shook her head. "Attorney."

"Really? I might need one after tonight." KY laughed.

Willie noticed that the man's friends over at the bar were no longer watching with concern, but they'd still be curious. Not that Willie and Ellie looked out of place in this bar. He saw several cowboy hats and some boots. He'd rodeoed here when he was young, so he knew Ellensburg.

Ellie shifted in her seat, knocking her purse to the floor. Earlier, she'd hooked the strap of the bag over the back of her chair. As it landed, she reached for it. KY lurched to the side, leaning down to help her, and practically fell out of his chair. He had to catch himself by grabbing the edge of the table. The beer glasses wobbled.

It took a few minutes for Ellie, with KY's inept help, to pick up what had fallen from her purse.

Willie sighed. He could see that if they were going to get anything out of KY, they'd better hurry. "You really didn't see a way to get rid of Zoey and Vernon and pay back Lowell Carter—all at the same time?" Willie asked after Ellie had retrieved her purse. Out of the corner of his eye, Willie saw that she was applying lipstick and taking her time doing it—and KY was watching with a drunken leer.

KY slowly dragged his gaze away from Ellie, as if confused for a moment. "That would make me awfully damned smart, wouldn't it?" Grinning, he asked, "You don't think I'm that smart, do you, *Deputy*?"

"Who then was behind it?" he asked.

KY shook his head. "You're right about one thing. If I ever get my hands on the person…" He looked up, locking eyes with Ellie. "I loved that woman. What they did to her…" He finished his beer and shoved to his feet. "Thanks for the drink." He cocked his head at Ellie. "You should come back sometime without the cowboy cop." He raised his almost empty beer bottle in salute and staggered back to his friends.

Willie took a sip of his beer, placed a tip on the table and rose. "Let's leave before he tells his friends I'm a cop and you're a lawyer."

Once in his patrol SUV, he turned to her. "You were amazing in there. I apologize for putting you in that situation."

She waved off his apology as she pulled her phone from her jean jacket pocket. "It was my choice. I knew how it would go."

"Still." He started the patrol SUV and pulled out of the parking lot. "What's your take on KY?"

"He could have done it. He knew all the players." She was scrolling on the phone in her lap. "He was also a little too proud of himself. If he did it, he's going to brag about it to someone. Truthfully, he doesn't seem smart enough to have planned it alone, though."

"Someone could have put him up to it. Paid him," Willie said, wondering what she was looking for on the phone. "If he's guilty and wasn't working alone, I'm betting he'll contact the person after our visit."

"He won't be calling anyone for a while," she said, and held up the phone in her hand. "I took his cell phone when I dropped my purse. It was hanging out of his side pocket. He didn't even realize he'd lost it."

Willie shook his head. "You really are something. You managed to get into the phone?"

"It's an old phone and he didn't have it password-protected," she said. "Probably didn't want the hassle when he was drinking. I'm not sure how much it's going to help, though. I only recognize one contact name on it." She looked over at him and grinned. "Lowell Carter."

"If I wasn't driving, I'd kiss you."

Eleanor knew he was joking, but still his words were like a beam of sunlight, warming her. It was the look in his eyes though that sent the missile of scorching heat to her center.

She dragged her gaze away to look out at the night as she reminded herself that she couldn't get too attached to this man. Once this wild ride was over, the cowboy would be galloping off into the sunset. She had no idea what she'd be doing when that happened, she realized.

Settling in for the long drive, she tried to make sense of what she was doing with this man. Her boss was dead. The memory came as a shock, one she knew she hadn't fully accepted. She couldn't even be sure that she still had a job. What surprised her was that she didn't feel that upset about the job and had conflicting emotions about her boss. McNamara had gotten her into this. Maybe he hadn't known how dangerous it was—until the shooting started. But he'd made working at the firm almost impossible after she'd rebuffed his advances.

Maybe giving her Vernon Murphy's case had been more punishment for rejecting him. Maybe everything he'd said to her at that table before the shooting had been a lie, and those bullets had been for her. Still, she hoped that she wasn't the reason he was dead.

She closed her eyes, realizing how exhausted she was after the long, emotional day. She worried they would never find out the truth. At some point, Willie would have to go home to Montana. At some point, she'd have to do what? Go back to her old life? Right now she couldn't bear the thought.

Eleanor woke to Willie's hand on her shoulder.

"Hey, Cinderella, we're back from the ball," he said.

She struggled to fully wake up, still caught in what she now knew had been a dream. She felt the dream slipping away like mist drifting across the Sound as she sat up. All she knew was that Willie had been in the dream—and she'd been naked. That was disturbing enough. "Where are we?"

Not Seattle. All she could see were pine trees and darkness, except for a lone light shining on a log house. *"Willie?"*

Chapter 14

Her tone alone warned him everything was about to hit the fan. He'd made good time, driving over the speed limit from Ellensburg. He kept thinking about his earlier words. "If I wasn't driving, I'd kiss you."

He would have kissed her. He had wanted to kiss her. He'd wanted a lot more than that, he'd thought as he'd looked over at her, surprised that she'd fallen asleep.

In that moment, he'd felt such a mixture of overwhelming emotions, most of them so alien to him, that he felt lost. It terrified him that he might get this smart, ingenious, amazing woman killed and he'd changed his plans. He'd taken the first exit, gotten back on the interstate and headed to the one place he knew would be safe for her.

"We're in Lonesome, Montana."

"Wha—" She was awake now.

"Come on, I want you to meet my brother James and his wife, Lori." He started to open his door, but she grabbed his arm.

"What is going on?" she demanded, those gray eyes clouded with anger.

He sighed and looked out into the darkness before he told her the truth. "The police chief in Seattle as well as my boss here made it clear that if I wasn't back in Lonesome by tonight, I was fired and headed for jail."

That didn't seem to be the answer she'd anticipated. "You're giving up?"

Willie met her gaze and smiled. "Unfortunately, it isn't in my nature to give up, on anyone or anything I care about."

She looked toward the house. "Then why— If you think—"

He didn't let her finish as he reached for her, cupping her chin and turning her to face him. "I realized I was going to get you killed. I couldn't bear that thought even before I started caring so much about you." He watched her reaction to his words.

When she spoke, some of her anger had dissipated. "So you kidnapped me?"

"I've taken you under protective custody for the night."

Ellie snorted. "You have no legal right to do that."

"Take me to court," he said, releasing her chin to open his door.

As he started to step out, she said, "Are you prepared to remove me bodily from this vehicle?"

He stopped and turned back to grin at her. "If I have to, I promise to try not to enjoy it."

She swore and threw open her door, bounding out. "You can't keep me here."

Willie climbed out and looked across the top of the SUV at her. The fire in her eyes stirred him as much as the curve of her hips in the jeans he'd bought her. This woman was going to be the death of him, he thought.

He softened his tone. "Come meet some of my family. At least for tonight, we're both safe. We can talk about it in the morning." She looked toward the house. His brother James had come out to stand under the porch light. He saw her surprise at the resemblance between them.

"How many of you are there?"

"Just four—that I know of," he joked. "Women did love my father and people say we've all taken after him."

She harrumphed but let him lead her toward the house and the brother waiting on the porch for them. He didn't kid himself. He'd seen that flash of fury in her eyes and known that she might never forgive him for this.

That realization hurt more than he wanted to admit.

Chapter 15

"You're probably going to need help getting those off." From the doorway, Willie saw Ellie sitting on the edge of the bed. He could tell from her expression that she'd already tried to remove the boots herself. She had a frustrated, angry look he recognized. E.L. Shafer wasn't a woman who enjoyed failing at anything. He suspected that was in part why she was still furious with him. He didn't have to guess what the other part was. He motioned to her boots as he closed the guest room door behind him.

"You're...impossible," she said as he approached her.

"I know." He hunkered down in front of her and pushed up her jeans. Wrapping his hands around her booted foot, he removed one boot, then the other. Setting them aside, he avoided her gaze.

She'd hidden her anger at him when she'd met James

and Lori before they were shown to the guest room and his brother and wife returned to bed. Ellie had been nice and polite, and he could tell that she liked Lori, but then everyone did. James had looked worried, just as he'd sounded on the phone when Willie had called to tell him that he was bringing Ellie to Lonesome.

"Do you think that's wise?" his brother had asked.

"I can't leave her in Seattle. It's too dangerous." He heard James's question in the silence that followed. "She's been a big help with navigating this huge city and filling in gaps in the investigation." More silence. "I care about her, okay?"

"You can't keep her. You do realize that, right?"

Earlier, Lori had apologized, saying that they had only one guest room. "But there's a couch in it that Willie can take or—"

"They'll figure it out," James had said, and taken his wife's hand. "Good night. We'll see you both in the morning."

Now he could feel Ellie watching him. He slowly raised his head. Her gray eyes shimmered as if filled with a light from inside. She hadn't cried, not even a tear, after the attack in the alley or after seeing her boss killed next to her.

Willie could see so much in her face now, emotions she'd held back since they'd met, emotions she'd kept locked down. He suspected she was a woman who'd been raised to always be in control. It was as if she'd been putting on that buttoned-up lawyer veneer like she did her power suit and heels each morning for years, and now felt naked.

He reached for her, drawing her to him, half expecting her to slap him—or worse, push him away. She did neither. She fell into his arms, pressing her face against his shoulder. He felt the quake of her silent sobs, felt the dampness, felt her give up any semblance of control as she held on to him as if in a violent storm.

Pressing his face into her hair, he closed his eyes, rocking her, he, too, in a storm of his own. He more than cared for this woman and it terrified him—and at the same time, just the sight of her filled his heart to overflowing. He would catch just a hint of her scent or make her smile or hear her laugh or feel her breath on his cheek and realize that he'd never felt this alive.

Having her in his arms—even for a few minutes…

She pulled back to wipe her tears on her shirtsleeve before she met his gaze. Their eyes locked and he couldn't catch his breath as she leaned toward him and pressed her lips to his.

As her lips touched his, Willie drew back. His eyes searched hers, but for only an instant, and then his mouth was on hers. Hungrily, he kissed her with a passion that could only match her own. Her lips parted as she opened up to him, surrendering to these feelings that had been plaguing her since he'd walked into her office. With this man it would be total surrender.

Eleanor had spent her life regimented, from how she interacted with her lawyer parents to how she attacked her classes at university and law school, and finally how she took on her job at the firm. Everything had been well-ordered, because the law had its rules to follow. She'd never considered stepping off the path, breaking those rules, changing her course.

Until cowboy deputy Willie Colt burst into that disciplined life with his untamed, boundless thirst for doing the right thing—no matter the consequences. He'd torn down barriers she hadn't even known she'd constructed. He'd brought into question everything about her life and how she had lived it. Especially her love life. She'd chosen men like herself, by-the-law lawyers who didn't have a wild bone in their bodies. Men nothing like Willie Colt.

He pulled her to her feet, his hands cupping her buttock as he deepened the kiss. Her nipples ached, hard-tipped and yearning for his mouth on them as he let go of her and slowly began to unsnap her Western shirt. With the sound of each snap being released she felt a bolt of heat pierce her center. Goose bumps raced across her skin. She craved the warmth of his big warm hands, his hard body.

She'd never wanted a man like she did this cowboy. As he opened her shirt, he pulled down her bra to suck a nipple into his mouth. She moaned with pleasure as he laved the tip with his tongue before moving on to the other breast while he unhooked her bra, slipped off her shirt and cast it aside.

Needing to feel his bare skin against hers, she pulled at the snaps on his Western shirt, making them sing as they opened. She pressed into him, her full breasts soft against his warm, hard chest. Hearing his moan, her desire mounting, she worked at the rodeo buckle on his belt, then at the buttons on his jeans as he stripped off her jeans and panties with the same urgency.

Kicking off his boots and jeans, he grabbed her and practically threw her onto the bed. She felt a laugh escape her lips before his mouth covered hers again. His hands roamed over her, touching places that sent shivers through her, intensifying everything. She thought she'd burst even before she felt his fingers gently work her thighs apart. Her head fell back with a cry of decadent desire as he gently stroked her.

It took only his touch to take her to the zenith. She cried out from the release only to feel it building once again as he moved up her body, his lips making their way to hers as he filled her, fulfilled her, taking her to unimaginable new heights before his release.

He collapsed beside her, pulling her over into his arms as they both fought to catch their breaths. Her body was still alive, her skin sensitive even to the air around them. His body, skin hot to the touch, felt like a warm fire next to hers.

When she met his eyes, she saw her own wonder mirrored in his. There were no words. She could feel a cool breeze coming in the open window, bringing the scent of pine from the remainder of the night. They didn't have to find words for what had just happened between them, she thought as she curled against him and fell into the best sleep she'd had in her life.

She woke to sunlight streaming into the guest room, almost believing that last night's lovemaking had been nothing but a dream.

Then she turned and met Willie's blue gaze and felt him reach for her yet again.

Chapter 16

Later that morning, James looked up as Willie came into the kitchen. All it took was one glance at his older brother for James to apparently know that he hadn't slept on the couch. He shook his head and said, "I hope you know what you're doing."

Willie scoffed at that. "Did you know what you were doing when you ran into Lori again?" he asked as he took a chair across from his brother at the table.

"You always swore that you were never going to fall in love."

"Who says I'm in…love?"

James laughed. "You're a goner and you don't even realize it yet."

Willie thought about last night. "I've never met anyone like Ellie…" He couldn't put the feeling into words this morning any more than he could last night. Nor did he want to. It felt too intimate, too personal, too intense and too new.

His brother chuckled. "There is no fool like a fool in love, especially in your case."

"What's this talk of fools in love?" Lori asked as she came into the kitchen. She looped an arm around her husband's neck and kissed his cheek before coming over to hug her brother-in-law. "Don't listen to him. I'm making pancakes and bacon. James, didn't you even offer your brother a cup of coffee?"

"We've been busy talking," her husband said.

"Don't let me stop you." Lori went behind the kitchen island and returned with a cup of coffee.

Willie thanked her and asked his brother, "What did you find out about Lowell Carter's finances?"

James seemed as glad of the change of topic as Willie. "He's facing a lot of EPA fines from the messes he left behind when he abandoned mining operations in a variety of states. A lot of his investors have pulled out, including Jonathan Asher."

"So Asher isn't involved with him anymore?"

"At least not that I could find," James said. "But his other investors probably aren't happy. Right now Cascade Extraction Corp is shut down, and from what I can tell, there isn't much if any money coming in—at least not from mining. By the way, the building outside of Lonesome wasn't the only one owned by the corporation that was torched in the past two years—and insurance collected on it."

"Maybe Angeline Carter is right about her husband trying to cash in on her life insurance policy," Willie said as Ellie came into the kitchen. He met her gaze, making her cheeks flush before she looked away. He couldn't help but think of the two of them tangled in the sheets again this morning. Nor had he ever felt like this before. It was as if he was floating. The cold shower he'd taken had done little to bring him back down to earth—a place he really needed to be right now. These newfangled feelings scared the hell out of him, and at the same time, he'd never felt happier.

Lori got her a cup of coffee, declining Ellie's offer to help with breakfast. "You just join the men. James said you've been a great help to Willie out in Seattle, so I'm sure you're interested in what James has found out."

"I'm not sure how much help I've been," Ellie said as she took her coffee over to the table. Willie could tell that she was touched by not just the hospitality but the acceptance of her being part of the investigation.

"So, how broke is Carter?" Willie asked.

"As broke as any man who made his fortune with other people's money," James said. "He won't go hungry."

"Do you think he was desperate enough to hire Vernon to torch his building, kill his fiancée and get the ring back?" Willie asked.

Before James could answer, Ellie said, "Vernon didn't get the ring. I don't think he even knew about it. He told me about his shock at seeing Zoey at the window and I believe him. He was scared. He knew he'd been set up to take the fall for her death. He'd run. He wasn't in on it."

The two men looked at her for a long moment before Willie nodded and said, "So, where's the ring?"

"Pawnshop?" James joked.

"Not if it's worth as much as Angeline Carter told her lawyer it is," Ellie said. "But she could have lied to my boss about it, although he believed her."

"Sounds like if you find the ring, you'll find your killer," his brother said.

"If the ring even exists," Ellie said, drawing both his and James's attention. "Did anyone see it on her finger?"

James made a quick call to Zoey's sister to ask about the ring. As he disconnected, he said, "There *was* a ring. A large emerald surrounded by diamonds. Apparently, Zoey had been afraid to wear it to work, fearing she might lose it. The sister said she looked for it in Zoey's apartment, but it wasn't there. She says that her sister must have been wearing it when she died."

"If she left it at home, wouldn't the police have found it when they were investigating her murder?" Eleanor asked.

Willie nodded. "So who has it?"

As the brothers' conversation turned to the ranch and the investigation business, Eleanor went into the kitchen, determined to help Lori. "Thank you for opening up your house to us in the wee hours of the morning."

Lori smiled and touched her arm. "Our home is always open to family."

"I'm not—"

"Not yet," the woman said with a laugh. "I've seen the way my brother-in-law looks at you. He's never looked at a woman like that, not ever. In fact, he's always sworn he was never going to fall in love, saying it was more dangerous than being a deputy or a PI."

Eleanor wanted to argue that neither of them had necessarily fallen in love. But she could no more explain this feeling than make excuses for why she'd ended up in his arms last night. She'd wanted Willie and had never wanted another man with that kind of intensity.

Lori's look softened. "I've known Willie my whole life. I've never seen him like this. I love seeing him so…happy. You have a glow about you as well," she said, smiling.

She didn't know what to say. Nor did she get the chance. Lori handed her a huge platter full of pancakes and bacon, then followed her out to the table carrying plates and silverware. The conversation changed to the antics of the wild Colt brothers in their youths.

Eleanor found herself laughing as she enjoyed the warmth in this house along with her breakfast. She listened as Lori told the story of how she and James fell in love, laughing over a sandwich she'd made him full of hot peppers.

"I ate it. Every bite," James said. "It hurt all the way down—and for days later, but it was worth it." A lovely look passed between husband and wife.

"I'm sorry you didn't get to meet our daughter, Jamie," Lori said. "My sister-in-law Bella picked her up this morning. Bella's pregnant and needed a baby fix." Lori laughed. "Did James tell you that we're expecting again? It's a boy." Her smile told it all.

Eleanor congratulated the happy couple and helped clear the table. As she and Lori filled the dishwasher, she thanked her again.

"You are welcome here anytime." She paused as if to study Eleanor. "I hope you'll be back. I worry about how dangerous this line of work is, but I can also see that all four of the Colt brothers love trouble. They just can't stay out of it." She shrugged and reached for Eleanor's hand. "Take care of yourself and Willie. I know he'd risk his life for you."

"That's what worries me," Eleanor said.

"Just be careful with his heart," Lori said, and squeezed her hand before letting go. "Please don't break it."

"I forget how much this place grounds me," Willie told Ellie. He'd brought her outside out on the porch and into the sunshine under an azure blue, cloudless sky. The air smelled of pine and the nearby creek. Birds sang from the tree boughs. There was no sound of traffic, no honking horns, no blare of sirens. There was only the whisper of the breeze sighing high in the tops of the pines.

"I can see that," she said. "This place and your family." She felt it as well. Here, she felt safe, as if insulated from the outside world. Seattle and the trouble there seemed a million miles away.

"While I'm in town, I need to go see my boss," Willie said with a sigh. "Would you mind following me in my pickup down to the sheriff's department?" At her confused look, he said, "I'm pretty sure that I'll be turning in the patrol SUV and my badge—either because I lost Vernon and didn't come right back to Lonesome, or because the sheriff isn't going to like that I'm going back to Seattle to finish what I started. I'll have to quit. It's possible that Sheriff Henson here tipped off whoever took Vernon." He shrugged. "I don't know whom to believe anymore."

"So you're going to need a ride," Ellie said, and cocked her head as if sensing what was coming.

He looked down at his boots for a moment, his Stetson in his hand, and said, "You know that I wish you'd stay here with my family so I know you're safe." Before she could open her mouth, he rushed on, "But if I've learned anything about you, it's that you are your own woman, with a damned good mind and good instincts. I respect that. It's up to you what you do next."

Eleanor had been ready to argue. For a moment she didn't know what to say. "Thank you." She stepped closer to cup his rough, stubbled jaw in her palm as she thought about their lovemaking. A quiver of desire threaded through her as she kissed him. Drawing back, she thought about what Lori had said. "I can't let you go alone. We're in this together, one way or the other."

He nodded, though she could see it was hard for him to accept. He reached into his pocket and dug out a set of keys. "You know how to drive a stick?"

"I suspect I'm about to learn," she said as she took the keys from his hand.

"I could ask my brother."

She shook her head. "I'll figure it out."

He smiled, his gaze locking with hers. "I'm sure you will," he said with a laugh. "Follow me. Not too close," he added, and grinned.

She hadn't seen anything of the area around James and Lori's house in the pines last night. As she followed Willie in the patrol SUV with a lot of jerks and stops that required restarting the pickup, she caught glimpses of mountain peaks and clear running creeks.

The trees opened to a two-lane blacktop. Willie turned onto the highway and minutes later a town appeared. Welcome to Lonesome, the sign read. She felt as if she'd been dropped into a Western film. The town was quaint with its brick and wood structures that seemed as if they were straight off a movie set.

Willie turned into the sheriff's department parking lot. After a couple of unsuccessful tries, she did as well in his truck. By the time she turned off the pickup's engine, she felt as if she was starting to get the hang of driving a stick. It made her smile. Although she couldn't imagine driving it in the city. Or possibly ever driving one again.

The feeling that this was all a dream and that she would soon wake up left her feeling despondent. She didn't want to wake up and have never known Willie Colt.

Just the thought of their lovemaking came with both pleasure and pain. Lori seemed to think that this could last, this wild fling with Willie Colt. All she could think was, a fish and a bird could fall in love, but where would they live?

She tried not to think about the future. All she knew for sure was that Deputy Willie Colt had turned her life inside out in a matter of days. Was it any wonder that her old life felt like a blur after everything she'd been through since the cowboy had walked into her office?

She made herself think about Seattle and her job— if she still had one. She figured one of the other partners had taken over managing the firm. She had no idea where that left her. Maybe out in the cold.

Her cell phone rang. Not the burner she'd used to call Phillip, but her own. She dug it out, thinking it would be Willie, since he'd been inside for a while. Maybe he'd been arrested. Maybe he needed bail rather than a ride.

She didn't recognize the number. Was it possible that Vernon could be calling her again?

She looked toward the sheriff's department—no sign of Willie—and quickly took the call. "Hello?"

Chapter 17

Sheriff Henson leaned back in his chair, his fingers entwined across his large extended belly, as he considered Willie. From the expression on the older man's face, this was going to get uglier.

"I knew you weren't going to work out," Henson said. "I've watched you Colt boys behaving like a pack of wolves for years." He shook his head. "But the mayor, bless her tender soul, asked me personally to give you a chance."

"I didn't realize Beth had done that," Willie said, touched. Mayor Elizabeth Conrad had gone to school with Willie's father. The two had been friends and maybe more. "I'll have to thank her."

Henson scoffed. "A little late for that, since I can't have a man on the force who doesn't follow orders."

"I came back as soon as I could."

The sheriff side-eyed him. "You caused a pack of trouble out there. I got a call from the police chief—"

"The bottom line is that they aren't doing anything to find Vernon Murphy."

"I'm sure it isn't a top priority for them," Henson said. "They have an entire city to keep safe. One two-bit arsonist probably isn't even on their radar."

"He killed a woman."

"Which might get him second-degree murder if he didn't know she was in the building. Face it, you blew this, Deputy Colt. It's on your head."

"That's why I have to go back. I have to—"

"You aren't going anywhere," the sheriff cut in.

"—find these people and bring them to justice," Willie continued, speaking over his boss.

Henson rocked forward in his chair, propelling himself to his feet. "Did you hear anything I said? Your job is hanging by a thread. I wanted to fire you, but the mayor…" He shook his head. "But if you go back to Seattle, you're out."

Willie nodded and rose from where he'd been ordered to sit. He pulled out his badge and laid it on the sheriff's desk. Then he removed his service revolver and put it beside the badge. "Guess I'd better quit then."

He told himself that he'd only taken this job because he'd thought he could find out more about his father's death from inside the sheriff's department. He'd never expected that he would like the job or that it would suit him, he thought as he removed his canvas jacket with the sheriff's department's insignia on it. He tossed the jacket on the chair he'd been sitting in.

"I didn't want it to be this way," Willie said, realizing how true that was. "But I have to see this through."

"You're just going to get yourself thrown in jail or killed," the sheriff called after him as Willie walked to the door. "Those Seattle cops aren't going to put up with your lone rider cowboy antics."

"I need to see you," Angeline Carter said without pre-amble. Eleanor had hoped it was Vernon. She realized how foolish that hope had been as the woman rushed on. "I called the office. They gave me your number. I can't believe what happened to Phillip. I don't know what to do." The woman's voice broke. "I'm terrified I'm next."

"Where are you?"

"At the Vashon Island house."

"Where is your husband?"

"I don't know." She began to cry. "Why would he kill my attorney?"

"We don't know that your husband—"

"I think he's already made several attempts to kill me. Two so-called accidents in my car. I swear both times, the brakes didn't work right. And now Lowell is acting so strangely. I think he's having a breakdown. I called the police, but they said they can't do anything until he commits a crime. To which I said, 'What about shooting Phillip?'"

Eleanor saw Willie come out of the sheriff's department. She noticed right away that he wasn't wearing his deputy jacket—nor his department-issued weapon. "Why would your husband want to shoot your attorney?"

"He accused me of having an affair with Phillip, of the two of us trying to steal his money, destroying his reputation… It's all so upsetting. He keeps talking about the ring he gave to his girlfriend like he thought I had it."

"Do you have it?"

Angeline let out a bark of a laugh. "How would I have it?"

Eleanor could think of several possibilities. "Why is it so important to him to get it back?"

"Because it's worth so much, according to him."

"Wasn't it insured?" she asked. "If all he cares about is the money..."

"I hadn't thought of that. He must not have insured it before he gave it to the woman. It isn't like it has any *sentimental value*." Bitterness tinged her words. "What a fool. Giving a bauble like that to someone so irresponsible? She probably lost it. Or sold it."

"Why would you say that?" Eleanor asked as she slid over to let Willie climb behind the wheel of his pickup.

"The police said that the ring wasn't found on the woman's body."

"Perhaps whoever bound her and left her in that building took the ring. In that case, whoever hired Vernon to kill her has it." Willie raised a brow as Eleanor said into the phone, "If that were the case, Mrs. Carter, it stands to reason that if your husband was that person, then he wouldn't be asking you about the ring."

Angeline sighed. "Phillip always said you were scary smart," she commented with a note of respect. "But I told you. Lowell's not in his right mind." She let out a sob. "He said he wanted to try to make our marriage work and I believed him. I forgave him and now..."

"Have you considered getting a restraining order, Mrs. Carter?"

"Please, call me Angeline. Mrs. Carter reminds me of Lowell's mother. Bless her soul." She blew her nose, sniffling for a moment. "I can't keep kidding myself. I need to go ahead with the divorce as soon as possible. With Phillip gone…"

"I'll find out who'll be taking your case," Eleanor said.

"That's why I'm calling. He gave me you."

The woman's words stopped her cold. "Who gave you me, Angeline?"

"Phillip. He told me that if anything happened to him, you were to take over. He always said that you were the best attorney at the firm. He didn't mention me to you?"

Willie listened as Ellie promised to meet Angeline Carter first thing in the morning at her office. "What was that about?" he asked after she disconnected.

"Phillip McNamara apparently wanted me to handle her divorce case—if anything happened to him."

"Apparently he *did* know how dangerous it was," Willie said. Ellie didn't respond. He saw that she didn't want to argue the point, probably because she didn't want to take McNamara's side. But he could tell that she felt guilty, as if she were responsible for getting him killed. "Don't blame yourself for what happened to him."

She swallowed as she glanced over at him. "You know I feel guilty?"

He turned to grin at her. Of course he did. In a matter of days, he'd gotten so close to E.L. Shafer that he felt he knew her better than she knew herself. Yet, he wanted to know more. He wanted to know everything about her. The woman intrigued the hell out of him and that scared him.

It was now more than keeping her safe. He couldn't bear the thought of leaving Seattle. Leaving Ellie. But he didn't see how this could end any other way.

Ellie met his gaze, but quickly looked away as if she'd glimpsed the emotional battle going on under the grin. "Angeline feels she needs to get her divorce immediately," she said. "She thinks Lowell is having a breakdown and she's terrified and doesn't know where he is. She seems to think that her husband is behind Phillip's shooting—and alleged attempts on her life—as well as hiring Vernon to kill his girlfriend."

He shook his head. "I'm sorry, but why would your boss want you to have Mrs. Carter's case? Was he that desperate to get you back to work? Or did he have reason to believe that someone might try to kill him?"

"I don't know. It's not unusual for a partner to choose an attorney as backup." He grunted in response. "Do I need to ask how it went with the sheriff?"

"Nope." Willie studied her as he said, "I'm going back to Seattle as a civilian. My badge wasn't worth anything out there anyway." He reached under the seat, pulled out a small bundle and unwrapped the weapon inside. He put it in the holster on his hip and took out a box of shells. "Are you serious about representing Angeline Carter, Ellie?" he asked.

"You said you wanted to talk to her. I think she knows more than she's telling, but I also believe that she's scared and maybe with good reason. She's convinced she needs the divorce pushed through because Lowell's trying to kill her before it's granted. I need to go back as her attorney and represent her."

He nodded. "What if representing her is what got your boss killed?"

She turned to lock eyes with him. "We both want this over, right?"

Was that what she wanted? "Not if you're dead."

"For some reason Phillip wanted me to handle this," she said. "It's crossed my mind that Angeline might actually know for a fact that her husband is behind all of this and told her attorney. She might even have evidence. Client-attorney privilege, Phillip couldn't tell me or the police. But if it's in her file I might be able to talk her into going to the police with what she knows—and providing any evidence she might have. I now have access to those files."

Maybe that was Phillip's reasoning, Willie thought. But wouldn't he have tried to persuade Angeline Carter to go to the police himself? Maybe he had and that was why he was dead.

"I don't like it," he said. "Like you said, whatever Angeline might tell you is covered by attorney-client confidentiality. What if she tells you something that puts you in even more danger?"

"We need answers," she said, determination in her voice. "Angeline is scared, but if she has those answers…" He could see that tough-as-nails lawyer he'd first met. "I need to do this. If Angeline has evidence that could put Lowell away, I need to convince her to turn it over to the police."

There was no doubt that Ellie could be persuasive. But this could put her in the killer's crosshairs. If she hadn't already been.

Willie started the pickup. He knew better than to try to talk her out of it. He told himself that he would just have to find Lowell quickly. He had a feeling that Jonathan Asher might know where he was. If not him, then Alex Mattson. There was a connection there. He just had to find out what it was and use it to his advantage.

His hope was that he might get some answers before

the day was over. Ellie would be meeting Angeline in the morning, so he had time.

It was late afternoon by the time they reached Seattle. Ellie had him take her to her apartment. Willie had been quiet most of the trip home. She'd been lost in her own thoughts as well. It felt as if they'd been spinning their wheels, getting nowhere. Vernon was probably dead. Phillip certainly was, and Eleanor couldn't help thinking that she might have been as well, if not for Willie.

"I know you don't like me going back to my apartment, or my office to meet with Angeline Carter tomorrow, but I can't keep hiding," she said as she opened her apartment door and they walked inside.

"Is that what we've been doing?"

She turned to look at him. "You know what I mean."

His expression softened. "I know this has been hard for you, but I can't say I'm sorry we met."

She stepped to him and kissed him, then pulled back to look into his eyes. "I'm not sorry, either." Didn't he realize how badly she wanted the danger part of this over? She didn't know what happened afterward, but she couldn't keep living like this, not knowing if she was going to live or die, waiting for it to happen.

It wasn't just the living in limbo, her life out of her control, and everything completely out of her comfort zone. It was the fear that this cowboy was going to get himself killed. Not that she didn't know that once they found the answers, he would be gone back to Montana.

She had to do something to take back the reins of her life, and being a lawyer was something she did well. Working with the law made her feel safe. She needed the rules and regulations—unlike Willie. Mostly she needed her job to fill in the huge hole that this cowboy was going to leave in her life. Just the thought of never seeing him again after this...

He pulled her to him, kissing her with a passion that made her knees weak with longing. As he drew back, he nodded as if he could see her inner turmoil in her eyes. "I need your promise that you won't step a foot out of this apartment until I come back." His tone brooked no discussion, so she nodded, even though she wondered where he was going. Earlier at the gas station, she'd heard him making a series of calls, leaving messages.

At her high-rise apartment overlooking the city, he quickly checked every room. The apartment looked exactly as she'd left it. She couldn't imagine that anyone had been able to get past the twenty-four-hour security downstairs. At least, no one had signed in since she'd been gone.

Eleanor watched Willie check for listening devices in her lamps. Under her kitchen stove hood, in her bathroom. She also saw him taking in the view in the expensive apartment as if comparing how differently they lived. She knew he'd lived on the road, sleeping in the camper part of his horse trailer at some rodeo fairgrounds.

She didn't need to be reminded of how dissimilar their backgrounds were. If it wasn't for Vernon Murphy, they would have never met. So, why had they? she wondered as she headed for her bedroom, needing to get a hot shower and change of clothes. Was she wishing that he would join her in the shower? Doubtful, since he seemed anxious to leave.

She'd just sat down on the edge of the bed to take off her boots when Willie appeared in the doorway.

"Want some help with the boots?" he asked as he moved to her. He knelt down and slipped them off. She knew she could have managed by herself since the leather had loosened up, but she didn't mind the feel of his hands or these few minutes with him.

When he looked up, she saw desire fire his blue eyes. He ran a hand up her leg inside her jeans, along her calf. She felt the aching need of her own desire for this man. His expression looked pained as his cell rang. He let out a curse and rose to his feet.

She watched him walk away, wanting to call him back, suddenly afraid she might not ever see him again as she heard him say, "I'm on my way."

Willie turned to see Ellie still sitting on the side of the bed. It took all his inner strength not to go to her, take her in his arms and make love, since common sense told him it could be the last time. The thought shook him to his core. He knew how dangerous meeting Lowell could be.

But it was Ellie he worried about. He knew he couldn't wrap her in cotton to keep her safe. But he wanted badly to, until this was all over. All his instincts told him that Lowell Carter was the key, and right now, he was in trouble.

He walked back toward her, stopping in the bedroom doorway. He thought about telling her who'd called and where he was going. But he could see that she was already worried. "I don't like leaving you here alone."

She cleared her voice and seemed to push the worry from her expression. "I will be fine. Call me as soon as you can, though."

"I had a gun in my glove box. I put it in your purse."

He saw her glance toward her purse, which she'd dropped on the table in the corner of the bedroom. "It's a point-and-shoot handgun. All you have to do is pull the trigger." He could tell by her expression that she didn't believe she could do that. He hoped she was wrong—should she need to fire it.

"Eleanor, I..." He realized he was going to tell her that he loved her. It was on the tip of his tongue. This woman had stolen his heart. But for so many reasons, he couldn't say the words. Not now. Maybe not ever. "Be safe."

He hated leaving her. But what he'd heard in Lowell Carter's voice was that he was finally going to hear the truth.

On the way down in the elevator, he replayed the phone call in his head, listening to the man's words as well as what Lowell hadn't been saying.

"I need to talk to you," Lowell said, *fear punctuating his hurried words.*

"I'm listening."

"Not over the phone. You have to meet me."

He thought he'd heard a foghorn in the distance. *"Why would I do that?"*

"I know who killed Zoey." The man's voice broke. He rattled off an address. *"You're the only person I can trust. Please. Hurry. You're my last hope."*

Willie walked across the lobby and stepped out onto the dark street. He felt mist on the breeze as he hurried to his pickup. The smell of the Sound and the scents of this city were starting to feel achingly familiar because they reminded him of Ellie.

He pushed that thought away as he climbed into his truck, punched in the address on his phone and drove toward the spot Lowell Carter had said to meet him—in the warehouse district along the wharf. He kept thinking about the man's tone of voice on the phone. Anxious and strained, as if someone was holding a gun to his head.

Chapter 18

Willie parked behind one of the warehouses and waited for his eyes to adjust to the dark. A foghorn sounded in the distance.

Outside the pickup cab, nothing moved in the still darkness between the warehouses. He opened his door and breathed in the dense, wet air smelling of fish and water. He was already armed with a handgun, but he wasn't taking any chances. He pulled the shotgun from behind the seat. It was loaded, since an empty gun was worthless in an emergency. He dug out the box of shells and put another four in his pocket.

He had no idea what he was walking into. That Lowell was in trouble, he'd suspected long before the phone call. The man had sounded scared. He was either hiding out or they already had him and were drawing Willie into a trap.

Quietly, he closed the pickup door. They would have heard him drive up, as noisy as the old truck was. He needed to buy a new one, but like a lot of rodeo cowboys, he had his superstitions. This pickup had gotten him to many a rodeo where he'd done well. To change trucks had seemed like a bad idea.

He hoped the pickup's luck held tonight as he cradled the loaded shotgun and moved around the warehouse toward the single light over the door of an adjacent building, where Lowell said he would be waiting.

Willie tried the door, not surprised to find it unlocked. He turned the handle and it creaked open just enough that he could see the huge empty space dimly lit. Why would Lowell want to meet here?

He shifted the shotgun to his right hand and pushed the door farther open. Empty. But beyond the vast space, he could see what appeared to be an office on the second floor. The light was on behind the shuttered windows.

Letting the door close behind him, he kept his eye on the office as he crossed the expanse, his footfalls the only sound in the cavernous space. He stopped at the bottom of the stairs and listened. No sound coming from the office that he could hear. Was Lowell alone? Willie didn't see anyone moving up there.

He glanced around, but there was little place for anyone to hide. He started up the stairs, his boots ringing on each metal step. All his instincts were on alert, all of them telling him this was a bad idea.

Sheriff Henson had called him a lone rider cowboy. It was true, but only because there was no one else he could call. He didn't trust the cops, nor did he trust Lowell's associates. Ellie was the only one he trusted, and she was home safe. There was no way he would have brought her out here, because all his instincts told him he was walking into a trap.

He was almost to the top of the stairs. He couldn't see into the office, but he could hear a noise inside like someone moving around. Swearing under his breath, he reached for the door handle, telling himself the only way it would be wired with explosives was if Vernon Murphy was in on all of this.

Eleanor had been lost in thought, unable to stop thinking about the call Willie had gotten—and the gun he said was in her purse. Where was he going? Who was he meeting? He hadn't told her because he hadn't wanted her to worry.

She scoffed at that. It was dangerous, that much she knew instinctively. She'd seen the way he looked at her before he left. For a moment, she'd thought he was going to say… She swallowed, her throat suddenly dry. Did he love her? Was that what he was going to say? Or was he going to say goodbye?

Her heart beat faster. Did he fear he wouldn't be coming back? She pushed off the bed, unable to accept the thought that something would happen to him and he wouldn't be coming through that door ever again.

She looked around the apartment, realizing she would be next. Willie thought so. It was why he'd gone out tonight, to try to end this. She moved quickly to her purse, opened it and lifted out the gun, surprised by how heavy it was. She'd never fired a weapon. Her parents refused to have a gun in the house. They were civilized people who used the law to fight their battles. They would have been horrified that she had a loaded weapon in her apartment.

She quickly put the gun back in her purse, shuddering as she remembered the loud report of the gunshots outside the café—and the damage the bullets had done to Phillip. She told herself that she would never be able to pull the trigger, as her phone rang.

Eleanor snatched it up, thinking it was Willie. "Tell me you're all right," she said without preamble.

"Of course I'm not all right," snapped the female voice.

"Mrs. Carter." She couldn't help the slight groan in her voice. She should have checked caller ID, but she'd been so sure, so hopeful, that it was Willie. If she had known it was Angeline Carter, she wouldn't have answered it.

"I thought you were someone else." Eleanor cleared her voice, trying to push down her disappointment and growing fear for Willie. "Has something happened?"

"I need to talk to you tonight," the woman said. "This can't wait until morning. I'm in Seattle. I can swing by your apartment and pick you up. Say twenty minutes?"

"No." Eleanor tamped down her frustration with the woman. "I'm sorry. I'll see you in the morning at my office, but not tonight. I'm…busy."

"My life is in danger," Angeline Carter snapped.

So is mine, Eleanor thought. "Go to a hotel. You'll be safe there. I'll see you first thing in the morning." She disconnected and, taking the phone, went into the bathroom to draw a bath. It was the only thing that calmed her. *Except for Willie Colt*, she thought as nerves made her restless. *Be safe. Come back to me.*

Sweating even in the cold of the warehouse, Willie held his breath and turned the knob. It took a moment for him to realize that no explosives had gone off. But the door refused to open any further. He pushed with his shoulder, inching it open until he saw the body on the floor.

Lowell Carter lay sprawled, his feet against the door, his ankles wrapped in duct tape, his wrists bound behind him. A wide strip of tape covered his mouth. The moment he saw Willie, he began moaning loudly as he tried to talk through the tape. But it was what Willie saw duct-taped to the man's chest that chilled him to his bones. Explosives!

Willie hurriedly reached down and tore the tape from the man's mouth and was reaching for his pocketknife to cut the explosives free, when Lowell cried, "There isn't time. This whole place is about to go up. Run!"

He looked from the man's terrified eyes to the bright red glow of the timer ticking off the seconds left and did the only thing he could. He turned, falling down the stairs as he ran. He had just reached the ground floor and was running for the outside door when the first explosion boomed behind him. A wall of heat hit him in the back, the force knocking him to his knees.

He knew at once that there were more explosions coming. Scrambling to his feet, he sprinted to the door, threw it open and lunged out into the darkness. If he could get to the other side of the adjacent warehouse next to the water...

The world behind him exploded in a fiery ball, the blast knocking him off the pier. He hit the water hard, the air forced from his lungs as he went under, the dark water dragging him deeper and deeper below the surface.

Chapter 19

After a long bath that hadn't helped calm or relieve her worry, Eleanor dressed, made herself a cup of coffee and began to pace the floor. Willie had promised that he would call. He hadn't. She checked the time again. He'd been gone almost two hours. Shouldn't she have heard something by now?

She made the decision. If she didn't hear from him soon, she was calling the police. She didn't know what else to do, because she couldn't shake the feeling that he was in trouble. She checked the time again and was reaching for the phone to make the call when there was a knock at her door.

Willie. That was why he hadn't called. He had been on his way. Her heart soared. She rushed toward the door, but then stopped a few feet short, frowning. She had twenty-four-hour security downstairs. There was only one way the person could have been let in. Unless the guard had recognized Willie from before…

There was another knock. She moved to the door, looked through the peephole and felt a start. A cop in uniform was standing outside her door. He knocked again.

"Who is it?" she called, her voice cracking. Willie didn't trust the police and yet she'd been ready to call them. Only because she hadn't known whom else to call. His brothers were miles away. Now there was a cop at her door?

"I'm here about Willie Colt," he called through the door. "I'm afraid he's been in an accident." Her heart leaped to her throat. She'd known something was wrong. She'd felt it. "He gave me your address and asked me to—"

She threw the door open. "Is he all right?"

The cop was about her age, short dark hair, anxious brown eyes. "He's in the hospital. He asked me to come get you."

If Willie sent him to get her, it had to be serious. "What happened?"

"Why don't I tell you on the way. We should hurry," the officer said. "My patrol car is right outside."

"Let me grab my coat." She stepped back in, leaving the door open, and got her purse and coat. Hurrying out, she closed and locked the door. Her heart thundered in her chest, a silent prayer on her lips. Willie had to make it. There was so much unsaid between them—at least on her part.

The cop led her down the hall and into the elevator. He pressed the button once, then twice. Impatient. Were Willie's injuries that serious that every minute mattered?

Her eyes filled with tears. She hastily brushed them away. She had to be strong. For Willie.

The elevator began to move. She leaned against the wall, closing her eyes as she prayed even harder. She could hear the officer moving around restlessly. She opened her eyes and noticed something she hadn't before.

He wasn't wearing his name tag on his uniform.

Willie couldn't breathe. His eyes flew open to cold, wet darkness. He was drowning. Again. Only this time, none of his brothers were here to pull him to the surface, to save him. He felt disoriented, his body aching. But the real pain was realizing he might never see Ellie again.

He looked up, seeing light, and frantically began to swim toward the surface. His chest ached for just one more breath, his heart ached for just one more day. As he burst through the surface, he gasped for air, lungs screaming, heart thundering in his chest. He had to get to Ellie.

As he swam to the edge of the dock, he hauled himself up onto it, ignoring the pain. He tried to make sense of everything that had happened since he'd arrived in Seattle. The sky was black with smoke, the warehouse smoldering in ruin. He could hear sirens in the distance as he spotted his shotgun where he'd dropped it before being thrown into the water.

He picked it up and staggered to his pickup parked a few warehouse buildings away. His only thought was Ellie. Pulling out his phone, he shook off the water and tried it. No dice. Anger and frustration surged through him, blurring the pain in his body as he climbed in and started the engine. He'd been set up from the moment he'd come to Seattle, and it was starting to really tick him off. He tried to put the pieces together, his mind fuzzy except for the obvious.

That explosion back there in the warehouse had Spark's name all over it, which meant the man had fooled him—and no doubt Lowell, too. But Willie couldn't believe that Vernon was acting on his own. He remembered the small, scared man he'd picked up at the police department. It hadn't been an act. He'd known someone would be coming for him, someone who terrified him. So, who was pulling the strings?

Willie had a bad feeling as he sped toward downtown. Ellie had been in danger from the get-go. He told himself that she was too smart to leave her apartment. But that didn't mean that whoever was behind this wouldn't figure out a way to get to her.

He'd put the gun in her purse, but would she use it? Just the thought of her in trouble brought pain more excruciating than being blasted into Puget Sound and almost drowning. He'd endured physical pain many times before. It had come with riding bulls in the rodeo.

But this pain in his heart? He didn't think he could stand it. This was why he'd sworn to never fall in love.

Ahead, he spotted her apartment building rising up into the dark sky as it began to rain.

Heart already pounding, Eleanor had a sick feeling in her stomach as she asked, "Officer...? I'm sorry, I didn't catch your name."

"Guess I forgot to put my name tag on before my shift," he said, reaching up and touching the spot where it normally would be. "My wife wasn't home when I left. She's the one who makes sure I'm presentable. I keep telling her I'm an adult and I don't need her help." His laugh sounded more nervous than humorous. "She'll never let me live this down."

Eleanor had dealt with all kinds of clients. Some lied better than others. The liars often talked too much, filling the silence with any word that came to mind.

The elevator reached the ground floor and the cop stepped off, holding the door open with his arm as he waited for her to exit.

Eleanor had no choice. If she refused to get out, he would get back in. The close confines of the elevator were the last place she wanted to be with this man even as she told herself she was wrong about him. He wasn't who she suspected he was. He wasn't lying.

She stepped out and let the door close behind her, but she didn't head for the doors out of the building. The lobby was empty at this time of the night. A guard should have been behind the security desk. He wasn't. That alone should have warned her since the guard would have had to have let the cop in.

At the windows facing the street, darkness pressed against the rain-streaked glass. She could feel the weight of the gun in her purse. Except she knew she couldn't get to it fast enough—even if she could shoot an officer of the law.

"You still haven't told me your name," she said, meeting his gaze, and saw that his hand was already resting on the weapon holstered at his hip. She knew she could run, just as she knew he would catch her before she reached the front door.

"I'm Officer Mattson. We need to get moving, Ms. Shafer," he said. "We're wasting valuable time."

Alex Mattson, the cop Vernon had confided in and

regretted doing so. Willie was convinced the cop was neck-deep in all this. Eleanor had no reason to doubt it. Out of the corner of her eye she saw him furtively un- snap his holster as he palmed the gun's grip at his hip.

Eleanor swallowed, her throat dry, her body feeling weak with fear. Even if she tried to run, she didn't think her legs would hold her. She'd been lured from her apart- ment by a man who wasn't taking her to Willie. Once he had her in his patrol car, who knew where he'd take her. Somewhere to kill her.

She started to turn toward the stairs that led down to the parking garage, willing her body to take flight. She could feel the adrenaline raging through her veins even before he drew his gun. She got only a few steps before he grabbed her arm, spinning her back into him. She felt the hard, cold barrel pressed against her side.

"We are going to walk outside to my patrol car. Please don't make this more difficult than it has to be." He didn't sound like a cold-blooded killer. She got the feel- ing he didn't want to do this. But she knew he would. He was afraid of whoever had sent him here.

"Willie Colt isn't waiting for me at the hospital, is he. Was he even in an accident?" she asked, surprised by the calm in her voice as he forced her toward the front door. She could see his cop car parked at an angle in the oval drive outside, where he said it would be.

"We're just going to ride down to the station. My boss needs to talk to you about Vernon Murphy. He has some questions and he knew you wouldn't come in un- less forced."

"You aren't a good liar, Alex. I know about your in- volvement with Jonathan Asher and Lowell Carter." She felt him stumble a little in surprise. "I also know that

Vernon Murphy confided in you while in jail, waiting to be extradited. He actually thought he could trust you. It must have been the uniform that fooled him."

"You don't know anything about me," he snapped. "You think I like this? I didn't want anything to do with any of this." He pushed open the door and they stumbled out onto the sidewalk and into the falling rain. She turned her face up to the raindrops as she rested her hand on her shoulder bag at her side. Once he had her in the patrol car she was as good as dead. She slowly began to open the zipper until she could get her hand inside to the gun.

"I know you invested in Lowell Carter's mining corporation and that it's in trouble," she said, walking as slowly as possible, as if unsteady on her feet.

"I put my life savings in it." She could hear the anger in the cop's voice. "Now I'm going to lose everything unless…"

Unless? The word hung in the air as he half dragged her by her arm toward the patrol car. His fingers bit into her flesh, the barrel of the gun still pressed against her side.

"Unless you do something for them." He'd made a deal with the devil. "Let me guess. You have to kill me." Her voice broke as she asked, "Did you also have to kill Willie?"

"No, Vernon—" He caught himself. "Just shut up, okay? I don't have a choice."

We all have a choice, she thought. But felt a wave of defeat wash over her. For a moment, she just wanted to give up. She'd been trying to stall, to keep the inevitable from happening, but if Willie was dead… She shuddered at the thought, knowing how Vernon took care of his end of things.

A sob rose in her throat as the pain seized her heart in a death grip. Grief flooded her, followed by rip-roaring rage. Mattson was a fool if he thought she'd just give up. She was going to fight to the death—just as she knew Willie Colt had done.

She spun into him so abruptly that she caught him off guard. The move broke his hold on her arm. He stumbled and she went for his gun. They wrestled for a moment, before his strength and training won out. He swore, wrenching the gun away, and shoved her toward the patrol car—no longer holding on to her.

But she could see his gun trained on her as she pushed her hand into her purse and wrapped it around the grip of the gun Willie had given her. She was going to have to shoot him, she thought as she took a step back and collided with the side of the patrol car. The cop was moving toward her, his weapon aimed at her heart. Her hand was shaking as she pulled the gun.

The roar of an engine made them both turn toward the sound as a pickup came barreling around the corner and headed right for them. She pulled the trigger.

Chapter 20

Willie felt his heart drop at the sight of the cop, the police car—and Ellie backed up against it in front of her apartment house.

He'd never gotten a good look at Officer Alex Mattson, but he knew that was who this had to be as the cop spun in his direction—his service revolver in his hand. Willie had his foot crushing the gas pedal to the floor, the old pickup engine a howl in his ears. He saw the cop raise his weapon—and fire.

The windshield shattered as Mattson's first bullet embedded into the passenger seat. Willie kept his foot to the metal. He saw the cop jerk, saw the gun in Ellie's hand as he closed the distance between them. The cop's second shot caught him in the shoulder, making him jerk the wheel. The pickup careened off to the right, clipping the cars parked there as he swung into the oval in front of the condo building. He struggled to hang on to the wheel, to keep from losing control, and was forced to let up on the gas.

He was only yards from Mattson when the cop started to fire point-blank at him. That was when Willie saw Ellie fire the gun again. Mattson seemed to scream in pain as the bullet hit him. He stumbled but didn't fall. For a moment he lowered his weapon, but then he spun around to turn the gun on Ellie.

Willie rammed the pickup into Mattson, heard the crunch of metal and bones and the thud of the cop's body as the truck rolled over him.

Then Willie was standing up on the brakes as the pickup skidded toward Ellie, whose eyes were wide as a deer's caught in headlights.

Eleanor knew she was in shock. She stared at the steam roiling out from under the hood of the pickup just inches from her. She'd seen Mattson go down, but now there was no sign of him. Through the pouring rain, she couldn't make out Willie behind the wheel through what little remained of the windshield.

Eleanor felt as if she was in a fog, drifting above the scene. She heard the driver's-side door open with a groan. Willie fell out, caught himself and lurched toward her. She stared in horror. He'd been shot at least once, the front of his shirt soaked with blood.

"You're going to be fine. Everything is going to be fine," he said, his voice rough with emotion as he moved to her. She still had the gun gripped in her hand, her limbs shaking. He stepped to her and gently pried her fingers from the weapon. "Everything is all right now."

He staggered. His bloody hand grabbed the side of

the police car for support but then slipped, and he slid to the concrete.

Feeling as if she was watching herself from a distance, she dropped beside Willie, pulled out her phone and called 911. Her movements robot-like, she did everything by rote, as if watching from somewhere else, while she pressed her coat to his wound to staunch the bleeding.

She heard herself saying, "You're going to be fine. Everything is going to be fine." They were his words, meaningless words. She heard the wail of sirens, the scream of an ambulance as it grew closer and closer.

It wasn't until she met his blue eyes as Willie was loaded into the back of the ambulance that she began to cry. Standing in the rain, she listened to the sound of the siren die away.

"Going to need to know what happened here," a police officer said, touching her arm to draw her attention. "Miss?"

She brushed at the tears mixing with the rain. "E.L. Shafer," she said. "I'm an attorney here in Seattle."

Willie woke in a hospital with a sense of déjà vu. He blinked, and for a moment thought he'd dreamed everything that had happened since driving out to Seattle to pick up Vernon Murphy. But as his eyes focused, he saw his brothers rise from where they'd been waiting in the shadows. One after another they came to his bedside.

He heard James pick up the phone and ask that someone let the doctor know that Willie Colt had regained consciousness after his surgery.

His mouth felt dry as dust. "Surgery?"

"You took a bullet, man," Davy said. "You don't remember?"

"Ellie?" It came out a whisper. Tommy got him a drink of water. He looked from one to the next, his fear growing. He didn't think she'd been hit, but he couldn't remember much. He tried again. "Ellie?" he asked, his heart in his throat.

"She's fine," James said as Willie tried to rise. "Take it easy. You'll see her soon. The cops had her for a long time, but she was released. Apparently, she knew a good lawyer. She didn't want to leave you, but we sent her home to change."

He remembered the rain and blood. Hers? Or just his? He remembered that dead look in her eyes as he'd pried the gun from her hand. He knew the pain in his chest had nothing to do with a gunshot. He'd dragged her into this. He would never forgive himself. Maybe if he'd never gone to her office...

"Speaking of cops, they're anxious to talk to you," James said. "They've been waiting out in the hall for you to wake up." As if seeing that Willie wasn't ready, he added, "They can wait a little longer."

He nodded, not surprised that the cops wanted to see him. The only person he wanted to see was Ellie. After what she'd been through, he had to know that she was all right. He thought about her returning to her apartment alone with Vernon still out there.

Willie tried to sit up again. "Ellie. Vernon is still—"

Tommy shook his head. "Vernon's no longer a threat. They found a second body in the debris at the destroyed warehouse. The body is believed to be Vernon's. He'd apparently been trying to get out of the building, but either had gotten trapped or miscalculated. Either way, he's gone."

Willie lay back. Vernon was dead? Lowell was dead. Was it possible that this nightmare was really over? That Ellie had no one to fear?

The hospital room door opened, and the doctor came in to shoo his brothers out. After checking Willie over, he said, "Are you up to talking to the police? They're very anxious to speak to you."

He nodded and the doctor sent them in. Chief Landry strutted in along with a younger cop, both looking like they wanted to cuff him and haul him off to jail. Willie had expected they would once he left the hospital.

"You're a dangerous man," the chief said in his gravelly voice. "Thanks to you we've been cleaning up bodies all day. Not only did you have no jurisdiction out here, but also you aren't even a deputy in Montana anymore. You're in a hell of a lot of trouble, cowboy."

"Do you want to hear what happened or did you just come in here to chew my ass?" Willie asked.

The chief puffed up for a moment before he signaled for the cop with him to make a video recording. Willie started at the beginning, making sure that his suspicions about the police department were in his statement even though the chief kept interrupting him.

He finished with being lured to the warehouse, finding Lowell Carter trapped there with explosives strapped to him and the timer about to go off.

"You somehow managed to get away," the chief said suspiciously. "How do you explain that?"

"I move fast when I have to," Willie said. "I knew I had to get to Ellie. I figured if I was set up, she probably was, too. If Lowell Carter wasn't behind this, then who did that leave? Vernon, Jonathan Asher, Alex Mattson. I knew one of them would try to get to Ellie."

"Vernon's dead. So is Mattson. You aren't suggesting that Jonathan Asher had anything to do with this?" Landry demanded.

"I know that Jonathan Asher had invested in Lowell Carter's mining company and was somehow involved with your officer Alex Mattson. Someone was giving Vernon Murphy orders."

"What makes you say that?" the chief demanded.

"He had nothing to gain by killing his boss or sending a cop to kill his lawyer. Asher stood to lose money if Angeline and Lowell divorced. Getting rid of the girlfriend, Zoey Bertrand, could have been the first step to make sure that didn't happen. But then I showed up to take Vernon back to Montana to stand trial. If I'm right and Asher hired Vernon, he couldn't have him testifying. Have you talked to Jonathan Asher?" He saw the answer on the chief's face.

"It appears he might have left the country," Landry said under his breath.

Willie nodded. "It makes sense. Asher had Vernon abducted and convinced him to keep his mouth shut and keep working for him. Lowell must have figured it out. Asher had to get rid of him, and apparently Vernon as well."

"Let's say you're right. Where does Attorney Phillip McNamara fit into all this?" the chief asked.

"I suspect McNamara wasn't the target." Bile rose in his throat. "The shooter was supposed to kill Attorney E.L. Shafer."

Landry shook his head. "For what possible reason?

I can't believe merely because she'd represented Vernon Murphy."

"No," Willie said. "At first I thought she was in danger because whoever hired Vernon would worry about what he told his lawyer. But in truth? She was in danger because of me. I dragged her into all of this." He was the reason she'd almost been killed.

He realized that Asher must have wanted to know what Vernon had told her—just as Phillip McNamara had wanted to know. But Willie didn't think they had wanted to kill her the night outside the pub. That was why they were going to drug her. Otherwise, the man in the alley that day could have easily killed her.

"It wasn't until she started helping me that her life was in danger," he said, feeling the gut-wrenching truth of it in his soul.

Landry shook his head. "What a hero."

"I should have figured it out sooner. If I had…" He didn't like to think how close Ellie had come to dying because he hadn't.

The chief motioned for the officer with him to stop the video recording. "I told you that you can't go around acting on your own." He began to read Willie his rights. "Once you're out of here, you're going to jail—if not prison." With that, the two cops left.

Before his brothers were allowed back in, two federal agents entered his room, making him groan. Willie repeated everything he'd told the chief of police, starting again with what had happened since he'd come to Seattle up to the grand finale in front of Ellie's apartment building.

"Just the whisper of a divorce had Lowell Carter's investors worried. From the get-go, I wasn't sure I could trust the cops. I didn't know then who had tipped off the men who attacked me and took Vernon."

"You believe you were set up."

"From the start," Willie told the agents. "Find Jonathan Asher and you'll find the man behind this whole mess. The chief said it appears he's left the country?"

"It does appear that way," one of the agents said. "We've taken Ms. Shafer's statement. She said you saved her life."

"She's wrong. I risked her life and almost got her killed. She's the one who saved mine."

Chapter 21

Eleanor pulled on her suit jacket and checked herself in the full-length mirror. She straightened her blouse collar before meeting her reflected gaze squarely. On the surface it would appear that last week hadn't happened, that this was just another workday, that everything about her life was the same.

She was still an attorney at the firm her parents had started, only now she was in power. To her shock, the majority of the senior partners hadn't liked the way Phillip McNamara had been running things. They'd been planning to get him out. Some of the senior partners had been the first ones her parents had hired. Loyal to the family, they'd voted for her to take Phillip's place. The news had come as a shock.

She'd dreamed of seeing her family name again on the masthead. More importantly, she'd dreamed of seeing the firm change and had fought for it with Phillip always shutting her down. Now she could hire female attorneys. She could turn the firm into what she knew it could be.

So, why wasn't she more excited now that it had happened? It wasn't just the way it had come about, with Phillip's death. She felt an ache low in her belly. Willie Colt. He'd ridden into her life, changed everything and then left, leaving a hole she'd been trying hard to ignore.

Admittedly, he hadn't simply left. His brothers had taken him home to mend. She'd wanted to go with him, but with the crisis at the firm, she'd had no choice but to stay in Seattle. Not that Willie had wanted her with him. If anything, he'd seemed happy to be leaving, as if he wanted to put this all behind him—her included.

"It's for the best," he'd said that day when he was released from the hospital. "Your life is here. Mine's in Montana." She'd seen him swallow, his blue eyes filled with regret? "I'm sorry about so much."

She hadn't known what to say. She hadn't been sorry about anything to do with him. Instead, she'd felt heartbroken.

Eleanor straightened. She had responsibilities. Being managing partner was what she'd worked so hard for all this time. She knew she could run the firm. She'd certainly watched her parents do it her entire life. So, basically, nothing had changed, she told herself.

Except she was no longer the woman Deputy Willie Colt had met that day at her office. She was stronger because of everything she'd been through. Stronger for having met Willie Colt, for loving him.

Before she stepped away from the mirror, she slipped

the top button of her blouse free. She was also no longer the buttoned-up attorney, thanks to Willie Colt.

"Now what?" James asked Willie once his gunshot wound had healed. "I heard Sheriff Henson stopped by?"

"To offer me my job back after he heard that I'm running against him in the next election for sheriff," Willie said.

"You're running for sheriff?" This was news to him.

"At least Henson thinks I am." Willie winked and smiled that devilish grin of his. It was good to have him back. They'd all missed him, even when he'd been back in Lonesome for weeks. He just hadn't been himself.

And still wasn't. There was something different about his older brother. He'd lost something out in Seattle. They all knew it had been his heart. James knew first-hand how that could hurt. He worried that his brother might never get over what had happened in the big city. He knew it had little to do with almost dying and a whole lot more to do with falling for the sexy attorney.

Ellie had called every day for a while, then once a week. Her calls had slowly dropped off since Willie hadn't been taking them. James had kept her up-to-date on his brother's recovery. They'd both pretended that was all she'd called about.

"You should reach out to her," James said now, even though neither had mentioned her name.

Willie's smile instantly disappeared, making James regret that he'd said anything. "Thanks for the advice, little brother."

"You can't pretend that nothing happened out there."

"I have the scars to always remind me."

"It's the scars we can't see that I'm talking about. Willie—" His words fell on deaf ears.

His brother got to his feet. "I got a call from a wrecking yard outside of Missoula. I might have found Dad's wrecked pickup. I know it's a long shot…"

"You're sure you want to see it?" James asked. Willie was clearly at loose ends, which was why he'd been investigating their father's death with a vengeance. None of them believed it had been an accident, but thanks to the sloppy work of then sheriff Otis Osterman, they'd never been able to prove it.

"If there is any chance that evidence was overlooked…"

James worried that his brother was in for more disappointment. He was so glad that Willie was feeling better. He didn't want to lose him again to that dark place he'd been in for weeks after returning from Seattle. "It's been almost ten years. What evidence could there still be?"

Willie shrugged. "I have some free time before I win the election. What else do I have to do?"

"I like your confidence. But you probably can't beat Sheriff Henson," James said with a laugh. "So you know you're welcome to come to work with us. We keep getting more investigative jobs all the time."

His brother shook his head. "Thanks, but if I don't win the sheriff seat, I'm not sure what I'm going to do yet. But don't worry about me." He patted James on the shoulder as he started out the door. "I'll call you if I find anything."

James couldn't help but worry about his older brother. Willie had healed nicely, Doc had said, but James had seen the change in him. As Willie had improved, Ellie had wanted to come to Lonesome, but James hadn't encouraged her. He knew it was the last thing Willie wanted.

"What's going on with you and Ellie?" he'd asked his brother once Willie had started feeling better.

"Nothing." Willie had gotten that closed-off look he always did when it was something he didn't want to talk about.

"She's worried about you." No reaction. "Did something happen between the two of you?"

"I almost got her killed, that's what happened," his brother had snapped. "I was so determined to solve the damned case." He shook his head. "I should never have gone out there. I should never have…" He looked away.

James knew how stubborn the Colt men could be. "You do realize that she's in love with you, right?"

"She'll get over it."

James had chuckled. "But will you?"

Willie had rolled over. "I need to rest. Close the door on your way out."

He'd left him alone and hadn't brought up Ellie again. But he couldn't help feeling bad for both of them. He remembered too well falling in love with Lori and how painful it had been until he'd opened up his heart to her and let her in.

Maybe there wasn't any hope for Willie and Ellie. Willie certainly wasn't going to move to Seattle, and according to his brother, she was now responsible for the firm her parents had built. Her life was in the big city and Willie Colt was no big-city cowboy.

It broke his heart because he could tell that a lot of his brother's pain had nothing to do with the gunshot wound.

Eleanor looked around the office, missing her old one. The views of Seattle and the Sound and even Mount

Rainier were incredible up here. She could understand why Phillip had wanted to hang on to it so badly.

She still didn't know how deeply he'd been involved with the Vernon Murphy case. Enough that it had gotten him killed? Or had those bullets been for her? She would never know. She suspected Willie knew, but he wasn't about to tell her. He wouldn't even talk to her when she called.

Pushing that thought away, she considered the remodel she'd had done on the office. There was nothing to remind her of Phillip and yet it felt as if he was still here—just as she felt her parents and had since law school. This was what they had always wanted for her. They would have been pleased, she thought.

But as she stood looking out at the Sound, her thoughts always turned to Willie. She'd talked to James earlier.

"I'm sorry, Ellie, he's not here. He got a call about our father's pickup being found at a wrecking yard in Missoula. He drove down to see if even after all these years, there was some evidence still in it."

"Sounds like him," she said, her voice betraying how much she missed him. He'd thrown himself into solving his father's death. "Determination isn't something he lacks."

"How are you doing? Enjoying your new office and position at the firm?"

"It's been busy. I never knew what the job entailed. Corralling attorneys feels like herding cats, not to mention trying to keep the partners happy. They seem to think I should have all the answers."

"I'm sure you're doing a great job." The conversation had died off and she'd said she had a meeting and got off the line. It was too painful talking to James. She kept remembering the night she'd spent in his and Lori's beautiful, cozy home on Colt Ranch. Lying in bed that night with Willie, she'd felt as if she'd belonged in Lonesome, belonged with the cowboy.

She walked back to her desk, hating the tears that burned her eyes. Willie had made his lack of intentions clear. His job in Seattle was over—and so were the two of them. Not that they had ever put a name to what they'd been. Lovers? Friends? Coconspirators? Colleagues?

Definitely lovers, she thought with that old ache. She'd hoped the pain would have gone away by now. Her friends encouraged her to date, but she had no interest. She knew there was no one out there like Willie Colt. And he was all that she wanted.

She got a message. The partners were waiting for her in the boardroom.

Chapter 22

The wrecking yard was huge. Willie had seen the rows and rows of old beaters miles away. It had taken him weeks of calling junkyards for fifty miles around Lonesome before he'd finally found his father's pickup.

"You're sure the plates on the pickup match?" he'd asked when an older man had called him back to say he thought he had the pickup Willie was looking for.

"Yep. Hit by a train, right?"

"Right," Willie said, grimacing inside at the thought of what he was going to see when he found it.

"A 2010 blue-and-white crew-cab Ford."

"That's it." He couldn't believe that he'd actually tracked it down. "I'm on my way." He'd hung up, telling himself not to get his hopes up. It had been ten years since his father's death. All that time the pickup had been sitting out in the elements. If there had been any evidence, it would be gone.

Yet nothing could keep him from going to see it. He knew it wouldn't be easy, a crash like that, knowing that his father had been inside that pickup when the train collided with it. But it was something he had to do. He didn't trust that former sheriff Otis Osterman had done a thorough investigation of the crash.

If anything, Willie suspected Otis would have covered up evidence. The sheriff had never liked any of the Colts, maybe especially their father, Del. Otis had been convinced that Del had been drunk and that was why he'd stopped on the railroad track with the train coming.

Willie and his brothers had never believed that, even though Otis swore he saw their father arguing with a woman outside a bar not long before the train wreck. Del had an occasional paper cup of blackberry brandy, but that was it. True, he'd been involved in a difficult case involving the hit-and-run death of a young boy. The coroner's report showed that Del had consumed some alcohol, but it wasn't over the legal limit at the time of his death, even though Otis also swore that an empty bottle of whiskey had been found at the accident site.

There were too many unanswered questions. But their father knew how dangerous that railroad crossing was. He'd always warned his sons about it. Where had he been going that night?

Willie couldn't help but hope that some of those answers might still be in his father's pickup as he drove to the small town outside of Missoula.

A skinny, weathered man somewhere in his late seventies came out of the small shack-like office as Willie drove up to the wrecking yard. He wore faded blue overalls over a red plaid flannel shirt and muck boots.

"Clyde Stanley?" Willie asked.

Pushing back the grimy trucker's cap on his gray head, Clyde gave Willie a nod and pointed to the south. Without a word, the older man headed out. Willie followed through this graveyard of abandoned vehicles. The wind whistled through the torn metal, kicking up dust, sending a stray tumbleweed blowing between the rows.

The pickup was on the side of a windswept hill, between an old Cadillac with fins and a smashed-in front and a van missing its engine.

Willie spotted the pickup and stopped walking. He stood a few yards away and had to swallow back the bile that rose in his throat. He'd seen wrecked vehicles after being hit by trains before, but they hadn't had his father inside. He took a deep breath and let it out.

"I can take it from here," he said, looking to his right, only to find that Clyde Stanley had already gone back to his office, leaving him entirely alone. The wind seemed to pick up as he approached the vehicle, whirling dust and dirt around him.

He tamped down any emotion, drawing on his strengths. It wouldn't be the first time he'd had to "cowboy up." It was something their father had taught them at a young age. Willie remembered his first rodeo. He couldn't have been much over two. He'd tried to ride one of the sheep. He'd fallen off, gotten trampled and his face pushed into the dirt.

Hurt and crying, he'd gone to his father. Del had checked him over, seen that he wasn't hurt badly and told him there was no crying. "If you're going to do this, you have to learn to 'cowboy up.' Later you can lick your wounds, but in the arena, you keep a stiff upper lip. Show them who you are. You're a Colt." He never forgot. His father's advice had gotten him through some tough times.

None had been tougher than what he'd gone through in Seattle. Just the thought of Ellie made his heart ache. That pain had to be far worse than seeing how and where his father had died. As he walked over to the pickup, he rubbed his healing shoulder and told himself he could do this.

The train had apparently hit the front part of the Ford, pushing the engine almost out the other side. It had also smashed in the driver's side, the metal buckling, with the steering wheel facing the passenger seat.

But rather than push the pickup down the tracks, the train had flipped it off to the side. Because of that, the passenger side hadn't been as badly damaged. He tried the door, but it refused to open. The crew-cab door directly behind it opened with a groan. The grinding sound was chillingly loud.

His father never carried much in the back seats. They looked almost brand-new. He peered over the front passenger seat to what had landed on the floorboard. In the police report he'd read a variety of items had been taken from the pickup. Tools, a handgun, a shotgun, some paperwork and reportedly a whiskey bottle.

Now all he could see was dirt that had blown in to form small dunes. Out of the corner of his eye, he saw the stained fabric of the front seat. He leaned back, swallowing hard, and looked at the back seat floor. Lots of broken glass, some stained with a dark smear that he knew was also blood.

What had he hoped to find after all this time? He

leaned against the seat, the wind howling through the missing window glass, and took a breath. There were no answers here. Not to why his father was on that road that night. Not to why he would have stopped on the railroad track. Not to his father's state of mind.

Maybe he had been drinking. Maybe the Billy Sherman case hit too close to home with his own sons. Unfortunately, Willie feared they would never know.

He started to turn away when he caught a glint of gold snagged at the edge of the door behind the passenger seat. He stared, thinking he was seeing things. It appeared to be a gold, horseshoe-shaped charm.

Reaching down, he tried to pick it up. That was when he saw that there was a thin gold chain attached. He pulled out his pocketknife and worked the chain out of the crack. Parts of the chain and charm were tarnished from the weather and the years. Holding it in the palm of his hand, he realized it was a little girl's necklace.

He frowned. What was it doing in his father's pickup? He rubbed his thumb over the charm attached to the tiny chain and saw that a name had been engraved inside the horseshoe.

DelRae.

Chapter 23

On his way back to Lonesome, Willie called his brothers and told them to meet him at the office. All three were waiting when he walked in. He could tell by their expressions that they were hoping he'd found the evidence they'd all been anxious for. He hated to disappoint them.

He wished at least one of them could help explain the little girl's necklace as he pulled it out of his jeans pocket and put it on his father's desk between them.

"What is this?" James asked, picking it up and holding it in the light. "Is that…" He was squinting at the engraving.

"DelRae. It's a girl's name," Willie said. "I found it on the floorboard of Dad's pickup."

James passed the necklace to Tommy, who studied it and passed it on to Davy. "I don't get it," Davy said.

"Neither do I," Willie said. "But you have to admit, it's too much of a coincidence. Dad's name is Del Ransom Colt."

"Not DelRae," Tommy pointed out.

"But close," Willie argued. "What if Otis Osterman was telling the truth about Dad arguing with a woman outside the bar that night?"

"This necklace looks like a child's—not a woman's," Davy said, dropping it back on the desk.

"Like the kind a parent might buy for a daughter," Willie said.

James sat down at their father's old desk. "Wait, what are you getting at?"

"What was the necklace doing in Dad's pickup?" Willie said. "What if there was a woman from Dad's past—and a child?"

"Slow down. Let's not jump to conclusions based on a tarnished piece of jewelry," James said, and paused. "I admit, though…the name DelRae does make me wonder, especially the odd way it's spelled."

"It's an unusual enough name that if there is someone out there…" Tommy had already stepped to his computer and was tapping away at the keys. "Would help if we had a last name."

Willie heard his brother curse. "What did you find?" he asked as he moved to Tommy's desk.

"There is no DelRae Colt, but Dad could have had other kids," Tommy said. His brothers looked at him but no one spoke. Their father had had another relationship none of them knew about? Del Ransom Colt wasn't one to have secrets. The question was, if they were wrong about that, did they want to know those secrets?

"How would we find DelRae?" Davy asked. "If she exists?"

"And are we sure we want to?" James said, voicing what they had all been thinking.

"What if she's the answer to what really happened that night on the railroad tracks?" Willie said. His cell phone rang. He checked it, already knowing it wouldn't be Ellie—not after he hadn't been taking her calls. Talking to her would hurt too much.

He could never let himself forget that he'd almost gotten her killed. As much as it hurt to end their relationship the way he had, he told himself it was for her own good. Her life was in Seattle. His was in Lonesome, Montana. What more was there to say?

His cell rang again. It was a number he didn't recognize. He could feel his brothers watching him with growing disapproval. They thought it might be Ellie.

He answered. A woman's voice told him the Federal Bureau of Investigations office was calling and to please hold while she connected the call.

"It's the FBI," he said as he took the call.

Eleanor had spent the past few days in meetings. She felt exhausted, but glad she was finally free to do some work of her own, when her assistant buzzed her.

"Mrs. Carter is here to see you," she said.

She sighed. "Mrs. Carter didn't have an appointment, did she?" For some time now, she'd felt distressed, especially when her mind wandered to Willie.

"Also, Police Chief Landry is here. He insists it can't wait."

Groaning silently, she said, "Have Mrs. Carter wait. I'll see Landry first."

Eleanor assumed the man had stopped by with news about Jonathan Asher. Why he'd share it with her, though, was questionable. Willie had suspected the man who resembled a bulldog had known more about Vernon Murphy's abduction than he wanted anyone to know. That was enough to make her nervous as the short, stocky man entered her office.

Willie's first thought was that the feds had found Jonathan Asher. When an agent came on the line, he listened, thanked the man for calling, and disconnected.

Looking up to find his brothers anxiously waiting to hear what was up, he said, "Jonathan Asher. They found his body. They're treating it as a homicide." He swallowed and then dropped the real bombshell. "The last time Asher was seen alive was the night Alex Mattson visited him."

"What are you saying?" James said.

"There's a good chance that he couldn't have been behind the killings because he was already dead," Willie said, his mind whirling. Someone had made it appear that Asher had packed up and left the country. If he was already dead… "That means I was wrong. It means…" He pulled out his phone and hurriedly called Ellie.

"I'm afraid I have a busy day ahead of me, Chief Landry," she said, not wanting to offer him a chair, hoping whatever he had to say would be quick.

But he took a seat anyway and looked around her office for a few moments before he finally spoke. "Nice view." It made her think of the first time she'd met Willie. He hadn't been all that impressed by her office or the view; he'd just been suspicious of whoever had hired her to defend Vernon Murphy.

Eleanor lowered herself into her chair, seeing that this wasn't going to be quick. "What can I do for you, Chief Landry?"

"Just thought you'd want to know," the man said in his gravelly voice. "The DNA report came back on that second body believed to have been Vernon Murphy's in the warehouse after the explosion." He met her gaze. "It wasn't his." He nodded as if seeing her surprise. "Vernon's still out there."

She recovered quickly from the startling and worrisome news. "I'm sure you are actively looking for him. Just as you are for Jonathan Asher." Why was this man sitting across from her right now, wasting time on the taxpayer's dollar?

"Thing is, we still have a killer on the loose. Got me thinking. You were Vernon's lawyer. Shared a lot of secrets, I bet. I asked myself, who benefited from all this?" He looked around her office again, glancing out the floor-to-ceiling windows to the glittering city below. "Look at you in this snazzy office. Things turned out pretty good for you, didn't they?"

The chief was right about one thing. She'd benefited from Phillip's death. Sighing, she looked around the office. It was gorgeous and everything she'd ever dreamed of having. Now the accomplishment felt hollow.

Her father had made no secret about wanting her to make it on her own. He'd wanted her to work her way up in the firm to partner, then managing partner. He'd trusted Phillip, a mistake they'd both made.

Her cell phone rang. She picked it up, surprised to see that it was Willie Colt calling. Her pulse jumped. Why was he calling? Had something happened? He'd made it clear that the two of them had nothing more to say to each other. Why call after all this time?

She looked up at the chief of police. "Are we about finished here, Chief Landry?"

"Do you still carry a gun, Ms. Shafer?" the chief asked.

Trying to hide her irritation, she declined the call and said, "No, I don't have a gun." She doubted she ever would again. The police had taken the one Willie had given her, the one she'd used to wound Officer Alex Mattson. The coroner had ruled that Mattson's death was due to heavy trauma when hit by a truck.

The chief nodded, openly studying her. The department had taken a blow that she doubted Landry would get over soon. "You don't seem all that concerned to hear that Vernon is still alive," Landry said. "Why is that?"

"I have no reason to be concerned."

He raised a brow, a smile pulling at his lips. "So you did get close to Vernon." His smile broadened. "Then again, while you might know his secrets, I'm wondering if he knows a few of yours. You that sure Vernon doesn't have a reason to want you dead, Ms. Shafer?"

She'd represented Vernon like she had her other clients. He hadn't wanted to be extradited and had begged her to find a way to keep him in jail in Washington. She hadn't been able to. Would he blame her if he really was still alive?

Eleanor cleared her throat and rose. "Chief Landry, I have work to do. Unless you've come here to arrest me…"

He locked gazes with her as if he thought he could intimidate her. He wasn't the first to try. He looked away as he slowly rose from the chair. "Don't let me keep you, then."

She watched him amble out the door and waited, listening for the elevator. She told herself that he was trying to scare her. She told herself that he was angry with Willie, and her as well, because of everything that had happened. They'd made the local police look inept.

She looked out at the rainy morning. Even the rain annoyed her now, she thought as she watched the latest storm streak the windows and blur her view. This had been her dream. *But dreams change*, she thought as she went back to her desk and tried to call Willie. The call went straight to voice mail. Maybe the call had been accidental. She didn't leave a message.

She realized that she'd forgotten all about Angeline Carter and hurriedly messaged her assistant.

I didn't want to interrupt while you were with the police chief, but Mrs. Carter said she couldn't stay and that she would catch you later, came the reply.

With Phillip gone, Angeline would probably be moving her business to another firm. That was probably why she'd stopped by, Eleanor thought as she tried to go back to work.

She kept thinking about Willie. What if it had been something important? She started to try his number again, but stopped. She'd called and left too many messages over the past few months, she thought shamefully. It was pathetic, her attempts to reach him.

Willie snatched up his phone without even checking to see who was calling. "Ellie?" He hadn't heard her voice in weeks. He'd thought he'd never hear it again. As part of his healing, he'd tried to put Seattle and the attorney into the past. The gunshot wound had been painful, but nothing like letting go of Ellie.

"It's James. Are you at the airport?"

"I just got here. I hope she calls before I board," he said.

"She probably tried to call you back," his brother said. "There's minimal cell service through the canyon."

He hoped his brother was right. He wouldn't blame Ellie if she never wanted to speak to him again. Since hearing about Jonathan Asher's remains being found, he was more than anxious to talk to her. He'd been frantically trying to put the pieces together. If not Asher, if not Lowell Carter, if not Vernon, if not Alex Mattson, then who the hell was behind this?

"Keep in touch. If Ellie calls here, I'll tell her you're on your way to see her," James said.

He thanked his brother, who'd spoken more to Ellie than he had the past few months. Just the sound of her voice made him hurt worse. Yet, every day he'd wanted to pick up the phone and call her and tell her how he felt about her.

There had to be some way to work this out. But then he would remind himself that he'd almost gotten her killed and all the other reasons they couldn't be together.

It would never work out, he kept reminding himself. Neither of them could survive in the other's environment. Ellie was a city girl. He was all country. She would hate Lonesome even if she found it quaint at first. There was no way he could navigate Seattle with all its traffic and people. He'd be miserable, and eventually they would resent each other. Nothing could kill love quicker.

He'd watched his brothers fall in love and almost lose the women they loved. He'd been determined never to feel that kind of pain by never falling in love. Love. He swore. He didn't even know if Ellie had felt the same way he did.

Good thing he hadn't bared his soul to her. What if she had been horrified by his confession? Or, worse, laughed before gently letting him down? He wasn't the kind of man she dated. The last thing she needed was a cowboy who didn't fit into her life.

He'd almost deleted her number from his phone. He was thankful now that he hadn't. But he should have left a message earlier. He heard his flight called and decided to try her office number.

Her assistant messaged that Willie Colt was on the line and that it was urgent.

Chief Landry's visit had made her more nervous than she wanted to admit. Learning that Vernon was possibly still alive…

She quickly took the call, no longer pretending that she didn't want to hear his voice. She tried to tamp down the hope that soared inside her.

"This is Eleanor," she said into the phone in her most formal tone.

"Ellie," he said. "It wasn't Asher."

She hadn't known what to expect, so it was no wonder that the words made no sense. "What?"

"I'm about to get on a flight to Seattle, so I don't have time to explain it all, but Jonathan Asher was murdered *before* the warehouse was blown up, *before* Lowell and Vernon died. He was apparently one of the victims."

Just the sound of Willie's voice sent a spike of regret and desire through her. But it was the other feeling that hurt the most. She'd fallen in love with this cowboy.

Tears burned her eyes. He'd called about the case. Of course it wasn't personal, just as she'd suspected. All he cared about was the case, so she said, "Vernon. The DNA. It wasn't his."

"I'm on my way out there," he said as if he already knew that or didn't hear. "If I miss you at work, I'll meet you at your apartment. Ellie?"

"Yes?" She held her breath waiting for him to say the words she'd yearned for—or anything close to *I love you*.

"I have to go or I'm going to miss my flight. Just be careful." He disconnected and she sat holding the phone. Tears welled and fell. She wiped at them. Angry with herself for the hope that had been so quickly smothered. Why would she foolishly think he would tell her he loved her after his silence the past few months? What was wrong with her?

Slowly she hung up the phone she was still holding. He'd caught her flat-footed. She'd hoped the call was about them. Instead, it was about the case?

Now he was on his way to Seattle? Willie was on his way to her. She couldn't do it, she told herself, even as she felt her heart bump in her chest at the thought of seeing him again. Elation mixed with dread at what was coming. It would be starting all over again. The fear. Willie back in her life—but only temporarily and only if one or both of them didn't get killed.

But if Jonathan Asher hadn't orchestrated everything… Vernon? No one thought he was smart enough, but what if they were wrong? What if he was behind everything—including making it appear he'd died in the last building he'd destroyed?

She shuddered. Would he have reason to come after her?

Eleanor tried to concentrate on work, losing herself

in legal paperwork as she had for years. It wasn't until her assistant announced she was leaving for the day that she realized she actually had lost herself for a while in her work. She looked to the wall of windows overlooking the city. The rain appeared to have stopped, though the sky was still gray with low hanging clouds.

She'd thought she would see Willie here when he arrived, keep it cordial, but she couldn't bear to wait here in this office. She rose, retrieved her coat and purse, and started for the door, then turned back. Picking up the phone, she called downstairs.

Herb, her favorite security guard, answered. "I'm expecting Mr. Colt to stop by. I'm headed down to the parking level. If I miss him, would you please tell him I'll be at my apartment?" Herb said he would be happy to.

Willie's short flight from Montana should have landed by now. She didn't want to think about what might happen between the two of them at her apartment. Or, worse, what might not happen.

Taking the elevator to the parking level, she almost talked herself into returning to her office. Even her apartment wasn't the same since Willie had burst into her life. She felt him everywhere, as if he was always with her now, deep in her heart.

The elevator shuddered and slowed as it neared the parking garage. Something clanked. A chill curled around her neck. The police chief had managed to put her on edge about Vernon. Landry would have been delighted to know that, she thought, and shoved away her discomfort.

She wondered if the chief had only come by her office to scare her. Landry wanted something on Willie Colt, that much was obvious. But there had been too much blowback on the police department once it was discovered that Alex Mattson had been involved. Also, it hadn't helped that Willie had solved the case—not the big-city law enforcement. It probably didn't hurt that the FBI had been involved or that she had said she would represent Willie if the Seattle police came after him. No charges had been filed on either of them.

She felt the elevator shudder to a stop on the parking level. As the door opened, the sound echoed through the nearly empty space. She saw a shadow fall across the concrete floor in front of the elevator. For one delusional moment, she thought it was Willie, but could he have made it from the airport already?

It wasn't Willie who suddenly filled the elevator's open doorway. Eleanor was so startled when she recognized the person that she didn't react fast enough. She no longer had a gun in her purse, but she did have pepper spray—a gift from Willie he'd had his brothers purchase for her before he'd left.

Unfortunately, she didn't have time to get to it before the business end of a gun was shoved into her face and she was pushed back into the elevator.

"Let's go up on the roof. The view is breathtaking."

Chapter 24

As the elevator rose toward the rooftop, Eleanor tried to catch her breath. Her heart thundered in her chest even as she told herself that this wasn't happening. She'd been through so much. This couldn't be how it ended—not with Willie on his way. Just the thought that she might never see him again…

She leaned against the elevator wall for support as she shifted her gaze from the gun to the woman holding it. "Mrs. Carter, what do you—"

"For crying out loud," Angeline Carter snapped. "Don't you think we should be on a first-name basis by now?"

She swallowed. "I don't understand what's going on."

"It's pretty simple. We're going up on the roof and you're going to jump."

A shiver ran the length of her spine. The woman appeared deadly serious. "Why would I do that?"

"Because you can't live with yourself after everything that has happened. First Phillip, then that cowboy breaking your heart."

"He didn't break my heart," she said as if that mattered right now.

"Oh, I know a broken heart when I see one. Lowell wasn't the first man who broke mine. Did you know that Phil and I used to be lovers?"

She shook her head.

"I talked him into investing in the mining business when Lowell was first getting it off the ground."

"Phillip never mentioned that." She realized how little she'd known about Phillip's...dealings, but she now suspected that was what had gotten him killed.

Angeline seemed to be studying her. "He didn't tell you I asked him to give you the Vernon Murphy case?"

Eleanor couldn't help her confusion with a gun pointed at her and this clearly unbalanced woman telling her she was about to jump off the roof of the office building. "Why would you do that?"

"Phillip, you silly twit. Weren't you listening?" Angeline spat and Eleanor realized that she hadn't been. Willie had said he would be here soon. Would he know how to find her, though? What if he went to her apartment first? Or Herb told him she'd already left?

"Phillip and I were more than lovers. We confided in each other. He told me about his affair with your mother."

"I really doubt—"

"He dumped me for her. But when I told your father about the two of them..." She smiled a cat-who-ate-the-canary smile. "I've always wondered if they were arguing about me when they had the car wreck that killed them. Or maybe it wasn't an accident at all."

Eleanor thought she'd be sick to her stomach. She had suspected her father hadn't been faithful, but her mother? Now this woman was insinuating the wreck that had killed them might not have been an accident? When she spoke, her voice was calm, and yet her heart thumped wildly in her chest. "Why are you telling me this?"

"Because we have so much in common. Phillip told me that he was in love with you. I knew he wanted you, since he couldn't have your mother. But I had no idea he felt so...strongly." The woman's words dripped with bitterness. *Hell hath no fury like a woman scorned.* "Then there was Lowell. He actually thought I was going to divorce him and let him walk away with half of what I'd built."

Eleanor fought to make sense of this. "I thought—"

"I just wanted Lowell to think I was divorcing him. I made Lowell. I got him the financing to start the business, I hosted the parties for investors and people in high places who would grease the wheels and also look the other way if necessary." Her voice rose with her anger, echoing in the small space. "I built that company. Not Lowell. I was fine with people believing I knew nothing about his business. But it was all me. He thought I was going to let him walk away with half of everything I'd built so he could be with that tart?" Her laugh held no humor.

The elevator came to a stop. The door opened. Angeline motioned with the gun. Eleanor felt a tremor of fear as the damp night air rushed in. *Keep her talking.* She didn't move. The last thing she wanted to do was step out this door and onto the open roof twenty floors above the city. She could feel the wind, strong up here, heavy with the scent of the Sound.

"You were the one who hired Vernon Murphy to destroy the building with Zoey Bertrand in it."

Angeline touched the tip of her nose with her free hand as she smiled. "Vernon has worked for me for years. I make sure he gets what he needs—a building to blow up here and there and he's as loyal as an old dog."

This sweet-faced, tiny woman who'd been wearing the guise of a victim was a heartless killer. "You killed Phillip."

"Me? I thought he was killed in a drive-by shooting. The man Vernon got for me wasn't much of a shot, since he was supposed to take out both of you—and your cowboy cop friend, too, if he was with you."

"Why?" Eleanor told herself that this made no sense. She understood why Angeline wanted her husband and his mistress dead. But her attorney?

Angeline's smile was all shark teeth. "Phillip was fine giving you Vernon's case as a favor to me—until it got dangerous. Then he started making threats. I had to remind him that I knew things about him—like the way he'd gotten control of this firm after your parents died. Bet you always wondered how he managed that."

Eleanor said nothing. Phillip had been the son her father never had. She'd just assumed her father had believed he would build the firm—just as he had—and make a place for Eleanor in it.

"Once you took off with that cowboy cop, he was beside himself with worry about you," Angeline said. "That's when I knew how deep his feelings were for you. He didn't have to tell me how much you're like your mother, but he did. I can't count all the times Phillip told me what a hellion you were when it came to the courtroom. Focused, cool, calm, calculated and brilliant. A true fighter, just like your mother. I knew you couldn't be bought off or dissuaded with reason or threats. I knew there was only one way to stop you—and your cowboy. I was going to have to kill you both—and Phillip, too, just like I did your mother."

Eleanor stared at her, unable to speak. "She was killed in a car wreck. How could you—"

"I grew up in a mining camp around equipment. Fixing the brakes to fail on your mother's car was child's play for me."

Her heart drummed in her chest, her stomach roiling. "Phillip knew."

Angeline's laugh was brittle as an old windowpane. "I'd always been able to hold what I knew about Phillip over his head, but he was threatening to tell you the truth—and to turn me in."

Eleanor shook her head. She'd had no idea what had been going on between her parents and Phillip. "So this is personal, an old grudge against my mother." This woman had already killed before. And would kill again, she reminded herself. There would be nothing stopping her.

Unless Eleanor could distract her long enough to get to the pepper spray.

"Of course it's personal," Angeline snapped, and motioned for Eleanor to get out of the elevator. "Especially since Phillip had decided to go to the authorities. Said I'd gone too far too many times. He wasn't going to let me destroy you the way I had your mother. Now get out. Don't think I won't shoot you where you stand."

* * *

Willie'd had James hire him an Uber for when his plane landed. By the time he got out of the terminal, a car was waiting for him. The driver had the address of Ellie's apartment building, but Willie realized she would still be at work. He gave the driver the law firm's address instead.

He could feel time slipping away too quickly. The flight from Missoula, Montana, to Seattle had been short once they were in the air. It was all the other wasted time that went with flying that drove him to distraction. He'd had too much time to think.

Mulling it all over, he saw now that he'd been a coward. He should have told Ellie how he felt. He'd had plenty of opportunities, but the longer they were apart while his gunshot wound healed, the more he'd talked himself out of it.

He promised himself that no matter how she felt, he would tell her the truth. He'd fallen in love with her. It had taken him a long time to admit it. Because everything was too complicated, he told himself. Love didn't solve the fact that they lived miles away from each other in very different worlds. Love didn't solve the fact that his job—if he won the election for sheriff—was dangerous. He'd be dragging her into trouble even if he didn't mean to.

Nor did love bridge the divide between the different paths they'd taken in this life so far.

So, why tell her that he loved her when there was no hope for a future for them?

Because he couldn't hold it in his heart any longer without admitting the truth. He loved her. And if she didn't love him…

The car stopped in front of her office building. He leaped out and ran toward the front door. The security guard was at his desk.

"I have to see Ellie... E.L. Shafer," he said as he ran toward the elevator. Short of the guard shooting him, nothing could stop him.

"She's not in her office," the man called as Willie hit the elevator button. The door opened and he stepped in, then stopped.

"She already went home?"

The guard shook his head. "She told me to watch for you. She was headed for her apartment, she said, but she didn't get out on the parking level. Instead, she must have changed her mind. I saw the elevator open, but she didn't get out. I had to take a call. When I looked again, the elevator was headed up to the roof. It's stopped up there."

He'd already hit the button for the top floor, the elevator door closing, before he realized what the guard had said. The roof. The elevator shot upward. Ellie had been planning to go to her apartment, but once she reached the parking garage, she changed her mind? Why would she suddenly decide to go up on the roof?

Because she wasn't alone.

Eleanor looked into the woman's eyes. Angeline was intent on killing her, one way or another. There was nothing squeamish about her. Maybe she hadn't killed anyone face-to-face before, but she'd sure plotted the killings of others, including her husband and her former lover. And if she was telling the truth, the murders of Eleanor's own mother and father.

"Won't shooting me be hard to explain to the authorities?" she asked, stalling for time as she tried to come up with a plan for survival. Herb would know that the elevator to the roof was stopped up here. He would eventually investigate.

But she feared he would be too late.

"I'm not going to jump," Eleanor said. "You're going to have to kill me here in this elevator."

"Why not? Did you really think I didn't have a backup plan?" Angeline laughed as she raised the gun slightly, leveling it at Eleanor's heart, her hand steady, her finger on the trigger. "You'll die, but I'll only be wounded and manage to call for help. I'll tell the cops it was Vernon who killed you and wounded me."

"You've thought of everything." She could see that it just might work. Angeline didn't look like a killer. That was what had gotten her this far.

With a nod, Eleanor stepped out of the elevator and was instantly buffeted by the wind. Behind her, she heard Angeline release the elevator. The doors closed, and it hummed downward. Herb wouldn't be coming up to check it.

Her fear intensified. She was truly alone on the rooftop with this unbalanced woman. The air felt laden with moisture, the darkness on the rooftop complete. She turned her face up to the night sky, afraid but determined not to die. Not here. Not now. Not with Willie on his way.

Just the thought though made her realize that if he did find her up here, Angeline would gun him down. Eleanor couldn't let that happen any more than she could let this woman push her off this roof.

"If all you wanted was to keep your husband from taking off with his mistress, you accomplished that with

Vernon's help," she said as she moved slowly across the massive roof. "Why keep killing?"

The closer she got, the more she could see. There was a short wall around the roof that she estimated was less than three feet high. Anyone could fall over it. For a woman like Angeline, pushing her over that wall would be child's play. She kept talking even though Angeline hadn't responded. "Vernon didn't know Zoey Bertrand would be in the building. Did he threaten to turn on you? Is that why you had him abducted?"

"You *are* smart," Angeline said. "Too bad you aren't as smart as Vernon. It took only a little persuading to get him to see reason once I kept him from being extradited."

Eleanor shook her head. "He's still wanted for arson and murder," she said over her shoulder.

"True, but what's some prison time compared to death?" Angeline jabbed her in the back with the gun, making her stumble forward.

Eleanor could see more of the lights of the city, feel a stronger wind near the edge of the roof, hear traffic below. "You really are an evil mastermind," she said, fighting to keep her tone calm, even complimentary. "My mother must have underestimated you."

"People always do."

"But all these deaths…"

"Come on, you've stalled enough. No one is coming to save you. I waited to make sure that your cowboy had left town. He got to you, didn't he?" She laughed. "Whatever you thought the two of you had, it was all in your mind. I know the feeling."

Eleanor feared she was right. Willie wouldn't be able to save her since only one elevator came all the way up to the roof. The other elevator would only take him to the top floor, from where he would have to take the stairs. He'd never make it in time to save her—or himself.

She was on her own. The thought sent both fear and regret through her. After falling in love for the first time in her life, she couldn't believe it would end like this— not knowing if Willie had felt anything and wondering if it was all in her mind, like Angeline had said.

Her heart was lodged in her throat as the woman pushed her toward the ledge and the twenty-story drop to the pavement below. From this height, cars would look like children's toys, people like ants.

Eleanor told herself that Angeline didn't know Willie Colt. Nor did she know the woman Ellie had become since meeting the cowboy. She turned just a little to look back at Angeline, drawing the woman's attention as she slid her hand into her shoulder bag and closed her fingers around the pepper spray.

She felt the wind in her face and knew that the pepper spray would be worse than worthless up here. It would blow back in her own face, blinding her, making it even easier for Angeline to push her off the roof.

The elevator Willie had taken didn't go to the rooftop. It opened on the top floor. It took him a few precious minutes to find the stairs to the roof. He scrambled up them, terrified of what he would find once he reached the rooftop.

He told himself that she might not be up here. That even if she was, she might be alone, and there was no need to panic.

But he knew better. She'd been leaving for her apartment. She knew he was coming to Seattle, coming to her. He felt a lump rise in his throat. He was coming back and not just to make sure she was safe, but to tell her what was in his heart.

As he took the stairs three at a time, he prayed he'd get the chance. He'd worked it out on the plane. If Lowell or Jonathan hadn't been behind this and Vernon was still alive...

He reached the door, shoved it open, gun drawn, and saw two figures near the edge of the roof. Ellie and the woman he knew had been behind this the whole time. Angeline Carter. She was shoving Ellie toward the edge of the roof. He started to take a step out when the wind caught the door, jerking it out of his hand.

Eleanor heard a door slam against the wall next to the elevator. Angeline heard it, too, both of them turning to look back. As Willie started to step through it, Eleanor yelled, "She's got a gun!"

Angeline swung the gun toward Willie and fired. The bullet tore into the stucco on the wall next to him, forcing him to duck back inside the stairwell as the elevator she and Angeline had ridden up in dinged. The door opened and a man stepped out. Vernon!

She wasn't the only one who'd looked back. Angeline had been distracted just long enough that Eleanor was able to spin around and grab the woman's wrist holding the gun.

Angeline was petite, small-framed, but much stronger than she looked. As the two wrestled for the weapon, Eleanor found herself being forced back the few yards to the edge of the roof. She could hear the traffic, feel the wind.

The report of a gunshot echoed over the roofline as

Eleanor fought to get the gun free. Out of the corner of her eye, she saw that she was getting dangerously close to the edge of the roof. She heard Willie call out her name, heard another shot.

Past Angeline, she saw Vernon rush Willie, barreling into him. She screamed his name as another gunshot filled the air, the handgun bucking in Angeline's hand. The woman smiled without looking back, as if she knew that Vernon would come through for her once again. Eleanor saw Willie stumble as the two fought. She let out a cry as she tried even harder to get the gun away from Angeline.

Shoved back, she tripped into the short wall at the edge of the roof. She quit trying to wrench the gun away and flung a hand back to keep from falling backward into the abyss.

No longer needing the gun, Angeline smiled and tossed it aside as she charged, throwing her whole body into it. In that split second, Eleanor hurled herself to the side, forced to lean out over the edge to miss a direct hit from the crazed woman. She felt Angeline's hand hit her hand, then saw the woman's eyes widen as she realized that instead of hitting Eleanor in the middle of her chest and pushing her over the edge of the roof, she'd only managed to brush her shoulder.

Angeline looked confused when her hand came away with the strap of Eleanor's shoulder bag. Eleanor had shrugged off the strap of her bag while falling across the top of the wall and fighting to find purchase against the wind and the chasm next to her.

That's when she saw the glitter of the emerald-and-diamond ring on the woman's finger as Angeline clutched the shoulder bag strap as if it was going to slow her momentum. As if it would keep her from going over the wall.

Her scream filled the air for a few moments before it faded away in the wind.

Lying on the narrow edge of the wall, Eleanor froze, terrified to move. She didn't dare breathe, let alone look over the wall to the street all those floors below. She could feel the wind rushing up the twenty stories at her. She clung to the wall beneath her with both hands, still afraid she was going over.

She feared she would have stayed there if Willie hadn't grabbed her, pulling her away from the ledge and into his arms. "Ellie. Ellie," he kept saying as he held her tight against him. "You're all right. You're all right."

"Angeline?" She knew the moment she heard the scream. Still she glanced back. Angeline Carter was gone. Icy horror seized her. Angeline had gone off the roof. Her momentum had carried her over the wall beyond the rooftop to plummet to the street below—taking only Eleanor's shoulder bag with her.

She felt her legs give out. Willie carefully lowered her to the roof floor. Dropping down beside her, he pulled her to him with one arm as he dug out his phone. She watched him, still stunned, as he called 911. She heard him say, "There's been a shooting on the roof at the law office of…" He gave the address. "We're going to need an ambulance."

An ambulance? She pulled back to look at him, afraid he'd been shot again.

He repeated the address to the operator.

That was when she glanced past him and saw the body lying on the roof, yards from them, unmoving. The ambulance was for Vernon. The wind brought the sound of sirens from far below. She closed her eyes and leaned into Willie, her fingers gripping the soft cotton of his Western shirt. She breathed him in and began to cry.

Chapter 25

Police Chief Landry rubbed a hand over the back of his neck. "I thought we were rid of you, cowboy. This time, you're going in a cell. You can't just keep coming back here like some Old West vigilante." He heard the alert on his computer that he had a call. He ignored it. "It was bad enough when you were out here wearing a badge." Another alert, also ignored, and another. The man's office door was flung open.

Two FBI agents burst in, flashing their credentials.

"We'll be taking this from here," the older of the two agents Willie had spoken with said. "Mr. Colt, if you'll come with me."

Landry put up a fight, but got nowhere before Willie was led down the hallway and out of the building. It was a short car ride to the FBI's regional office.

"Feel like we've been here before," the older agent,

Frank Rice, said. "Going to need your statement. We already have Ms. Shafer's."

He told the agent how he'd had his doubts. "Angeline Carter didn't seem like the brains behind this. But once I knew Jonathan Asher was already dead before the explosion that killed Lowell Carter, and that the second body found after the warehouse explosion wasn't Vernon's, I knew it had to be her. She brought Asher in when her husband was starting up the business. He must have realized after Mattson's visit that Angeline was the one who hired Vernon to blow up the building and kill Zoey Bertrand. He must have made the mistake of thinking he could cash in on that knowledge." Willie shrugged. "I think that once Angeline started tying up loose ends, she couldn't stop."

"The loose ends being?" the younger agent asked.

"E.L. Shafer and Vernon Murphy. He'd done everything she'd asked of him, but now he had to go and so did his attorney." He saw the two agents exchange a look. "By the way, how is Vernon?"

"He'll live. Maybe even long enough to stand trial. We have him in protective custody. Thank you for not killing him."

Willie shrugged. It had been touch and go. "He almost killed me, but I'm sure he'll be able to answer any questions you have about Angeline and this whole mess."

"Will you be staying around Seattle?" the older agent asked.

He shook his head. "No offense, but I'll be heading back to Montana after I take care of some personal business here." He rose, put his Stetson back on his head and started toward the door.

"I think it would be best if you stayed out of Seattle,"

the younger agent said. "You seem to have gotten on the wrong side of the chief of police. I wouldn't even jay-walk in this city if I was you."

Willie nodded. "Thanks for the advice. I was think-ing the same thing myself." He'd worn out his welcome in the big city and that, too, made it hard to finish what he'd started here.

Eleanor looked around the long conference table at the men gathered there. She knew this meeting had been coming for some time and yet she could feel her parents' disapproval as well as Phillip McNamara's.

"Thank you all for being here," she said as she stood and cleared her voice. "As you all know, my parents were founding attorneys at this firm. Upon their death they put senior partner and managing attorney Phillip Mc-Namara in charge. I now have that position."

A couple of the attorneys moved restlessly. Others stared at her, appearing half-afraid of what she was going to say.

She knew what she wanted to say, but she couldn't walk away that easily. "There are going to be some changes. For starters, we're actively going to hire more female and diverse attorneys. I'll be staying in charge of the firm until the changes are implemented and I can manage things with an occasional in-office visit. That means some of the other senior partners are going to have to step up."

"You're leaving the firm?" one of them asked.

"Not leaving. I'll still be keeping track of what's hap-pening here—just not from the managing partner's of-fice down the hall. I have a list of potential candidates whom I'd like to see in this firm. I'll be sitting in on final interviews."

She looked around the boardroom and saw resignation as well as disfavor.

"We don't really need any personnel other than replacing you and Phillip," one of the senior partners said.

"I'll be offering some suggestions on replacing several of the attorneys recently brought into the firm," she said. Phillip had liked it being an all-boys club. She thought of her mother, who would have done exactly what Eleanor was doing.

With that, she adjourned the meeting, walking out. She could hear the murmur of disapproval from some but nods from others. She smiled. Almost losing her life upstairs on the roof had made her even more determined to live the rest of her life on her terms.

When she reached her office, she found Willie Colt standing at her windows, Stetson dangling from his hand, his gaze on the city stretched out in front of him.

Willie turned as he heard Ellie come into her office. She didn't seem surprised to see him. He watched her move to her desk, put down the folder she'd been carrying and face him.

"Did we have an appointment?" she asked.

He smiled at that and, tossing his hat on one of the chairs, moved around her desk. She turned toward him as he approached. He stopped within inches of her. "We have some old business we need to take care of." She raised an eyebrow but said nothing. They hadn't seen each other since what went down on the rooftop. "I left here once before without you, determined to put you and this city behind me. I'd watched my brothers fall in love."

He winced. "And while it turned out fine after a time, it looked like pure hell at first. I saw the pain of falling in love and I wanted nothing to do with it."

Her gray eyes locked with his own as she waited.

"I was afraid that if I told you how I felt, you'd tell me you didn't feel the same," he continued. "But more than anything, I just didn't see how this could work between us. You this big-city lawyer, me a former deputy now running for sheriff. Our lives couldn't be more different. Until recently, I was a rodeo cowboy living on the road in my horse trailer camper and you a successful attorney living in a high-rise penthouse apartment. Not to mention we live in different states. You see the problem?"

"When you put it that way, I do," she said. "So, what solution did you come up with, former rodeo cowboy turned candidate for sheriff?"

He reached out and took her shoulders in his calloused hands. As he did, he noticed that while she was wearing a suit that he knew cost more than his horse, the top button of her silk blouse was undone and so was the next one. He met her gray gaze and couldn't help but smile. *In for a penny, in for a pound*, he thought. The one thing he wasn't doing was walking away again until he told her how he felt.

Eleanor held her breath. She could see the answer in his blue eyes, but she still needed, more than anything, to hear the words.

"I'm in love with you." He shook his head as if he couldn't believe he was finally saying it. "I love you and I want you and I'm damned sure going to do whatever I have to so we can be together."

She let out the breath she'd been holding. She shook

her head. "I've been waiting for you to say those words. I was worried you never would."

He nodded. "Me, too."

She smiled. "I love you, too, Willie Colt." She felt the tension leave his hands holding her shoulders.

He let out a laugh. "Damned if I can stand being away from you. You're all I've thought about. I've tried to forget you." His hands moved from her shoulders to cup her face. A calloused thumb moved slowly over her lower lip, his gaze following the motion. Then he leaned forward and kissed her, pulling her into his arms as if he was never letting her go.

The kiss was full of promise, full of desire and passion, full of the love she'd seen in his eyes, heard in his words. She leaned into him, filled with glorious emotions. She'd missed him so much and had begun to believe that she'd never see him again. But then he'd rushed to Seattle to save her.

He drew back, still holding her as he looked into her eyes and asked, "What are we going to do?" His voice, so full of emotion, touched a chord inside her.

So much had happened up on that rooftop. She'd come close to dying, all the other near misses nothing compared to lying on that short wall, clinging to life. How could she have not made some big decisions about the rest of her life after that?

"Well," she said, the effects of the kiss still raging through her bloodstream. "There is only one thing we can do."

"If you want me to move to Seattle, I will," he blurted out.

She laughed, shaking her head. "I've already made arrangements so I only have to come to Seattle to take care of business a few times a month. The firm is mine, I now have controlling interest."

"But what about your life here?" he asked. "Your apartment?"

"I'll keep it for when I have to come out." She reached for his face, cupping it in her hands. "As for my life? The only life I want is with you. But there is one thing you should know. My parents left me more than the firm. I'm rather...wealthy. Is that a game changer?"

He began to laugh, throwing back his head, before settling his gaze on her again. "I guess this means we won't have to live in my horse trailer camper," he joked. "I own Colt Ranch with my brothers. If this sheriff gig doesn't work out, I was thinking about buying some cattle and making it a real ranch. There's a spot on the land that I thought would be perfect for a house overlooking the river. But if you don't want to live that close to my kin—"

She silenced him with a finger on his lips. "After meeting Lori and James, I know I'm going to adore all of your brothers and their wives. I'd love to build on the ranch. Remember? I'm an only child without any family. I've already fallen in love with some of yours. Just the thought of raising our children so close to their cousins..." She stopped and met his gaze. "You do want kids, don't you?"

He drew her close. "I can't wait to make babies with you, Ellie. Or do you want me to call you Eleanor?"

Laughing, she said, "I kind of got used to Ellie. At least the way you say it."

He kissed her again, then pulled back. "My brother James gave me something." He reached into his jacket pocket and pulled out a small velvet box. She felt her heart jump. "I thought he was delusional offering me Grandmother's ring. I wasn't even sure you'd have me, let alone that we could work out a living arrangement."

Willie looked from the box to her as he dropped down on one knee. "E.L. Shafer, will you marry me?"

"She said yes?" James let out a hoot that brought Lori hurrying in from the kitchen as he put down his phone. "Willie asked Ellie to marry him, and she said yes." He saw Lori's eyes fill with tears and moved to take her in his arms. "You called it. When I gave him our grandmother's ring, he looked at me as if I'd lost my mind. I think he was afraid that she didn't feel the same way he did."

"I knew that she would say yes, if the darned fool ever got around to asking her." Lori hugged him and stepped back. "She's going to be my sister-in-law. When is the wedding? Where will it be?" As if seeing that her husband hadn't asked, she shook her head. "Men, you never ask the right questions. I have to call Bella and Carla. This is so exciting. Then I'll call Ellie and find out." She rushed from the room.

James smiled to himself, happy for his older brother. He'd never thought Willie would ever take that leap, but he was glad it was with someone like Ellie. He wished as he often did that his father was here to see this. All of them back at the ranch, all of them happy and married. Del would have loved having grandchildren.

He brushed away the regret, glad that things had worked out for Willie. They were going to have a great Christmas this year with all of them at home. His son would be born by then, his daughter old enough to be tearing into the presents under the tree. This was how it should be, he thought, family all together.

As he picked up the phone to call his brothers, he thought about what Willie had found in their father's wrecked pickup. The girl's necklace with the name Del-Rae engraved on it. Willie was right. They had to find out whom it had belonged to.

He hadn't wanted to get his brothers' hopes up, but he knew that once Willie and Ellie's wedding was over and they were settled in, it would be time for Colt Brothers Investigation to dig deeper into their father's death. Until they found out the truth, it would always hang over them. They had to make sure they got justice for the father who'd raised them.

The wedding was planned for fall on the river not all that far from the property where Willlie and Ellie's house was under construction. It was a beautiful autumn day, the Montana sky a clear blue, the river sparkling in the sunlight and golden leaves fluttering on the nearby aspens.

Eleanor stood in front of the full-length mirror at Bella and Tommy's lodge. All around her were the women she'd come to love like sisters. She felt enveloped in this warm, loving family. Her three soon-to-be sisters-in-law were her matrons of honor. They'd been fussing over her all morning, often all four of them brought to tears of happiness.

"I really thought Willie would be the Colt who never married," Bella said as she straightened Eleanor's veil. "I know he felt responsible for his brothers after they lost their father. Mr. Tough Guy."

"The strong, silent type," Lori agreed. "He always

took on more than he should have. But once James quit the rodeo and got the investigation business going, I think Willie realized that he didn't have to worry about his brothers as much."

"He was never going to marry," Carla said, and turned to Ellie. "Until he met you. You can't believe how miserable he was when he came back from Seattle. We could all tell that it wasn't the gunshot wound that was hurting him. It was leaving you."

Her sisters-in-law all agreed. "The problem was he's a Colt, stubborn as a post," Bella said, making them laugh.

"A post?" asked Lori. "I think the expression is as dumb as a post."

"That, too, sometimes," Bella said. "Dumb as a post when it comes to love. Look at Tommy. I swear he took his sweet time getting around to asking me to marry him."

"Davy, too," Carla agreed. "How awful is it that it takes a near-death experience to get these men to realize that they can't live without us?" They all laughed and looked at each other.

"Now we get to raise our children together," Bella said, giving Ellie a hug.

There was a tap at the door. "We're ready for you," James announced through the door.

Eleanor went to the second-story window and looked out. She found Montana breathtaking, but nothing warmed her heart like seeing Willie all decked out in his Western attire, waiting to marry her by the river. Tears of joy burned her eyes. She bit them back as she gave thanks. What would her parents have thought about her marrying a cowboy and newly elected sheriff?

The thought made her smile as she turned back to the

women who'd become the family she'd always longed for. "Let's do this," she said.

Eleanor couldn't wait to marry Willie Colt. She felt a rush of happiness. She'd found a real home and a real cowboy to curl up next to every night. She had to be the luckiest woman alive as she walked toward Willie and their bright, beautiful, loving future.

* * * * *

RESCUE AT CARDWELL RANCH

Chapter 1

From the darkness, he heard the sound of high heels tapping quickly along the pavement, heading in his direction, and smiled. This could be the one.

If not, he would have to give it up for the night, something he couldn't bear doing. For days his need had been growing. He'd come here tonight because he couldn't put it off any longer—no matter how dangerous it was to hunt this close to home.

Since it had gotten dark, he'd been looking. He hated to think of the women he'd let get away, women in their tight skirts and low-cut blouses, women who'd just been asking for it.

But waiting for the right woman, he'd learned, was the smart thing to do. It took patience. Tonight, though, he found himself running short of it. He'd picked his favorite spot, the favorite spot of men like himself: a grocery-store parking lot at night. Once he'd parked next to her car—he knew it was a woman's car because she'd left her sunglasses on the dash and there was one of those cute air fresheners hanging from the mirror—he'd broken the bright light she'd parked under.

Now the area was cast in dark shadow—just the way he loved it. He doubted she would notice the lack of light—or him with his head down, pretending to be packing his groceries into the trunk of his large, expensive vehicle. Women were less afraid of a man who appeared to have money, he'd discovered.

At the sound of her approaching footfalls, he found it hard not to sneak a peek at her. *Patience.* This would be the one, he told himself. He already felt as if he knew her and could easily guess her story. She would have worked late, which was why she was still dressed as she had been this morning, in high heels. She wasn't pushing a cart so she wasn't shopping for her large family.

Instead, he guessed she was single and lived alone, probably in a nice condo since she drove a newer, pricier car—the kind independent, successful single women drove. By the sound of her footfalls, she carried only one small bag of groceries. He could already imagine his hands around her throat.

The footfalls grew closer.

He'd learned a long time ago not to act on impulse. Snatch the first one he saw and bad things happened. He had a scar to prove it. That run-in had almost cost him dearly. Not that she'd gotten away. He'd made sure of that. But she'd wounded him in more ways than one. It was why he'd come up with a set of rigorous guidelines he now followed to the letter. It was the reason, he told himself, that he'd never been caught.

He closed his eyes for a moment, imagining the look in her eyes when she realized she was about to die. This woman *had* to be the right one because his need had grown to the point of urgency. He went over his guidelines, the memory of his only mistake still haunting him.

He wouldn't let himself be swayed by an alluring whiff of perfume. Nor would he risk a woman carrying anything that could be used as a weapon at a distance like an umbrella.

Then there was her hair and attire. It would surprise most women to know that what made her his target was her hairstyle. There was a reason women with short hair were not common prey of men like him. Give him a woman with a ponytail—a recent trend that filled him with joy—or a braid or even a bun—anything he could bury his fingers in and hold on for dear life.

Clothing was equally as important. She had to be wearing an outfit that would come off easily and quickly because he often didn't have a lot of time. Of course, he always carried a pair of sharp scissors, but a woman in a blouse and a skirt made his life so much easier, even with a blade handy.

Now as the sound of the high heels grew closer, he readied himself with growing anticipation. He was betting this one was wearing a nice short skirt and a button-up blouse. Tonight, he could even handle a matching jacket with the skirt. No blue jeans, though. They were such a pain to get off.

Her cell phone rang. She stopped walking. He groaned since if she'd been just a little closer, she would have already been in his trunk, her mouth duct taped as well as her wrists and ankles.

He cursed her cell phone even though it often made

things easier for him. Women who were distracted—either digging in their purses for their keys or talking on their cell phones or unloading their groceries—were oblivious to the fact that he was already breathing down their necks.

He silently urged her phone call to end. Just a few more steps and he would grab her by the hair, overpower her and have her in the trunk of his car before she even knew what was happening. Once he got her to the place he had picked out down by the river…well, that was when the real fun would begin.

His next victim was still on the phone. She sounded upset, so upset that she'd stopped walking to take the call. She would be thinking about the call—not him right next to her car.

The call ended. She began to walk again, right toward him. He doubted she'd even noticed him bent over his car trunk, pretending to be taking care of his groceries.

He heard her vehicle beep as she unlocked it. Any moment she would walk within a few feet of him on his right. He would have only an instant to make his decision. An instant to see what she had in her hands, what she was wearing, how long her hair was. Even with his meticulous planning, there was always the chance that this could be the one woman who would surprise him. The one who would fight back. The one who would get away and ruin his perfect record.

His heart began to pound with excitement. He loved this part. None had ever gotten away—even the one who'd scarred him. He was too smart for them. They were like sheep coming down a chute to slaughter, he thought, as he looked up and saw her start past him.

Chapter 2

McKenzie Sheldon came out of the grocery store thinking about work. Not work, exactly, but one of the men at her office.

She was going to have to do something about Gus Thompson. The warnings she'd given him had fallen on deaf ears. The man had reached the point where he was daring her to fire him.

Shifting the single bag of groceries to her other arm, she began to dig for her keys when her cell phone rang. She stopped and pulled out her phone, saw it was her receptionist and said, "What's up, Cynthia?"

"You told me to call you if I was having any more problems."

McKenzie let out an angry breath. "Let me guess. *Gus*. What has he done now?" she asked with a disgusted sigh.

"I'm sorry, Ms. Sheldon, but he won't leave me alone. If I work late, *he* works late. He always insists on walking me to my car. I've told him that I'm not interested, but it seems to make him even more determined. I make excuses to avoid him, but—"

"I know. Trust me. It isn't anything you're doing."

"He scares me," she said, her voice breaking. "Tonight I looked out and he was waiting by my car. I'm afraid to try to go home."

She started to tell Cynthia that she didn't think Gus was dangerous, but what did she know? "Is he still out there?"

"I don't know." Her receptionist sounded close to tears.

"Call the police. Or if you want to wait, I can swing by—"

"I don't want you to have to do that. I'll call the police. I wanted to talk to you first. I didn't want to make any trouble."

"Don't worry about that. Gus is the one making the trouble. I promise you I'll take care of this tomorrow." She heard her receptionist make a scared sound. "Don't worry. I won't mention your name." She thought of the night she'd looked out her window at her condo. Gus had been sitting in his car across the street. He'd seen her and sped off, but she'd wondered how many other nights he'd been out there watching her house. "I should have fired him a long time ago."

"But he's your best salesman."

McKenzie let out a humorless laugh. "Hard to believe, isn't it?"

"Still, I wouldn't want to be blamed for him losing his job."

"You won't. Trust me. I have my own issues with him." She snapped the phone shut, angry with herself for letting things go on this long.

She had talked to Gus after that incident outside her house. He'd shrugged it off, made an excuse and she hadn't seen him again near her place. But that didn't mean he hadn't been more careful the next time. There was just no reining Gus in, she thought as she found her keys and started toward her car.

She wasn't looking forward to tomorrow. Gus wouldn't take being fired well. There would be a scene. She really hated scenes. But this was her responsibility as the owner of the agency. Maybe she should call him tonight and hire security until she could get Gus Thompson's desk cleaned out and the locks changed on the doors at the agency.

With a sigh, she hit the door lock on her key fob. The door on her SUV beeped. Out of the corner of her eye, she barely noticed the man parked next to her, loading his groceries. His back to her, he bent over the bags of groceries he'd put in his trunk as she walked past him.

She was thinking about Gus Thompson when the man grabbed her ponytail and jerked her off her feet. Shocked, she didn't make a sound. She didn't even drop her groceries as his arm clamped around her throat. Her only thought was: *this isn't happening.*

Hayes Cardwell felt his stomach growl as he walked down the grocery-store aisle. The place was empty at this hour of the night with just one clerk at the front, who'd barely noticed him when he walked in. The grocery was out of the way and it was late enough that most people had done their shopping, cooking and eating by now.

His plane had been delayed in Denver, putting him down in the Gallatin Valley much later than he'd hoped—and without any food for hours. He still had the drive to Big Sky tonight, one he wasn't looking forward to since he didn't know the highway.

Being from Texas, he wasn't used to mountains— let alone mountain roads. He was debating calling his brother Tag and telling him he would just get a motel tonight down here in the valley and drive up tomorrow in the daylight.

He snagged a bottle of wine to take to his cousin Dana Savage tomorrow and debated what he could grab to eat. The thought of going to a restaurant at this hour—and eating alone—had no appeal.

In the back of the store, he found a deli with premade items, picked himself up a sandwich and headed for the checkout. His Western boot soles echoed through the empty store. He couldn't imagine a grocery being this empty any hour of the day where he lived in Houston.

The checker was an elderly woman who looked as tired as he felt. He gave her a smile and two twenties. Her return smile was weak as she handed him his change.

"Have a nice night," she said in a monotone.

"Is there a motel close around here?"

She pointed down the highway to the south. "There's several." She named off some familiar chains.

He smiled, thanked her and started for the door.

McKenzie had taken a self-defense class years ago. Living in Montana, she'd thought she would never need the training. A friend had talked her into it. The high-

light of the course was that they'd always gone out afterward for hot-fudge sundaes.

That's all she remembered in the split second the
man grabbed her.

He tightened his viselike grip on her, lifting her off
her feet as he dragged her backward toward the trunk
of his car. The man had one hand buried in her hair, his
arm clamped around her throat. He was so much taller,
she dangled like a rag doll from the hold he had on her.
She felt one shoe drop to the pavement as she tried to
make sense of what was happening.

Her mind seemed to have gone numb with her
thoughts ricocheting back and forth from sheer panic
to disbelief. Everything was happening too fast. She
opened her mouth and tried to scream, but little sound
came out with his arm pressed against her throat. Who
would hear, anyway? There was *no* one.

Realization hit her like a lightning bolt. The parking lot was empty with only one other car at the opposite end of the lot. With such an empty lot, the man
who'd grabbed her had parked right next to her. Also
the light she'd parked under was now out. Why hadn't
she noticed? Because she'd been thinking about Gus
Thompson.

She saw out of the corner of her eye that the man
had moved his few bags of groceries to one side of the
trunk, making room for her. The realization that he'd
been planning this sent a rush of adrenaline through her.

If there was one thing she remembered from the
defense class it was: *never let anyone take you to a second location.*

McKenzie drove an elbow into the man's side. She
heard the air rush out of him. He bent forward, letting

her feet touch the ground. She teetered on her one high heel for a moment then dropped to her bare foot to kick back and drive her shoe heel into his instep.

He let out a curse and, his hand still buried in her long hair, slammed her head into the side of his car. The blow nearly knocked her out. Tiny lights danced before her eyes. If she'd had any doubt before, she now knew that she was fighting for her life.

She swung the bag of groceries, glad she'd decided to cook from scratch rather than buy something quick. Sweet-and-sour chicken, her favorite from her mother's recipe, called for a large can of pineapple. It struck him in the side of the head. She heard the impact and the man's cry of pain and surprise. His arm around her neck loosened just enough that she could turn partway around.

McKenzie swung again, but this time, he let go of her hair long enough to block the blow with his arm. She went for his fingers, blindly grabbing two and bending them back as hard as she could.

The man let out a howl behind her, both of them stumbling forward. As she fell against the side of his car, she tried to turn and go for his groin. She still hadn't seen his face. Maybe if she saw his face, he would take off. Or would he feel he had to kill her?

But as she turned all she saw was the top of his baseball cap before he punched her. His fist connected with her temple. She felt herself sway then the grocery-store parking lot was coming up fast. She heard the twenty-ounce pineapple can hit and roll an instant before she joined it on the pavement.

From the moment he'd grabbed her, it had all happened in only a matter of seconds.

*   *   *

Hayes stepped out into the cool night air and took a deep breath of Montana. The night was dark and yet he could still see the outline of the mountains that surrounded the valley.

Maybe he would drive on up the canyon tonight, after all, he thought. It was such a beautiful June night and he didn't feel as tired as he had earlier. He'd eat the sandwich on his way and—

As he started toward his rented SUV parked by itself in the large lot, he saw a man toss what looked like a bright-colored shoe into his trunk before struggling to pick up a woman from the pavement between a large, dark car and a lighter-colored SUV. Both were parked some distance away from his vehicle in an unlit part of the lot.

Had the woman fallen? Was she hurt?

As the man lifted the woman, Hayes realized that the man was about to put her into the *trunk* of the car.

What the hell?

"Hey!" he yelled.

The man turned in surprise. Hayes only got a fleeting impression of the man since he was wearing a baseball cap pulled low and his face was in shadow in the dark part of the lot.

"Hey!" Hayes yelled again as he dropped his groceries. The wine hit the pavement and exploded, but Hayes paid no attention as he raced toward the man.

The man seemed to panic, stumbling over a bag of groceries on the ground under him. He fell to one knee and dropped the woman again to the pavement. Struggling to his feet, he left the woman where she was and rushed around to the driver's side of the car.

As Hayes sprinted toward the injured woman, the man leaped behind the wheel, started the car and sped off.

Hayes tried to get a license plate but it was too dark. He rushed to the woman on the ground. She hadn't moved. As he dropped to his knees next to her, the car roared out of the grocery parking lot and disappeared down the highway. He'd only gotten an impression of the make of the vehicle and even less of a description of the man.

As dark as it was, though, he could see that the woman was bleeding from a cut on the side of her face. He felt for a pulse, then dug out his cell phone and called for the police and an ambulance.

Waiting for 911 to answer, he noticed that the woman was missing one of her bright red high-heeled shoes. The operator answered and he quickly gave her the information. As he disconnected he looked down to see that the woman's eyes had opened. A sea of blue-green peered up at him. He felt a small chill ripple through him before he found his voice. "You're going to be all right. You're safe now."

The eyes blinked then closed.

Chapter 3

M c Kenzie's head ached. She gingerly touched the bandage and closed her eyes. "I'm sorry I can't provide you with a description of the man. I never saw his face." She'd tried to remember, but everything felt fuzzy and out of focus. She'd never felt so shaken or so unsure.

"Is the light bothering you?" the policewoman asked.

She opened her eyes as the woman rose to adjust the blinds on the hospital-room window. The room darkened, but it did nothing to alleviate the pain in her head. "It all happened so fast." Her voice broke as she remembered the gaping open trunk and the man's arm at her throat as she was lifted off her feet.

"You said the man was big."

She nodded, remembering how her feet had dangled above the ground. She was five feet six so he must have been over six feet. "He was…strong, too, muscular." She shuddered at the memory.

"You said he was wearing a baseball cap. Do you remember what might have been printed on it?"

"It was too dark." She saw again in her memory the pitch-black parking lot. "He must have broken the light because I would have remembered parking in such a dark part of the lot."

"Did he say anything?"

McKenzie shook her head.

"What about cologne?"

"I didn't smell anything." Except her own terror.

"The car, you said it was large and dark. Have you remembered anything else about it?"

"No." She hadn't been paying any attention to the car or the man and now wondered how she could have been so foolish.

The policewoman studied her for a moment. "We received a call last night from your receptionist about a man named Gus Thompson."

McKenzie felt her heart begin to pound. "Gus works for me. You aren't suggesting—"

"Is it possible the man who grabbed you was Gus Thompson?"

McKenzie couldn't speak for a moment. Gus was big. He also had to know, after numerous warnings, that she was ready to fire him. Or at least, he should have known. Could it have been him? Was it possible he hated her enough to want to hurt her? "I don't know."

"We found a car registered to him, a large, dark-colored Cadillac. Did you know he had this car?"

"No. But his mother recently died. I think he mentioned she'd left him a car."

"He never drove it to work?"

"No, not that I know of." Again, she hadn't been paying attention. She knew little about Gus Thompson because she'd chosen not to know any more than she had to. "I saw him parked outside my house one night. I spoke to him about it and I never saw him again, but I can't be sure he didn't follow me sometimes." She thought of one instance when she'd noticed him driving a few cars behind her. But Bozeman was small enough that it hadn't seemed all that odd at the time.

The policewoman raised a brow. "You never reported this?"

McKenzie tried to explain it to herself and failed. "I guess I thought he was annoying but harmless."

"Did you ever date him?"

"Good heavens, no."

"But Gus Thompson probably knows your habits, where you go after work, where you shop?"

She nodded numbly. Gus could have followed her many times and she wouldn't even have noticed. She'd been so caught up in making her business a success....

The policewoman closed her notebook. "We'll have a chat with Mr. Thompson and see where he was last night at the time of your attack."

"He wasn't at the office last night when you sent a patrolman over there?" she asked.

The policewoman shook her head. "He'd already left. Your receptionist was unsure when."

McKenzie felt a shiver, her mind racing. Could it have been Gus who'd attacked her? She swallowed, her throat raw and bruised from last night. Gus was big and strong and she knew he resented her. To think she'd almost reassured Cynthia that Gus wasn't dangerous. He could be more dangerous than she would have imagined.

"I used to work with his mother when she owned the

agency," she said. "I inherited Gus. He is my best sales-man, but I know he felt his mother should have left him the business and not sold it to me."

The policewoman nodded. "This could have been building for some time. We'll see what he has to say."

She had a thought. "I hit the man last night several times, but I'm not sure I did enough damage that it would even show." She described the ways she'd hit him.

"Don't worry. We'll check it out. In the meantime, you'll be safe here."

As the policewoman started to leave the room, McKenzie said, "The man who saved me last night..." She had a sudden flash. *You're safe now.* She blinked. "I'd like to get his name so I can thank him."

"He asked that his name be kept out of it."

She blinked. "Why?"

"There actually are people who don't want the noto-riety. I can contact him if you like and see if he might have changed his mind. What I can tell you is that he just happened to fly in last night and stop at that gro-cery store on his way to see family. Fortunately for you."

"Yes. Fortunate." She had another flash of memory. Warm brown eyes filled with concern. *You're safe now.*

"The doctor said they're releasing you this afternoon. We're going to be talking to Mr. Thompson as soon as we can find him. Maybe going to the office isn't the best idea."

"I *have* to go into work. I was planning to fire Gus Thompson today. Even if he wasn't the man in the parking lot last night, I can't have him working for me any longer."

"Why don't you let us handle Mr. Thompson. We have your cell phone number. I'll call you when he and his personal items are out of your business. In the meantime, I would suggest getting new locks for your office and a restraining order for both yourself and your business."

She must have looked worried because the officer added, "You might want to stay with friends or relatives for a while."

"I have a client I need to see tomorrow south of here. I could go down there tonight and stay in a motel."

"I think that is a good idea," the policewoman said.

"Look what the cat dragged in," Tag Cardwell said as Hayes walked into the kitchen on the Cardwell Ranch. "We were getting ready to send the hounds out to track you down."

"Hey, cuz," Dana said as she got up from the table to give him a hug and offer him coffee. It was his first time meeting his cousin. She was pretty and dark like the rest of the Cardwells. As Tag had predicted, he liked her immediately. "We thought you'd be in last night."

"Ran into a little trouble," Hayes said and gladly took the large mug of coffee Dana handed him.

"That's Texas-speak for he met a woman," his brother joked.

Hayes told them what had happened and how it was after daylight before he left the police station. He didn't mention the strange feeling he'd had when the woman had opened her eyes.

"Is she all right?" Dana asked, clearly shocked.

For months, Tag had been talking up Montana and its low crime rate among all of its other amazing wonders.

"She regained consciousness in the ambulance. Last I heard she was going to be fine—at least physically. I'm not sure what a close call like that does to a person."

"Have the police found the man?" Dana asked, and hugged herself as if feeling a chill. Hayes thought about what his cousin had been through. She had personal experience with a psychopath who wanted to harm her.

"Unfortunately, the police don't have any leads. I wasn't able to get a license plate or even the model or make of the car the man was driving." He felt exhausted and stifled a yawn. He'd been going on nothing but adrenaline and caffeine since last night. "Hopefully, the woman will be able to give the cops a description so they can get the bastard."

"You look exhausted," Dana said. "I'll make you breakfast, then Tag will show you to your cabin. You two don't have anything planned until late afternoon, right?"

"Right," Tag said. "I'm taking my brother to see the restaurant space I found."

"Then get some rest, Hayes. We're having a steak fry tonight. Our fathers have said they are going to try to make it."

"That sounds great." He wasn't sure he was up to seeing his father. Harlan Cardwell had only been a passing figure in his life. Tag, who was the oldest, remembered him more than the other four of them. Harlan had come to Texas a few times, but his visits had been quick. Being the second to the youngest, Hayes didn't even remember his uncle Angus.

Hayes felt emotionally spent, sickened by what he'd witnessed last night and worried about the woman. He kept seeing her staring up at him with those eyes. He mentally shook himself as Dana put a plate of silver-dollar-sized pancakes with chokecherry syrup in front of him, along with a side of venison sausage and two sunny-side-up eggs.

He ate as if he hadn't eaten in days. As it was, he'd never gotten around to eating that sandwich he'd purchased at the grocery store last night. After he'd been plied with even more of Dana's amazing buttermilk pancakes, his brother walked him out to his rental SUV.

"So how are the wedding plans coming along?" he asked Tag as they got his gear and walked up a path behind the barn into the pines to his cabin.

He'd flown in a month early to talk his brother out of opening a Texas Boys Barbecue joint at Big Sky. The five brothers had started their first restaurant in a small old house in Houston. The business had grown by leaps and bounds and was now a multimillion-dollar corporation.

All five of them had agreed that they would keep the restaurants in Texas. But in December, Tag had come to Montana to spend Christmas with their father and had fallen in love with both Montana and Lily McCabe. Nothing like a woman and a little wilderness to mess with the best-laid plans.

It was now up to Hayes, as a spokesman for the other three brothers, to put Tag's feet firmly back on the ground and nip this problem in the bud.

"It's going to be an old-fashioned Western wedding," Tag was saying, his voice filled with excitement. "I can't wait for you to meet Lily. She's like no woman I have ever known."

Hayes didn't doubt it. He'd never seen his brother so happy. All of the brothers had the Cardwell dark good looks. Add to that their success, and women were often throwing themselves at one of them or another. Except for Jackson, none of them had found a woman they wanted to date more than a few times. They'd all become gun-shy after Jackson had bitten the bullet and gotten married—and quickly divorced after he found out his wife wanted nothing to do with their newborn son.

Hayes couldn't wait to meet this Lily McCabe to find out what kind of spell she'd cast over his brother—and possibly try to break it before the wedding.

Gus Thompson had never been so angry. The bitch had called the cops on him. He glanced toward the empty receptionist's desk at the front of the real-estate office. It didn't surprise him that Cynthia hadn't come in today. Stupid woman. Did she really think he would blame *her*?

No, he knew Cynthia didn't do *anything* without checking with her boss.

So where the hell *was* McKenzie Sheldon? No matter what was going on, she was usually at work before him every morning. *She must have had a rough night,* he thought with a smirk.

Where was everyone else? he wondered as he checked his watch. Had they heard about the police coming by his house last night?

When the front door opened, he turned in his office chair, the smirk still on his face since he'd been expecting McKenzie. He felt it fall away as he saw the cops. Hadn't it been enough that an officer had shown up at his door last night, questioning him about stalking the receptionist at the office? Now what?

"Mr. Thompson?" the policewoman asked. Her name tag read P. Donovan.

"Yes?" he asked, getting to his feet. He saw them look around the empty office.

"Are you here alone?"

"Everyone seems to be running late this morning,"

he said, and wondered why that was. Because they'd all been given a heads-up? Gus noticed the way both cops were looking at him, scrutinizing him as if he had horns growing out of his head.

"We'd like to ask you a few questions," the woman cop said. "Ms. Sheldon has asked us to first see that you remove your belongings from the premises."

"What?" he demanded. "The bitch is *firing* me? Has she lost her mind?"

P. Donovan's eyes went hard and cold at the word *bitch.* The word had just slipped out. He'd known McKenzie had it in for him, but he'd never dreamed she'd fire him.

"I'm her biggest-earning salesman," he said as if there had been a mistake made and he hadn't made it. Neither responded. Instead, he saw the male cop looking around. "What?"

"Are there some boxes in the office you can put your belongings into?" the cop asked.

Hadn't either of them been listening? "She can't do this." Gus heard the hopelessness in his voice. He hated nothing worse than the feeling that came with it. He wanted to break something. Tear the place up. Then find McKenzie Sheldon and punch her in the face.

The male cop had gone into a storage room. He came back with two boxes. "Please take only those items belonging to you personally. We'll watch so we can tell Ms. Sheldon."

Gus gritted his teeth. McKenzie didn't even have the guts to face him. Well, this wasn't the last she'd see of him. He'd catch her in a dark alley. He started to shovel the top of the desk off into one of the boxes, but the male cop stopped him. T. Bradley, the name tag read.

"Leave any inventory you've been working on."

He grabbed up his coffee mug and threw it into the box. The couple of tablespoons of coffee left in the cup made a dark stain across the bottom. The same way McKenzie's blood was going to stain the spot where they met up again, he told himself.

His personal belongings barely filled one box. That realization made him sad and even angrier. This business should have been his. When he was a boy, he used to sleep on the floor of the main office when his mother had to work late. This place had been more like home than home during those years when she'd been growing the business.

"Is that everything?" P. Donovan asked.

He didn't bother to answer as T. Bradley asked for his key to the building.

"Ms. Sheldon has taken out a restraining order against you," the cop said. "Are you familiar with the way they work?"

He looked at the cop. "Seriously? Do I look like someone who is familiar with restraining orders?"

"You are required to stay away from Ms. Sheldon and this building. If you harass her—"

"I get it," he snapped, and handed over his key. As he started toward the door, T. Bradley blocked his way.

"We're going to need you to come down to the police station with us to answer a few more questions."

"About what?" The receptionist, bloody hell. "Look, I haven't done anything that any red-blooded American male doesn't do. I like women." He realized they were staring at him. "Come on. She liked it or she wouldn't have led me on."

"Whom are you referring to?" P. Donovan asked.

He frowned. "Cynthia. The receptionist. She was threatening to call the cops last night, but I didn't really think she'd do it. Why would you ask me that? Who else called the cops on me?"

"Didn't she ask you to leave her alone?" the woman cop asked.

He shrugged. "I thought she was just playing hard to get."

"What about Ms. Sheldon? Did you also think she was just playing hard to get?" T. Bradley asked.

Gus closed his eyes and sighed. So she'd told them about that time she'd caught him in her neighborhood. "There's no law against sitting in your car on a public street. I didn't even realize she lived in the area. I was looking at the house down the block, okay?" Not even he could make the lie sound convincing.

"Let's go," P. Donovan said and led him out of the building as if he were a criminal. In the small parking lot, he saw his colleagues waiting in their vehicles for the police to take him away.

He wanted to kill McKenzie.

"Please open the trunk of your car, Mr. Thompson," T. Bradley said as Gus started to put the box in the backseat.

"Why?" he demanded.

"Just please open it," P. Donovan said.

He thought they probably needed a warrant or something, but he didn't feel like making things any worse. He cursed under his breath as he moved to the back of the vehicle and, using his key, opened the trunk. It was empty, so he put the box in it. "Satisfied?"

It wasn't until T. Bradley rode with him to the police station and they had him inside in an interrogation room that they demanded to know where he'd been last night after he'd left the office.

"We know you didn't go straight home," P. Donovan said. "Where did you go?"

So much for being Mr. Nice Guy. Through gritted teeth, Gus said, "I want to speak with my attorney. *Now.*"

Chapter 4

He'd failed.

Failed.

The word knocked around in his mind, hammering at him until he could barely think.

You got too cocky last night, you and your perfect record.

It wasn't his fault. It was the woman's. The fool woman's and that cowboy with the Southern accent who'd rescued her.

That rationale didn't make him feel any better. He'd had one woman who'd fought back before, he thought, tracing a finger across the scar on his neck. But he hadn't let her get away and she'd definitely paid for what she'd done to him.

The possibility of not only failure, but getting caught was what made it so exciting. He loved the rush. But he also loved outsmarting everyone and getting away with it. Last night should have gone off without a hitch. The woman was the perfect choice. He'd done everything right. If he hadn't had to knock her out... Even so, a few more seconds and he would have had her in the trunk. Then it was a short drive to the isolated spot he'd found by the river.

His blood throbbed, running hot through his veins, at the thought of what he would have done to her before he dumped her body in the Gallatin River. He had to kill them for his own protection. If he were ever a suspect, there couldn't be any eyewitnesses.

Except last night he'd left behind *two* eyewitnesses— the woman and the cowboy. Had either of them gotten a good look at him or his vehicle? He didn't know.

A costly mistake. He mentally beat himself for not waiting until he could leave town before grabbing another one. The northwest was like a huge marketplace, every small town had perfect spots for the abduction and the dumping of the bodies. Small-town sheriff's offices were short on manpower. Women weren't careful because people felt safe in small towns.

Also, he had the perfect job. He traveled, putting a lot of miles on the road every year with different vehicles at his disposal. He saw a lot of towns, learned their secrets at the cafés and bars, felt almost at home in the places where he'd taken women.

But last night, after a few weeks unable to travel, he'd been restless. The ache in him had reached a pitch. His need had been too strong. He'd never taken a woman in his hometown. One wouldn't hurt, he'd thought. No, he hadn't been thinking at all. He'd taken a terrible chance and look what had happened.

He gingerly touched the side of his head where she'd hit him with whatever canned good had been in her grocery bag. Fortunately, other than being painful, the bruise didn't show through his thick hair. His shin was only slightly skinned from where she'd nailed him with her high heel and his fingers ached. No real visible signs of what she'd done to him. Not that he didn't feel it all and hate her for hurting him.

It could have been so much worse. He tried to console himself with that, but it wasn't working. The woman had made a fool out of him. It didn't make any difference that he shouldn't have gone for so long since the last one. But it had begun to wear on him. Otherwise, he would never have taken one this close to home. He would never have taken the chance.

The television flickered. He glanced up as the news came on. This was why he couldn't let them live, he thought, as he watched the story about a botched abduction at the small, out-of-the-way grocery store the night before. He waited for the newsman to mention the woman's name and put her on camera to tell of her heroic rescue by the cowboy. He wanted to see the fear in her eyes—but more than anything, he needed her *name*.

The news station didn't put her on air. Nor did they give her name or the cowboy's who'd rescued her.

Furious, he tried several other stations. He'd gotten a good look at her last night after he'd punched her and had her on the ground.

But he foolishly hadn't bothered to take down her car license number or grab her purse. He hadn't cared who the woman was. She'd been nobody to him. But now he was desperate to know everything about her. All the others, he'd learned about them after their bodies were found. It had never mattered who they were. They'd already served their purpose. Now it was inconceivable that he didn't know the name of the only woman who'd ever gotten away.

Without her name, he wouldn't be able to find her and finish what he'd started.

Standing in the hospital room half-dressed, McKenzie tried to still her trembling fingers. The morning sun was blinding. Her head still ached, but she'd kept that from the doctor. After the police had left, he'd made her spend the night in the hospital for observation. Today, though, she had to get back to work. It was the only thing that could keep her mind off what had happened. Worse, what could have happened if someone hadn't stopped the man.

"Let me," her sister said and stepped to her to button the blouse.

She stood still, letting her big sister dress her—just as she had as a child. "Thank you. I wouldn't have called but I needed a change of clothing before I could leave the hospital."

Shawna shook her head. She was the oldest of nine and had practically raised them all since her mother had been deathly ill with each pregnancy, especially with her last baby—McKenzie.

"Mac, I would expect you to call because I'm your *sister* and, after what you've been through, you need your family."

She didn't like needing anyone, especially her big sister. "I didn't want to be any trouble."

Her sister laughed. "You have always been like this." She straightened McKenzie's collar. "You've never wanted to be any trouble. So independent. And stubborn. There. You look fine."

She didn't feel fine. From an early age, just as her sister had said, she had been fiercely independent, determined to a fault, wanting to do everything herself and driven to succeed at whatever she did. She was still that way. Nothing had changed—and yet, after last night, everything felt as if it had.

It was as if the earth was no longer solid under her feet. She felt off-balance, unsure—worse, afraid.

"Are you sure you're ready to leave the hospital?" Shawna asked, studying her.

"The doctor says my head will hurt for a while, but that I should be fine. I need to get to the office and reassure everyone. I had to fire one of my employees today." She swallowed, her sore throat again reminding her of the man's arm around her neck. Had it been Gus Thompson? The thought made her blood run cold. "I'm sure everyone is upset."

"You can't worry about them right now. You need to think about yourself. Just go home and rest. I can stop by your office—"

"No, this is something I need to do myself." She saw her sister's disappointment. Shawna lived to serve. "But thank you so much for bringing me a change of clothes."

"What do you want me to do with the clothes you were wearing?" she asked, picking up the bag. Her pretty new suit was blood-splattered from the now bandaged head wound. So was the blouse she'd been wearing.

"Throw them away. I don't want them."

She felt her older sister's gaze on her. "There doesn't seem to be anything wrong with the suit or the blouse. Once I get them clean... It seems a shame—"

"Then drop them off at Goodwill."

Her sister nodded. "Are the police giving you protection?"

"They really can't do that. Anyway, there's no need. If it was someone I know, then they don't believe he'll try anything again with them involved. And if it was random…then the man could be miles from here by now."

Shawna didn't look any more convinced than McKenzie felt. "I guess they know best."

"I'm going to stay in Big Sky tonight. I have a client I need to see up there this afternoon so I'll spend the night and come back tomorrow."

"Do you want me to go home with you to your condo and wait while you pack?"

She thought of her empty condo. "No. That's not necessary." But even as she said it, she was already dreading facing it alone. "I know you need to get back to your job." She stepped to her sister and hugged her. Shawna had never married. But she kept busy with three jobs as if needing to fill every hour of her day doing for others.

"You've done enough," McKenzie said. Her big sister had always been there for her from as far back as she could remember. It made her feel guilty because she felt her sister had been robbed of her childhood. Shawna had been too busy raising their mother's babies.

"If you need anything…"

"I know." Sometimes she felt as if Shawna had made a life in Montana so she could watch over her. All the other siblings had left, stretching far and wide around the world. Only she and Shawna had stayed in the Gallatin Valley after their parents had passed.

But her big sister couldn't always protect her. Before last night, McKenzie would have said she could protect herself. Last night had proved how wrong she was about that.

Gus Thompson would never forget the humiliation he'd been put through at the police department. "Don't you know who I am?" he'd finally demanded.

They had looked at him blankly.

"My photo is all over town on real-estate signs. I am number one in this valley. I sell more property than any of the hundreds of agents out there. I'm *somebody* and I don't have to put up with this ridiculous questioning."

"You still haven't told us where you were last night." The woman cop was starting to really tick him off.

He looked to his attorney, who leaned toward him and whispered that he should just tell them since it would be better than their finding out later. "I went for a drive. I do that sometimes to relax."

"Did you happen to drive by the River Street Market?"

"I don't remember. I was just driving."

"We searched your car… Actually, the car that is still registered to your mother, and we found a gas receipt." The woman cop again. "You were within a quarter mile of the grocery last night only forty-two minutes before the incident involving Ms. Sheldon."

"So what?" he snapped. "Aren't you required to tell me what I'm being accused of? Someone steal McKenzie's groceries?"

"Someone attacked and attempted to abduct Ms. Sheldon."

"Trust me. The guy would have brought her back quick enough." Neither cop smiled, let alone laughed.

He raked a hand through his hair. "Why would I try something like that in a grocery-store parking lot when I could have abducted McKenzie Sheldon any night right at the office?"

His attorney groaned and the two cops exchanged a look.

"Come on," Gus said. "I didn't do anything to her. I swear." But he sure wanted to *now*. Wasn't it enough that she'd fired him? Apparently not. She wanted to *destroy* him. Something like this could hang over his head for years—unless they caught the guy who really attacked her. What was the chance of that happening? Next to none when they weren't even out looking for him.

He pointed this out to the cops. "Get out there and find this guy. It's the only way I can prove to you that I'm innocent."

They both looked at him as if they suspected he was far from innocent. But they finally let him go.

Once outside the police station, Gus realized he didn't know what he was going to do now. Of course, another Realtor would hire him. The top salesman in Gallatin Valley? Who wouldn't?

Unless word got around about Sheldon's attack—and his firing. Everyone would think it was because he was the one who'd attacked McKenzie. How long would it take before everyone knew? He groaned. Gossip moved faster than an underpriced house, especially among Realtors.

McKenzie Sheldon better hope she hadn't just destroyed his reputation—*and* his career.

"I'm anxious for you to see the building I found for the very first Big Sky Texas Boys Barbecue," Tag said later that afternoon. "The Realtor is going to meet us there in a few minutes."

Hayes had taken a long nap after the breakfast Dana had made for him. He'd awakened to the dinner bell. Dana was one heck of a cook. Lunch included chicken-fried elk steaks, hash browns, carrots from the garden and biscuits with sausage gravy.

"This is the woman who should be opening a restaurant," Hayes said to his cousin.

"Thanks, but no, thanks," Dana said. "I have plenty to do with four small children." As if summoning them, the four came racing into the kitchen along with their father, Hud, the local marshal. The kids climbed all over their father as Dana got him a plate. It amazed him how much noise kids seven to two could make.

Tag's fiancée, Lily McCabe, came in looking as if she was already family. She declined lunch, saying she'd already eaten, but she pulled up a chair. Introductions were made and five minutes later, Hayes could see why his brother had fallen in love with the beautiful and smart brunette.

"We'd better get going," Tag said, checking his watch. He gave Lily a kiss then rumpled each child's hair as he headed for the door. Hayes followed, even though there was no purpose in seeing this building his brother had found for the restaurant.

They weren't opening a barbecue place in Big Sky. He wasn't sure how he was going to break it to his brother, though.

The road from the ranch crossed a bridge over the Gallatin River. This morning it ran crystal clear, colorful rocks gleaming invitingly from the bottom. Hayes watched the river sweep past, the banks dotted with pines and cottonwoods, and wished they were going fishing, instead.

At Highway 191, Tag turned toward Big Sky and Hayes got his first good look at Lone Mountain. The spectacular peak glistened in the sun. A patch of snow was still visible toward the top where it hadn't yet melted. This morning, when he'd driven to the ranch, the top of the peak had been shrouded in clouds.

"Isn't it beautiful?" Tag said.

"It is." All of the Montana he'd seen so far was beautiful. He could understand why his brother had fallen in love with the place. And with Lily McCabe.

"Lily was nervous about meeting you earlier," Tag said now, as if reading his mind. He turned toward Lone Mountain and what made up the incorporated town of Big Sky.

Hayes could see buildings scattered across a large meadow, broken only by pines and a golf course. "Why would she be nervous?"

"She was afraid my brothers wouldn't like her."

"What is the chance of that?" Hayes said. He had to admit that Lily hadn't been what he'd expected. She was clearly smart, confident and nice. He hadn't found any fault with her. In fact, it was blatantly clear why Tag was head over heels in love with the woman.

But Lily had reason to be nervous. She was backing Tag on the restaurant idea. A math professor at Montana State University in Bozeman, she didn't want to move to Texas with her future husband. A lot was riding on what Tag's brothers decided. Their not wanting a Montana barbecue place had nothing to do with liking or disliking Lily.

"Is she going to meet us at the restaurant building

site?" Hayes asked, wondering how involved the bride-to-be was planning to be in the barbecue business. After the fiasco with Jackson's wife, the brothers had decided no wives would ever own interest in the corporation. They couldn't chance another ugly divorce that could destroy Texas Boys Barbecue. Or a *marriage* that would threaten the business, for that matter.

"No, she's doing wedding planning stuff," Tag said. "Who knew all the things that are involved in getting married?"

"Yes, who knew," Hayes agreed as his brother turned into a small, narrow complex. He saw the For Sale sign on a cute Western building stuck back in some pine trees and knew it must be the one his brother had picked out.

"Good, McKenzie is already here," Tag said just an instant before Hayes saw her.

He stared in shock at the woman he'd seen the night before. Only last night McKenzie had been lying at his feet outside a grocery store as her would-be abductor sped away.

Chapter 5

"Hayes, meet McKenzie Sheldon, Realtor extraordi-naire," Tag said. "McKenzie, this is my brother Hayes."

McKenzie smiled, but she wasn't sure how convincing it was. Her sister had tried to talk her into moving this meeting to another day. Maybe she should have listened. She hadn't felt like herself all day.

While she'd tried to put what had happened last night out of her mind, she kept reliving it. Now she felt jumpy and realized it had been a mistake to take the attitude "business as usual" today.

But she couldn't bear the thought of hanging out at the condo all day when she knew nothing could take her mind off last night in that case. Her first stop had been the office where she'd assured everyone that Gus Thompson would no longer be a problem. While she was there, the locksmith came and changed all the locks, which seemed to reassure some and make others at the office even more nervous since Gus hadn't gotten along with any of his coworkers.

Then she'd gone to her condo, packed quickly for overnight and driven to Big Sky to meet her client. She'd worn a plain suit with a scarf to cover the bruises on her neck, but the gash on her temple where the man had slugged her still required a bandage if she hoped to hide the stitches.

As she caught her reflection in the empty building window, she saw with a start that she looked worse than she'd thought. How else could she explain Hayes Cardwell's reaction to her? His eyes had widened in alarm as he put out his hand.

He looked like a man who'd just seen a ghost. He'd *recognized* her. How was that possible when he'd only flown in yesterday?

"Pleased to meet you, Ms. Sheldon."

Tag had told her that his brothers shared more than a love of barbecue. The resemblance was amazing. Like Tag, Hayes Cardwell had the dark hair and eyes, had the wonderful Southern accent and was handsome as sin.

She thought of Ted Bundy as she took Hayes Cardwell's large hand, hers disappearing inside it, and saw his dark gaze go to the bandage on her head. "I had a little accident last night."

"You're all right, though?" He still held her hand. She could feel herself trembling and feared he could, too.

She put on her best smile. "Fine." Then she finally met his gaze.

His eyes were a deep brown and so familiar that it sent a shudder through her. Even though she'd told her sister that there was nothing to worry about, she was well aware that the man who'd attacked her last night could be closer than she thought.

He'd stayed home from work saying he didn't feel well, even though he knew that might look suspicious if he was ever a suspect. But he was too anxious and upset over last night to go to work today.

There'd been nothing of use in the morning paper, only a short few paragraphs.

Police say a man tried to abduct a 28-year-old woman about 10:35 p.m. last night in the River Street Market parking lot.

The man attacked the woman as she came out of the market and attempted to put her into the trunk of his vehicle. He is described as over six feet with a muscular build. He was wearing a dark-colored baseball cap and driving a newer-model large car, also dark in color.

If anyone has information, they should contact the local police department.

He knew he should be glad that the information was just as useless to the police. She hadn't gotten a good look at him, which was great unless they had some reason to withhold that information. That aside, nothing in the news was helping him find the woman.

Too restless to stay in the house, he decided to go for a walk in his northside neighborhood to clear his head. The houses were smaller on this side of town, many of them having been remodeled when the boom in housing came through years before.

House prices had dropped with the mortgage fiasco, but so many people wanted to live in his valley that prices had never reached the lows they had elsewhere. He was glad he hadn't been tricked into selling his house for top dollar. He could have found himself in a house he couldn't afford. Instead, his small, comfortable home was paid for since he lived conservatively.

Everything about his lifestyle looked normal on paper. He'd attended Montana State University right there in Bozeman. He'd bought a house after he graduated with a degree in marketing and had gone to work for a local company. He was an exemplary employee, a good neighbor, a man who flew under the radar. If caught, everyone who knew him would be shocked and say they never would have suspected him of all people.

As he walked around his neighborhood, he saw that more houses were for sale. It made him upset to think that his older neighbors were dying off because more college students would be moving in. Constant temptation, he thought with a groan.

He promised himself the next time he took a woman it would be in another town. Even better, another state. He couldn't take the chance so close to home ever again. If there *was* another time. Last night's botched abduction had left him shaken. She'd jinxed things for him. If he didn't find the woman and fix this—

At a corner he hadn't walked past in some time, he saw that another house had gone on the market. But that wasn't what made him stumble to a stop next to the strip of freshly mown lawn.

There she was! He could never forget that face and now there she was. Right there on the real-estate sign in the yard, smiling up at him as if daring him to come after her.

McKenzie Sheldon of M.K. Sheldon Realty.

"Are you all right?"

McKenzie nodded, even though she was far from all right. Did she really think she recognized this man? She hadn't seen the face of the man who'd tried to abduct her so she couldn't have seen his eyes. This man's eyes were…familiar and yet she'd never met him before, had she? Would she look at every man she met and think he was the one who'd attacked her?

Hayes Cardwell was staring at her with concern and something else in his expression. Compassion?

It was the very last thing she needed right now. Tears welled in her eyes. She felt lightheaded and groped for the wall behind her for support.

"If you'd prefer to do this some other time," Hayes said.

She shook her head. "No, I'm fine. It must have been something I ate." In truth, she hadn't eaten anything since the day before. No wonder she felt lightheaded. But she'd toughened it out through worse, she told herself, remembering when she'd taken on the agency.

Tag Cardwell hadn't seemed to notice her no doubt odd behavior. He was busy looking in the windows of the building, anxious to get inside and show his brother the space.

"I think you're going to like this location for your restaurant," she said, turning away from Hayes Cardwell's dark, intent gaze and what she saw there. "Let me show you. It's perfect for what you have in mind."

Her fingers shook so hard, she didn't think she was

going to be able to put the key in the lock. A large, sun-tanned hand reached around her and gently took the keys from her.

"Let me do that," Hayes said. His voice was soft, his Southern accent comforting and almost familiar.

She was going mad. She could smell his male scent along with the soap he'd used to shower that morning. He was a big man—like the man last night who'd attacked her. She touched her bruised throat and closed her eyes against the terrifying memory.

He opened the door and she stumbled in and away from him. Her cell phone rang and she was startled to see that it was the police department.

"I need to take this. Please have a look around." She scooted past Hayes and back outside, leaving the two men alone inside what had been a restaurant only months ago. Her phone rang again. She sucked in a deep breath of the June mountain air and, letting it out, took the call. As she did, she prayed the man had been caught. She couldn't keep living like this.

"Ms. Sheldon?" the policewoman asked.

"Yes?"

"I spoke to the man who intervened last night during your attack. He still would prefer to remain anonymous."

"You're sure he wasn't involved?"

"Involved? No. The clerk at the store was a witness. He was leaving the store when he saw the abductor try-ing to lift you into the trunk of his car. The man saved your life."

"So why is this so-called hero so determined to re-main anonymous?"

"As I told you, he's in town visiting relatives. He doesn't want the notoriety. But I can assure you, we checked him out. He just happened to be in the right place at the right time last night."

McKenzie felt as if she could breathe a little easier. "I'm sorry he won't let me thank him, but I certainly appreciate what he did. Is there any word on…?"

"No, but we are looking at Gus Thompson. We brought him in. He doesn't have an alibi for last night."

"You really think it was him?" She shuddered, remembering. He was about the right size and he *had* acted more than a little creepy in the past.

Behind her, the door opened. She heard Tag and his brother come out.

"Thank you for letting me know," she said to the patrolwoman and disconnected. "So what do you think?" she asked, but one look at their faces and she knew Hayes hadn't liked the place.

Tag had been so excited about the building. She could get it for him at a good price since the owner was anxious to sell. But she could see that Hayes was far from sold.

"We can't really make a decision until all my brothers see the place," Tag said. Hayes said nothing.

She could feel the tension between the two men. "Well, let me know. This property won't stay on the market long. I'll lock up." She moved past Hayes to turn out the light and lock the door.

When she came back out, the brothers were leaving. She shivered as she felt someone watching her. Her gaze shot to Hayes, but he was looking off toward the mountains and his brother was busy driving.

I'm losing my mind. Hayes Cardwell wasn't her attacker. So why, when she thought of his brown eyes, did some memory try to fight to surface?

* * *

Gus Thompson was going to see McKenzie no matter what anyone said. When he'd come out of the police station and climbed into his vehicle, he hadn't known where to go or what to do. He had to save his career, and McKenzie was the only one who could do that.

Restraining order or not, he *would* see her.

He had racked his brain, trying to remember where she said she had a showing today. Something about a listing in Big Sky. A former restaurant. He'd quickly checked to see what commercial restaurant space was under the multiple listings at Big Sky and laughed out loud when he'd found the restaurant with ease.

It didn't take much to find out what time she was showing the place. He'd called the office, changed his voice and pretended to be the person she was showing the restaurant to. Within minutes, he'd found out that McKenzie would be at the restaurant this afternoon at two to meet the Cardwells.

For a few minutes after he'd hung up, he'd tried to talk himself out of driving up to Big Sky. The last thing he needed was for her to call the police before she heard him out. It appalled him that she thought she could just fire him and he'd go away. Well, she was dead wrong about that.

Unfortunately, the forty-mile drive had taken longer than he'd expected. Summer traffic. He'd forgotten about the damned tourists so he hadn't been able to beat McKenzie to the restaurant—which had been his intent.

Fifty minutes later, he'd parked next to a small grocery in a space where he had a good view of the restaurant with the M.K. Realty sign out front. He'd arrived in time to see two men pull up in an SUV only moments after McKenzie.

He'd been forced to wait, telling himself it might work out better. He would grab her after her showing. He could get a lay of the land before he did anything stupid. More stupid, he thought, thinking of Cynthia, the receptionist. She wasn't even that cute.

While he had no patience for waiting, he was surprised when the showing only took a matter of minutes. He had to laugh. Boy, had that not gone well. And now McKenzie had just lost her best salesman. She would definitely regret firing him, probably already did.

He saw his chance when the two men McKenzie had shown the property to got into their SUV and drove away. The restaurant location was somewhat secluded, separated from the other businesses by pine trees.

Once he got her alone, she'd be forced to listen to what he had to say.

As he started his vehicle, planning to park behind her car so she couldn't get away, he saw her looking around. Was she worried he might show up? Or was she looking for the man who'd attacked her last night? Her gaze skimmed over him in his vehicle where he still sat, motor running. He looked away, glad he'd driven his silver SUV that looked like everyone else's around here.

When he'd dared take a peek again, she was headed for her car. He couldn't let her just drive away. His best chance of talking to her was here rather than back in Bozeman.

Gus shifted the SUV into gear. He told himself all he wanted to do was tell her what he thought of her firing him, of accusing him of attacking her, of treating him like an employee rather than appreciating what he did for M.K. Realty.

He just needed to have his say. He wasn't stupid enough to touch her. Or threaten her. He had the right to have the last word. She couldn't just get rid of him in such a humiliating way and think he was going to let it pass.

But as he'd started to drive up the road to the empty restaurant, another vehicle pulled in and parked next to her car. Annoyed, he saw that he would have to wait again. He hadn't come all this way to give up. He killed his engine with a curse. If he couldn't get to her now, then soon. She would hear him out, one way or another.

McKenzie hated the scared feeling she had as she hurried to her car. Her gaze took in the activity lower on the hillside. She told herself she'd just imagined someone watching her. Down the road, there were families in vans with laughing and screaming children, older people trying to park in front of one of the small businesses that dotted the meadow, a young couple heading into the grocery store.

Everywhere she looked there were people busy with their own lives. It was June in Montana, a time when in Big Sky, it seemed everyone was on vacation. No one had any reason to be watching her.

Still, she gripped her keys in her fist until her hand ached as she neared her car. She wanted to run but she was afraid that like a mad dog, the person watching her would give chase. She couldn't see anyone watching her and yet the hair rose on the back of her neck. The afternoon sun had sunk behind Lone Mountain. Shadows moved on the restless breeze through the pines next to the building.

Fear was making her paranoid, but she couldn't shake off the feeling that the man from last night hadn't left town. Nor had he forgotten about her.

She reached the car, opened the door and climbed in, fumbling in a panic to get the door locked. The moment she did, she realized she hadn't looked in the backseat. Her gaze shot to the rearview mirror. She swiveled around. The backseat was empty.

Hot tears burned down her cheeks. She began to shake uncontrollably.

At the sound of a vehicle approaching, she brushed at her tears and tried to pull herself together. She was trying to put the key into the ignition, when the tap on her side window made her jump.

Her head swung around and she found herself looking up at Hayes Cardwell. She cursed herself. He would see that she'd been crying. She felt a wave of embarrassment and anger at herself.

"Are you all right?" Hayes mouthed.

She lowered the window a few inches. "I—"

"I know. That's why I came back. There's something I need to tell you."

"If it's about the restaurant space—"

"The police called me and asked me again if I would mind if they told you that I was the man who found you last night at the grocery store."

She felt her eyes widen in alarm. "You—" The brown eyes. A flicker of memory. *You're safe now.*

"I can't imagine what you're going through, that's all I wanted to say. I was worried about you. But I didn't want you thinking…"

She nodded, unable to speak around the lump in her throat. He'd seen her reaction to him. It was the reason he'd decided to tell her. He didn't want her thinking he was the one who'd hurt her. Her eyes burned again with tears.

"Call the police. I understand why you would suspect me. I'll be over here when you finish if you want to talk or anything." He stepped away from her car.

She put the window up and dug out her phone. When the patrolwoman came on the line she asked, "The man who saved me last night? Was his name Hayes Cardwell?"

"So he *did* contact you."

"It's true?"

"Yes. He and his brothers own a chain of—"

"Barbecue restaurants in Texas."

"That's right. He also works as a private investigator in Houston. Like I said, we checked him out thoroughly. Plus, we have an eyewitness who saw him rescue you."

"Thank you." She disconnected and, pulling herself together, climbed out of the car.

Hayes was standing at the edge of the building, looking toward the Gallatin River. In the afternoon sun, the surface of the water shimmered like gold. The scent of pine wafted through the June air. There was nothing like Montana in the summer.

"I'm so sorry I suspected you." He'd never know how much. "The police told me that I owe my life to you. Thank you."

He turned to look at her, kindness in his dark eyes. "No, please, don't feel bad. I didn't tell you so you could—"

"Thank you?"

He shrugged, looking shy. "I just happened to be in the grocery store."

"I didn't mean to make you uncomfortable."

"I'm afraid I'm the one who made you uncomfortable. I apologize for staring earlier. I was just so surprised to see you again."

She nodded and touched her bruised neck, remembering the man's arm around her throat and fighting for breath.

"Are you sure you should be working this soon after what you've been through?" he asked.

"I needed to keep my mind off…everything."

"Is it working?"

She gave him a weary smile. "No," she said and looked away. "I've felt jumpy all day and I haven't been able to shake the feeling that someone is…watching me." She glanced around again, the feeling still strong. She shivered, even though the afternoon was warm.

What if the man from last night wasn't through with her? Wasn't that what had been in the back of her mind all day?

Hayes looked past her. He saw people coming and going at a nearby small business complex. No one seemed to be looking in this direction, though.

"You say you feel as if someone's watching you?"

She nodded. "I know I'm just being paranoid—"

"Your best defense is your instincts. Don't discount them."

She stared at him and tried to swallow the lump in her throat. "You think he'll come after me again?"

"I don't know. Is there any way he knows who you are?"

"I... The police think it might be a man I worked with. I fired him today. I have a restraining order—"

Hayes scoffed at that. "Restraining orders can't protect you from a predator. Where are you staying?"

"I checked into a motel up here for the night—"

He shook his head. "My cousin Dana owns a ranch not far from here. She recently built several guest cabins. I'd feel better if you'd consider staying there—at least until the police have a chance to catch this man." Hayes knew from experience that there was little chance they would catch him—unless he did turn out to be this man she'd fired.

"I couldn't impose."

"You wouldn't be imposing, trust me. My cousin Dana loves a full house and you would be doing me a favor."

She cocked a brow. "How's that?"

"I wouldn't have to worry about you the whole time I'm in town."

McKenzie smiled. It was a nice smile, a real one, and he was suddenly aware of how attractive she was. She had long hair the color of caramel. Most of it was pulled up with a clip at the nape of her neck, but a few strands had escaped, framing a face that was all girl-next-door—from the sprinkling of freckles that dusted her cheeks and nose to the wide-set tropical-blue eyes. But it was her mouth that kept drawing his attention. It was full, her lips a pale pink. Right now she worried at her lower lip with her teeth.

She had the kind of mouth a man fantasized about kissing.

He roped in his thoughts, telling himself not to make a big deal out of this coincidence. But he couldn't shake the memory of the first time he'd looked into her eyes. And now here she was, Tag's real-estate agent. As a private detective, he'd never bought into coincidences. This was definitely one that had him thrown off-balance.

"You'll like my family and you'll be safe." After that, he didn't want to think about it. Maybe the police would get lucky and catch the man.

"Are you sure about this? I know you didn't want to be involved..."

"I *am* involved," he said and smiled. Maybe more involved than he should be, he thought. "Do you need to stop by your motel to cancel your reservation?"

"I hadn't checked in yet. I can call."

"Why don't you follow me to the ranch, then, and meet the Cardwells. Trust me. You're going to love them and feel at home there."

"What?" Tag said as they stood in the ranch house living room later. "McKenzie is the woman you saved?"

Hayes nodded.

"Talk about a small world. So you decided to bring her back to the ranch?"

"Look, I know you're upset with me about the restaurant—"

"I'm just trying to understand what you're thinking. Since you're only going to be here a couple of days, how do you intend to keep this woman safe?"

"I don't know what I was thinking, okay? She was scared. When I went back and found her, she was losing it, all right? She thought someone was watching her."

Tag looked skeptical.

"I think she was probably imagining it, but she's

terrified this predator will come for her again. Who wouldn't be?"

"You did the right thing," Dana said from the doorway. "I'm glad you brought her here. It isn't like we don't have plenty of room. I put her in the cabin next to yours, Hayes. She can stay as long as she wants."

"With the wedding coming up July Fourth—"

Dana cut Tag off. "Your brothers can always bunk together if they haven't caught the man who attacked her by the time Jackson, Austin and Laramie arrive. I told her she is welcome to stay as long as she wants to and that is that."

Tag didn't look happy about it. "It makes it pretty awkward since, from what I can gather, we aren't going to buy the restaurant space."

Dana looked to Hayes. "Is that what you and your brothers have decided?"

"We're still discussing it." That wasn't quite true but he really didn't want to get into this right now. If he couldn't talk his brother out of this, then he'd contact the rest of the guys and let them deal with it. His job had been to come up here and check out the situation and if at all possible, put an end to it.

"Why don't you take McKenzie for a horseback ride?" Dana suggested to Hayes. "It's beautiful up in the mountains behind the ranch and it will take both of your minds off your problems."

He was glad for anything that let him escape more discussion about the restaurant, so he jumped at it. "Good idea."

He found McKenzie standing outside on the wide Western porch, leaning on the porch railing and looking toward the mountains beyond. At his approach, she turned to smile at him.

"Thank you," she said, turning to him. She'd changed out of the suit she'd been wearing earlier into jeans and blouse. "This place is beautiful. I feel…safe here and I adore your cousin Dana."

"Everyone does. I thought you'd like it here. That was the plan. Dana suggested a horseback ride up into the mountains. What do you say?"

"Really? I'd love to." She sounded so excited he couldn't help but smile. He was reminded again of that moment last night when he'd looked into her eyes and felt…something.

"Great. Dana said she has two gentle horses that should be perfect for us greenhorns."

"Speak for yourself," McKenzie said. "I grew up riding and I suspect you did, too," she said, eyeing him. "Or is that Stetson and those boots just for show?"

He laughed. "I've ridden a few horses in my day."

Dana came out of the house then with a pair of boots she thought would fit McKenzie. They all visited as she led them up to the corral and got them saddled up for their ride.

Hayes noticed that McKenzie's step was lighter. He felt uncomfortable playing hero protector, but he preferred that to worrying about her. He'd learned as a private investigator to follow his own instincts. If she felt she was being watched, he knew there was the chance she probably was.

Chapter 6

He couldn't believe his good luck at finding McKenzie Sheldon's face on that real-estate sign. He took this as an omen that things were going to work out, after all.

Whistling all the way back to his house, he planned his new strategy. From the description the newspaper had run of the attacker, he felt assured that McKenzie hadn't gotten a good look at him. Which meant she wouldn't know him if she saw him again. But he had to be sure before he moved forward.

He checked the real-estate listings and found an open house she was hosting on Sunday, day after tomorrow. But to his delight, he saw that she was going to be the featured speaker at a real-estate conference being held at the university right here in town tomorrow.

He imagined that she was scared after last night. He just hoped she didn't cancel her speech or her open house or have someone else host it. Given the fight she'd put up last night, he had a feeling she wouldn't. He liked that about her and couldn't wait to see her again.

Excited now and much relieved, he felt better than he had since his failure the night before. But he wouldn't be satisfied until he fixed this.

From as far back as he could remember, he couldn't bear failing. He supposed that was his parents' fault. They'd expected so much of him—too much. He would have given anything to make them happy, and he'd certainly tried for years. But he'd only disappointed them time and time again.

The thought left a bitter taste in his mouth.

His parents weren't the only ones. He'd also disappointed his girlfriends. The thought of them made his stomach roil. He'd never known what they wanted from him. It was this secret that women kept among themselves. They would get that self-satisfied smirk on their faces, mocking you for failing.

"I should have expected as much from you," his high school girlfriend used to say. And when he begged her to just tell him what she wanted, she would add, "If you don't know, then there is really nothing more I can say."

The bitches had played their games with him throughout high school and then college. He'd tried to understand them. Even with his longest relationship after college, four years, he'd continued to disappoint. Nothing was ever good enough. And the nagging…

That was really when things had started to change. After his breakup following four years of torture, he'd picked up a woman at the bar and taken her for a ride out into the country. All he'd wanted was sex and a little peace and quiet. But it had proven too much to ask.

She'd started going off on him, about how she should have known at the bar that he was a loser. He'd told her to get out of his car.

"Out here? No, you take me back to the bar where I left my car right now," she'd said.

He remembered looking at her. How ugly women were when they scowled like that. "Get out of my car right now or I am going to kill you."

She'd started to argue, but something in his expression had stopped her. She got out and began to cry, yelling obscenities as he backed up to leave. "I'm going to tell on you! Everyone is going to know about you!"

He'd hit the brakes, then threw the car into first gear and hit the gas as she began to run. That had shut her up. He'd chased her down the road until she'd had the sense to run into the trees. He'd been so calm as he'd turned off the car and gone into the trees after her.

She'd been easy to catch.

That was when he'd officially quit trying to please other people. Now he only worried about making himself happy. And what would make him happy was finding McKenzie Sheldon and finishing what he'd started.

McKenzie shifted in her saddle as she stared across rows of mountaintops to the sunset. The waning sun had left streaks of pink, orange and gold that fanned up into Montana's big sky.

"It's breathtaking." She turned to look at Hayes. "Thank you for bringing me up here. You were right, your family is so inviting, especially Dana. This was so kind of her."

"She is one in a million, no doubt about that."

"You all seem so close. My family is spread out all

over the place. I only have one sister here in town and I don't see her much. My fault. I work all the time." She let out a sigh.

"I never met the Cardwell side of my family until this trip," Hayes said. "My mother left my father when us boys were very young and took us to Texas to live. We only saw our father on occasion, so this is my first time in Montana—and meeting my cousin Dana."

McKenzie couldn't help being surprised. "You seem so at home here."

He chuckled at that. "Montana does that to a person. Look at my brother. He intends to stay, restaurant or no restaurant."

"You're opposed to opening a Texas Boys Barbecue here?"

"It's complicated."

"I'm sorry, I shouldn't have asked." She looked toward the sunset and breathed in the sweet scent of the tall pines around her.

"No, it's fine. It's just that we started small, in an old house in Houston, and the business just…mushroomed. My brother Laramie has a head for that end of it and runs the corporation so the rest of us can pursue other careers."

"I understand you're a private investigator in Houston?"

He nodded. "Maybe it's just me, but our little barbecue joint has grown into something I never wanted it to be. Adding another one in Montana… Well, it was never in the plans. We swore we would at least keep them all in Texas."

She said nothing, hating that she had a dog in the fight. This was something the brothers would have to sort out among themselves. Meanwhile, she feared Tag would lose the restaurant space and clearly he had his heart set on his own business in Big Sky.

"It makes it all the more difficult because there are five of us," Hayes said. "Do you come from a large family?"

She laughed. "Nine children."

His eyes widened in surprise. "Imagine all of them having to agree on something."

"Impossible."

Hayes nodded, but he looked upset by the situation.

"Your brother is still going to marry the woman he loves and stay in Montana no matter what happens with the restaurant, right?"

"Seems so. I just hate to disappoint him, but it isn't as if he needs a job."

"Some people just enjoy working," she said, realizing how true that was. She couldn't imagine retiring, say, ten years from now even though she probably could. What would she do all day if she did?

"I suppose we should head back," Hayes said as the sky around them began to darken. The breeze stirred the thick pine boughs and McKenzie felt a chill, even though the day was still warm. "Sorry to dump my problems on you."

"Yes, I have more than enough of my own," she joked. "Seriously, it was nice to think about someone else's for a while."

"I'm glad you're staying here on the ranch. Dana has invited us for a cookout tonight. You'll get to meet the rest of the family."

"I don't know how I will ever be able to repay her," McKenzie said.

"Just being here makes her happy since I think she gets starved for female companionship with all these Cardwell men around."

As they rode back toward the ranch, she couldn't help but notice the pines shimmering in the waning light. In the distance, she could see Lone Mountain, now a deep purple.

She couldn't remember a time she'd enjoyed a man's company the way she did Hayes Cardwell's. He wasn't hard to look at, either, she thought with a hidden smile, surprising herself. No man had turned her head in a very long time. And he really had taken her mind off last night.

But as they rode into the darkening ranch yard, she felt another shiver and tried to shake off that feeling of being watching again.

Hayes noticed how quiet McKenzie was at supper. Fortunately, his father and uncle hadn't been able to make it to the ranch so she'd only had to meet a few of the family members. He could tell she was exhausted. The ride, though, had put some color back into her cheeks.

After dinner, the two of them headed for their respective cabins on the mountainside behind the house and he asked, "Would it be possible for you to take a few days off? I'm anxious to have a look around the area and thought you might want to come along."

He could see that she saw through his ruse right away.

She smiled politely, though, and said, "I am speaking at a real-estate convention tomorrow at the university before several hundred people."

That had been his fear. "You can't get someone else to do it for you?"

"Are you kidding?" She laughed. "This has been planned for months."

He nodded. "So it's been widely publicized."

She frowned. "You can't think that the man who attacked me would come to something like this, hoping to harm me."

He wasn't sure what to think. "I don't like it because it will be hard to protect you in a crowd like that."

"Hayes—"

"If you're going to tell me that you don't want my protection, save your breath. I'm going with you."

"You'll be bored to tears."

"I hope so. I'm sure your speech will knock 'em dead, but with any luck, it will be uneventful."

"This conference is important. It's about growth in Montana, especially in this Big Sky area," she said as they neared her cabin.

Moonlight filled the canyon, casting long shadows from the pines. A breeze stirred the boughs, sending the sweet scent of pine into the night air. Overhead stars glittered above the canyon walls.

McKenzie met his gaze and smiled. "Good for *both* of our businesses, actually. There's a lot of money that has moved into Montana. A Texas barbecue restaurant at Big Sky wouldn't have made it maybe even five years ago. Now, though?" She raised an eyebrow.

"I know you aren't just saying that to sell the building we looked at."

"That building would already be sold if your brother hadn't put down money on it," she said.

Hayes's brow shot up. "Tag put money down on it?"

She realized she'd let the cat out of the bag. "I'm sorry, I got the impression it was his own money and merely to hold it until you could all see it."

"I knew he had his heart set on this, but…" He shook his head as they reached her cabin.

A small lantern-shaped light cast a golden glow from the porch over them and the wooden lattice swing that moved restlessly in the light breeze. Dana and Hud had the half-dozen guest cabins built to look as if they'd been there for a hundred years. They were rustic on the outside but had all the conveniences of home inside.

"I hope you and you brothers can work this out," McKenzie said.

"Me, too."

"Thank you again for everything," she said as she looked past him toward the old two-story ranch house below. "I've loved getting to know some of your family and the horseback ride… Well, I can't tell you how much I needed it, needed all of this."

"You know, Dana said you are welcome to stay as long as you want."

She smiled at that. "That is very sweet of her, but with Tag's wedding just weeks away… No, I need to get back to work."

"I understand. What time is this conference tomorrow?"

McKenzie told him and reluctantly agreed to his following her to her condo and then to the university.

"I hope you didn't think I was trying to strong-arm you into the restaurant site," she said.

He shook his head. "I didn't. McKenzie, I was thinking we should have dinner some night before I return to Texas."

"I would enjoy that."

He waited for her to enter the cabin and turn on a light before he started through the pines to his own cabin. As he walked, he pulled out his cell phone and called his brother Laramie. It was such a beautiful June night and he wasn't tired at all. If anything, he didn't want the night to end. He couldn't remember being this...

For a moment, he didn't recognize the emotion. Happy. He laughed to himself. He felt...happy.

"Tag has his heart set on opening a restaurant here," he said without preamble when his brother Laramie answered.

"We already knew that. What did you think about the location he picked?"

"What is the point of discussing that if we don't want to open one in Montana?" he demanded. "Wait a minute. He called you, didn't he?"

Laramie sighed. "He wanted to make sure I was flying in for the wedding in a few weeks so I could see the site and we could talk. You didn't tell him what we decided, I take it? Is this just a case of you not wanting to play the bad guy?"

"No, I'm actually reconsidering." Hayes told himself it had nothing to do with McKenzie Sheldon and much more to do with Montana. He was falling for the state. He wouldn't be here long enough to fall for the woman, which was another reason not to stay too long. Fate might have thrown them together, but then again, he didn't believe in fate, did he? "Tag made some good points."

"So would the location work?"

"The location is fine. Actually better than fine. And maybe Big Sky is ready for Texas barbecue, but is this really something we want to do? What's next, Wyoming? Minnesota?"

"Tag said that people from all over the world visit Big Sky and a lot of the homeowners have sophisticated tastes."

Hayes laughed. "You aren't really implying that our barbecue requires a sophisticated taste."

"Maybe not, but our beans definitely do."

They both laughed.

"So tell me about his fiancée," Laramie said.

"She's pretty, supersmart, has a great job and owns her own home here in Big Sky. And she's definitely wild about our brother."

"Sounds like our Tag hit a home run."

Hayes sighed. "She's nice, too. I liked her."

"I heard you found a woman up there, as well."

"*Found* being the operative word." Hayes told his brother what had happened.

"Crazy. I thought there wasn't any crime up there."

"Low crime. Not *no* crime." He'd reached his cabin. As he climbed up the steps and sat down on the porch swing, he said, "I'm thinking I might stick around for a while." It surprised him that he'd voiced what had been in the back of his mind.

"So it's like that," Laramie said.

"It's…complicated."

"Be careful, Hayes," his brother warned. "You know what Jackson went through with his marriage."

He did. His wife had left him right after their son was born, only to come back three years later and try to take Ford away from Jackson. "Could you fly up now instead of before the wedding?"

"Not going to happen. Let's remember that I'm the brother who keeps Texas Boys Barbecue Corporation going."

"We never forget that," Hayes said. Laramie was the business major, the brother who'd gladly taken the reins when the business had begun to take off. True, it had grown more than any of them had anticipated since then, but Laramie was still the best brother to be in charge. And there was that added benefit that none of them forgot. Laramie allowed the rest of them to do whatever they wanted, never having to worry about money.

"You know how thankful we all are that you took it on," he said, not that Laramie needed reassurance. His brother loved what he did and continued to make the corporation more than profitable.

"What about Austin?" Hayes had to ask.

Silence, then Laramie said in a worried tone, "He's on a case down by the border. I haven't been able to reach him for several weeks now."

Hayes let out a curse. When Austin got on a case, it was all-consuming. They often went for weeks, even months, with no word from him. He only seemed to take on the most dangerous cases. They'd almost lost him more than once.

"I thought he was working fewer hours for the sheriff's department."

"You know him better than that," Laramie said. "I'm sure he will do everything possible to make the wedding, though."

Hayes sure hoped so, but of the five of them, Austin was the loner of the family and possibly the most stubborn. "When are Jackson and Ford flying in?" He knew Jackson and his five-year-old son wouldn't miss the wedding, even though weddings were the last thing Jackson was interested in attending after his marriage had gone so awry.

"A few days before the wedding. Ford is excited about riding horses at the ranch. Apparently, cousin Dana promised him his own horse while he's up there."

"So what do you want me to do about Tag and the restaurant site?" Hayes asked.

"If you've already weakened, I'd say it was a done deal."

As Hayes disconnected, he thought about walking back to McKenzie's cabin and telling her to get the paperwork for the restaurant site ready. It was pretty much a done deal if Laramie was getting behind it.

But he stayed on his cabin porch. He could tell her tomorrow or maybe even the next day. It would give him an excuse to see her again. Not that he needed one. What was that old Chinese proverb? *He who saves a life is responsible for it.*

The woman brought out his protective instincts. He knew it was because she was so strong, so determined, so capable of taking care of herself under normal circumstances. But the man who'd attacked her had shaken her world and left her afraid and vulnerable.

Hayes told himself that whoever had tried to abduct her in the grocery-store parking lot was probably long gone.

But what if he wasn't? What if it was this man she'd fired?

He swore softly under his breath. It seemed that tomorrow he was going to a huge real-estate conference where a predator could be anyone in the crowd. And to think he'd actually considered leaving his gun in Texas, asking himself, *what were the chances he would need it in Montana?*

Chapter 7

The moment they reached what McKenzie called the "field house," a huge, circular, dome-shaped building on the Montana State University campus, Hayes saw the parking lot and knew this was going to be a security nightmare.

As they entered the building, they were surrounded by people, many of them coming up to McKenzie. There were pats on the back, handshakes, people brushing her arm in welcome as she made her way down to the exhibits.

"Are you all right?" McKenzie asked when they finally got to M.K. Realty's booth.

"It's not me I'm worried about."

"You've been scowling since we got here," she said. "Haven't you ever heard of safety in numbers?"

She seemed to be at ease, as if she'd forgotten the attack, but Hayes wasn't fooled. He could see past the bravado. She was putting on a show, determined that her attacker wasn't going to change anything about her life.

But he already had. She either was pretending otherwise or the reality of it hadn't hit home yet.

"Sorry," he said. "I'll try to lighten up. Or at least look as if I have."

She gave him a grateful smile and squeezed his arm. "I really do appreciate that you're here."

Let's see if you do when this day is over, he thought, wondering how he was going to keep her safe in a place this packed with people.

As she had a word with her employees at their booth, he watched the crowd. He had some idea of who he was looking for. A large man, over six feet, strongly built.

He'd had a few cases involving these types of men. While he knew the general type, there were always exceptions. He wasn't going to make the mistake of trying to pigeonhole this one.

The place was filled with men, most of them alone. Any one of these men could be here to hurt McKenzie. The thought rattled him so much that he didn't hear her saying his name. When she touched his arm, he jumped.

She gave him a pleading look. She was trying so hard to hold it together. She didn't need him wigging out on her.

"He could be miles from here," she whispered as she stepped close. He felt her breath on his ear and shivered inwardly. Just the light scent of her perfume had his pulse thrumming.

Today she'd worn a business suit with a white blouse under the jacket that accentuated her olive skin and the thin silver necklace around her neck. At the end of the chain, a small diamond rested between the swell of her breasts. She'd put makeup on the bruises at her neck, hiding them enough that no one would notice. Diamond studs glittered on each of her earlobes with her hair pulled up off her long, slim neck.

She'd chosen a shade of lipstick that called attention to her full mouth. No way could this woman possibly blend into this crowd.

"Are you listening to me?" she asked.

He nodded, although his thoughts had been on the way the suit skirt hugged her shapely behind, dropping below her knees to her long legs and the matching high heels on her feet. McKenzie was the whole package. Any man in his right mind would want this woman.

As it was, somewhere in this building could be a man completely out of his mind who, if he got the chance, would hurt her and bury her in a shallow grave somewhere.

"Why don't you stay here? You'll be able to see me from here." She pointed to a raised area where she would be giving her speech.

Before he could object, she took off through the crowd. He went after her, fighting his way through the throng of people. He caught a glimpse of her head as she neared the platform and knew he wouldn't be able to catch up to her before she was on stage.

McKenzie couldn't help being irritated with Hayes. She needed his strength right now. Seeing the worry in his eyes only made her more aware of what had happened to her two nights ago.

But she'd put it behind her, convinced the man had been traveling through town and was now miles from here.

She cut through the crowd, not stopping even to say hello to people she knew. She was in the people business. It really did matter who you knew when you sold real estate, she was thinking as she neared the side of the raised platform and the podium and microphone waiting for her.

Rows of chairs had been placed in front and were already full. She'd been honored when asked to speak. Some of the older Realtors resented her because she'd climbed so fast.

She thought of Gus Thompson's mother. She'd been McKenzie's mentor and had taught her the ropes.

"Of course they don't like it," she'd said once when McKenzie had mentioned that some of the Realtors had given her the cold shoulder. "Just keep your chin up and don't lose sight of where it is you want to go."

It had been good advice. She hadn't made enemies along the way and was glad of that. Instead, she'd kept her nose to the grindstone, working hard and now knew she had the respect of her peers. Several of the older Realtors gave her a nod as she passed.

She made her way to the stairs at the back of the platform near the wall and had started up the stairs when her hair was grabbed from behind. Her head jerked back. She heard the sound of something sharp cutting through her hair an instant before the pressure on it was released.

Fighting to keep from falling back down the couple of stairs she'd climbed, she swung around, thinking she must have caught her hair on something.

There were people everywhere but none were paying any attention to her. Nor could she see anything that might have caught in her hair.

Her hand went to her long, blond mane. In the middle of the back of her head she felt a place where a huge chunk of her hair had been chopped off only inches from her scalp.

She looked down to see a few long strands on the stairs along with the clip she'd used to put her hair up this morning.

Her body began to shake. Someone had grabbed her from behind and chopped off a huge chunk of her hair? It was inconceivable. But then so was what had happened to her the night in the grocery-store parking lot.

On the stage, one of the Realtors was checking the microphone as she got ready to announce the guest speaker.

McKenzie looked again at the people milling past. No one seemed to pay her any mind. No one had a hank of her hair in his hand. But she knew it could have been any one of them.

She quickly stepped back down the stairs to retrieve her clip. Her fingers trembled as she pulled her hair up as best she could and anchored it with the clip.

She could do this. She would do this. She wouldn't be scared off. She wouldn't let whoever had done this win.

Something was wrong. Hayes watched McKenzie walk onto the stage smiling. But he knew her smile and that wasn't it.

His heart began to pound. He shouldn't have let her out of his sight. The darn woman. She was so stubborn, so sure she could handle this on her own. She hadn't been out of his sight for more than a few moments—not until she'd gone behind the raised platform.

Whatever had happened must have occurred there. But with so many people around…

He watched her walk up to the microphone. He could

see her trying to pull herself together. She looked down at her notes. Even from a distance he thought he saw her hands trembling.

She laid her notes down on the podium and leaned toward the microphone. Her voice was clear and true as she looked up at the crowd gathered to hear her speak.

Hayes had admired her, but right now he was in awe of her courage and fortitude. He could practically see the determination in her shoulders, in her voice, in those amazing eyes of hers. She stood there and gave her speech with probably more spirit than she would have if something hadn't happened before she'd stepped up to that microphone.

She was beautiful, a woman to be reckoned with, and Hayes knew he wasn't the only man in the audience who thought so.

When she finished, she was met with applause and even a standing ovation.

She beamed, raising her chin into the air, her eyes bright. The look on her face filling him with fear.

If the man who'd attacked her was somewhere in that crowd watching her, McKenzie was letting him know she wasn't scared of him and that she was far from defeated.

It was the kind of challenge that would only antagonize her attacker—and get her killed.

Hayes was waiting for her as she descended the stairs behind the platform. She saw his expression and had to look away to keep from breaking down. He knew. How, she had no idea.

He took her arm without a word and led her toward the closest exit. She kept a smile on her face, nodding to people she knew. Hayes didn't slow down until he had her out the door and almost to his rental car.

"What happened?" he asked the moment he had her safely in the passenger seat with him behind the wheel.

She reached up and unclipped her hair. It fell past her shoulders except for the part that had been whacked off. She put down the car's visor mirror and got her first look at the damage that had been done.

Hayes let out a curse.

The savagery of the act more than the loss of the hair brought tears to her eyes. "It will grow back. It's just hair."

He let out another oath. "He's telling you that he's not done with you. He's telling you—"

"I know what he's telling me," she snapped as she turned to face him. "It's just hair. He won't get that close to me again."

Hayes pulled off his Stetson and raked a hand through his own hair as if he was too angry to speak.

"You can't give him another chance at you," he said after a moment. "Today? It was too dangerous. You need to cancel your appointments until the police find this guy."

"What I need is a haircut."

His expression softened as he met her gaze. He must have seen how close she was to tears and how badly she was fighting not to cry. "Where do you want me to take you?"

"A friend of mine owns a salon. I'm sure under the circumstances she will be able to squeeze me in."

"After that, we need to talk," he said as he started the car and pulled out of the lot, wondering if her attacker was watching them drive away.

* * *

He put the fistful of McKenzie Sheldon's hair to his nose and smelled the sweet scent. She'd probably shampooed it this morning in the shower. He let himself imagine her standing under the warm spray for a moment. He would never see her like that, arms raised as she gently worked the shampoo into her long, blond hair.

Rubbing the hair between his fingers, he studied it in the light of the men's room. It was hard to know the exact color. Pale summer sun, he thought. Too bad he couldn't show the hair to someone who would know what to call it.

He would keep the hair. Maybe he would tie a ribbon around it. Not even an hour ago, it had been growing on her head. That thought stirred the need within. He ached with it and wasn't sure how much longer he could go without fulfilling it.

Someone came into the men's room. He put the hair into the pocket of his jacket, careful not to let any of it escape. He'd lost some of the strands on the stairs as it was. He didn't want to lose any more.

The idea of cutting her hair hadn't even crossed his mind until he'd grabbed hold of it as she'd started up those stairs. He'd wanted her to stumble. Maybe even fall. He had needed to know if she would recognize him when she saw him. The idea of her falling into his arms was just too mouthwatering to pass up.

He'd told himself that just touching her again would be enough. But then she'd gone behind that platform out of sight of the cowboy she'd come with, the same one, he suspected, who'd saved her at the grocery-store parking lot.

Seeing his chance, he'd grabbed her hair, felt its silky

smoothness… He always had his scissors with him, sharpened to a lethal edge. When he'd grabbed her hair, felt it in the fingers of his right hand, his left had gone for the scissors.

At that moment, he'd wanted a piece of her—since that was all he was going to get until he could catch her alone.

Now, feeling better than he had since the night he'd failed, he left the bathroom one hand deep in the pocket of his jacket where he kept the scissors, the other gently caressing her hair. It was enough for today, he thought, anxious to get out of the building so he could be alone.

Soon, McKenzie Sheldon. Very soon and it will be more than your hair that I have my hands on.

"Are you sure you don't want me to take your open house today?" Jennifer Robinson asked when McKenzie called the office.

"No, I can handle it, but thanks, Jennifer." She wasn't looking forward to the open house. Someone had tried to scare her yesterday.

Now she looked at her short curly hair in the mirror. Hayes had complimented her hairdo when she'd come out of the salon. "It looks good on you."

She'd always hated her natural curly hair, brushing it straight every morning after her shower. It felt odd, the loss of weight she'd become used to. She raked her hand through the curls and told herself she liked it better short—a lie, one she told herself every time she remembered the sudden feel of her head being pulled back, then the sound of something sharp cutting through her long hair before her head snapped forward again.

It had happened so fast.

And could again, Hayes had reminded her. She knew he was angry with her for taking off yesterday without him with her—and for not hiding out. He didn't want her hosting this open house today. He didn't understand. She couldn't hide. She refused to let this man take away everything she'd worked so hard for.

"At least come back to the ranch tonight," Hayes had pleaded yesterday after the conference. "I can keep you safe there."

She'd been scared and shaken enough that she'd agreed to go back up the canyon to Cardwell Ranch rather than return to her condo. Her evening had been so relaxing and enjoyable she'd never wanted to leave. Dana's husband, Marshal Hud Savage, had cooked steaks outside on the grill and they'd all eaten on the wide porch to enjoy the beautiful night.

She'd been completely captivated by the Cardwells, especially Hayes. He had an easygoing way about him that appealed to her. It amazed her that she'd thought there was anything threatening about him. It was his eyes. She'd remembered them from the night of the attack. They had been comforting. Just like his words. *You're safe now.*

Only she wasn't.

She reminded herself of that as she drove from Big Sky into Bozeman, determined to get on with her life.

"At least let me take you to your open house," he'd argued.

"You can't be with me 24/7 and I refuse to hide under a rock. He's trying to scare me."

"Until he tries to abduct you again and kill you. McKenzie, he knows who you are."

His last words had sent an icy chill through her. *He knows who you are.*

But she didn't know who he was. He could have been anyone in that crowd yesterday.

Angry with herself for letting her thoughts take that turn, she told herself she would put the attack behind her. Big words, she thought as she drove up in front of her condo and just sat there, engine running, surprised how hard it was to face going inside. She knew it was crazy. The attack hadn't even happened here. And yet she had the crazy fear that he would be inside, waiting for her....

Getting out of her SUV, she gripped her keys as she made her way to the front door. She noticed her neighbor had already gone to work. A quiet had settled over the four units. She'd picked this condo because of all the pine trees and the creek that meandered past it.

Now, though, the thick pines made her nervous and the babbling stream quickly put her nerves on edge. She got the key into the lock and pushed open the door.

She wasn't sure what she'd expected to find. Maybe the place ransacked. Everything looked exactly as she'd left it. She stepped in. An eerie silence settled around her. She'd always loved coming home. The condo had been decorated simply with light colors that made the rooms feel welcoming. She'd always felt at peace here.

Now, however, she opened her shoulder bag and took out the pepper spray she'd bought yesterday. Holding it, she moved quickly through the two-story condo, checking closets and bathrooms and even under beds until she was sure she was alone.

She was trembling more from fear than from the effort of searching the spacious condo. The fear made her angry with herself. She couldn't keep living like this.

When her cell phone rang, she jumped. Stilling her heart, she took the call. It was her sister.

"How are you doing?" Shawna asked.

"Fine." The lie seemed to catch in her throat. "Not as well as I'd hoped."

"If you need company—"

"No, I'm keeping busy. I have an open house today."

"Work as usual, huh? That's my little sis. Well, if you need anything, you know to call."

"I will. Thank you."

As she hung up, she saw that Gus Thompson had left a message. She braced herself and played it.

"We need to talk. Call me."

Just the sound of his voice made her stomach ache. What did he think they needed to talk about? And why was he so insistent? She still couldn't believe he was the man who'd attacked her, but maybe she just didn't want to. She'd worked with him for years. Surely she would have known he was dangerous, wouldn't she?

McKenzie quickly showered and changed for her open house, determined not to let Gus or anyone else keep her from her work. She had a business to run. She had to go over everything she needed, afraid that as distracted as she was, she would forget something important. The open house needed to go off just right. This was a major sale for a contractor she liked working with, so she hoped to get an offer before the day was out.

Hurrying so she could get to the house early, she exited her front door and was just pulling the door closed after her when the man stepped out of the shadows.

Hayes swung by the restaurant site before heading to McKenzie's open house. He wanted to see the traffic flow in the area and take another look around. The other day, he'd been distracted and determined they weren't buying the space. But after talking to his brother Laramie, he'd tried to reach Austin. He'd been told that Austin was on a case and couldn't be reached. He couldn't help worrying about him.

He felt at loose ends. His attempt to talk McKenzie out of hosting the open house today had fallen on deaf ears. Did she really think that by pretending none of this was happening it would stop this bastard? All she had to do was look in the mirror to see just how close the man had gotten to her—again.

He'd been shocked last night after dinner when she'd told him about the open house, but he'd tried not to argue with her. He'd seen the way she could dig her heels in. Look at what had happened yesterday. Maybe his concern *had* put her in more danger. He was determined not to let that happen again.

"Can't someone else host it?" he'd suggested.

"I could get someone else to do it, but…I can't." She'd shrugged as if it was hard to explain.

"I get it," he'd said. "You're like my brother Laramie. We've offered to help with the load, but…"

"He has it handled."

"Yep, and he does a fine job of it. I noticed that you own your realty company." She was young to have accomplished so much so quickly. He wondered if she'd had help and decided not. It was that tenacity about her that intrigued him. But also frustrated him because her determination not to let her attacker interfere with her life put her in danger.

"It was a lot of hard work, but when you want something badly enough…" Her voice had dropped off and he'd realized she was thinking about the man she'd fought off repeatedly the night of her attack. Neither would have given up. If Hayes hadn't come out of the store when he had…

"What kind of open house is it?" he'd asked to derail her thoughts—and his own.

"A brand-new, state-of-the-art, spacious, three-thousand-square-foot executive home overlooking Bozeman with beautiful views of the Spanish Peaks."

He'd laughed and she'd joined him. He was glad she could laugh at herself.

"I did sound like a Realtor, didn't I?" She sighed. "Bad habit."

"Let me guess. All restaurant-quality appliances and granite countertops in the massive kitchen. I had the flu recently and found myself watching some of those home shows on television. Talk about over the top."

She'd nodded in agreement. "You do see a lot of…extravagance in some of the homes in this area, too. Gold faucets, heated driveways, dual master suites."

"You love what you do," he'd said as if he'd just seen it.

She'd smiled, tears in her eyes. "That's why I can't let him stop me."

"Or me stop you," he'd said, and she'd nodded before she'd leaned over and gently placed a kiss on his cheek.

Their eyes met and locked and for one breath-stealing moment he'd almost taken her in his arms, even though he knew he wanted a lot more than a kiss. Fortunately, or unfortunately, they'd been interrupted by the kids running in to say good-night as they headed to bed.

The moment had been lost, filling him with regret

and relief at the same time. His life was in Houston. He reminded himself of that now.

Determined to get at least the barbecue joint settled, he called Jackson. Ford answered the phone. The five-year-old sounded so grown-up. Hayes tried to remember the last time he'd seen his nephew. It had been too long, that was for sure.

"Hey, kid," he said. "What have you been up to?"

Ford was a chatterbox on the phone. Hayes listened to stories about sports, the trouble his nephew had gotten into and how they would be flying to Montana for his uncle Tag's wedding to some girl before Ford launched into an excited story about the horse Dana had picked out for him to ride once he got to Montana.

Finally, Hayes had to ask if he could speak to the boy's father.

Jackson came on the line.

"How much of that can I believe?" Hayes joked.

His brother laughed. "Ford's into Texas tall tales I'm afraid, just like his uncles. What's this I hear about Laramie supporting the Montana restaurant?"

"I talked to him last night. Tag's convinced him. I have to admit, I've weakened, as well."

"What about this future bride?"

Hayes could hear the concern in Jackson's voice. He'd gotten burned badly. He didn't want to see his brother Tag go through a divorce.

"She's nice. I liked her. She's got plenty of her own money, a good job, a nice house up on the mountain behind Big Sky. Clearly, they are crazy about each other."

Jackson snorted. He knew crazy.

"I'm standing in front of the restaurant space right now. I think we should move ahead with this."

Jackson sounded surprised. "What changed your mind?"

"I actually think it's a good business decision. Also, I guess I want to do this for Tag."

"Is everyone else in agreement?"

"Can't reach Austin. Nothing new there." But he figured Austin would go along with whatever was decided. He had little interest in the business, too involved in being a sheriff's deputy and saving the world.

"As long as Tag's new wife isn't involved in the business in any way, I'm good with it," Jackson said. "I still have time to meet her and see what I think before he can get the place open."

No one was more cynical than Jackson.

"I think this is the right thing to do," Hayes said, checking his watch. "I'll tell the Realtor when I see her."

Gus was glad he'd scared her. He took enjoyment in McKenzie's shock and fear. How did she think he felt being interrogated by the police and suddenly out of a job?

"Gus." She said his name on a frightened breath, her hand going to her chest as she stumbled back against her closed condo door.

He'd seen her lock it so he knew she wasn't going to be able to get back inside away from him until he had his say. He closed the distance, forcing her up against the door, towering over her. She'd cut her hair. It surprised him. He'd always thought she liked it long. He wondered what had precipitated this? Out with the old, in with the new? Had she already replaced him at the agency?

"What do you want?" Her voice actually squeaked. Where was that ball-breaking woman he'd worked for the past six years?

"What do I *want?*" he repeated. "I want to know why you're ruining my life."

Some of her steel returned to her voice. "This isn't the place to talk about this."

He laughed. "Where would that place be, McKenzie? You've taken out a restraining order against me so I can't go near the office or you."

Some of the color came back into her face. "It should be obvious why I had to do that."

"Because you think I'm some kind of psycho? Do you really think I attacked you in a grocery parking lot?"

"I don't know. Were you at the conference yesterday?"

"Why? Were you attacked again?" He smirked. "Do you really think I can show my face at a real-estate conference right now?"

He could tell she didn't believe him. "I thought I saw you there."

"Well, you were wrong. The same way you were wrong to fire me."

"I'm sure I wasn't the first person you've stalked. You've been harassing my receptionist. I told you that if I had to warn you again..."

He looked at her in disbelief. "Maybe I was *interested* in you, did you ever consider that? I came by your house that day to ask you out, but about the time I finally got up my nerve, you saw me. Your expression... Well, let's just say I knew my answer."

The woman he'd known was back. Anger flared in her eyes. She moved away from the door, forcing him to take a step back. "It's too bad you didn't take no from Cynthia."

He felt off-balance, something she'd made him feel

way too many times. "I don't expect you to believe this, but she led me on. She liked me flirting with her."

"Up to a point, I'm sure that was true."

"And yet you fired *me*."

"It was a combination of things, Gus, not just a couple of incidents and you know it. You've always resented working for me."

He nodded, finally seeing it. His own anger boiled to the surface. "You were just waiting for my mother to die so you could get rid of me. As long as she was alive, you wouldn't dare."

"That isn't true." McKenzie looked at her watch, dismissing him. The old McKenzie Sheldon, businesswoman, had come back. "You're going to make me late for an open house and there really is no point to this discussion. I'm not changing my mind. If you promise to leave me alone in the future, I will write you a recommendation, not that you need one. You're a great salesman. Just stop trying to sell yourself to women who aren't in the market."

"That's it?"

"You brought this on yourself, Gus." She slipped past him.

He had no choice but to let her go. As he watched her drive away, he felt as if she'd punched him in the gut. He knew the best thing he could do was leave her alone, take the recommendation and start looking for another job.

But this still felt unfinished to him.

He stood outside the open house for a moment, wondering who could afford such a home—and what the commission would net McKenzie Sheldon. Probably more money than he made in months. He would never admit that that alone made him want to hurt this woman. The woman was obviously very successful. It would seem small of him to want to destroy her simply out of jealousy.

But a part of him had to admit, he liked to target successful women. He liked bringing them down. He smiled to himself, thinking how many of them he had made beg for their lives. They weren't so arrogant and sure of themselves then.

People were coming in and out of the open house. Beautiful June days probably brought more people out than stormy, wintery ones, he thought. He waited and fell behind a group of five. Being a salesman at heart himself, he quickly sized them up. The elderly married couple looked serious about home buying. The two women behind them were just gawkers. The lone man who'd led the way looked like another Realtor.

Once inside, he cut away from the others. The elderly couple made a beeline for McKenzie and the flyer she was handing out. He only got a glimpse of her. The last thing he wanted to do was get caught staring at her.

His plan had worked beautifully. He would wait until there were a lot of other people going through the house so he blended in. But at some point, he would have to get close enough to McKenzie Sheldon so he could look into her eyes and find out whether or not she recognized him.

Even a hint of recognition and he would get out of there. The best plan was to park a few blocks away and walk. Not that he expected her to chase him out to his car. Or even scream.

The house was no surprise. Every room was large and over the top with expensive features and furnishings. He wandered around, saw the older couple inspecting the fixtures and heard the two women oohing and ahhing over the kitchen.

As spacious as the house was, he felt claustrophobic and knew he couldn't take much more of this. He was working up his nerve to return to the main entrance and get one of the brochures from Ms. Sheldon, when he came around a corner and almost collided with her.

She pretended the encounter hadn't startled her, but he'd seen the terror flash in her eyes. Nice eyes, more green than blue today. Those eyes widened and for just a moment, he feared she'd recognized him. She was blocking the hallway and his way out. A fissure of panic raced along his nerve endings. Perspiration dampened his shirt and hairline.

He told himself that if she opened her mouth, he'd hit her. There wasn't anyone else around. He'd punch her hard enough to knock her out and then he'd push her into one of the bedrooms and leave quickly. He balled up one fist and took a breath.

But she didn't scream. The flash of terror had only lasted an instant then she'd looked relieved and relaxed a little.

"Sorry," she said. "You startled me."

Not as much as I did a few nights ago. He looked right into those aquamarine waters. Not even a hint of recognition. He almost laughed since just an instant before he'd been planning to knock her senseless and make his escape.

"I'm sorry," he said. "We both must have been distracted."

"How do you like the house?" she asked, covering her initial reaction to him.

"It's beautiful." *Just like you.* She blew him away. She

was much more striking than her photo on the real-estate signs. There was a sweetness about her. Strength? Oh, he knew her strength and her determination only too well. Sweet, strong and successful—his perfect woman.

"You might want one of these." She held out a flyer.

"Yes," he said and smiled. "Thank you. Oh, and do you have a business card?"

She brightened. "Of course. I usually have one stapled to the flyers. I forgot this morning. I have one in my purse if you'd like to follow me." She headed back toward the entrance. He followed her, admiring the part of her body he had some history with.

From under an entertainment counter, she pulled out her purse, removed a business card and handed it to him. The card was thick, nicely embossed. He rubbed it gently between his fingers. A business card told a lot about a person.

He carefully put it into his shirt pocket and folded the flyer she'd given him.

"Is there anything else I can help you with?" she asked.

"No, I think I have everything." He smiled. "But you'll be hearing from me."

McKenzie was just about to ask the man for his name when the front door opened and her attention was drawn away as she saw Hayes Cardwell come through the door.

A mixture of pleasure and relief filled her at the sight of the big cowboy. He wore jeans, a Western shirt and a gray Stetson over his longish dark hair. Unlike yesterday, he looked more relaxed.

Almost instinctively, she started to move toward him, but remembered the man who'd shown an interest in the house. She turned her attention back to him. "I look forward to hearing from you if you have any questions about the house or would like to see any others."

"Next time, I'd like to bring my wife along. I'll give you a call," the man said, glancing at Hayes before he quickly moved off.

McKenzie turned to Hayes. She always felt she had to be "on" at open houses. Even though she loved her job, sometimes it wasn't just her high-heeled shoes that made her hurt. Her face often ached from smiling so much.

"Decided you wanted a kitchen with all stainless-steel appliances and granite countertops?"

"Can't imagine living without them."

She chuckled at that. "You're saying you don't have them at your house in Houston?"

"I live in an unremodeled house in the older part of Houston."

She cocked an eyebrow at that.

"I have…humble tastes."

"Nothing wrong with that," she said. "Excuse me a moment." McKenzie saw a few more people she needed to talk to before they left. The elderly couple sounded interested. She gave them her business card. As she started to go look for Hayes, she saw the man she'd spoken to earlier before Hayes had come in.

The man was walking away when he suddenly stopped and turned to look back at her as if he'd known she'd be there framed in the front window, watching him. He gave a slow, vague kind of smile. She quickly stepped back out of sight, even though she feared he'd seen her. His smile had almost been mocking, as if he'd put one over on her.

She'd dealt with enough people at open houses that

she had a pretty good sense of who was genuinely in the market for a house and who wasn't. The man had seemed interested and yet he hadn't asked any questions about the house—unlike the elderly couple. Maybe he *had* just been putting her on.

McKenzie went to find Hayes, annoyed with the man and herself. He might have fooled her once, but she would be watching for him at her next open house.

Hayes looked around the large residence, killing time until the open house was over. Several men came through. Any one of them could have been McKenzie's attacker.

At four o'clock, he found McKenzie finishing up with a couple and waited as she packed up to leave.

"Dinner. You name the restaurant," he said.

"I really should—"

"Work?" He saw her hesitate. "I figured since we both need to eat…"

She brushed a lock of hair back from her face. She'd dressed up for the open house, taking extra pains with her appearance. Probably to give herself more confidence. But under the surface, he would see that she was still running scared.

"Hayes, I appreciate what you're trying to do…."

"*Eat?* I like to do it three times a day, if possible."

"You know what I mean." She sighed. "You can't protect me forever, especially since you will be leaving soon."

He nodded. "So that must mean I'm just hungry, don't you think?"

She laughed. "Are you always so determined?"

"Always." He led the way out of the house and waited

while she locked up. "By the way, how long do we have on that restaurant space at Big Sky?"

"Changed your mind?" she asked as they walked toward their vehicles.

"Tag isn't changing *his* mind." They'd reached his rented SUV. "Why don't you leave your car," he suggested. "I'll be happy to bring you back after dinner."

"Okay. Just let me put my things away."

He watched her put the flyers in the passenger seat and helped her place the Open House signs in the trunk. But as they finished, he noticed her look past him and frown. He turned but didn't see anything out of the ordinary.

"Is everything all right?" he asked.

"Hmm," she said distractedly. "Just someone I saw earlier at the open house. He must live in the neighborhood. It's nothing."

They ate a nice dinner, talked about everything but her attacker. Not that it kept the man from being present. Hayes doubted the attack was ever far from either of their minds.

He'd hoped McKenzie would be staying in the cabin at Cardwell Ranch, but she couldn't hide out, given her career. Not that a woman like her would let herself hide out forever, anyway, and the man might never be caught. Still, he didn't like the idea of McKenzie staying in her condo alone.

He'd told his brother he was staying until the wedding. It was only a few weeks away and if they were going ahead with the restaurant, he could help out. At least that was his excuse. In truth, he couldn't leave McKenzie. Not yet, even though she was right. He couldn't stay forever. Maybe it was best for her to start adjusting to living with never knowing when the man might reappear in her life.

"Dinner was wonderful," she said as they left the restaurant. "And a great idea."

"Thanks. I'm just full of great ideas," he said with a chuckle. "Like this one. I wish you would come back up to the ranch tonight."

She shook her head as he pulled up behind her car where they'd left it earlier for the open house. With the houses so far apart, the neighborhood was dark in the huge spaces between streetlamps. No lights burned in the house she'd shown earlier. With the houses bordered by tall, dense trees or high hedges, there were lots of places for a man to hide, he thought.

How many houses just like this did she show alone? He hated to think. In other places, he'd heard that real-estate agents now worked in twos to be safer. But this was Montana. People felt safe here.

"Thank you for the offer," she said. "I appreciate it, but I have a lot to do tomorrow."

He nodded, not surprised.

She opened her car door. "Have your brother give me a call about the restaurant space."

So that was how it was going to be? Business as usual? The woman was stubborn as a mule. She refused to take some time off, leave the state or at least town for a while. There was no way he could keep her safe and he couldn't just walk away.

He got out and caught up to her, catching her hand to turn her toward him. "I have a favor." She raised a brow. "I need a date for the wedding."

"Your brother's wedding?"

"Yes."

She shook her head. "I'm not your responsibility. I told you, you can't keep me safe."

"It's more complicated than that," he said as he touched her cheek. "From the moment I first looked in your eyes..." His words died off. She was staring at him. He shook his head. "Maybe I can't get you out of my mind—"

"I know what you're up to."

"I doubt that," he said, and leaned toward her, his hand looping around the back of her neck as he gently drew her to him. "Because if you could see what I was up to, then you'd know I was about to kiss you."

He brushed his lips over hers, then pulled back to gaze into her eyes. He'd been captivated by those eyes two nights ago. That hadn't changed. "Sorry, I couldn't resist."

"You don't have to treat me as if I'm made out of glass and might break," she said. "I'm a little battered right now, but I'm resilient and strong, a lot stronger than I look."

"Is that right?" He looped an arm around her waist and pulled her to him right there in the street between their vehicles. He kissed her like he meant it this time. Her full lips parted in surprise. Her sweet, warm breath comingled with his own. She let out a soft moan as he tasted her. Drawing her even closer, he deepened the kiss, demanding more.

McKenzie came to him, fitting into his arms as she answered his kiss with passion. He felt desire race in a hot streak through his veins. He didn't want to ever stop kissing her.

But when she pulled back, he let out a shaky breath. "Wow," he said and laughed.

She sounded just as breathless. She met his gaze in the moonlight. "Hayes, what is this?"

"*This?* This is crazy. Worst possible timing ever."

McKenzie nodded agreement.

"And yet, from the first moment I looked into your eyes…"

She shook her head. "I…I really can't.… Hayes, I'm not sure of anything right now and quite frankly, I'm suspicious of your motives."

"My motives for kissing you? It was just a kiss, right?"

She studied him openly in the dim light.

"Quite the kiss, though, wouldn't you say?" he asked, grinning.

She smiled at that. "Quite the kiss."

"Glad you agree. I'm still going to follow you home and make sure you're all right."

She looked as if she wanted to put up a fight, but no longer had the energy to. "Thank you," she said as she turned and started for her car. He watched her. She seemed a little wobbly on her high heels, strange for a woman who lived in them. He hoped the kiss had smacked her silly the way it had him. He'd kissed his share of women, but none had lit a fire in him the way McKenzie's kiss had.

As she reached the car, she hesitated. He saw her glance back at him, then reach for something on her windshield. His pulse leaped. Something was wrong. He was running toward her as she took what looked like a folded sheet of paper from under the wiper blade.

Chapter 8

McKenzie had been shaken even before she found the note. The kiss had her whirling. It had been a while since a man had kissed her. She couldn't recall anyone who'd made her surrender so completely to a kiss before, though. She'd felt...*wanton,* and that wasn't a word she would have used about herself. She'd also felt out of control and that scared her.

Hayes had her blood running hot. He'd sparked something in her that made her ache for more. That alone was enough to turn her already crazy world upside down. She'd been content with her career, with her life, with an occasional date. Hayes had changed all that in just one kiss. Now she wanted...Hayes Cardwell. Bad timing or not.

But she questioned whether he was interested in her as a woman. Or if he was just hardwired to protect the woman whose life he'd saved because he was a Texas cowboy and a gentleman.

When she'd found the note under her windshield wiper, at first she'd thought it was an advertisement.

Instead, scrawled words had been written on the sheet of paper.

I'm watching you.
This time you won't get away.
I am going to miss your long hair.

The paper began to shake in her fingers. She had *felt* him watching her. It hadn't been her imagination. He was out there and he wasn't through with her.

She read the words again, all easily visible in the diffused light from the closest streetlamp. All her bravado fell away. The man wasn't giving up. He was out there. Maybe even watching her right now, wanting to see her fall apart.

McKenzie slumped against her car as she looked out into the darkness, unable to pretend any longer that she wasn't terrified. She'd thought she could go on as if nothing had happened. As if nothing kept happening.

Suddenly, Hayes was at her side, his arms coming around her. "What is it?" His gaze took in the sheet of paper trembling in her fingers. Using his sleeve, he took it from her. "Get in my car. I'll call the police."

She nodded and started for his rental SUV. Earlier, she'd told him how strong and resilient she was. She didn't feel either right now. She wanted to lose herself in his strong arms. For so long she'd made her way alone, determined not to lean on anyone, not to need anyone.

Right now, she needed Hayes—and more than just to protect her.

Behind her, she heard him on the phone. Her gaze swept through the dark neighborhood. A breeze stirred the tree boughs, throwing shadows everywhere. Was he out there watching her? Enjoying tormenting her?

McKenzie quickened her step, gr bbed the passenger-side door handle and flung it open. She practically threw herself into the car, slamming the door behind her. Heart pounding, she tried to catch her breath. Anger mixed with fear, a deadly combination that had her wiping furiously at her tears.

She'd never felt helpless before. It was a horrible feeling, one she couldn't bear. Somehow, she had to make it end, and falling into bed with Hayes wasn't the answer as much as she would have liked to.

As Hayes finished his call and climbed into the SUV behind the wheel, she turned to him. "I have to find this man."

"I've called the police. They're on their way. They'll see if they can get a print off—"

"He won't have left fingerprints on the note he left for me. He's too smart for that." She shook her head. "Nor do I believe the police will find him. That's why I have to."

Hayes stared across the seat at her. "What are you saying?"

"I need to set a trap for him."

He held up a hand. "Hold on."

"No, I can't let him continue to torment me. I have to find him and put an end to this, one way or another."

Hayes didn't know how to tell her, but decided honesty might be the best approach. "I would imagine he

will find you before you find him." He saw her reaction
to his words. "He's fooling with you because you made a
fool of him the other night. He has only one option. He
needs to right this. Which means there's a really good
chance that he isn't some psycho passing through town
who just happened to see you the other night. He's a
hometown psycho who isn't finished with you."

Her lower lip quivered for a moment before she bit
down on it. "You sound as if you've dealt with this kind
of…person before."

He nodded. "I've crossed paths with several. They're
calculating, cunning and unpredictable—and extremely
dangerous."

She leaned toward him and he was reminded of their
kiss. He could smell her clean scent and remembered
the feel of her in his arms. "Help me set a trap for him.
I don't want to wait until it's on his terms."

"It's not that easy—"

McKenzie drew back. "I'm sorry. I shouldn't have
asked. You have your brother's wedding and you're leaving town—"

"Do you really think I can leave you now?" He
thought of that strange feeling the moment he'd looked
into her eyes three nights ago—not to mention the kiss
just moments before. He took her hands in his, reveling
at the touch of her skin against his. This woman made
him feel things he'd never felt before, never dreamed he
would ever feel.

"I can't let you go after this man alone. I'm staying
until I know you're safe." He wasn't sure he could leave
even then and that scared him more than he wanted to
admit.

He thought of his brother Tag coming to Montana

for Christmas and falling for Lily. Now Tag was getting married and talking about settling in Big Sky. Hayes had thought his brother was nuts to leave behind everything like that.

Hayes felt as if his head were spinning. All he knew for sure was that he had to protect this woman—whatever it took. He couldn't think beyond that, didn't dare.

"I won't be safe as long as he's out there. You said so yourself. I don't see that I have a choice."

A car turned onto the street. The headlights washed over them. Hayes glanced in his rearview mirror as the cop car pulled up behind them.

Hayes didn't have a choice, either. He leaned over and kissed her quickly before climbing out with the note that had been left on her windshield. Like her, he doubted there would be fingerprints on it. Just as he doubted the police would be able to find this man, given how little they had to go on.

The only thing Hayes didn't doubt was that the psycho would be coming for McKenzie.

The police officer bagged the note her attacker had left and promised to let her know if they found any prints. McKenzie could see that Hayes wasn't holding out any more hope than she was.

The cop walked around the neighborhood, shone his flashlight into the bushes and trees, but to no one's surprise, found nothing.

"He's right," Hayes said after the officer left and he walked her back to her car. "The best thing you can do right now would be to take a long vacation somewhere far away from here."

They stood under Montana's big sky. Millions of stars

glittered over their heads and a cool, white moon now buoyed along among them. The June night had turned crisp and cool. This far north even summer nights could chill you. Especially if there was a killer on the loose.

"Do you really think the man would forget about me?" She didn't give him a chance to answer because they both knew that answer. "I can't run away. I would always be looking over my shoulder. No, I have to end this here and soon."

Hayes groaned. "How did I know you were going to say that?"

She shrugged and met his gaze, losing herself in his dark eyes. It would have been easy to get on a plane with him and go to Texas and pretend none of this had happened.

But it *had* happened. Not to mention, she had a business here, people who were counting on her. She wasn't going anywhere—not that Hayes had given her the Texas option to begin with.

She felt strangely calmer as she leaned against the side of her car and looked at the Texas cowboy standing by her. Once she'd settled down enough so she could actually think clearly, she'd made the decision quickly—just as she'd done with her business.

She couldn't wait around for this horrible man to try to abduct her again and do nothing. If Hayes wouldn't help her, then she would figure out something on her own. She'd been on her own and done all right. She wasn't going to let one crazy psycho change that.

"I have another open house tomorrow." She held up her hand before Hayes could argue. "As you said, he knows who I am. He also knows where I am going to be. For all I know he was one of the people who came through the house earlier. I could have talked to him." She shuddered at the thought and hugged herself.

"I wouldn't be at all surprised that he was one of the men who came through today," Hayes said. "Seeing you feeds whatever it is that drives him. He likes seeing you scared. He'll play with you until he's ready to make his move, until an opportunity presents itself."

She was no fool. She was still scared, but knowing that the man wanted her scared made her determined not to let her fear hold her back. "So you're saying it could be a while before he makes his move?"

"Possibly. Unless you give him the opportunity he needs—like at an open house. You do realize this is speculation based on what I know about men like this. As I said earlier, they're unpredictable. I could be completely off base. There is no way to know what he will do next."

She nodded, considering this. "He feels safe because I didn't see his face the night he attacked me. If you're right about what drives him, he won't be able to stay away."

Hayes took off his Stetson and raked a hand through his thick, dark hair. She recalled the feel of those fingers when he'd taken the nape of her neck in his hand during their kiss.

"If you're determined to do this, then I'm staying down here in the valley tonight. I'm also going to the open house tomorrow," Hayes said.

She shook her head. "He won't make his move as long as you're around."

He stuffed his hat back down on his head and stepped to her to take her shoulders in his hands. "He's just waiting for the chance to get you alone again. He will make that happen with or without me around because he knows I can't watch you all the time. I'll be there tomorrow, like it or not."

McKenzie knew she didn't have the strength to tackle this tonight. "All right," she agreed. She had mixed feelings about having Hayes around. On one hand she would definitely feel safer, but he was a distraction she couldn't afford right now. She had to think clearly.

"He'll come to the open house tomorrow."

Hayes nodded in agreement. "That would be my guess. He's trying to build up his confidence. Being around you and you not knowing how close he is...well, that will make him feel more in control."

"Is there any way to get photos of everyone who comes through the open house?"

"Consider it done. I'll also talk to the police about running the license plates of those who show up."

She smiled at him. "I do appreciate what you're trying to do to keep me safe." She sobered as she looked into his handsome face. "I don't like involving you in this. If this man is as dangerous as we both suspect—"

"Don't worry about me. I'll follow you to your condo. But first let me check your car."

McKenzie watched him look under and around her car before popping the hood and checking the engine. "You can't think he'd put a bomb under my hood."

"Not really. But I do think he might disable your car so it stalls on the way to your condo and while you're trying to figure out what is wrong..."

She got the idea. Distraction. That's how she'd fallen into the man's snare the first time. A memory of the dark night at the grocery-store parking lot flashed before her. She'd been fiddling with her keys, her mind on the phone call and Gus. Gus, she thought with a silent curse. Maybe she should have called the police after she found him on her doorstep at the condo. Was this note merely him trying to scare her? Or was it from the man who'd tried to abduct her?

As she looked out into the darkness, McKenzie wasn't sure who would be caught in the trap she hoped to set for her would-be abductor. Whoever he was, she didn't feel him out there watching her. But he had been there. A psycho who, for whatever reason, had set his sights on her.

At her condo, McKenzie unlocked the door while Hayes surveyed the neighborhood. He hated that there were too many places for a man to hide. Also, because Bozeman was so small, he had to assume that the man knew where she lived.

He had McKenzie remain by the door until he could check to make sure they were alone in the condo. The place was neat and clean and sparsely furnished. He got the feeling that she didn't spend much time here other than to sleep.

The lower floor consisted of a kitchen, dining room, living room and half bath. Upstairs he found a full bath and two bedrooms. Just the right size for a single woman who worked all the time.

"Can you tell if anyone has been here?" he asked her when he returned to where he'd left her downstairs just inside the door.

She glanced around, clearly startled by the question. "I don't think so. How would he have gotten in?"

"I didn't see any forced entry, but if the man is some-one you know and has access to your keys…"

"You mean like an old boyfriend?" She shook her head. "No one has a key to my condo. Nor can I recall anyone having access to my keys."

"Good." He met her gaze. "Do you own a weapon?"

She swallowed and looked uncomfortable. "I have pepper spray, Hayes." His name seemed to come of its own volition. She appeared surprised as if she, too, had just realized that she'd never said it before. "I also have a spare bedroom, if you want to…" She looked away.

"Thanks," he said without hesitation. He was planning to stay, whether she liked it or not.

"The spare bedroom—"

"I know where it is," he said.

She nodded. "I can't take being afraid all the time."

"We'll find him." Even as he said it, Hayes hoped he wasn't promising something he couldn't deliver. He *would* find him, but before the man got to McKenzie? That was what worried him.

She glanced at her watch. "Would you like a drink? I could use one." She headed for the kitchen.

He followed. As she pulled out a bottle of wine from the refrigerator, he said, "I'm going to need to know about everyone who came through the open house today—at least all of them you can remember. Do you have something I can write on?"

She poured them each a glass of wine before removing a notebook and pen from the small desk in the corner of the kitchen. They sat down in the living room on furniture that felt and smelled new. He doubted she had many—if any—guests over, including men. No time to date, he suspected.

That also explained why the man who had attacked her had chosen her. A businesswoman with a lot on her mind. She was a classic case of the perfect female victim. Had the man been following her? Or had he picked her at random? Hayes wished he knew. It would help find the bastard.

"Okay, from when the first person came in after you got to the open house…"

She nodded, took a sip of her wine and began to go through them. He quickly weeded out the women and most of the couples.

"There was that one man near the end…" She stared thoughtfully into space for a moment. "You might have seen him. I was talking to him when you arrived."

Hayes recalled a tall man with a head of thick, brown hair and light-colored eyes. He looked like a former football player. In fact, Hayes recalled wondering if the man had played for the Bobcats while attending Montana State University. He'd been wearing a Bobcat jacket.

"Early forties, big, not bad-looking?"

She nodded. "He seemed interested in the house— until I saw him later when he was leaving."

Hayes frowned. "What changed your mind?"

"You're going to think I'm silly, but he hadn't driven to the open house. I realized he must live in the neighborhood."

"He could have parked some distance away."

She nodded. "I suppose, but as I was watching him walk away, he seemed to sense me watching him and turned. It was his expression… This is where you're going to think I'm nuts, but he turned to look back, right at me as if he knew I would be there watching him, and the look on his face…" She took a drink of her wine. "It was as if he'd put something over on me."

Hayes felt a fissure of unease move through him.

"You think it could have been the man who attacked you?"

"He was big enough." She shook her head. "I don't know. He mentioned that he had a wife."

"Probably to put you at ease."

"Maybe. It's just that he seemed…nice, gentle even, almost shy."

"Ted Bundy seemed the same way to *his* victims."

McKenzie finished her wine and poured them both another glass. "Why would he take a chance like that, not just coming to the open house, but actually talking to me?"

"Maybe he wanted to see if you recognized him."

She cupped the wineglass in her hand as she felt a shudder move through her. "Is it possible I was that close to him again and I didn't know it?" That alone terrified her. Could she really not sense the danger?

"It's why the cops take video of people at crime scenes and funerals. Criminals like to return to the scene of the crime. In your case, be close to one of their victims."

"He is safe—until he tries to abduct me again." She shivered. "If he doesn't try again, he'll have gotten away with it." She felt her eyes suddenly widened in alarm. "There have been others, haven't there?"

"More than likely. But that can help. If we find out who this man is, maybe we can place him wherever those other abductions took place."

"You think he *killed* them."

Hayes didn't answer. He didn't have to. "I'm sure the police are looking into other abductions or missing persons around the area…. I'll check with them tomorrow. Tell me about tomorrow's open house."

"It's out in the country. It's fairly…isolated."

"Then I'm definitely going to be there. Don't worry, I'll be discreet. You won't even know I'm around. I'll want to go out earlier than you. Will you be going to your office in the morning even though it's a Sunday?"

"Yes. My job isn't eight to five. Nor five days a week."

"Neither is mine, so I get it," he said, and finished his wine. His gaze met hers and she felt that bubble of excitement rise inside her, along with a longing that she knew only this man could fill. She wanted him, but not like this. Maybe once this was over…

As if sensing her thoughts, he said, "It's late. We should get some rest." He got to his feet.

"The bed is made up in the spare room. There are towels in the bathroom cabinet…."

"Thank you. I'm sure I have everything I need."

Wasn't that what the man at the open house had said?

Hayes met her gaze. "I'll be right down the hall if you need me."

She nodded. She *did* need him. It was that need that kept her silent as she watched him head upstairs. She heard him go into the bathroom and turn on the shower. She could hear water running and closed her eyes at the thought of Hayes naked in her shower. The Texas cowboy had done something no other man had. He'd reminded her she was a woman, a woman with needs other than her career.

McKenzie poured herself another glass of wine, finishing off the bottle. Normally, she had only one glass before bedtime. Tonight, she didn't mind indulging. Better to indulge in wine than in what she would have liked to indulge in. Her life was complicated enough without getting any more involved with Hayes Cardwell than she already was.

The wine made her feel lightheaded. Or was that her fantasies? Upstairs, Hayes came out of the bathroom. She heard him walk down the hall to the spare bedroom. She waited for him to close the door, but he didn't.

Shutting her eyes, she tried not to think about him lying in bed just down the hall from her own bedroom. A wild yearning raced through her as out of control as a wildfire. Her need quickly became a burning desire as it mixed with the wine already coursing through her veins.

McKenzie had always prided herself on thinking logically. She assessed every situation, looked at it from every angle then made a decision based on the facts—not emotion.

With Hayes, she knew she wasn't thinking rationally. She wanted him, needed him, like no man she'd ever met.

But she wouldn't act on it. Couldn't. At least until the crazy after her was caught. Even then, she wasn't sure she could let herself go. She'd been so wrapped up in her business that she hadn't given much thought to men. Now she couldn't stop thinking about Hayes Cardwell, but she would force herself to. She needed her wits about her and if she gave in to whatever this was between them… The thought made her ache.

She wouldn't let herself go there.

Feeling on moral high ground, she took the empty bottle and the glasses into the kitchen. She tossed the bottle in the trash and hand-washed the glasses, dried them and put them away before she went up to bed. Alone.

* * *

Hayes woke to the sound of a phone ringing. He'd had a devil of a time getting to sleep, knowing McKenzie was just down the hall—and that there was a psychopath out there after her. If the man who'd come to the open house was her attacker, then he was definitely brazen. He was practically daring them to catch him.

The phone rang again. He heard McKenzie fumbling to answer it.

"Hello?"

Silence.

"Hello, who is this?"

Hayes was out of bed and down the hall to her room in a matter of a few strides. He reached for the phone. She handed it to him, those amazing eyes of hers wide and terrified. All the color had drained from her face and the hand that relinquished the phone had trembled.

He could hear heavy breathing as he put the phone to his ear. The man on the other end of the line chuckled softly. To his surprise, McKenzie jumped out of bed and ran to the window.

"Who is this?" Hayes demanded.

The chuckle died off. He could almost hear the anger in the breathing just before the call was disconnected. He checked caller ID. Blocked.

"It was him," McKenzie said, turning from the window. She wore a short cotton nightgown that left little to the imagination—not that Hayes's imagination needed any help.

He'd always thought of himself as a strong man. But right now he felt helpless against emotions that threatened to overpower him when he looked at this woman. "McKenzie." He said her name as if that alone could put distance between them and keep him from taking her in his arms.

She turned to him, her voice breaking as she said, "I heard something else besides his breathing." Her gaze locked with his. "I heard my neighbor's wind chimes. He called from those pines below my bedroom window."

Chapter 9

Gus Thompson was lost. He'd driven around town tonight feeling as if his life were over. The last place he'd wanted to go was home to an empty house. He still couldn't believe everything had changed in an instant.

He was thirty-eight years old. Not even in his prime. He would get another job. At least that's what he told himself. And yet just the thought of approaching other Realtors had turned his knees to jelly. He'd never had to actually ask for a job before. His mother had seen that he had jobs from the time he was sixteen. Nepotism wasn't something he'd ever thought about—until now.

If his mother were alive, she would have put in a call, got him on somewhere and he'd just show up for work. She'd had those kinds of connections. Even better, his mother would have made McKenzie pay. Her wrath would have rained down like a firestorm on M.K.

Realty. She might even have put dear McKenzie out of business just for spite.

But his mother was gone and he was jobless and lost. And all because of McKenzie Sheldon.

He hadn't known where he was driving until he found himself in her neighborhood. Parking down the block, he'd cut the engine, having no idea what he was going to do when she returned. Their "talk" earlier had left him cold. He needed more from her than a lukewarm recommendation. He was a great salesman, but if there were even a whiff of gossip that he was difficult to work with or that he hit on women in the office, it would kill the deal.

McKenzie had to hire him back. It was the only way.

As that thought settled over him, he'd seen her come up the street and pull into her drive. He'd started to get out, afraid how far he would have to go to get her to agree to rehire him, when an SUV had pulled up in her drive next to her vehicle.

Gus had ducked back into his car as he watched the Texas cowboy get out. McKenzie and the man headed for her front door. "What the—" They'd disappeared inside. A few minutes later, the cowboy had come back out and driven his vehicle into her garage.

It was the same cowboy he'd seen her with at Big Sky. The same man he'd followed to the Cardwell Ranch only to have neither appear again even after Gus had waited an hour.

Determined to wait this time, though, he settled in. The cowboy would leave before daylight, he told himself. He must have fallen asleep because something awakened him. He sat up to find it was the middle of the night. All the lights were off inside the condo—just like the other condos on the block.

Angry and frustrated and feeling even worse, he was about to leave when he noticed something odd. A man had been sitting in an old panel van up the street. Gus watched him get out and head into the trees next to McKenzie's condo. A few moments later, Gus saw a light flash in the trees. Not like a flashlight. More like a small screen, making Gus suspect the man was making a call on his cell phone next to her condo.

How many men did McKenzie have on the string? he wondered. Definitely the cowboy.

So who was the man in the trees? His heart began to pound as he realized it could be the same guy who'd attacked her.

Before he could react, the man came out of the trees, walking fast. He jumped into the van. Gus hurriedly started his car, a plan crystallizing as he drove. If this guy was McKenzie's attacker and he could catch him, she would have to give him back his job.

Hayes, dressed only in jeans, ran back to his room and grabbed his gun after the call and what McKenzie had heard on the other end of the line. He raced down the stairs and out the front door. If she was right, the man had been right outside her condo in the dense trees.

But as he reached the trees, he heard tires squeal and looked out on the street as a large car sped past. This time, though, the car passed under a streetlamp and he was able to get the license plate number.

Back in the condo, he found McKenzie wrapped in a fluffy white robe and matching slippers. She stood hugging herself at the front window.

"Did you…" Her words died off as she saw his expression. "He got away."

"I got his license plate number as he was speeding off." Hayes was already dialing the police. He asked for the same officer who they'd talked to earlier and told him about the phone call and the car.

"Give me a minute," the cop said as he ran the plate. "The car belongs to Ruth Thompson. Wait a minute. It's the same car Gus Thompson admitted to driving the night Ms. Sheldon was attacked."

"She has a restraining order on him."

"I see that. I'll make sure he gets picked up."

"Thank you." Hayes hung up and turned to look at McKenzie. "Did you actually see him in the trees?"

She shook her head. "He was just a shape. Large."

"The car that I saw racing away was Gus Thompson's mother's." She groaned. "Is it possible he also made the phone call?"

She seemed to think for a moment. "The man didn't say anything, he just…breathed." She closed her eyes and sighed. "It would be like Gus to try to torment me. He's furious that I fired him. So you think it wasn't the man who attacked me?"

"Not unless that man was Gus Thompson."

"What the devil?" He looked in his rearview mirror, surprised that the car he'd seen earlier was still following him. He knew it couldn't be either McKenzie Sheldon or the cowboy he'd seen her with before. So who was it?

Not the police or they would have already pulled him over.

He had spotted the tail right away, but hadn't thought anything of it. He had too much on his mind to care.

What was the cowboy doing at her house? He could only imagine. He gritted his teeth, remembering the male voice on the phone. The Texas accent had been a dead giveaway. It had to be the same cowboy, the one who'd rescued her at the grocery-store parking lot. The same one he'd seen her with before. And now the man was in her condo with her? Close enough he'd gotten on her *phone?*

A wave of disgust and fury washed over him like acid on his skin. He'd never taken women out of any kind of anger. If anything, it was about control. So this scalding fury made him feel impotent. He had to do something about this situation and soon.

But how could he get control again—and quickly? If he acted out in anger, he would be more likely to make a mistake, one that could cost him dearly. No, he had to rein in his emotions. He couldn't let this woman and her hero cowboy get to him.

But even as he'd thought it, he felt his blood boiling. How dare the two of them! It was as if they were laughing behind his back. Mocking him. Now the cowboy had something that belonged to him. The woman was *his,* not some stupid bystander's who'd come to her rescue.

He had to think, plan. The woman had known he was outside her window. How? He remembered the way she'd stood at the window at the open house, watching him leave. He'd sensed her watching him. Had she also sensed how close he was to her tonight?

Or had it been something else? That's when he remembered the wind chimes. He'd noticed them when he'd been waiting in the trees. They had been tinkling lightly so he hadn't paid much attention. But right when she'd answered the phone, a gust had caught them…

She'd heard the wind chimes. The woman was more astute than any of the others, a worthier prey. It should have filled him with pride since she was now his.

The only thing spoiling it was the cowboy.

He thought of how he'd planned it, borrowing the old van he sometimes used at work, waiting until she'd be asleep before he'd called. He'd wanted to wake her, to catch her off guard. He hadn't known she wouldn't be alone.

A curse on his lips, he glanced again in his rearview mirror. The car was still with him! The driver had been staying back, but clearly following him. It was one reason he hadn't gone home. Instead, he'd been driving around, trying to clear his head and ditch the tail. But the fool was still with him.

It couldn't be the cowboy, could it? No. Then who? He reached under the seat for the tire iron he kept there, and was about to throw on his brakes and see just who was following him when he caught the flash of cop lights behind them.

Fear turned his blood to slush—until he realized that the cop wasn't after him, but whoever had been following him. He kept driving up another block before he turned and circled back. He had to know who'd seen him at the condo. Who was stupid enough to put himself in jeopardy?

Fortunately, as he drove by, neither the cop nor the man bent over his car's hood being handcuffed paid any attention to him.

The man being arrested wasn't the Texas cowboy, but he did look familiar.

After Hayes left the condo this morning, McKenzie locked the door behind him as he'd ordered. She was still upset that the man who'd called last night had been right outside her condo. *He knew where she lived!*

But if the man was Gus… She still couldn't believe that even though the police had called to tell her that the car Hayes had seen speeding away belonged to Gus Thompson and that Gus had been arrested, but was expected to be out on bail soon.

"I really don't like you doing this open house," Hayes had said this morning before he left. "This nutcase is going to strike when you least expect it."

"Then I will have to be on guard all the time."

Once ready for the open house, she called to remind him that she had to stop at her office.

"I'll meet you there," he said.

"That really isn't necessary."

"I'll be the judge of that."

Only Cynthia and another real-estate saleswoman were in the office this morning. The others either had open houses or had taken the day off. She'd always felt a sense of euphoria when she walked into her office. She'd worked hard for this agency and felt a sense of pride that she'd done it alone through hard work.

But today she felt edgy. She couldn't forget for a moment that she was being hunted like an animal. It set her nerves on end and made her start whenever the phone rang.

McKenzie knew she had to pull it together. Last night she'd been angry, filled with a determination to track down this bastard and stop him. But in the light of day, she was too aware of how ill-prepared she was. She'd gotten lucky the other night and had been able to fight the man off—at least long enough that Hayes had seen what was going on and had saved her.

She couldn't count on his saving her again. That's what he was trying to tell her earlier at the condo.

And yet when she saw him drive up, she'd never been so happy to see anyone. "I told you I was driving myself," she said, glancing at the clock. The open house wouldn't start for several hours.

"There's somewhere we need to go." He sounded mysterious, but she followed him out to his SUV and climbed in. He drove out into the country, down a narrow dirt road until they were back into the foothills away from town.

When he stopped, she glanced around. "What are we doing?"

"You really think you're ready for this?" he asked as he pulled out a gun.

She felt her eyes widen in alarm. He held the gun out to her. "You ever fired one before? I didn't think so. You think you can kill someone?"

"Is this really necessary? I have pepper spray that I carry—"

"Pepper spray isn't going to stop this guy. I've seen the way you grip your keys when you get out of the car. If he gets close enough to grab you, your keys aren't going to stop him, either. You're going to have to kill him or he is going to kill you."

She stared at the gun for a moment. Then she swallowed the lump in her throat as she reached for it. Her hand trembled. She stilled it as she got a good grip on the pistol.

"Will you show me how to fire it?"

He'd raised a brow. "You really think you can do this?"

"I don't think I have a choice, do you?"

He took the gun from her. "Come on, then." Climbing out he led the way to a gully where he set up a half-dozen rusted beer cans on rocks. "Familiarize yourself with the gun. Here is how you load it. Here is how you fire it."

Turning toward the cans, he showed her how to hold the gun and take aim. She did as he had done, looked down the barrel and pulled the trigger. The gun kicked in her hand, the shot going wild.

"Don't close your eyes when you pull the trigger," he said.

She tried again, holding the gun tighter. The next shot was closer. The third one pinged into a can, knocking it to the ground. She felt a surge of satisfaction, missed the next shot, but centered the cans on the next two.

Feeling cocky, she turned to look at him. "Well?"

"You killed a few old beer cans. You will have only a split second to make the decision whether to pull the trigger or not—and that's if you can pull the gun fast enough when the man surprises you," Hayes said. "He'll be counting on those few seconds when you hesitate."

"Where are you?" Tag asked, not long before noon. "I checked your cabin. It hasn't been slept in."

Hayes was driving north, leaving Bozeman and traveling out into the country past wheat fields broken by subdivisions. "I stayed at McKenzie's last night. Quit smirking. Nothing happened—at least not what you're thinking."

"Oh?"

He found the road he needed and turned down it. The sun had cleared the mountains to the east this morning and now splashed the valley in gold. "This guy who attacked her is still after her. She's determined to find him before he finds her. I'm helping her."

"Did you read something on a fortune cookie that says if you save someone's life, you're responsible for it?"

"I can't just leave her," Hayes said as he saw the house come into view.

"Really? That's all it is, just you needing to play hero?"

"I can't get into this right now. I'll call you as soon as I know something definite, but I might be staying until your wedding. Also, I told McKenzie we will take the restaurant building at Big Sky. I haven't talked to Austin but—"

"Was this McKenzie Sheldon's doing? Never mind. Whatever the reason you've changed your mind, I'm glad. You won't be sorry."

"I hope not."

"Now try not to get yourself killed before my wedding."

As Tag hung up, Hayes sped up the SUV, driving past the house and up the road for a half mile before he turned around and headed back, going slower this time.

The ranch-style house was huge, sprawled across twenty acres with a guesthouse, barn and stables behind it, along with an assortment of outbuildings. All kinds of places for a person to hide. He noticed there was also a dirt road that went up into the Bridger Mountains behind the house.

As he drove on by the house a second time, he called McKenzie. "Get someone to do the open house for you. It's too dangerous."

Gus had been arrested last night for violating the restraining order. But McKenzie had received a call earlier, warning her that he was already out on bail.

What had Hayes upset was what else the policewoman had told her. "He swears he saw a man beside your condo last night using a cell phone. He says he was chasing the man when he was arrested."

"Did he get a good look at the man?" McKenzie had asked.

"He says he didn't."

The policewoman hadn't believed Gus about any of it.

Hayes didn't know what to believe. Gus could be behind both the note on McKenzie's car and the call last night. Gus was angry, according to the police, which gave him reason to want to torment his former boss, even if he wasn't the man who'd attacked her.

"It wasn't Gus," she'd again said this morning on the drive back from shooting the gun.

"But Gus would know about the convention speech and the open house," Hayes had argued. "And he was definitely at your condo last night."

"You said he sped away. You didn't see another car?"

He hadn't been looking for another car once he'd seen Gus speeding away.

"I went by Gus Thompson's house," he said now. "He's not there. This open house is in the paper with your name on it, right?"

"It's not Gus."

"Okay, then if true, I would say you have two angry men after you now. Which is yet another reason you shouldn't do the open house."

"The police are going to have a car in the area of the open house."

"The area is too large and there are too many places a man could be hiding."

"*You'll* be there."

Her words hit him at heart level. "Why do you think I'm so worried?"

"I trust you."

Her first mistake. He opened his mouth to speak, but shook his head, instead. A part of him was touched by her words. Another part was afraid he would fail her.

"Hayes?"

"I'm still here."

"I know. I'm grateful."

He sighed. "Let me know when you leave the office for the open house. Keep your phone on. I won't stop worrying until I know you made the drive safely. Then, once you get here, I can really start worrying."

"So you agree with me that he'll show?"

"He'll be here. He couldn't possibly pass up such a perfect location with all these places to hide. The question is where."

Gus was no longer angry at McKenzie. He was *furious*. She hadn't really had him *arrested?* Not when he was following the man who he assumed had attacked her.

When he'd first gotten released from jail he'd thought about just letting the crazy bastard get her. She deserved it, right?

After a while, though, he'd tamped down his fury, focusing instead on the look he'd see on her face when he caught her stalker. When he *saved* her.

He dug the handgun from the drawer beside his bed. He'd bought the pistol at a gun show years ago. The gun was loaded, but he grabbed another box of ammunition.

As he walked through the kitchen, he grabbed a sharp knife. He put the knife in the top of his boot. Today he'd worn jeans, hiking boots, a long-sleeved shirt. He had some dirty business to get done today.

In the garage, he walked past his mother's car to his SUV. He felt like a commando going into battle. The man after McKenzie had been at her condo last night. That had been a gutsy move. So Gus figured, given where the open house was being held, that the man would show. All Gus had to do was get there early for a place to hide out and wait. It would be like shooting fish in a bucket—barrel, whatever.

He'd checked out the house and grounds when the ranchette had first come on the market, so he knew where to park the SUV so it wouldn't be noticed. There was literally a forest that backed up to the property. He knew the perfect spot where he would be able to see anyone coming.

McKenzie grew more anxious as she neared the ranchette. She remembered what Hayes had said last night. But her car seemed to be running fine. However, she was relieved when she reached the turnoff to the house.

She didn't see Hayes anywhere around, but then again, she didn't expect to. He was here, though, she assured herself. The property was twenty acres, just as Hayes had said. While she'd seen the place before, she found herself looking at it from a totally different perspective than she had the first time.

Now she saw all the places a man could hide and wait for that moment when she was alone. And she would be alone some of the time because the asking price of this place was high enough that she didn't expect a lot of viewers.

Fear rippled over her, dimpling her skin and giving her a chill as she got out at the turnoff to put up the Open House sign. She couldn't help looking over her shoulder, hurrying to get the sign up and back into her vehicle as quickly as possible.

She was shaking by the time she climbed behind the wheel again. Did she really think she could do this? To catch this man she would eventually have to come face-to-face with him. He had to be caught in action. Her heart began to pound at the memory of his arm around her throat, the way he'd picked her up off her feet—

Turning down the road, she heard another vehicle. An SUV turned down the long drive behind her. She glanced at the car's clock. Her first viewer was early. As she pulled in, she saw that the car had slowed as if to study the place at a distance. Hurrying, she climbed out, taking everything with her as she moved toward the empty house. Her heart hammered in her chest as she opened the door and felt a blast of stale, cold air hit her.

She had to calm down. Taking a few breaths, she reminded herself how far she'd come. She hadn't gotten her success by being a wimp. She straightened her back as she put down the flyers and turned to watch the SUV cruise slowly up the road toward her. The sun glinted off the windshield so she couldn't see the driver.

This could be him.

Or he could already be in the house waiting for me.

Chapter 10

Last night had been a close call. Some fool had chased him. Fortunately, the police had pulled the man over. He'd gotten a good look at the man's familiar face but it wasn't until he got home that he placed him. He'd seen Gus Thompson's face enough times when he'd been perusing the real-estate ads looking for McKenzie Sheldon's smiling face.

Just the thought of her made him feel better. But he couldn't ignore the fact that the man had given him chase last night. Did McKenzie now have *two* men protecting her? That made his stomach roil. It was bad enough that the cowboy kept getting in his way. Now this other fool?

To settle himself down, he thought about the open house and Ms. Sheldon. He would see her again today. Unfortunately, just seeing her wasn't helping much anymore. He needed more. He smiled in memory of the terror he'd seen on McKenzie Sheldon's face last night when she'd found the note and what he'd heard in her voice when he'd called and woken her up.

But even that wasn't enough. He had to get his hands on her.

True, she had needed a reminder that he was still here, that he was still coming for her. It had been a dangerous thing to do, calling attention to himself that way. But he relished in the fear, both his own and, of course, hers.

He'd been curious to see, after the note and the phone call, whether or not she would go ahead with the open house today. The listing was out in the country, miles from town and enough acreage and buildings that not even her cowboy or Gus Thompson, real-estate salesman extraordinaire, could keep her safe.

She'd proven to be a worthy opponent. But today would tell if the woman was equal to the challenge.

He'd already decided that he had to show up at the open house. She might be suspicious of him after yesterday since he'd been one of only a handful of men who'd come alone to the open house.

Today he would assure her she had nothing to fear from him.

After all, the one thing he could do well was *act* normal. He'd spent his life fooling people—even those closest to him. He knew exactly how he would play it and couldn't wait.

Hayes felt his stomach tighten as viewers began to arrive. When he'd spoken to the police earlier, they'd agreed to run the plates of those attending the open house. They'd asked the sheriff's department to send a car out to the area, as well.

Given the price of this so-called ranchette, he'd thought that number would be low. He'd been surprised by the turnout.

Most were just curious, he was betting. But some actually appeared to be interested, walking much of the grounds, looking in the many structures. He'd heard that expensive houses in the area had continued to sell, even during the recession. It was easy to understand why people fell in love with Bozeman's charm, along with the beautiful valley, the nearby mountains and inexhaustible outdoor entertainment.

He took down each license plate number and snapped a photo of the people attending. He had a half dozen written down when the man drove up. He recognized the man right away as the one he'd seen talking to McKenzie the day before at the open house. Was this her attacker? He was dressed in jeans, boots and a Western shirt and had a cocky way about him.

As the man climbed out of his SUV, he glanced around as if taking in the place for the first time, then he headed for the front door.

McKenzie had been talking to a middle-aged couple and turned to find the man directly behind her.

"I'm sorry. I didn't mean to startle you." He held out his hand. "Bob Garwood."

McKenzie battled back her initial surprise and took his hand. It was cool to the touch, the handshake firm. She even found her voice. "It's nice to meet you, Mr. Garwood."

"Please, call me Bob." He let go of her hand and glanced around the living area. "I like this much better than yesterday's listing. How many acres?"

"Twenty. Most of it is now leased for hay."

He nodded. "That's great." His gaze came back to hers. "Mind if I take one of those?"

She handed him a sales flyer. Her hand was hardly shaking.

"Sheldon, right? McKenzie Sheldon. I almost called you last night. You gave me your card with your cell phone number, remember?"

She nodded numbly. If this was the man who'd attacked her, then he *had* called her last night. In fact, he'd been outside her condo. Her heart began to pound harder.

He smiled. "This might seem a little forward, but I wanted to ask you to dinner sometime."

"I don't date clients."

His smile broadened as he pulled out his card and handed it to her. "Good thing I'm not a client yet."

With that he walked away, his gaze going from the sales flyer in his hand to the house as if he seriously was looking for something to buy. She glanced down at the card. Robert Garwood. Apparently, he sold high-tech workout equipment for gyms.

"Are you all right?"

She jumped before she recognized the voice and turned to find Hayes behind her. "How long have you been here?"

"Long enough to hear him ask you for a date."

She let out a nervous laugh. "Maybe that's all he was doing, just hitting on me."

"Maybe. I'll run his name. Bob Garwood, right?"

She nodded as a few more cars pulled up out front. Two women climbed out of one vehicle, a couple out of another and one man, alone.

"You remember him from yesterday's open house?" Hayes asked.

The men's faces were all starting to blend together. "I think so."

"I'll be close by if you need me," he whispered and left.

McKenzie braced herself as the man who'd just arrived looked up at the house, then started up the walk. She recognized him as being one from yesterday's open house. As she took a closer look at the couple, she realized the husband also looked familiar.

"Holler if you need me," Hayes said and left out the back way.

McKenzie jumped as the front door opened. She plastered a smile on her face as the group entered. The lone man took a flyer, gave her a nod and moved off through the house behind the two women. The husband she recognized from the day before came up to her.

"You're a busy woman," he said. "Didn't I see you yesterday at an open house in town?"

She nodded, wondering if he really didn't remember. He was large and there was something about his light blue eyes that made her feel naked. He was the one who'd acted as if he was pulling something on her yesterday.

His gaze locked with hers and she felt a shiver move through her. She tried to repress it as she handed him a sales flyer.

He nodded, his gaze still on her as if he was trying to place her.

McKenzie tried to pull herself together. She'd been so determined last night, so sure she wanted to trap the man. But being this close to a possible suspect...

He was still looking at her.

"Jason?"

"Sorry," he said, turning to the woman with him. "I was just lost in thought for a minute there." He let out a self-deprecating laugh. "I'm Jason Mathews. This is my wife, Emily."

She shook the wife's hand, then Jason Mathews's. He had a firm handshake and held her hand a little too long, making her even more nervous.

"I was surprised when Jason suggested we buy something larger," Emily said. She was a small woman with dark hair and eyes. Her handshake had been limp and cold. As she spoke, she kept looking at her husband. "We own a house in town that's paid for, but I would love a place in the country. This might be too much for us, though. I hate to even ask what it costs."

Jason Mathews smiled at his wife. "Well, let's have a look. You might be surprised what we can afford." He gave McKenzie a conspiratorial wink and handed her his card before leading his wife toward the kitchen.

McKenzie tried to catch her breath as she glanced down at the card in her hand. Jason Mathews. Under his name was: Antiquities Appraiser and his business number.

She groaned inwardly as she realized how foolish she had been. The man apparently really was interested in buying a house. With a sigh, she turned to welcome more people into the house.

But every man who came in alone to see the ranchette made her wonder if he was the one she had to fear.

There were too many people here. He finally found himself alone next to one of the outbuildings and took a breath. He couldn't believe how smooth he'd been when he'd seen McKenzie Sheldon again. It had taken some of the sting out of failing. He couldn't wait to get her alone.

Talking to McKenzie Sheldon had his blood running hot, though. He felt his need growing, worse this time because of his failure. Just the thought of his hands on her bare skin— The things he would make her do. The things he would do to her.

A flash of light caught his attention. He stepped back into the shade of the building and cupped his hands to look up the hillside toward the forest. There was someone up there in the barn loft. The flash must have been binoculars. A cop? Or that damned cowboy?

He'd known the cowboy would be here protecting McKenzie. It irritated him, but would give him such satisfaction when he stole the woman from the cowboy right in front of his eyes. He smiled just thinking about it.

In the shadow of the building, he waited and watched, hoping for a glimpse of whoever was hiding up in the barn loft. Finally, his patience paid off. He caught a glimpse of a face and swore.

It was that man who'd followed him last night from McKenzie's condo, the same man he'd witnessed getting arrested. Obviously, Gus Thompson had gotten out of jail.

He didn't need to speculate on who the man was looking for. Stupid fool.

A hot well of need rushed through his blood. The women he took fulfilled a variety of his needs on several levels. At first, killing them had been just a precaution, but over time he'd begun to enjoy that part, as well.

If he couldn't have McKenzie just yet, well, maybe he could satisfy at least one of his yearnings.

* * *

Gus caught movement out of the corner of his eye. He had found the perfect spot in the barn loft. Through a small window, he had been able to watch the property as well as the comings and goings at the house. He'd picked the barn because he'd known that few people would come all the way up the hillside to the big barn, let alone climb up to the hayloft.

A few had made the hike but only given the barn a cursory look. The stables were much more interesting, and even some of the outbuildings. But since the place was immaculate, all the buildings painted white with dark green trim, it was easy to see that everything was well maintained.

He could sell this place in a heartbeat, he thought with aching regret. What did McKenzie know about selling this property? It should have been his listing.

He was thinking that when he saw movement off to his right in the pine trees. Gus turned, fear making his movement jerky. He'd forgotten why he was here for a moment and that kind of distraction was just when the man who had attacked McKenzie would take advantage.

But to his surprise, there was no one in the pines next to the barn. The breeze stirred the branches, casting shadows over the dry needles on the ground.

He reminded himself that he couldn't get caught here by anyone or he would be going back to jail.

He might have convinced himself that he'd imagined the movement if he hadn't heard a sound below him. As his heart began to pound, he pulled the pistol he'd brought and moved cautiously toward the hole in the floor where the ladder came up.

He'd lied to the cops about the man he'd seen at McKenzie's condo. Even though it had been dark and the man had been dressed in a hooded black sweatshirt, he'd gotten a pretty decent look at him in the streetlamp. Once he saw him again, he'd know him.

He heard nothing below him. He thought about going down the ladder when he realized there was another way up into the loft—a second ladder on the other side of the large stack of hay.

Gun ready, he cautiously moved in that direction. The smell of the hay and dust filled his nostrils. As the floor beneath his feet creaked, he couldn't hold back the sneeze. He stopped and listened again. No sound other than the breeze in the pines nearby.

There was no one. He felt both relieved and disappointed. His only hope of getting his job back was saving McKenzie, he thought as he heard a slight rustle in the stack of hay next to him.

Hayes mentally kicked himself as he walked the perimeter of the property one last time. The open house had ended almost an hour ago but there were some visitors who were just now leaving. He'd texted McKenzie just moments ago. She'd texted back that she was fine. He tried to relax since the stragglers were either couples or several groups of women. No lone male. At least not one who he'd seen.

Earlier he'd found tracks coming from the road behind the house. But with the property bordering the forest, there were too many places to hide for him to search for a vehicle. He couldn't be sure that the tracks weren't from the owner or one of the people viewing the house and property.

He'd also found a place where someone had stood

for a while on a rise with a view of the house. The boot tracks were men-sized, but they could belong to anyone. He felt as if he were looking for a needle in a haystack. He couldn't even be sure the man who'd attacked McKenzie was even here.

Since arming her with the gun, he'd had his misgivings. The gun had been more about making him feel better than any real protection for her. Now he hoped he hadn't made things worse and she shot some innocent fool who surprised her.

But he couldn't watch her all the time. Was it wrong to want her to have a fighting chance? Whether or not the gun would give her that…well, he couldn't say. It would all depend on when her attacker decided to strike again.

He was about to head for the house when something caught his eye. For a moment, he almost ignored it. He was anxious to get to McKenzie. The last of the viewers were leaving. That would mean she was alone.

Staring up at the barn, he saw what had drawn his attention. The barn had four small octagonal windows across one side on the loft level. He saw now that there was something in one of the barn windows that hadn't been there earlier.

Hayes glanced down the hillside toward the house, torn. Whatever was in the barn window probably was nothing. He needed to get to McKenzie. And yet… He quickly texted her.

Everyone gone?

Yes.

He could almost feel the relief in that one word.

Lock all the doors and wait for me.

Pocketing his phone, he walked quickly up the hillside toward the barn.

Earlier it had been hot, but now with the waning sun, the air felt cool. He could smell the pines, hear the breeze rustling the boughs. As he neared the barn, he slowed. A prickling at his neck made him pull his weapon before he stepped into the cool, hollow darkness.

The inside of the barn was empty. He glanced overhead to the loft, then at the ladder. There was fresh manure on several of the steps. Someone had been up there, someone who'd come in through the corral where the horses were kept.

At the foot of the ladder, he saw that there was another way up into the loft—a second set of stairs, these much easier to climb. Moving to them, he began to climb, the only sound inside the cavernous barn the pounding of his heart.

Hayes slowed near the top, weapon ready. The moment he peered over the top, he saw the man sprawled on the loft floor, the strewn hay around him discolored with the man's blood.

As he eased up through the opening to the loft floor, he saw that the man's throat had been sliced from ear to ear. From the color of the blood straining the hay, he hadn't been dead long.

Hayes hurriedly surveyed the area, then careful not to contaminate the scene, checked the man's wallet and identification.

Gus Thompson, the man McKenzie had fired.

Chapter 11

As Hayes came through the door, McKenzie turned, clearly startled. Hayes saw her hand go to the gun in her bag, but stop short when she recognized him. Relief washed over her features as she dropped the bag and stepped into his arms.

"You're shaking," he said as he hugged her to him.

"The deputies wouldn't tell me anything, just to stay in the house. I saw the ambulance. I was so afraid it was you. What happened?"

"It's Gus Thompson. I found him in the barn on the property."

"Gus?"

"He's dead. He was…murdered."

McKenzie shook her head in obvious disbelief as she stepped out of his embrace. *"Murdered?"*

"The sheriff's department is investigating. That's all I can tell you."

She looked as stunned as he'd been when he'd ID'd the dead man. "What was Gus…?"

"Your guess is as good as mine."

"If he was the one who attacked me…" Her voice trailed off. "He wasn't."

"It doesn't appear so, but he definitely seemed to be stalking you. It could be he crossed paths with your attacker."

"So my attacker was here! He was someone who came through the house."

"Maybe. As I told you, with a property this size, he may have sneaked onto the place without anyone seeing him."

"Except Gus." She shivered. "I can't believe he's dead."

"I'm sure the deputies will want to question you about who came through the open house."

"But I don't know *anything*. A half-dozen men came through alone, but that isn't unusual."

"What about that man who asked you out? Bob Garwood."

She shook her head. "He's not the first man who came to an open house hoping to get a date with the Realtor. There were other men who could have been the one who attacked me." She described several of the men who'd come through. "There was one, Jason Mathews. He gave me a funny feeling, but he came through with his wife, Emily, so…."

"I'll check him out along with the others but there is a good chance the man who killed Gus didn't come into the house."

"You took down all the license plate numbers?"

"I did. I've turned them over to the sheriff's department." He hated to get her hopes up. If he was right about this man, the killer had gone years learning how to not get caught. He was good at this and he knew it. "We might get lucky, though."

McKenzie had stopped trembling, but she was still shocked and shaken. After she'd talked to the deputies, Hayes had followed her back to her condo. She'd worked so hard, determined to be successful and independent. She hadn't wanted to need anyone. Now her carefully built world was coming apart at the seams, and it scared her more than she wanted to admit how dependent she'd become on Hayes Cardwell.

She had to get control of her life again. That meant she needed answers—even those she knew she didn't want to hear. "You said you were going to do some research to see if other women... There have been others, haven't there?"

"Maybe you should sit down," he suggested as they moved into the living room.

She shook her head, crossing her arms over her chest as if she could hold back the fear that filled her. "Just tell me."

"More than two dozen have disappeared over the last ten years. The more recent ones match your profile."

"*My* profile?"

"Successful, single businesswomen who work late, shop late, have a lot on their plates."

She tried to swallow the lump in her throat. "I'm his type, that's what you're saying. Did any of them...?"

"None got away. I believe you might be the first."

"Then they are all…"

"Still missing."

She tried not to imagine the other women. "In other words, they're probably dead." She waited, seeing that he knew more than he was telling her.

"Several have turned up in shallow graves. They all went missing mostly out West. I suspect this man travels with his job. Since you have been the only one who he attempted to abduct in this area, I think there is a good chance that he lives here." At her frown, he added, "Predators don't normally hunt in their backyards. Too dangerous."

"But he *did.*"

Hayes nodded. "With what I know about his type, he probably can go for a length of time and then something just snaps or builds to the point where he can't help himself."

"So I just happened to be in the wrong place at the wrong time."

"Probably."

"But now he knows who I am and if I'm the only one that ever got away…"

"That's why you can't stay here."

She shook her head. "How long do you think I can hide from him, Hayes? I have a business to run. I need to work."

He shook his head. "I don't have all the answers."

"I know." She looked into his kind, handsome face. He hadn't asked for any of this. All she wanted to do was bury her face in his strong chest. In his arms, she felt safe. But Hayes wouldn't always be there to hold her and protect her. It was one reason she had to know everything she could about the man after her.

"You talked to the police about Gus?" She saw the answer on his face. "Tell me."

"The coroner said Gus was hit with a piece of pipe. The blow wasn't enough to kill him, but probably knocked him down, at least stunned him long enough for the killer to..." Hayes met her gaze. "Are you sure you want to hear this?"

"I got the man killed."

"That's not true and you know it. You had a restraining order against him. If Gus had stayed away, he would still be alive today."

She stepped to the window, her back to him, her mind reeling. "What was Gus doing in that barn?"

"The police think he was spying on you. They found binoculars near the window and a bag with candy bars. It was the bag I saw in the window fluttering in the breeze that made me go up to the barn. He had hooked it on a nail next to him. When the breeze came up..."

She turned to look at him. "Why would he spy on me?"

"You said he wanted to talk to you. Maybe he thought he could get you alone and convince you to give him back his job." Hayes shook his head. "Who knows."

"The police think his killer was the man who tried to abduct me, don't they?" She didn't wait for him to confirm it. "Gus swore to the police that he followed him last night after the man called me from down in the pines by the wind chimes. If he was telling the truth, maybe he wasn't there spying on me but looking for the man. But why would Gus do something like that?"

"Maybe he wanted to play hero and it got him killed."

"If he was looking for my attacker, that means he could recognize him. *Gus lied to the police.*" That shouldn't have surprised her. It would be just like Gus. Tears filled her eyes. "This is all because I fired him."

Hayes stepped to her and took her in his arms. She didn't fight it. She rested her cheek against his chest, soaking in his warmth, hoping to chase away the chill that had settled in her, even for a little while.

"McKenzie, none of this is your fault. Gus made some very poor decisions. That's what got him killed."

"Playing hero, isn't that what you called it?" she asked as she pulled back to look into his dark eyes. "So anyone who tries to protect me—"

"Don't," he said, as if seeing where she was headed with this.

She shook her head and stepped away from him. "He'll come after you next. I can't let that happen."

"I'm not Gus. He wasn't trained for this. I am."

"I want you to go back to Texas."

"Ain't happenin'," Hayes said. "I'm staying right here and there is nothing you can do to drive me away, so don't even try."

She looked up at him, her eyes brimming with tears. "I couldn't bear it if anything happened to you because of me."

He reached her in two long strides and took her shoulders in his hands. "Nothing is going to happen to me. Or to you. We are going to catch this guy." He could see that she didn't believe that. He wondered if he did himself.

"I thought if we set a trap for him… I thought today…" Tears spilled down her cheeks. She had a swipe at them. "It was a stupid idea and look what happened because of me."

He could see her fighting to be strong. He'd never met

a more courageous woman. "It wasn't stupid. He was there, just as you'd thought he would be. Unfortunately, Gus was, too. Listen, I have a plan. It's dangerous—"

She laughed, but there was no humor in it. "More dangerous than waiting around for him to attack me again after what he did today?"

"If I am right about this man, he's had some experience at this. He'll *expect* a trap. He knows the police and now sheriff's department are involved. I'm sure he knows I'm involved, as well."

"What are you saying? That he'll lie low for a while?"

He nodded. He didn't want to tell her that killing Gus would have relieved some of the killer's…tension. The man would be satisfied for a while. "But whatever drives him will eventually reach the point where—"

"He'll try to grab some other woman!"

"No. He can't move on until he's finished with you."

"You don't know that."

"Not positively, but based on what I know about these types of predators…" He held her gaze. "But understand. The longer he goes, the more dangerous he will be."

"Then you need to go back to Texas. Like you said, he knows you're involved. If he killed Gus because he thought he was in the way…"

"Who knows what happened with Gus. The truth is, I believe you're the only one who will be able to satisfy his need."

McKenzie swallowed. "This plan you have…"

"Right now, you're too accessible. He can fill some of his need too easily by simply seeing you and seeing that you're afraid or cutting off part of your hair as a souvenir. You need to hide out for a while. The longer we let him dangle, the more his confidence will decline.

He won't know where you've gone. Then when you sur-face again…he'll make mistakes."

She felt her eyes fill with tears. "At least that's what you're hoping for."

He nodded, not telling her what else he was hop-ing for.

"So I hide out until…until what?"

"Until he can't take it any longer." Hayes pulled her into his arms and stroked her back. He was hoping that he would find the bastard before that happened. "You have to trust me." He drew back to look into her eyes. "Do you trust me, McKenzie?"

She nodded.

"Then the two of us are going to Cardwell Ranch."

He licked at a spot of blood on his wrist that he'd missed and smiled. When he closed his eyes he could feel the warm flow of blood running over his fingers. But the best part was the look in Gus Thompson's eyes when the man realized he was going to die—and with his own knife.

The fool had gone for a knife in his boot after his gun had been taken away from him. It had been too easy to cut his throat. True, killing him had been a risky thing to do, especially killing him in the barn loft. But the dried hay would make it hard for forensics to find any-thing. Not to mention all the people who had tromped through that place.

He was reasonably sure he'd pulled it off without a hitch. He'd wiped off most of the blood on his hand in the hay, having cut the man's throat from behind him. Then he had slipped out of the barn to wash his hands in the hose on the back side of the barn.

He'd been careful not to leave any footprints next to the faucet. The police would suspect that he had to clean up. The creek would probably be their first choice, the hose behind the barn too obvious.

Either way, he'd managed to clean himself up and leisurely walk back to the house without causing anyone to take note of him.

All in all, it had been an amazing day. He felt better about everything. Now all he had to do was finish McKenzie Sheldon and life would be back to normal. Well, as normal as his life could be, under the circumstances.

But he was in no hurry. Killing Gus Thompson had filled his growing need. Now he could just relax and watch McKenzie sweat. With her former salesman's death, she would be terrified. He chuckled. And her cowboy would realize he was no match for him.

Soon he would call and ask to see a house. He knew exactly which one he would want to see. When he'd gotten home from the open house, he'd searched the paper and internet for a listing in the area that would work to his advantage.

As he picked up her card and ran his fingers over the dark engraving, he had no doubt that Ms. McKenzie Sheldon would accommodate him in every way possible.

Chapter 12

Dana met them at the ranch house door. "I am so glad you decided to come back."

McKenzie couldn't help being touched by the warm welcome, but she still had misgivings about being here. It must have showed in her face because Dana hugged her and said, "I have something I want to show you in the kitchen," leaving the men in the living room. Because it was late, the children were already in bed. The large, two-story ranch house was quieter than McKenzie had ever heard it.

"I know that you didn't want to come here," Dana said, the moment the kitchen door closed behind them.

"Only because there is a killer after me. I couldn't bear it if I brought my troubles here and put your family in danger."

"We've had our share of trouble at this ranch, believe me, and I'm sure we will again," Dana said. "For me this place has always been a sanctuary. If it can be for others…" She smiled and took McKenzie's hands in her own. "Then I'm glad. My mother loved this ranch, fought for it. It's that Old West spirit that lives here in this canyon. Hayes did right bringing you back here."

McKenzie wasn't as sure of that. But she had to admit, she felt safer here and more at home than she did even in her condo as the two of them joined the men.

"We're going down to the Corral tonight," Dana said as if the idea had just come to her. "You dance, don't you, McKenzie?"

She started to shake her head.

"Not to worry," Hayes said. "I'll teach you Texas two-step."

"It's Saturday night in the canyon," Tag said. "You really do not want to miss this. Isn't that right, Lily?" His fiancée laughed and agreed.

McKenzie couldn't help but get caught up in their excitement. "Saturday night in the canyon. How can I say no?"

Hayes smiled at her. "It's going to be fun, I promise."

She didn't doubt it. The Cardwells were a family that had fun; she could see that. She found herself smiling as they all piled into a couple of rigs and drove up the canyon to the Corral Bar.

"I forgot to mention that my father and uncle are playing in the band," Dana said as they got out.

McKenzie could hear the music, old-time country, as they pushed through the door. The place was packed, but Hayes pulled her out onto a small space on the dance floor, anyway.

The song was slow, a mournful love song. He took

her in his arms, drawing her close. She'd danced some in her younger days, mostly with her sisters, though.

Hayes was easy to follow and she found herself relaxing in his arms and moving with the music.

"You're a fast learner," he whispered next to her ear, making her smile.

They danced the next couple of songs, the beat picking up.

"Are you having fun?" Hayes asked.

She was. She laughed and nodded as he spun her, catching her by the waist to draw her back to him. She loved being in his arms and it wasn't just because she felt safe there. She was falling for Hayes Cardwell.

"Here, you need this after that last dance," Tag said, handing each of them a beer as they came off the dance floor. "Some nice moves out there, little brother." He winked at Hayes. "Who knew he could dance?"

"He is a man of many talents," McKenzie agreed as she tried to catch her breath. Just being around Hayes made her heart beat faster and her pulse sing. When he looked at her like he was doing now… "He just taught me the Texas swing."

"Come to Texas and I'll teach you all kinds of things," Hayes said, meeting her gaze and holding it.

She laughed that off but she could tell he was serious. Texas? She didn't think so. She hadn't spent years working her tail off to get her business where it was to pack up and move.

And yet when she looked into his dark eyes, she was tempted. She told herself it had only been an off-handed remark. They hardly knew each other. A woman would be crazy to pack up and move clear across country because of a man, wouldn't she?

* * *

Hayes could have bitten his tongue. He'd seen his brother's surprised expression. He'd been joking. Or at least he thought he had when he'd started to suggest it. But by the time the words were out of his mouth…

He shook his head and took a long drink of his beer. From the moment he'd looked into McKenzie Sheldon's eyes he'd been spellbound. He couldn't explain it but the woman had cast a spell on him.

The band took a break and Dana and McKenzie headed off to the ladies' room together. He decided it was as good as any time to go over to say hello to his father and uncle.

"I heard you were in the canyon," his father said, giving him a slap on the back. Harlan Cardwell was still strong and handsome for a man in his sixties.

Tag had bonded with their father on his visit to Montana last Christmas. Hayes only had vague memories of occasional visits from his father while growing up.

"Good to see you," he said, then shook his uncle Angus's hand. The two had been playing in a band together, Tag had told him, since they were in high school.

"I've gotten to know Dad better," Tag had said when their father's name had come up. "He's a loner, kind of like Austin. He and his brother are close, but Uncle Angus doesn't even see his own daughter Dana that much."

"So you're saying our uncle is just as lousy a father as our own?" he'd asked Tag. "That's reassuring."

"I'm saying there's more to them. Dad cares, but neither he nor his brother, it seems, were cut out to be family men."

Several locals came up to talk to Harlan and Angus.

Hayes told his father he would catch him later and went to find McKenzie.

Hayes had always wondered about his father. What man let his wife raise five boys alone? Not that their mother wasn't one strong woman who'd done a great job.

"That's your father?" McKenzie asked, studying the elderly cowboy.

"That's him." Hayes had only recently learned that his father and uncle had spent most of their lives working for various government agencies. Both were reportedly retired.

He didn't want to talk about his father. "About earlier when I suggested you come to Texas…"

"I might come down just to see what all the fuss is about sometime," she said and quickly added, "Just to visit."

Fortunately, the band broke into a song. McKenzie put down her beer and, taking her hand, he led her back out on the dance floor.

As he pulled her into his arms, though, he couldn't bear to think about the day he would have to go back to Texas without her.

"Are you all right?" Hayes asked as they walked toward their cabins after they'd closed down the Corral. Tag had stayed behind to talk to Hud on the porch, while Dana had gone into the house to see how the kids were. Her sister Stacy had come up from Bozeman to watch all the kids for them.

The night was cool and dark in the pines. Only the starlight and a sliver of white moon overhead lit their way through the dense trees. In the distance, McKenzie thought she could hear the river as it wound through the canyon. It reminded her of the music back at the bar and being in Hayes's arms.

"I'm fine," she said and breathed in the sweet summer night's scents, wishing this night would never have to end.

He took her hand, his fingers closing around hers, and instinctively she moved closer, their shoulders brushing.

"I enjoyed visiting with your father tonight. He seems sweet." She glanced over at Hayes. "He said he wants to get to know his sons. I can tell he's sorry he missed so many years with the five of you." She saw that it was a subject he didn't want to talk about. There was hurt there. She wondered what it would take to heal it. With Hayes in Houston and his father here, well, that was too many miles, too much distance between them in more ways than one.

"I had a great time tonight," she said, changing the subject. She didn't want anything to ruin this night. She felt still caught up in the summer night's festivities. If anything, she had fallen even harder for the Cardwell family tonight.

"Me, too. So you aren't sorry I brought you here?"

She laughed as she looked at him. He wore his gray Stetson, his face in shadow, but she knew that face so well now that she knew he was pleased she'd had fun. "I'd rather be here with you than anywhere else in the world tonight."

He squeezed her hand then drew her to a stop in the pines just yards from her cabin. A breeze swayed the boughs around them, whispering softly, as he pulled her to him. The kiss was warm and soft and sweeter than even the night.

"McKenzie, that isn't just the beer talking, is it?" he joked.

She cupped his face in her hands, drawing him down to her lips. All night she'd wanted his arms around her. All night she'd wanted him. As she put into the kiss the longing she had for him, he dragged her against him with a groan. Desire shot through her blood, hot and demanding.

When she finally drew back, she whispered on a ragged breath, "I want you, too, Hayes Cardwell, and that isn't the beer talking."

They were so close she could see the shine of his dark eyes in the starlight. Without another word, he swept her up in his arms and carried her into the cabin.

As the cabin door closed behind them, Hayes lowered McKenzie slowly to her feet. His need for her was so strong that he would have taken her right there on the floor. But not their first time, he told himself as he looked into her eyes, losing himself in the clear blue sea.

"Last chance," he said quietly.

"Not a chance."

She started to unbutton her blouse, but he stopped her, moving her hands away to do it himself. He was determined to take it slow. As he slipped one button free, then another, he held her gaze. Her blouse fell open. He slowly lowered his eyes to her white-laced bra against the olive of her skin.

He brushed his fingertips over the rise of her breasts. She moaned softly as he dipped into the bra. Her nipple hardened under his thumb, making her arch against his hand. Her skin felt as hot as his desire for her. He released the front snap of her bra, exposing both breasts. Need burned through him, making him ache.

He'd wanted her for so long. When his gaze returned to her face, he saw her own need in her eyes. In one swift movement, she unsnapped his shirt, making the snaps sing. She pressed her palms to his chest.

He felt heat race along his nerve endings. He bent to kiss her then drew her against him, feeling her full breasts and hard nipples warm his skin and send his growing desire for her rocketing.

His mouth dropped to her breast, his tongue working the nipple. His hand slipped up under her skirt and her panties. She arched against him, rocking against his hand until she cried out and sagged against him.

He unhooked her skirt. It dropped to the floor. Her white lace panties followed it. Naked, she was more beautiful than he could have imagined. He swung her up in his arms again and carried her into the bedroom. As he started to lower her on the bed, she pulled him down into a hot, deep kiss and then her hand was on the buttons of his fly.

Lost in the feel of her, he made love to her slow and sweet, but it took all of his effort to hold back. The second time, he didn't hold back. They rolled around on the bed, caught up in a passion that left them both spent.

Later, as they lay on the bed staring up at the skylight overhead and trying to catch their breath, he looked over at McKenzie. She was smiling.

Patience. He knew things would be hot for a while with the cops, which meant there was no going near McKenzie's condo or office. Killing Gus came at a cost. Now he had to live with the consequences.

Tonight he sat on his porch considering his options. One would be to go back to work. It would look better should he find himself on the suspect list. Anyone who'd been to the open houses would be scrutinized. He wasn't worried. He looked great on paper.

Gus hadn't told the police anything—just as he'd sworn before he died. He'd had to make sure the police didn't have the license plate number of the van he'd been driving that night outside McKenzie's condo. Gus hadn't given the police even the make of the vehicle he'd been driving. He couldn't believe his luck—or Gus Thompson's stupidity. Gus was the only one who could have identified him and now he was dead.

Luck was with him. It buoyed him in this difficult time. He could last a couple of days without seeing McKenzie, without going near her. Unless there was another way.

The idea came to him slowly, teasing him in its simplicity. The only way he could get to McKenzie Sheldon sooner would be if her attacker were caught. He thought of the men he'd seen at the open house. A couple of them had looked familiar. In fact, there was one he knew. He was the right size. All it would take was a couple of pieces of incriminating evidence to be found at the man's house. The police would think they had their man.

So would McKenzie Sheldon.

There would be no reason for her not to go back to work as usual.

He felt good as he got up and went to bed. When he closed his eyes, he relived every moment from the time he hit Gus Thompson and knocked him to his knees until he saw the life drain out of the man. It had been a good day.

But he couldn't stop himself from dreaming about the day he would take McKenzie Sheldon for his own. Normally, he only spent a few hours with each one. Too much time increased the chance of being caught.

With McKenzie, though, he wanted to take his time. He would have to find some place where they could be alone for more than a few hours.

McKenzie lay in the bed, the stars glittering like tiny white lights through the skylight overhead, Hayes Cardwell lying next to her.

"So I have to know," McKenzie said, rolling up on one elbow to look at him. "What makes good Texas barbecue?"

Hayes smiled over at her. "Are you serious?"

"Come on. You can tell me your secret. Isn't that how you and your brothers got your start? It has to be some kind of special barbecue."

He nodded as he rolled up on his side to face her. "You have to understand. We were raised on barbecue." He closed his eyes for a moment and sniffed as if he could smell it. "You've got to have the smoke," he said as he opened his eyes and grinned at her. "And that takes a pit and a lot of patience. Most people don't know this, but cooking whole animals over smoldering coals is thought to have originated in the Caribbean. The Spanish saw how it was done and called it barbacoa. It's been refined since then, of course, and every region does it differently. Texas is known for its brisket, cooked charred black and bursting with flavor."

She laughed. "What makes your brisket so special?"

"We cover them with special seasonings and then

smoke them for twelve to eighteen hours in wood-burning pits."

"Secret seasonings, right?"

"You better believe it. But wait until you taste our barbecue sauce."

"I can't wait. Am I going to get a chance to taste it?"

"Count on it," Hayes said and kissed her. It was a slow, sexy kiss that sent a throbbing ache of desire through her. She knew it wouldn't take much to find herself making love with him again. He'd been so tender the first time. The second time he'd taken her in a way that still had her heart pounding.

Just the thought brought with it the remembered pleasure. But as intimate as their lovemaking had been, she needed to know more about this man. She'd put her life into his hands. She felt as if he had done the same.

"I heard you started with just one small restaurant," she said.

He nodded. "We opened the first place in an old house with the pit out back. It was just good ol' traditional barbecue like we grew up on. You can take a cheap piece of meat and, if you cook it properly and with the right wood, it becomes a delicacy. One whiff and I can tell whether hickory, post oak or mesquite was used. But in the end, give me a piece of marbled pork shoulder and I will make you a tender, succulent pulled pork sandwich like none you've ever had before. The secret is that you've got to have smoky pork fat."

She smiled at him, hearing the pride in his voice. "Coleslaw?"

"Of course. You have to slather some sweet slaw on the pulled pork along with our spicy barbecue sauce to cut the richness of the pork. We also do a mean Southern potato salad and you are not going to believe our beans."

She had to laugh. "You're making me hungry."

"Me, too." His gaze locked with hers, making it clear it wasn't just barbecue he was hungry for.

"So the business just took off."

He nodded, almost sheepishly, as if embarrassed by their success. "None of us saw that coming."

Just like they hadn't seen this coming, she thought as Hayes kissed her. This time she let nature take its course. She couldn't bear the thought, though, that with a killer after her, this could be the last time they made love.

"What's going on, Hayes?" Tag demanded.

Hayes started as his brother stepped out of the trees next to his cabin a few hours before daylight. He was surprised and more than a little irritated. "Have you been waiting for me this whole time?"

"Don't try to avoid the question. What's the deal with you and McKenzie Sheldon?"

Hayes thought about telling him it was none of his business. But since the five brothers had been little, they'd taken care of each other. He knew his brother was asking out of concern, not idle curiosity.

"I don't know."

"This is moving a little fast, don't you think?" his brother asked.

"Oh, you're a good one to talk, Tag. You come up here for Christmas and the next thing we know, you're engaged to be married and want us to open a barbecue joint up here."

"I fell in *love*. It happens and sometimes, it happens fast." Tag studied him for a moment. "Are you telling me that's what's happening to you?"

Hayes looked out at the mountains, now dark as the

pines that covered them, then up at the amazing big sky twinkling with stars. Had he ever seen a clearer sky— even in Texas?

"What if I am falling in love with her?" he demanded.

Tag laughed and shook his head. "The Cardwells just can't do anything the easy way, can they? Bro, there is a killer after her and probably after you, as well, now."

"Don't you think I know that? I have to find him before..." He pulled off his hat and raked his fingers through his hair. "I have to find him."

"Okay, and then what?"

Hayes met his brother's gaze. "I don't know. I think about Jackson and his marriage—"

"It doesn't have to end up that way," Tag said as he followed him into the cabin. "Jackson was blinded by first love. He didn't see that all she really wanted was his money. Does McKenzie Sheldon want your money?"

"No." He let out a chuckle. "I'm not even sure she wants me for the long haul."

It was Tag's turn to laugh. "I've seen the way she looks at you. You're her hero."

"Yeah. That's what bothers me. I'm no hero. What happens when she realizes that? Worse, what if I get her killed?"

Chapter 13

Hayes looked toward the house where McKenzie and Dana had just disappeared inside.

"Sorry I came down on you like I did last night," Tag said. "It's none of my business."

In the clear light of day, Hayes now understood why his brother had been so upset with him the night before. "Last night shouldn't have happened. It's all my fault. I should never have let it go as far as it did. My life is in Texas."

"Shouldn't you be telling her this instead of me?" his brother asked.

Hayes barely heard him. "Her life is here. She's spent these years building up a business she is proud of. I couldn't ask her to give that up. Not that I would. Not that things have gone that far."

"Take it easy, bro. You made love to her. You didn't sign away your life in blood."

"I take making love seriously."

Tag laughed. "We all do."

"You know what I mean."

"Did you tell her you loved her?"

"Of course not."

"Because you don't?"

"No, because we barely know each other. I don't even know how she feels or how I do, for that matter."

Tag shook his head. "You're falling for this woman."

He could see Dana and McKenzie inside the house. They seemed to be having a heart-to-heart. He could almost feel his ears burn just thinking what McKenzie might be telling his cousin about last night.

"If you care about her, you should tell her," Tag said. "It sounds to me like you need to figure out how you feel about her."

"It's complicated."

"It always is," Tag said. "But God forbid if anything happens to her, you'll never forgive yourself if you don't tell her."

Dana had packed them a picnic lunch and offered to help saddle horses for the ride up the mountain to the lake. "It's beautiful up there. Crystal clear and surrounded by large boulders. There is one wonderful rock that is huge and flat on top. Have your picnic up there. Or there is a lovely spot in the pines at the edge of the water. I think that is my favorite."

McKenzie gave Dana a hug. "Thank you."

"My pleasure." She smiled as she looked out the window to where her two Cardwell cousins were standing by the corral after a huge Montana breakfast of chicken-fried venison steaks, hash browns, biscuits with milk gravy and eggs peppered with fresh jalapeños from Dana's garden.

Tag was handsome as sin, but nothing like Hayes, McKenzie was thinking.

"He's special, isn't he?"

She gave a start, but didn't have to ask who she was referring to.

"Hayes reminds me of Hud." Dana met her gaze. "He's a keeper."

"His life is in Houston."

"So was Tag's," she pointed out with a grin. "It wouldn't hurt to have two Cardwell cousins up here, making sure this barbecue restaurant is a success. Wouldn't hurt to have a private-investigative business here, either."

"You're a shameless matchmaker," McKenzie joked.

"Just like my mother. Did I tell you that she made a new will before she died, leaving me the ranch? Unfortunately, she was killed in a horseback-riding accident and no one could find the will. I almost lost the ranch. If Hud and I hadn't gotten together again I would have never found the will and been able to keep this place."

"Where was the will?"

"In my mother's old recipe book marking the page with Hud's favorite cookie recipe," Dana said and laughed. "Love saved this ranch."

McKenzie had to laugh, as well. The more she was around Dana Cardwell Savage, the more she found herself wanting to be a part of this amazing family. For a few moments, she could even forget that there was a killer after her.

* * *

The high mountain lake was just as beautiful as Dana had said it would be, Hayes thought as he swung down off his horse.

"It's breathtaking," McKenzie said as she dismounted and walked to the edge of the deep green pool.

"*You're* breathtaking," Hayes said behind her.

She smiled at him over her shoulder, then bent down and scooped up the icy water to toss back at him. He'd told himself that last night had been a mistake, that he wouldn't let it happen again. But right now all he could think about was McKenzie being in his arms again.

The droplets felt good, even though he jumped back, laughing. He loved seeing her like this, relaxed and carefree as if she didn't have a care in the world. He doubted she'd ever been like this—even before the attack. The woman had been driven in a single-minded determination to succeed. He couldn't help but wonder if any of that mattered now. Was it the attack that had changed her? Or could it possibly be that she had feelings for him? Long-lasting feelings?

He'd spent the morning on the phone with the police and doing some investigating online. The police had run the license plates of those who had attended, but with Gus Thompson's murder, they weren't giving out any information. All they'd told him was that they were checking into everyone who'd been there both for the attack on McKenzie *and* Gus Thompson's murder.

Hayes had run checks on the two men who had provided McKenzie with their names.

Would her attacker be so brazen as to give her his real name, though?

The first name he ran was Bob Garwood. The man

had a military background, special ops, and had received a variety of medals before being honorably discharged.

If anything, it showed that he had special training, something that could be an advantage for a man who abducted women and killed them.

Bob Garwood had no record, not even a speeding ticket. He looked clean. Maybe McKenzie was right and he *had* been merely looking for a date the two times he'd come to her open houses.

Or maybe not, Hayes thought, as he saw that Bob Garwood owned a gym-equipment business. Did that mean he traveled? Hayes bet it did. The company he owned was called Futuristic Fitness, promising to sell the most up-to-the-moment, technologically advanced equipment on the market. That could explain why the man was in such good shape.

The next name he ran was Jason Mathews. He was an antiquities appraiser, another job where he no doubt traveled. Like Bob Garwood, Jason Mathews looked clean. He was married, owned his house and volunteered for several charitable organizations—not that any of that cleared him, Hayes thought, reminded of Gacy who dressed as a clown at charitable functions.

The police hadn't found anything suspicious about any of the other viewers who'd attended the open house from what he'd been told. They were still investigating.

Hayes had finally given up in frustration. He couldn't even be sure that McKenzie's attacker had driven to the open house. He could have come by foot; in fact, that seemed more likely since when he stumbled upon Gus Thompson, he hadn't hesitated to kill him, even though it was a dangerous thing to do.

"I guess swimming is out," McKenzie said wistfully.

"Not necessarily," Hayes answered as he began to pull off his boots. He could use a cold dip in the lake. Not that he thought it would help. "Dana packed towels as well as a blanket." He raised a brow and McKenzie laughed as she hurriedly began to undress.

"Last one in has to unpack the lunch."

The call came forty-eight hours later. The police had received an anonymous tip from a neighbor. When they'd gone to a man by the name of Eric Winters's house to talk to him, they'd spotted incriminating evidence in his car and gotten a search warrant. Inside the house, they'd found the knife believed used to kill Gus Thompson along with items believed to have belonged to female victims that he'd kept as souvenirs—including McKenzie's red, high-heeled shoe.

McKenzie began to cry when she got the news as she thought of his other victims. The name Eric Winters meant nothing to her. Even when the police described the man to her, she couldn't place him, but apparently he'd come through the open house for the ranchette. He'd just been one of a dozen men who could have been her attacker.

"So it's definitely him?" she asked, weak with relief.

"Given the evidence we found at his house, we have the man who attacked you. Your shoe will have to be kept as evidence."

"It's all right. I won't be wearing those heels again, anyway. Thank you so much for letting me know." For so long she'd thought they would never find him, that she would always be looking over her shoulder. She hung up and turned to look at Hayes. Her eyes welled again with tears as she said, "They got him," and stepped into Hayes's arms.

Dana threw a celebratory dinner complete with champagne that night. "Stay," she pleaded when McKenzie thanked her for everything and told her she would be moving out of the cabin in the morning.

"I wish I could stay. I love it up here, but I have a business to run. I've been away from it for too long as it is." The business had been her world just a week ago. It had taken all of her time and energy as well as her every waking thought. Until Hayes, she hadn't realized what she was missing.

But now he had no reason to stay and she had no reason not to return to her life, even if it did suddenly feel empty.

"And Hayes?" Dana asked, as if sensing her mood.

McKenzie looked across the room where the men were gathered. "I guess there is nothing keeping him in Montana now," she said.

Dana lifted an eyebrow in response. "You could ask him to stay... Otherwise, he'll be back next month for Tag's wedding...."

McKenzie smiled at her new friend. "He *has* asked me to be his date."

Dana grinned knowingly. "That's if he can stay away from you until the wedding. I guess we'll see."

"I guess we will," she agreed. The thought of the wedding buoyed her spirits a little, but there was no denying it. Things had changed. *She* had changed. While she had to get back to work, it wasn't with the same excited expectation that she usually felt at the prospect. True, she would never feel as safe as she had, not in Bozeman, not in her condo. But it was more than that.

She'd fallen for the man, for his family, for even this ranch lifestyle. Not that she was about to admit that to him or his cousin, for that matter. As she'd told Dana, Hayes had a life in Houston. She had a life here. He hadn't asked to get involved. He hadn't even wanted her to know he was the one who'd saved her that night, she reminded herself.

As Hayes turned to look at her, he smiled and she felt her heart rise up like a bubble. She smiled back, fighting tears.

Where was she?

The words had been rattling around in his brain for four days now. It had taken the police several days to arrest Eric Winters. But now two more days had passed. Hadn't the police told her that her attacker had been caught? What was she waiting for? She should be back at work—and so should he. He couldn't afford to take much more time off. As it was, people were starting to notice. He couldn't keep saying he was taking off time to look for another house.

Unfortunately, his Realtor had disappeared. He'd expected her to hide out for a while after poor Gus Thompson's death. But that was almost a week ago. She hadn't been staying at her condo. Nor had she been going to her office. When he'd called the office, he'd been told that she couldn't be reached. He'd declined another real-estate agent, saying he had talked to Ms. Sheldon and only she could answer his questions.

From the exasperated tone of the receptionist's voice, he gathered that he wasn't the only one trying to reach her. Like him, surely she couldn't be away from work too long. Not a woman like her. She must be champing at the bit to return. These days away must be driving her insane.

Her absence was certainly pushing him over the edge. He didn't know how much longer he could stand it. He had to find her and finish this.

His instincts told him that she was with the cowboy. Before he'd killed Gus Thompson, he'd found out that the cowboy's name was Hayes Cardwell and that he was from Houston, Texas. He was considering opening a restaurant at Big Sky.

Cardwell. Wasn't there a ranch up there by that name? That had to be where McKenzie Sheldon was hiding. It would be too dangerous to go to the ranch. No, he had to find another way to flush her out.

He picked up the phone and called her office. He'd been careful not to come on too strong with the receptionist. He hadn't wanted to call too much attention to himself. But this time— "M.K. Realty, may I help you?"

"I sure hope so. I've been hoping to reach Ms. Sheldon, but now another house with another Realtor has come up—"

"I would be happy to put you through to her—"

"I've already left messages for her."

"Ms. Sheldon is at her desk this morning. I'll put you right through. May I say who's calling?"

Hayes looked out the office window at the Houston skyscape. Just hours ago he'd been in the Gallatin Valley looking out at the mountains as his plane banked and headed south. Now here, he couldn't believe there had ever been a time that this had felt like home.

"What's bothering you?" Laramie demanded behind

him from his desk. "If you still have doubts about opening a restaurant in Montana—"

"It's not that," he said, turning away from the view. The offices for Texas Boys Barbecue had started out in a corner of an old house not all that long ago. Now, though, it resided in a high-rise downtown with other corporations that pulled in millions of dollars a year.

"What is it, then?" Laramie demanded. "You've been acting oddly since you walked into my office."

"It's nothing." He didn't want to talk about McKenzie. It only made it harder. Better to put her and Montana behind him. "Have you talked to Austin?"

"You really want to talk about Austin?" his brother asked as Hayes took a seat across from him. "I've never seen you mope around over a woman before."

"I'm not—"

"Have you talked to her?"

Hayes gave up denying his mood had nothing to do with McKenzie. "She sounds like she is back at work and doing fine."

"And you probably told her you are back at work, too, and doing fine, right?"

He made a face at his brother. "She's happy with her life."

"Is that what she told you? Hayes, do you know anything about women?"

He had to laugh. "Not really. But I'm not sure you're the man to give me advice. Have you dated a woman more than once?"

"Very funny. One of you has to say it."

"Say what?"

Laramie groaned. "That you're in love. That is the problem, you know. You've fallen for the woman." He raised a hand. "Don't even bother to deny it. The question now is what are you going to do about it? Mope around and feel sorry for yourself or go get your woman?"

Hayes started to tell him how off base he was, but he saved his breath. "Just fly up there and go riding in on my white horse? Then what? I have a house, an office and a job here in Houston."

"Are you serious? You would let a simple stumbling block like those things keep you from what you really want? What did you do with my brother Hayes who has always gone after what he wants?"

"I've just never wanted anything this badly and I don't even know if I can have her," he admitted and not easily.

"Only one way to find out. Better saddle up and get yourself back to Montana." Laramie picked up the phone. "Take the corporate jet. I'll have the pilot standing by."

"Ms. Sheldon?" He couldn't believe she was actually in her office, actually on the other end of the line. "I'm so glad to catch you in your office."

He'd been following the story about Eric Winters in the newspaper and on the evening television news. The man hadn't even been able to get out on bail. And now they were saying he could be a serial killer, having abducted and killed women all across the West. McKenzie must feel so safe, believing her attacker was finally behind bars.

"My wife and I are interested in seeing one of your houses. I was hoping you would be able to show us the residence as soon as possible. My wife was very impressed by you when we met you a while back. I told her I would see if you were free to show the house yourself. I know you own M.K. Realty." He'd learned that acknowledging that he knew who he was dealing with often worked.

"When were you thinking of seeing the house?" she asked, even though he could tell she had been ready to give him to someone else at the agency.

"My wife is very anxious. She doesn't want this house to get snatched up by someone else. I would imagine that now is too soon?" He heard her surprise. Before she could draw a breath, he said, "It's the one you have listed as executive, high-end home with a million-dollar view."

"I'm familiar with the house."

"I believe it also has a several-million-dollar price tag. I can't tell you what I would have to contend with if we lost it before my wife even got a chance to see it."

"We can't have that," she said and he knew he had her. "I suppose I could show the house in, say, an hour?"

"I really appreciate this. My wife and I will meet you out there, if that is all right." This was working out even better than he'd hoped.

"I look forward to it. I'm sorry. I didn't catch your name."

"It's Jason. Jason and Emily Mathews."

"Yes, I remember we met at several of my showings." She sounded uneasy and he knew he had to mention the murder.

"I was so sorry to hear about your colleague being killed. That was such a shock. I'm glad the murderer has been caught. You just don't expect that kind of thing in Montana."

"It's rare, fortunately," she said and quickly changed the subject. "I'll see you soon, then, Mr. Mathews."

"Please call me Jason."

Chapter 14

The moment McKenzie got off the phone she walked over to one of the cubicles.

"Jennifer, would you be able to take one of my showings this afternoon?"

The real-estate agent looked up in surprise. McKenzie had never asked any of them to take her showings until this moment.

The woman blinked then said, "I'd be happy to. Are you not feeling well?"

McKenzie almost laughed. "It's just that I have one before it that could take a while. Also I don't want you going alone. See if Rafe can go with you. I've decided from now on, we won't be showing houses alone if at all possible, but definitely any that could run over after dark."

"But aren't you showing one now alone?" Jennifer asked tentatively.

"It will be all right this one time. I'm meeting a man and his wife at the Warner place."

"I'm sure Rafe can go with me."

"Great. Thanks for doing this." As she walked back to her office, McKenzie felt relieved. She had the other showing covered and after today, she would start relying more on her staff. If being gone had taught her anything, it was that she was not indispensible. For so long, she'd thought she had to do everything herself and yet when she'd returned after being gone for a week, she found that the agency was doing just fine.

There'd been numerous calls for follow-ups on houses she'd shown, but her staff had taken care of all but a couple of them. One of those was probably Mr. and Mrs. Mathews. Jason Mathews came across as the kind of man who only dealt with the boss or owner. Well, she was taking care of that one now.

McKenzie felt as if a weight had been lifted off her shoulders and at the same time, she couldn't help feeling a little sad. She hadn't heard from Hayes other than a quick phone call from the airport after he'd landed in Houston.

She'd gotten an agency call she'd had to take so she'd been forced to cut the call with Hayes short. When she'd tried to call him back, she'd gotten his voice mail. She hadn't left a message. What was there to say?

He'd asked how it felt to be back at work. She'd lied and said, "Great."

She'd asked him if he was glad to be home. He'd said he was.

That pretty much covered anything they had to say to each other, didn't it?

Outside her office, dark clouds had moved in. Thunder rumbled in the distance. The weatherman had warned that they might get some summer storms over the next few days.

Packing up her things, she headed for the door, also surprising her staff. She was always the first one in the office and the last to leave. As she walked out to her car in daylight, she couldn't help thinking of Hayes and Cardwell Ranch.

Was Hayes missing it and her as much as she was him? She pushed the thought away. She'd see him next month for Tag's wedding. The thought lightened her step even when it began to rain.

He was waiting for her. Anticipation had his heart racing. He'd failed once. He couldn't let that happen again.

Arriving early, he'd waited and gone over all the things that could go wrong. She might see that he hadn't brought his wife and panic, taking off before he could stop her. Or she might send someone else. Maybe even more possible, she might bring an associate.

He just couldn't let anything happen that would allow her to get away. Again.

He'd taken even more precautions since his failure with her the first time. He'd secured a place for them nearby. He couldn't chance transporting her any distance. Knowing Ms. Sheldon the way he did, she would be one of those women who got loose in the trunk, broke out a taillight and signaled for help.

Another precaution he was taking was knocking her out quickly. He'd opted to use a drug. He couldn't take the chance he might hit her too hard and kill her before all the fun began. It felt like cheating, drugging her, but he'd lost her once. That wasn't going to happen again.

That's why he'd carefully chosen this huge monster of a house in the middle of the valley—and the abandoned house through the trees, only a short walk away.

Normally, he just dragged them out into the woods. But McKenzie Sheldon wasn't getting his quick and dirty usual fare. No, she was going to get the full treatment and that meant he would need a room inside a house.

He'd found one near the house he'd told her he wanted to view. He was counting on her not telling anyone where she was going. He was counting on it, based on the fact that she was the boss and that she would no longer be afraid since as far as she knew, her attacker was still behind bars.

The hard part would be getting her away from this house quickly and to their private spot. He would have to act fast, taking her in her car then coming back for his own car.

At the sound of a vehicle approaching, he tensed. McKenzie Sheldon was right on time. He checked the syringe in his pocket. Now, if she was alone, then nothing could stop him. He carefully adjusted the large straw hat balanced on the back of the passenger seat. From a distance it would appear his wife was sitting in the car waiting.

He glanced in his rearview mirror. It was McKenzie and she was alone. He smiled excitedly as he opened his car door and stepped out. All he needed was a few precious seconds and she'd be his.

Hayes thought about what his brother had said on the flight to Montana in the corporate jet. He also thought about McKenzie Sheldon's well-ordered life.

Like him, his career had taken up the greater part

of his life. But that, he realized now, was because there hadn't been anything else that had interested him.

Now, his career, as important as it was, wasn't the first thing he thought of when he awakened in the morning. But was that true of McKenzie?

He'd seen her checking the messages on her phone, especially after a few days at the ranch. She'd been worried about her business. Not that he could blame her. She'd been such a major part of the agency he doubted she thought it could survive without her.

Hayes called McKenzie's office the moment the jet touched down outside of Bozeman, but was told she'd left work early.

"Have you tried her home?" the receptionist asked when he gave her his name. Word must have gone around the office that she'd spent almost a week with him up the canyon at Cardwell Ranch.

"She's already gone home?"

The receptionist laughed at his surprise. "I know it isn't like her. She even asked one of the associates to show a house for her this afternoon. We all thought she might have a date or something."

A date? He heard the woman try to swallow back her words.

"I mean we thought she was going out with you." Another gulp. "Is there a message I can give her if I hear from her?"

"No." He'd disconnected, wondering what he was doing flying to Montana. A *date?*

Well, what do you expect? he asked himself. *It wasn't as if you asked her to wait for you or even told her how you felt.*

Still, he hadn't been gone *that* long.

He tried her cell but it went to voice mail. On impulse, he called the office back and asked to speak to the sales associate who McKenzie had gotten to cover for her.

"This is Jennifer Robinson."

Hayes introduced himself and asked if she knew whether or not McKenzie was showing a house.

"She is, the Warner place."

That was the McKenzie Sheldon he knew, he thought with a sigh of relief. "Can you tell me how to find the Warner place? If she just left, I might be able to catch her."

McKenzie saw the large, newer-model expensive car parked by the house as she came up the drive.

Jason Mathews got out as she approached. She remembered him from the open house where Gus was killed. For a moment, she almost drove on through the circular drive and left.

You have nothing to fear. Your attacker was caught. Not only that, he brought his wife, right? As she glanced to the passenger seat, she saw a large summer straw hat and remembered that Emily Mathews was a tiny woman. Relief washed over her.

For a moment, though, she was sorry she hadn't brought another agent with her. Her heart just wasn't in this, even though the sale would mean a very large commission. This was one of a number of houses in this area that the bank was anxious to get sold after a rash of foreclosures.

Having two agents go on every showing wasn't the best use of manpower. Also, she knew the nonlist agent would complain about losing money. Still, she wanted her agents to be safe and she would have gladly shared the commission.

Shutting off the car, she turned toward the passenger seat to dig the house keys out of her purse. To her surprise, her car door opened. She turned, startled to find Jason Mathews standing next to her car.

"I appreciate you taking the time to do this today," he said.

She tried to find her voice as she told herself he was just being polite, opening her door like that. "Just let me get the keys."

As she picked them up, she gripped them like a knife. Hayes's words came back to her that keys weren't much of a weapon because by then the attacker would be too close. Women lost their advantage up close because they were often the weaker sex.

At that moment, she was sorry she'd given Hayes back the pistol she used to have in her purse. She still had the can of pepper spray, but it would be in the bottom of her purse, not easily accessible.

All these thoughts hit her in a matter of seconds before Jason Mathews said, "I'll get Emily. She is anxious to see this house. Great location since she likes the idea of no neighbors within view."

He stepped away from the car and McKenzie felt herself breathe again. She chastised herself as she climbed out, dragging her purse out after her.

As she headed toward the house, she saw that Mr. Mathews was leaning into the car talking to his wife. For a woman who was anxious to see the house, she certainly was taking her time getting out of the car.

McKenzie headed for the front door of the house, just assuming the two would follow. Whatever discussion was going on between them, she didn't want to eavesdrop.

When her cell phone rang, she stopped partway up the wide front steps to dig the phone out of her purse. Busy thinking about Mrs. Mathews and hoping this hadn't been a wild goose chase, she didn't bother to check to see who was calling. "Hello?"

"McKenzie Sheldon? This is Officer Pamela Donovan with the Bozeman Police Department. I don't want to alarm you."

Alarm her? Surprised, she didn't hear Jason Mathews come up behind her until she felt the needle he plunged into her neck.

Hayes's rental car was waiting for him with the map inside just as he had requested. The Warner place, as Jennifer had called it, was about five miles outside of town to the south.

That meant it was at least fifteen miles from the airport. The worst part was the traffic. While nothing like Houston's, he'd managed to hit the valley during the afternoon rush hour. Just his luck.

He'd left a message with both Jennifer and the receptionist to have McKenzie call him if they heard from her. That's why when his phone rang he thought it would be her.

He was thrown for a moment when he realized the female voice on the other end of the line was the policewoman who'd worked with McKenzie after her attack.

"Yes, I remember you, Ms. Donovan."

"I just tried to reach Ms. Sheldon."

It was the worry he heard in her voice. "Is there a problem?"

"I didn't want to alarm her, but there is some news about the man we arrested in her attack. It might not mean anything—"

"What is it?" he asked as he drove toward the Gallatin Range of mountains to the south.

"McKenzie Sheldon isn't with you, by any chance, is she?" the policewoman asked.

"No. I was just on my way to the house she's showing. Why?"

He heard her hesitate before she said, "I just tried to reach her. We were cut off."

Unconsciously, he found himself driving a little faster. "Why were you trying to reach her?" Again the pause. "Officer—"

"There is some question whether or not the man we have in jail for her attack is guilty," the deputy finally said. "I can't get into it, but the dates of the other abductions aren't adding up for him and there is some question about the evidence we found in his house."

His heart pounded. "The dates. They don't add up for him, but they do for someone else, someone who was at the open house where Gus Thompson was killed, right?"

"When we went to bring Jason Mathews in for questioning, his wife told us that he'd had to leave town for a few days."

Hayes swore under his breath. "I was told at McKenzie's office that she was showing a house to a husband and wife." He prayed that was true and that the man sans the wife wasn't Jason Mathews. "I'm on my way there now." He gave her the directions he'd been given.

"We'll have a patrol car there as soon as possible."

Disconnecting, he drove as if his life depended on it,

all the time mentally kicking himself for ever leaving. Worse, for never telling McKenzie how he felt about her.

McKenzie woke to darkness. She tried to open her eyes but her lids felt too heavy. For a moment she couldn't remember anything. She cracked an eyelid open as she attempted to move. Her hands were bound with duct tape at the wrists in front of her, her feet were bound at the ankles and she was strapped to a wheelchair.

A shot of adrenaline rocketed through her as memory came back in a wave of nausea. The prick of the needle, the horror of what was happening as she slumped against Jason Mathews, the fleeting glimpse of the empty car except for the carefully positioned summer straw hat on the back of the passenger seat.

She looked around, terrified to see where he'd brought her.

"Well, hello," Jason Mathews said from where he stood nearby. "Nice to have you back."

With relief she saw that she was still dressed, but that several of the buttons on her blouse were open. She shuddered at the thought of this man's hands on her as she lifted her gaze. The room was small. A walk-in closet or maybe a pantry. Were they still at the Warner house? She didn't think so, but all of these high-end houses had similar features.

Drugged, it took her a moment to realize he hadn't gagged her. She opened her mouth and tried to scream. The sound that came out was weak. She tried again, stopping only when he erupted into a fit of laughing.

"No one can hear you. There's no one around for miles. Not that I mind hearing you scream. I plan to make you scream a whole lot more before this day is over."

His smile curdled her stomach. She tried to fight down the terror that weakened her as much as the drug he'd given her. Her mind raced. Had she told anyone at the office where she'd gone? Yes, Jennifer. She'd told her she was meeting a husband and wife at the Warner place. Not that there would be reason for anyone to start looking for her for hours. More like days.

Her heart dropped at the thought as the man stepped in front of her, forcing her to raise her gaze to his.

"Finally, we are alone," he said, smiling. "I was worried it wasn't ever going to happen. We are going to have so much fun. Well, I am," he added with a laugh. "First I want to show you the house. It is only polite, since you showed me several houses." He stepped behind her and, kicking off the wheelchair brake, propelled her out of the small room into a larger one.

She saw that she'd been right about the space he'd had her in being a walk-in closet, even though there were no shelves or rods on the walls yet.

"The master bedroom!" he announced with a flourish. "I haven't had time to decorate, or even get a bed, so we'll have to make due."

Dust coated the floor. She frowned, trying to make sense of where they were. Not in the Warner place. She'd shown it before and it had been clean, although empty for some time like a lot of other houses in the neighborhood this far out of town. Were they in one of those houses? Some had been abandoned by the contractors when they'd gone broke and the banks had been slow to move on selling them.

Her gaze stopped on a pile of items in the corner of the room. Terror turned her bones to mush at the sight of the duct tape, handcuffs, gag ball and an array of sex toys, including a whip.

She closed her eyes, dropping her head, unable to look. She couldn't let herself give in to this. She had to find a way to escape. This wasn't the way she was going to die, not in this dirty, abandoned house with this madman.

"You need to wake up," he said next to her ear.

She didn't open her eyes. She needed to get away from him. She needed a weapon. She needed even half a chance. She could still feel the drug in her bloodstream. It made her limbs feel lifeless, her reflexes slow.

While driven, she'd still always been a realist. No one was going to save her and she didn't see any way to save herself, bound the way she was. He'd done this before. He knew what he was doing. And since she'd gotten away from him once, he had made sure she wouldn't this time, she thought as she tested the tape on her wrists and ankles.

He was going to kill her.

But not until he hurt her. She had seen the cruel glimmer in his eyes as soon as she'd looked at him moments before. For whatever reason, he liked hurting women. It must make him feel superior, not that his reasons mattered.

"I must have given you too much of the drug," he said, sounding disappointed, even angry. "I don't want you to miss a minute of the fun so you are going to have to wake up."

She kept her eyes closed. Let him think it was the drug.

The slap made her eyes fly open and slammed her head back against the webbing on the wheelchair seat. His face was inches from her own now, his breath rank as he laughed.

"I thought that might bring you out of it," he said with another laugh, and stepped behind the chair again. "Pay attention or the next time, I'll have to do something much more painful to get your attention."

He wheeled her through a door and into the large master bath. Her heart stopped at the sight of a roll of plastic in the bathtub and several new blue tarps spread over the floor. "That's for later. I want to put that part off as long as possible this time. You deserve my best after what you've put me through."

She heard the underlying anger in his voice. It made her blood run cold. He planned to hurt her for as long as he could keep her alive. A sob caught in her chest. "Why?" she cried, hating to let him see how terrified she was.

He laughed as he shoved her into the bedroom again then whirled the wheelchair around to face him. The blade of a pair of scissors caught the light, shimmering in his hand. She gasped and tried to draw back as he moved in closer.

"Why?" he asked mockingly. "Because I can."

The knife blade cut through the tape holding her to the chair an instant before he stepped behind the wheelchair and unceremoniously dumped her into the middle of the master bedroom floor. The sound of the blade cutting through the tape reminded her of it cutting through her hair.

"Tour over," he said. "It's time for the fun to begin."

She looked up at him from the floor where she lay on

her side, bound and helpless. If she couldn't get away, then there was only one thing to do. She had to make him so furious that he killed her quickly.

Chapter 15

Hayes hit a rain shower near the mountains. It was still spitting rain as the Warner place came into view. The massive house sat on a small rise with a stand of aspens and pines behind it. From the third floor, he would guess there was a three-hundred-and-sixty-degree view of the valley. The house was just as Jennifer at the agency had described it. Massive, tan with matching stone and a circular driveway. The driveway was empty.

"No!" he yelled and slammed his fist against the steering wheel as he slowed. She couldn't have already come here, shown the house and left, unless... Once off the narrow paved road, the circular drive was an intricate pattern of cobblestones. Unfortunately, Montana winters had done their worst, breaking some and dislodging others. His tires rumbled over them as he neared the elaborate front door.

Unless the couple she was supposed to show the house to had called and canceled. He tried her number again. Again, it went straight to voice mail. Still, he was about to grasp onto that theory like a life raft when he saw the muddy footprints.

Hayes threw on the brakes. The rain had stopped. His windshield wipers scraped loudly across the dry glass. He shut them off, then leaving the rental running, got out.

The prints appeared to be muddy boot tracks. What had caught his eye was how they had trailed onto the cobblestones from the side of the house.

So she had shown the house to someone? He started to follow the tracks along the side of the house. The landscaping had never been finished except for a little out front. Peering in a window, he found the house was empty. It had that never-lived-in look and he was reminded of something McKenzie had told him about overbuilding back in the early two thousands. Building contractors had gone broke, leaving grandiose spec houses for the banks to deal with. This appeared to be one of them.

As he neared the back of the house, he expected the tracks to head for the rear entrance, assuming they must be from whomever McKenzie had shown the house to.

But the tracks veered off into the trees. Strange. The hair rose on the back of his neck as he realized the tracks had been heading out of the woods behind the house—and ended on the cobblestones out front.

What the hell? He'd put on his gun and shoulder holster after the call from the policewoman. He checked his gun now as he realized what he was seeing. Whoever had recently come to the Warner place from the trees hadn't walked back. They'd driven.

"Does your wife know?"

He'd never let the others talk. He'd kept their mouths duct taped. He hadn't needed to hear their screams. The eyes were more than windows into the soul. He had been able to see their terror as their eyes widened in disbelief. None of them had been able to believe it was happening to them. When the realization that they were about to die finally hit them, it, too, was in their eyes. He hadn't needed to even hear more than their muffled screams.

"If Emily really is your wife, then she *must* know," McKenzie said. "No woman could be that stupid."

"Don't talk about my wife. She doesn't know anything," he snapped.

"She probably turns a blind eye, just thankful it isn't her."

"Emily isn't like that. She's sweet and kind and… If she knew…" His voice trailed off, the thought too horrifying. Emily loved him. She trusted him. She looked up to him. She wasn't like these successful bitches who looked down their noses at him. If only she had come along years ago before…the others.

"I bet she can smell it on you when you come home. Does she make you shower? Or does she like it, the smell of another woman's pain on you?"

"Enough!" he bellowed, his voice echoing in the cavernous empty room. "You don't know anything about it."

"Don't I? You know she can see it building up inside you, then you leave and when you come back…" She met his gaze, hers hard as stone. "Believe me, she knows."

He kicked her, catching her in the stomach and flipping her over. A painful cry came out of her so he kicked her again, shutting her up except for the second groan of pain. He flipped her back over to face him as he dropped down beside her and cupped her face in his hands, pulling her a breath's distance from his own face.

"You want to know why I do this? Because of women like you. You think you're so smart. Bitches, all of you. But once you realize that you're mine to do with whatever I want, then you change your tune. Like the others, you will cry and whine and plead with me."

She spit in his face.

He screamed in fury, releasing her to slap her as hard as he could. Her head snapped back, smacking the floor. He hurriedly wiped her saliva from his face with his sleeve, cringing at the horrible feel of it on his skin. "I am going to kill you!" he yelled. "I'm going to—"

"Big man, killing a woman who is bound and helpless. This is what makes you feel better? If you were a real man—"

He snatched up the whip from the corner of the room and swung it at her. She tried to roll away from him, only managing to flip over once before the cattails sliced the back of her blouse open along with her skin. She screamed.

As Hayes entered the dark stand of trees, he pulled his weapon. Droplets from the rain still shone in the bright green leaves of the aspens and dripped down occasionally as he followed the tracks.

He hadn't gone far when the trees opened a little. He glimpsed the backyard of another house. Around him, everything was deathly quiet. He didn't even hear a birdsong, just the drip of the trees.

Hayes moved along the edge of the trees until he could see the front of the house. No vehicles and yet the tracks were fresh. Two sets. Both disappearing into the garage. His heart began to pound faster as he worked his way toward the back of the house, keeping out of sight of the rear windows.

He passed an old greenhouse, the door dangling open. Inside he would see where the vegetation had taken over, but rather than being green, everything appeared crusted with a thick layer of dust. It was the kind of thing that had creeped him out when he was a kid exploring old houses with his brothers.

He moved past the greenhouse and through an old garden spot, the dried cornstalks giving him cover until he was within a dozen yards of the back entrance to the house.

The muddy tracks ended on the back step. He drew out his phone and called 911. He was headed for the door when a scream pierced the silence.

The back door wasn't locked. That was because the man inside hadn't been expecting company? Or had set a trap for him? Hayes took a chance, slipping through and moving fast through the big, empty house.

He couldn't tell where the scream had come from, but there were tracks in the dust on the floor. One set of man-sized footprints and two narrow wheel tracks. What the hell?

"Not so mouthy now, are you?" Jason said as he crouched down next to her.

The initial pain had been incredible. She'd never felt anything like it and could no more have held back the scream as she could have quit breathing.

Worse, she knew this was just the beginning. She could feel blood soaking into her blouse, running down her back.

He was kneeling next to her, his face close, so close she could feel his breath on her again. It took all her courage to look up into his face, knowing what she would find there. Satisfaction. He knew now that he could break her. There had probably never been a doubt in his mind. She was the fool for thinking she could trick this man into killing her.

He smiled. "I'm sorry. Did you have something else you wanted to say?"

As he started to move back from her, she swung her arms up, looping her bound wrists around his neck. She brought him down hard, pulling him off-balance and slamming his face into the floor next to her.

McKenzie knew it had been a stupid thing to do. She knew it wouldn't knock him out. If anything, it would only make him more furious and more determined to make her pay. She'd acted out of pain and fear and desperation.

He let out a bellow of pain and fury. She tried to slam his face down again, but he broke free of her hold, swinging wildly at her. She managed to roll away after only one blow, quickly rolling a second time so her back wasn't turned to him when he stumbled to his feet.

Dazed, his nose appearing broken and bleeding, he stared at her for a moment. He was breathing hard and looked unsteady on his feet. As he started toward her, she swung around on her butt and kicked him, knocking his feet out from under him.

He went down hard, hitting the wood floor with an *uhftt*. This time, he got up much faster and even as she tried to push herself back into the wall, he was on her, grabbing a handful of her short hair to drag her out into the center of the floor again.

"You have no idea what you've done!" he screeched at her as he held one hand to his bleeding nose and groped in his pocket with the other hand. Something silver flashed in his free hand an instant later.

McKenzie saw the scissors blade gleam in the late-afternoon light an instant before he lunged at her.

Hayes hadn't gone far into the house when he heard what sounded like a battle going on overhead. Of course, McKenzie would put up a fight just as she had the night she was attacked in the grocery-store parking lot, fighting for her life.

Rushing through the massive house, he finally found the stairs. What he saw brought him up short. There were no footprints in the dust on the steps and for an instant he stood confused, fighting to make sense of what he was seeing. He could hear sounds of a fight going on upstairs and yet—

That's when he spotted the elevator and the tracks leading into it—the same ones he'd found just inside the back door—a man's muddy boot prints and the two narrow wheel tracks.

He took off up the stairs at a dead run, weapon drawn. McKenzie's scream filled the air as he topped the stairs. He followed the sound, still running, breathing hard, knowing he would kill the man. Blinded with rage, he wanted to tear the man limb from limb. Hayes had never felt that kind of anger. It scared him and yet it also fueled him as he ran toward the heartbreaking sounds. He just prayed he would reach McKenzie before the madman killed *her.*

* * *

As Jason Mathews lunged at her with scissors, he let out a roar. She caught a glimpse of the insanity burning in his eyes. He came at her like a wounded animal, only this animal didn't just want to fight back. This animal yearned for retribution as only a human animal can.

He came at her so fast, she didn't get a chance to swing around with her feet. He came at her face, slashing the blades wildly. Had he simply tried to stab her, she might not have raised her hands to protect herself. But then again, she might have instinctively. She would never know.

She felt the blades slash across the backside of one wrist where she was bound by the thick tape. Because of that, she didn't feel the pain at first. She'd drawn her feet up as he'd struck her and managed to kick out at him, catching him in one knee. She heard screaming and thought at first it was her.

His leg buckled and he came down on top of her. She tried to roll out from under him, but he was too heavy. He had her pinned to the floor as he tried to struggle to his feet.

He rose just enough that he could get the scissors between them. He was going to kill her. Not the way he had wanted. But he could no longer hold back. She saw it in his expression as he struggled to rise.

Defeat, it was in his eyes, as well as disgust and pain. His nose was still bleeding and there was a bruised spot on his forehead from where it must have connected to the floor. The bright red blood had run down onto his white shirt.

How would he explain that to his wife?

That crazed, terrified thought came out of nowhere. The random thought of a woman about to die.

Hayes. The thought of him came with such regret she felt tears well in her eyes. She didn't want to die without at least telling him that she'd fallen in love with him.

Jason steadied himself as he timed his next thrust, this one aimed at her heart. They were both breathing hard, his breath making a loud almost snoring sound because of his broken nose. Neither of them heard the pounding of footfalls in the hallway.

Jason raised the scissors, meeting her gaze with one of rage and pain. He looked as if he was about to cry. McKenzie wanted to look away, but she couldn't. Her eyes locked with his. He almost looked afraid of her. He just wanted it to be over, she thought and realized that killing her this way wouldn't give him what he needed so there would be other women—and soon. That thought filled her with more sorrow than the thought of her own imminent death.

With the look of a man about to drive a stake into a vampire's heart, he grabbed the scissors in both hands and brought the blades down.

The sound of the gunshot was like an explosion, even in the large master suite. Another shot filled the air. Then another and another.

McKenzie had accepted that she would die. She'd told herself not to fight it as Jason drove the scissor blades down at her heart. But the gunshots into his back threw off his aim and gave her a few seconds to shift her body to the side. The blades came down into her side in a searing pain. Her cry was lost in the echo of the gunshots.

Hayes thought of the first time he'd laid eyes on McKenzie Sheldon. She'd been lying on the ground bleeding and then her eyes had opened....

He shoved the madman's body off her and dropped to his knees next to her.

"McKenzie!" There was blood everywhere. He couldn't tell how much of it was hers as he felt for a pulse, praying with every second that he would feel one. "McKenzie?"

He found a pulse and tried to breathe a little easier as McKenzie's eyes blinked open. What was it about those eyes? "McKenzie. Sweetheart. How badly are you hurt?"

She shook her head and tried to smile through the pain. "The bastard cut me. His name is Jason Mathews. He—"

"Don't try to talk," he told her. He could hear sirens in the distance. "You're going to be all right. You're safe now."

She closed her eyes as he took her hand. He thought about the first time he'd told her that. It had been a lie. She hadn't been safe. But she would be now, he thought as he looked over at the dead man.

Outside police cars and an ambulance had pulled up. He didn't want to let go of her hand, but he did only long enough to go to the window and direct the EMTs up on the elevator.

As he dropped down onto the bloody floor next to McKenzie again, he realized he was shaking. He thought about what he'd seen the moment he'd cleared the bedroom doorway. McKenzie bound up like that on the floor and that man standing over her, a pair of long-bladed scissors clamped in his hands, the man's beaten face twisted in a grimace—

That was all he remembered until he was on his knees next to McKenzie. He didn't remember pulling the trigger, couldn't even say how many times he'd shot the man.

That thought scared him. He'd been in the P.I. business for ten years. He considered himself a professional. He'd never lost control before.

Suddenly the room was filled with cops and EMTs and a stretcher. He let go of McKenzie's hand and moved back out of the way.

"Is she going to be okay?" he asked as two EMTs went to work on her.

"She's stable. We'll know more once we get her to the hospital."

Hayes wanted desperately to ride in the ambulance with her but one look at the cops and he knew he wasn't going anywhere. "Mind if I call my brother so he can go to the hospital to be with McKenzie until I can get there?"

Chapter 16

McKenzie woke with a start. As her eyes flew open, she saw the woman standing next to her hospital bed. Had she been able to forget yesterday's horror, she might not have recognized the woman at first.

But she hadn't been able to escape Jason Mathews, even filled with anesthesia in the operating room or later in a sedated sleep. He'd followed her into her nightmares.

"Emily Mathews?" She tried to sit up but the woman placed a hand on her shoulder, holding her down on the bed. McKenzie looked up into Jason's wife's face. A pair of dark brown eyes stared back at her.

"I had to see you," the woman said in that small, timid voice McKenzie remembered from the day at the ranchette showing. "Jason's dead, you know."

Dead, but far from forgotten. She tried to sit up again, but she was weak from whatever she'd been given after the surgery. Her side hurt like the devil from where she'd been stabbed. She saw that one of her wrists was bandaged and there was something plastered to her back under her nightgown that burned.

She felt foggy, as if caught between a nightmare and reality. Was this woman even really in her room or was this yet another nightmare?

As she felt the pain and recalled what the madman had done to her, she knew she wasn't dreaming.

"Here, let me do that," Emily said as McKenzie reached for the nurse call button. The woman didn't press it to call a nurse. Instead, she moved it out of her reach.

Fear spiraled through her, making her feel as if she might throw up. Jason was dead but this woman... She tried to sit up again. "What are you—"

The door burst open. McKenzie fell back with such relief that she could no longer hold back the tears. "Hayes." There'd been only one other time she'd been so happy to see him and that had been yesterday. She reminded herself that he'd also saved her the first time they'd met, as he rushed to her bed and took her hand.

"Are you all right?" he asked.

She couldn't speak. Tears rolled down her cheeks as she tried to swallow down the fear that had settled like a dull ache in her chest.

Behind him was a male police officer. "Mrs. Mathews, you shouldn't be in here."

"I had to come," Emily said in her tiniest voice.

"Well, you need to leave now. You're upsetting Ms. Sheldon," the cop said.

"Of course," the woman said, and turned to look at McKenzie. "I'm sorry."

McKenzie thought for a moment that she had misunderstood the woman's intentions. Maybe Emily had only come here to tell her how sorry she was for what her husband had done. But then she looked again in the woman's eyes. There was no compassion. The only emotion burning there was fury.

The woman was sorry, but not for the reasons anyone else in the room thought.

As the policeman led Emily out of the room, she turned to Hayes. "She *knew.* She knew the whole time. Her only regret was that I lived and he died."

Epilogue

"You're going to get sunburned."

McKenzie opened her eyes to look over at Hayes and smiled. "The sun feels so good."

Hayes sat up and reached for the suntan lotion. Since they'd been in Texas, the color had come back into McKenzie's cheeks and she'd gotten a nice tan. She looked healthy, even happy. But he knew she hadn't forgotten her ordeal. Never would. Neither would he.

The scars weren't just on her body, he thought as he rubbed the cool lotion on her back. He'd been surprised when she hadn't wanted to see a plastic surgeon about having the scar on her back removed or the others.

"What would be the point?" she'd said. "For me, it will always be there. Anyway," she'd said, tracing one along his shoulder, "we all have scars."

He remembered each of his scars that he'd gotten

growing up with four brothers as well as the ones he'd gotten working as a P.I. Life was dangerous. Sometimes you got lucky and survived it.

"I'm going to be all right, you know," she said when he'd finished applying the lotion.

"I never doubted it."

She sat up to look out at the Gulf of Mexico, her back to him.

"You are the strongest, most determined woman I know."

She smiled at him over her shoulder. She had the most amazing smile. Her hair was even shorter than it had been in Montana. He liked it, but wondered if she missed her long hair. She hadn't known that men like Jason Mathews targeted women with long hair. Women exactly like her. She hadn't known a lot about killers, but she did now.

"I like Texas," she said as she took a deep breath of the gulf air.

He waited, anticipating a "but" before he said, "That's good. You haven't seen much of it yet. It's a big state."

She was watching the waves as she had other days, lying in the sun, wading in the water, seemingly content to spend her days on the beach. The hot sun beat down on the white sand while the surf rolled up only yards from their feet, just as it had all the other days.

Only today, Hayes felt the change in her.

"I've had an offer on the agency," she said after a long moment.

He held his breath, not sure what he wanted her to say. He'd known she couldn't be content spending the rest of her life as a beach bum. That wasn't her. It wasn't him, either. Their lives had been in limbo for weeks now.

He'd known she needed time and had been determined to give it to her.

She turned around to face him, sitting cross-legged on the towel. Her skin was tanned, her high cheekbones pink from the sun, her amazing eyes bright. She looked beautiful. She also looked more confident than he'd seen her in a long time.

"I spoke with your cousin Dana. She wanted to know what our plans are for the wedding."

The sudden shift in subjects threw him off for a moment. "You still want to go to Tag and Lily's wedding?"

"Of course. He's your brother and I adore Lily." She frowned. "You do realize this—" she waved an arm, a motion that encompassed the Galveston beach "—this has been wonderful but only temporary, don't you?"

He nodded. "I've just been waiting for you to get your strength back."

She smiled and placed a cool palm on his bare leg. "What about you?"

"What about me?"

"I know you can afford to spend the rest of your life on this beach if you wanted to, but I don't think that is what you want to do, is it?"

"No, I need to work. Not for the money so much as for the work itself."

She licked her lips, catching her lower lip between her teeth for a moment. He felt a stirring in him, his desire for this woman a constant reminder of how much he loved her and that he hadn't yet told her.

The timing had felt all wrong. He wanted her strong. He wanted that unsinkable McKenzie Sheldon back before he laid that on her.

Now as he looked into her eyes, he saw that she was back.

"There is something I have to tell you," he said as he took both of her hands in his and got his courage up. His parents' marriage had failed. His brother Jackson's, as well. He wasn't sure he ever believed in love ever after, but he damned sure wanted to now.

McKenzie smiled, amusement in her eyes. "Is it that hard to admit?"

He chuckled. "I've been wanting to say it for weeks. I just had to wait until I was sure you were going to be all right."

"I'm all right, Hayes."

"I can see that." He gripped her hands, his gaze locking with hers.

McKenzie looked into his dark eyes, afraid of what he was going to say. They hadn't talked about the future. She knew he'd made a point of not pushing her. He'd given her time to heal and she loved him for it.

"I love you."

She laughed. "And I love you. I have for a long time."

He let out a relieved breath and pulled her into his arms for a moment. "I want to spend the rest of my life with you. I don't care where it is as long as we're together."

"Are you saying you would go back to Montana with me?"

"If that is what you want. I could open a private-investigation business in Bozeman or even in the canyon. Dana was telling me about a ranch near hers that was going on the market. I would need a good real-estate agent to handle things."

She couldn't believe what he was saying. "After staying at the Cardwell Ranch, I'm spoiled to live anywhere but the canyon. Could we really do this?"

"Only if you agree to marry me." He looked into her eyes again. "But be sure. This is a no-holds-barred offer till death do us part with kids and dogs and horses and barbecues behind the house."

She laughed as she threw herself back into his arms, knocking them to the sand. "Yes," she said as she looked down into his handsome face. "Yes to all of it."

"And I haven't even made you any Texas Boys Barbecue yet." He flipped her over so he was on top. "Woman, you are in for a treat."

She sobered as she looked up at him. "You've saved my life in so many ways," she said as she touched his cheek. "Do you think it was fate that night that we met?"

"I don't know. But I think I knew the moment I first looked into your eyes that you were the only woman who could get this Texas boy out of Texas."

He kissed her with a promise of good things to come as the surf rolled up to their feet and Montana called.

* * * * *